"Just your usual 'I've got an immensely wise alien in my head who wants me to become and international man of mystery' story. Which is to say, a page-turning homage to other classic SF like Hal Clement's *Needle*. Recommended."
    Steven Gould, author of the Jumpers *series*

"A fast-paced, high-action SF mix of Jason Bourne meets the Hero's Journey, jam-packed with dark conspiracies, wild romance, ancient aliens, and a secret, globe-spanning war. Loved it!"
    Matt Forbeck, author of Amortals *and* Hard Times in Dragon City

"This book is high-octane spy vs spy action with a sly sense of humor. Pure pleasure from beginning to end. Highly recommended!"
    Ann Vandermeer, Hugo Award-winning editor of Weird Tales

"Filled with non-stop action and brilliant asides on the history of our species, the book is sure to thrill and amuse."
    Ken Liu, Nebula Award-winning author of The Paper Menagerie

"Tipping his hat to both science fiction novels and comic books, Chu delivers a narrative that is at times pulse-pounding, laugh-out-loud funny and thoughtful. Part James Bond, part Superman, part *Orphanage*. There's something here for everyone."
    Myke Cole, author of Control Poir

WESLEY CHU

The Lives of Tao

ANGRY ROBOT

ANGRY ROBOT
A member of the Osprey Group

Lace Market House,
54-56 High Pavement,
Nottingham, NG1 1HW
UK

www.angryrobotbooks.com
Passengers

An Angry Robot paperback original 2013
1

A catalogue record for this book is available
from the British Library.

ISBN: 978 0 85766 328 3
Ebook ISBN: 978 0 85766 330 6

Set in Meridien by THL Design.

Printed and bound by CPI Group (UK) Ltd, Croydon, CR0 4YY

To my parents, Mike and Yukie Chu

CHAPTER ONE
ENDGAME

I once wrote "Whatever has come to be has already been named, and it is known what man is, and that he is not able to dispute with one stronger than he." The humans refer to that stronger being as God. I was referring to myself.

Huchel, Genjix Council – Eastern Hemisphere,
the Quasing of King Solomon

The five most egotistical personalities in history. Go.

"That's easy. You, Genghis, Alexander, Napoleon, and Kathy's nephew."

The one at Cambridge?

"He reminds me every time I see him."

Not a bad list, but I think Genghis Khan's inclusion is well deserved.

"Patting yourself on the back? I guess listing you and Genghis is a bit redundant."

Hardly. We should move to another spot. Our view here is obstructed.

Edward Blair looked at the sandy blond-haired woman in the charcoal suit sitting across the bar. Their eyes met, and a hint of dimples appeared on her face, accompanied by a small suggestive smile as she tugged on something around her waist and signaled the bartender. "The view's just fine where we're at, Tao." Edward swirled the golden brown liquid in his glass and sipped with confidence. He kept his gaze on her and winked. He was rewarded with a wink and a slight blush before the bartender arrived and blocked his view.

We have more important things to do than play this silly game.

Edward finished his scotch and ordered another. "Oh, I forgot. We're talking about how great Genghis was. Fact is, buddy, his work has been duplicated and expanded upon, just look at Alexander. And last time I checked, Mongolia plays a pretty insignificant role on the twenty-first century world stage."

Alexander is an unfair comparison. It is easy to build an empire when you inherit an army.

"Well, by size, the old British Empire won. At least they're still around. So there you go, bigger and longer. Size and durability count after all. Ask my wife." Edward turned away from the bar and looked out the window at the dizzying array of lights emanating from the streets below, a complex grid of bright lines reaching out as far as the eye could see. The night sky was growing darker as large rolling clouds smothered the moon and the stars.

He could feel the gentle swaying on the ninety-fifth floor as strong winds battered the John Hancock Center, rocking it ever so slightly. Springtime in Chicago half a klick above the ground was unpleasant at best. "Good thing we didn't glide in," he muttered, taking another sip of scotch and feeling its warmth spread through his body. "You'd think criminal masterminds would choose more isolated bases of operations than the top of skyscrapers. What happened to the good ol' days when they lived on deserted islands in the Pacific?"

Resorts and skyrocketing beachfront property prices happened. Besides, criminal masterminds are people too. They need groceries and cable like the rest of us. It also does not let us get cute with our plans.

Edward leaned forward and his eyes followed one of the metal beams that crisscrossed the building. That much was true. Sneaking into a base on top of a skyscraper in the center of a metropolis was just as difficult as infiltrating a remote island. Security on the ground level was tight, and the weather made an air drop too risky. Short of blowing up the building, Edward had limited options in their rules of engagement other than through the Signature room on the ninety-fifth floor, one above the Genjix base. "What about Napoleon?"

What about him? He should not even be on the list.

"He was crowned emperor. That's worth something."

Anyone can bestow a title upon himself. Calling yourself a genius does not make it so.

"You call yourself a genius all the time."

By human standards? Not hard.

"Napoleon didn't do too badly for himself. You're a bit biased; you two never got along."

Almost conquering Europe does not an emperor make. He was a brilliant general, but his short tenure disqualifies him for the hall of fame.

"You're penalizing him because of his administrative skills?"

Paper-pushing is an integral part of empire ruling. Consider–

"Excuse me, sir, the general manager would like to buy you a drink," the bartender said, placing another glass of scotch onto the counter.

Edward turned back toward the bar and smiled again as the woman sitting across the room earlier moved to the seat next to him, one hand on a martini and the other extended.

"Simone," she purred. "I hope you don't mind. I ordered you an eighteen instead of the twelve."

Edward looked down at his drink and grinned. He took her hand and shook it, lingering longer than appropriate. "Blake Emanuel. I'll have to return the favor in some other way." The two chatted intimately for the next twenty minutes, moving closer and closer together.

Edward, I hate to ruin your sport, but our window is closing. The codes expire in two days, and we are not getting anywhere here. I regret not insisting on gliding in.

"In this weather? You must have more faith in my flying skills than I do. Now, keep quiet and let me focus on Simone here. I need to keep my architect story straight."

Twenty years together now and you are still incorrigible.

"Intergalactic civil war wasn't exactly on my career track out of West Point, Tao."

Wish I never found you?

"You know the answer to that."

His earpiece crackled. "Abelard, are you in position?"

"That's cute. Remind me to have a few words with Marc about these dumb code names when I get back."

I find it fitting. Quite a compliment actually.

"Things didn't exactly end well for Abelard and Heloise, if I remember how that tragedy went. I hate it when he listens in."

It is Jeo's nature. Marc just picked up the habit.

Smiling all the while, Edward excused himself and left Simone at the bar, walking to the back of the lounge toward the restrooms. He waited until he was alone in the hallway before entering a door marked "Personnel Only." In the kitchen, he hurried past the workers before they had a chance to stop him and exited through another door into a back room. "Roger, Marc. Stand by." He pulled out a set of keys attached to a band and began to try them on the locked door.

How did you know she was the manager with the keys?

"They were dangling on her waist, and she was far too authoritative with the bartender."

Clever, Edward. I stand corrected.

"Twenty years together, Tao. Have a little faith."

The door clicked open and Edward sprinted through a barren hallway past a bank of elevators on one side to the stairwell on the other. He hurried down several flights to a non-descript metal door. He slipped on a pair of thin black gloves and broke a small vial over the handle. Edward watched the corrosive acid burn through the lock and whispered, "Marc, green to proceed. How's it looking topside?"

"It's bumpy up here, but we're taking a nice scenic tour of the skyline. Rendezvous on the roof at your go. You have one shot at this, so make it count."

"Evac 0100. Don't be late."

"Acknowledged, Abelard. Over and out."

"Tao, you keeping track of the time?"

As always, I am your alarm clock.

"Is something up with Marc? Past couple of missions, he seemed ambivalent about everything. Like the time we guarded the Spanish prime minister, I don't think Marc cared if the man died."

That is Jeo for you. He hates this planet more than the rest of us, but I have known him for a long time. He has always been reliable.

"You hate Earth, Tao?"

You have to put it in perspective to where we came from. Kind of like visiting your tax accountant.

"Got it. Still, I wish he wasn't such a downer." Edward caught the handle as it burned off and placed it on the floor. He opened the door a sliver and scanned the area inside. Dark Brazilian wood floors, antique lamps, and plush Victorian furniture decorated both sides of a long hallway. Books filled rows of shelves on one wall; a large polished marble bust of Plato was prominently displayed between two elevator doors. "Did we get the right floor?"

I believe so. Chiyva's fingerprints are all over it. How typical of him to have a bust of himself. And I see his taste has not changed much since the nineteenth century.

Staying flat to the wall, Edward crept to the end of the corridor and peered around the corner.

Two guards to the right side. Surveillance camera moving at twenty-second sweeps in the corner.

"Twenty seconds, huh? Not a lot of room for error. Gun?"

No, keep it quiet. No need to raise a fuss yet. Camera is moving now. Go!

Pulling out a knife from its holster, Edward exhaled, rounded the corner, and took off running. Hugging the right wall, he stayed low, covering ground quickly as he charged the two unsuspecting men. Once in range, he shifted to the left wall for a better angle and, with a flick of his wrist, threw the knife. It whistled as it shot past the first guard and into the neck of the second. The man gasped and went limp. The remaining guard turned to look at his fallen companion just as Edward closed in and rammed his fist into the man's ribcage.

Fifteen seconds on the camera.

The guard doubled over as Edward grabbed his head and snapped his neck. Before the body had fallen to the floor, Edward had already moved to the other body and pulled out his knife.

Not bad for a forty year-old dog.

"Like I said, durability counts."

Touché. Get the bodies in. Ten seconds on the camera.

Edward took out a modified keycard, slid it through the electronic lock, and opened it with a soft click. He dragged the bodies with him into a darkened room filled with rows of computers. The room was cool and hummed with a low resonance from dozens of machines and a loud ventilation shaft. "Did the camera catch anything?"

Two seconds and change. The mark is Trixlix GeTr715.

Edward's eyes ran down the list of servers until he found GeTr715 tucked near the rear of the third row on the bottom rack. "Hello, mark," he whispered in satisfaction. "Let's see if you're worth leaving Simone upstairs." Edward pulled out a small cable from his belt and plugged it into the server. "Codes accepted. Starting extraction now." The monitor above the server blinked to life, and Edward's fingers blurred as he typed, digging for the information he needed. His trained eyes jumped from directory to directory, grabbing bits and pieces of different files. "It seems the rumors about this fabled Penetra program are true. It does exist."

Verify.

Edward went into the folder and opened the files inside. "Hmm," he paused, shaking his head. "My secretary can organize information better than this."

Worry about their formatting skills another time. Copy the blueprints and get out of here.

Edward's eyes widened as he scanned the contents. "Found the blueprints, but look at this provisions list and these chemical stockpiles. I thought this was a surveillance prototype. Could it be a biological weapon? How are they getting past customs? I wish we had lobbyists this good. Initiating upload. Wait, backup access control list just tripped. We're getting kicked out."

The security file probably just alerted a platoon of guards. Get what we have and go.

His earpiece crackled, "Edward, we've just confirmed the data stream. On our way to pick you up now."

"Confirmed. Over and out." Edward unplugged the cord and scrambled toward the exit. Hearing heavy footsteps, he stopped and retreated back to the rows of servers just as a group of guards entered the room.

No armor. 1911s by the looks of it. Laser scopes. Three, no, four guards. None appear to be Genjix.

"Must be the hired help."

Take them out fast.

One of the guards turned on the lights and the rest fanned

out, each moving from aisle to aisle. Shouts of "Clear!" could be heard as they made their way toward him. Edward pulled out his Glock pistol and crept toward the edge of an aisle. As an arm came into view, he trapped it with one hand and threw his elbow into the guard's face, dropping him to the floor. The scuffle alerted the others and they converged on his position.

Another guard appeared at the other end of the aisle and opened fire. Bullets ricocheted off the metal frames of the shelves. A searing pain erupted in Edward's left arm and his hand went numb. Falling flat to the floor, he took quick aim and finished his target with three quick shots to the chest.

Grazing shot. Shake it off. Get to the extraction point!

Edward reloaded the Glock and ran out to the hallway. Sirens blared all around him. He sprinted back toward the stairwell, hearing sounds of approaching footsteps close behind. He burst through the door and ran up the stairs. A group of guards soon followed close behind. Bullets flying past his head, Edward craned his neck over the railing, grabbed a grenade from his side, pushed the timer for one second, and tossed it over the railing. The resulting explosion knocked him off his feet and everything went dark for a split second. Water sprinklers activated and began to spray the room. Shaking his head to clear the cobwebs, Edward pulled himself up and continued up the stairs.

"I'm getting too old for this."

What happened to "durability counts"? We can worry about putting you out to pasture after this mission.

Another group of guards appeared two flights above him and opened fire. Edward threw himself against the wall just as gunfire rained down upon him. "Get me another way up to the top."

Through the door. Get to the roof from the other stairwell.

Marc's voice came through the earpiece so loud Edward

winced. "We've landed on the roof. Resistance heavier than anticipated. Hurry!"

"I'm working on it!" Edward yelled as he burst through the door out of the stairwell and came face to face with an attractive young woman. She wore an expensive tan suit and had her hair tied in a high ponytail. If it was any other time, he would stop and try to chat her up. But it wasn't any other time. He grabbed her and jammed the Glock into her side. "Sorry, darling, this probably isn't the best way to make a first impression."

It is Yrrika.

Edward sighed. "Really? Yrrika always picks the pretty ones." Without hesitation, he pulled the trigger. She had only a moment to gasp before falling to the floor. Her body shimmered as the Genjix emerged and floated into the air.

Let us hope Yrrika does not find a new host in time. Down to the end of the hallway, make a right, third door on the left.

"Do you remember the time I tried to pick up Yrrika's previous host?"

In Istanbul? I warned you not to. You were a fresh twenty-five year-old agent and she was sixty. How did that work out for you?

"You could have told me she was a judo champion."

She was not. You just were not that good back then. Some of the hardest lessons are the best.

Edward took off running. The alarm was getting on his nerves and he heard footsteps all around him. There was no telling how many other Genjix hosts were here. He sprinted down the hall to the other stairwell and scrambled up to the roof. With the amount of heat behind him, Marc better be ready to take off any second. Edward slammed his body into the exterior door and barreled onto the rooftop. Losing his balance, he tumbled forward and rolled into a kneeling position, pistol trained forward.

The roof of the John Hancock Center in Chicago was a mess of black shadows and cluttered metal structures bathed in ghostly red by lights from its two towering antennas. To his left was a row of large fans; in front a set of stairs that led up to another platform; and to his right the helicopter. Cold winds howled overhead. Edward stayed low and made his way toward his ride home, slipping from shadow to shadow.

Where are the other agents and why is the helicopter not prepped to leave? Something is wrong.

Edward ran to the cockpit and found two of his agents slumped over the controls. One more was dead outside. The windshield was shattered, the cockpit smashed, and a small fire raged in the holding area.

Is it operable?

"Of course not, there's no cockpit anymore! Let's see if the emergency chute's still there."

Fortunately, the compartment in the rear housing the parachutes was intact. He strapped on a chute, tied it around his waist, and checked the release.

Are any of the bodies Marc? If so, we need to see if Jeo survived. We cannot leave him here.

Edward turned the bodies over and tore off their helmets. Then he went back outside and checked the lone agent there. "They're all standards. Where's Marc, damn it!"

Edward, all three died of headshots.

A chill shot down Edward's spine. He didn't care if he was up against James friggin' Bond. No one was good enough to tap three headshots in rapid succession... unless he was at close range. The only body missing was Marc. Was it possible? Faction changing was a time-honored tradition in the war, but Tao and Jeo had been comrades since Rome was nothing more than a bunch of huts on a muddy hill. However, as much as Edward hated to admit it, he couldn't come up with an explanation other than betrayal, and he didn't have the luxury at this moment to unravel the mystery. If this was true, he was in immediate danger.

Edward ducked behind the wreckage and blended into the darkness. Staying low, he made his way to the eastern side of the roof, using the assorted structures, ventilation generators, and air ducts as cover until he reached the edge of the building. He looked out at the black void that was Lake Michigan. The John Hancock Center was not tall enough for a safe paradrop, so his only chance would be a water landing. It would be frigid this time of year. "Base jumping is not my idea of a solid escape plan," he muttered, looking over the edge at the streets below.

There has been worse. Remember Budapest and the sewage tunnels?

Edward shuddered. "Don't remind me." He stepped up to the ledge and prepared to jump. Suddenly, sharp jabs of pain exploded in his back, nearly knocking him over the side. He collapsed onto the roof. Only the parachute and his body armor saved his life. Edward groaned as he tried to lift his head.

"Don't move, Edward," a familiar voice said from behind him. "I can't let you escape."

Snap out of it. Voice coming from behind you to the left. An image of a generator Edward passed moments before flashed in his head.

Edward rolled over and looked at his partner of the past two years. "Isolated rooftop; nice trap. What's going on, Marc? We're not paying you enough?"

With a stony expression, Marc shook his head and motioned with his rifle. "It's not that I don't believe in the Prophus cause anymore, it's just that I don't care. I'm tired of this stupid war."

"We're all tired of this war," Edward yelled over the howl of the wind. "It doesn't mean we just throw in the towel and change teams, you dumb bastard." He inched himself up to a sitting position.

Marc's face contorted in anger. "And you know what? You're right; I'm not getting paid enough. At least the Genjix know how to treat their people right. We don't get paid crap! No one bothered to tell me that I'd be working for nothing, so a bunch of aliens can return to some mud-ball planet! There's nothing in it for any of us. Not you, not me. Hell, I didn't even have a choice. I just got drafted by Jeo when he decided I was his type! Why are we even up here doing this crap if we'll be long dead before anything happens?"

"It's not just about you, Marc. You know what happens if we lose. Does Jeo feel the same way?"

Marc chuckled nervously. "Jeo? Hell, he's the one that convinced me that it's all a bloody waste." His face softened, showing a small semblance of remorse. "Look, man, it's not personal. I'm sure you and Tao know that. But if I have to be involved, I want to be on the winning side, and since no one trusts anyone anymore, you're my ticket in. I have to deliver you to Sean. He asked for you specifically."

Edward's body throbbed from the pain and his left arm felt useless. However, he wasn't about to surrender to this junior varsity agent. He watched Marc's breathing, pacing his nervous quick breaths and the slight up and down motions of the rifle. Then just as Marc inhaled, Edward lurched to the side and fired. Bullets sprayed the spot where he'd been moments before and he heard a satisfying cry of pain as Marc dropped his rifle and fell to one knee.

Edward crept behind a generator, grimacing. He had a couple of cracked ribs for sure. Peering over the top, he saw an injured Marc retreat back into the shadows, holding onto his bleeding shoulder. Edward took off the backpack and inspected the contents. The parachute was riddled with bullets.

"We're in trouble, Tao. We just lost our escape route."

I am working on a backup plan now.

"Work faster, Tao! We got more peons coming." Indeed, the door opened and several guards poured onto the roof. He would be discovered in moments. Marc limped out of his hiding spot and joined the guards as they fanned out to search for Edward.

We seem to be out of options. Surrender.

"That's your backup plan? You know I can't do that. If I surrender, they'll kill me anyway just to get to you. You'll die."

Then we go down fighting.

"No, that's not an option either. If I die here, you'll be trapped on the roof and be lost. They'll know if you take one of the guards and just kill him as well."

Edward...

"Edward," Marc shouted. "You've got one way out. Let's not waste your life. Come on, we can discuss terms. You don't need to die up here."

"Think they'll spare our lives as part of the terms?"

Jeo would. Chiyva or Zoras will stab you with whatever utensil they are eating with the instant you are in arm's reach.

"Price of fame, I guess." Edward peered over the side of the generator at the floating beams from the flashlights dancing over the roof's surface. It was just a matter of time. "There's one other choice then."

No, Edward. We will find another way.

Edward sighed and looked at the sky. The clouds had passed and a single star came out of hiding, sparkling in the otherwise black night. The harsh wind had died down as well and he felt a calmness come over him. "Tao, it's the only way. At least one of us will make it out of here. You'll have a much better chance of surviving if there are potential hosts around."

There has to be another way.

"We don't have time for another way. You know this is the right thing to do. Just promise me you'll get that son of a bitch Marc someday."

There was a brief silence.

I swear it by the Eternal Sea.

"Say goodbye to Kathy for me. Tell her I love her."

I will, my friend.

Without another word, Edward stood up and sprinted toward the edge. His heart was beating out of his chest as he reached the edge of the roof and leaped out as far as he could. The city opened beneath him to an explosion of lights.

CHAPTER TWO
REBIRTH

Tao cherished his last precious moments with his host as Edward plummeted down the side of the John Hancock Center, a bittersweet luxury as they said their goodbyes. His friend was characteristically stoic about the inevitable, having made peace with this eventuality years ago.

Goodbye, my friend. Return to the Eternal Sea in peace. Your soul will live on through me, and your death will not be in vain. I will always remember you.

"Take care of yourself, Tao. Win the war for me, buddy."

Then darkness.

And piercing bitter cold.

The expulsion hurt. It always did. No matter how many times he left a host, Tao was never prepared for the crushing shock of the thick atmosphere. He ebbed in and out of consciousness, and then found himself looking down at the body of his fallen friend.

Unable to sustain himself for long without the warm cocoon of a host, Tao struggled to keep his gaseous form together as the winds battered him. His translucent turquoise membrane stretched and expanded as if an irregular beating heart, floating side to side as the heavy oxygen currents pushed and pulled in every direction. He had only minutes before he would succumb to the near freezing temperatures of the planet's harsh environment. It was a grim reminder of why he was so desperate to return home.

The Genjix would have men down here in moments. Their scanners could track Quasing outside of hosts. Tao surveyed his surroundings. In front of him, Michigan Avenue was relatively still at this hour, save for a few passing cars. Behind him, the ominous structure of the John Hancock Center stretched high up into the sky, eerily black and quiet.

Tao decided to take his chances south and swam along the side of the street. Though time was not on his side and the choices were slim, he was determined to be selective with potential hosts. His first candidate was an old vagrant sleeping on a bus stop bench. Tao swam up and examined him: weak skeletal structure, multiple abrasions over the membrane, uneven shallow breathing. Without another thought, Tao moved on. No use in trapping himself into someone so old and unsuitable. There must be a healthier host more open to influence even at this hour!

He continued south on Michigan Avenue, passed the Water Tower Plaza to Chicago Avenue, turned east at the Museum of Contemporary Art, and studied a stray dog picking through a dumpster in the alley. It was a large mix, possibly mastiff and pit bull with strong jaws, powerful legs, and an intelligent alertness to his eyes. Tao guessed it was no older than three or four. He considered the animal a moment before moving on. It had been centuries since he was desperate enough to occupy an animal host and he wasn't far enough gone to concede the need yet.

Looking back, he saw a group of four men running toward him in the distance. They had found him! If they got close enough, a gunshot would tear him apart. A Quasing could not outrun a human in their natural state. Hiding was out of the question. The scanners would find him as long as he was within their radius. Tao would have to stay out of sight until he found a suitable candidate. He pressed on.

He doubled back to Michigan Avenue and continued south. A minute later, he found an excellent candidate walking alone on the other side of the street. She was an athletic female, late twenties, a shade under two meters in height, and about fifty kilos. The host was a little old, but at this time of the night, there weren't going to be many younger. Tao made his move and swam as fast as he could toward the candidate. Careful to avoid oncoming traffic, Tao crossed the street, staying low to the pavement to avoid the stronger air currents.

The young woman had stopped and was standing on the side of the road, looking in both directions. A car sped by in front of him, creating a breeze that sucked him off his course. He lost precious seconds struggling to regain control. Just as he reached her and was about to inhabit the new host, she hailed a cab, got in, and rode off.

No! Tao brushed the setback aside and kept moving, intent on surviving the night. His membrane was starting to crack from the cold, and like a human drowning in the ocean, he was wearing down. He reached Ontario Street and moved west, hoping for signs of life. Several times, he considered heading back for the dog, but knew he would not make it in time. A group of people was on the other side of the street, but traffic was too thick to risk crossing. Even at a slow pace, any impact from a vehicle would finish him in this delicate state.

A loud bang echoed in the distance and the car window near where Tao was floating shattered. Behind him, two more Genjix were taking aim. He didn't have much time. The Genjix forces were still two hundred meters back, but closing fast. Tao turned the corner and fled down the street. His only option now was to find a host while out of the Genjix agents' visual range, and then get the host away from this area before they caught him in their surveillance net.

A figure stepped out of a building at the far end of the block and walked toward him. Tao knew this was likely his last chance, so he swam hard toward his target, going against the currents that tossed him like a sailboat in a storm. The cold was overpowering, daggers of pain shooting throughout his membrane. If he was a human, screams would not express the agony he was experiencing, being crushed and ripped apart simultaneously from inside out. It would be so easy to let go, to just let his core dissipate. It would be final rest, a well-deserved one.

Tao lost consciousness, drifting off into the blackness, and for a moment, he felt a sensation of numbness so sweet that it overwhelmed him. If this serenity really was the end, maybe there was nothing to dying after all. The Quasing gave little thought to death, and Tao cared even less than most. But now, he enveloped himself in this beautiful numbness that was the end of his existence. If he had known previously that the end was so beautiful...

But that would mean the Prophus lost.

And the Genjix won.

Tao would die. Edward would die. Edward was dead. And the Genjix would succeed. The memories of every one of his brethren fallen to the Genjix flashed through his mind. He thought of the consequences if the Genjix won. Earth, a planet and her inhabitants he had grown to cherish, would lay in ruin in their wake. His work was unfinished. With a silent howl, Tao snapped back into consciousness and looked at the figure just off to the side, about to get into a car. He pushed forward harder than he ever pushed before. There was too much at stake to give in. Tao was almost upon the person now and prepared to transition into the new host's body. Then the new host got into a car and slammed the door shut.

Not again. It was over. There was no one else around, and he hadn't the strength to go any further. Tao floated outside the car and watched as the driver started the engine. Time had run out and he would die. It seemed unfitting in a way, to end his life with such a small whimper. Suddenly, the door opened and the man leaned out, head bent over the side.

Not believing his good fortune, Tao slid inside and focused on his new host as he prepared to make his move. The portly man was in his early thirties by the looks of the skin pigment, a tad under one hundred twenty kilos, and quite a bit under two meters. He had a stressed skeletal structure and a heart condition, most likely from the excess weight and a very low muscle to fat ratio. He also had an unsafe level of alcohol in his system, enough to impair motor skills. An adventurous or a foolhardy man to be sure. Both were traits Tao could take advantage of.

Now, he regretted ruling out the dog. At least with the animal, he could influence it to take him back to the Prophus. This human would require a bit more work to train and get up to speed. Well, Tao did not have the luxury to second-guess himself. He had to make do with what was in front of him.

He focused once more and made the final push into his new home. The shift into a new host was difficult as always. The skin was the most difficult to absorb through, though not as hard as some of the other creatures he had inhabited. A few, like the dinosaurs with their exterior bone plating, were impossible to push into without finding soft points. Others – like the insects of today – did not have the mass or fluid structure in their bodies to be proper hosts, missing the right mix of enzymes and nucleic acids needed to sustain a Quasing.

After several seconds and a laborious effort, Tao completed the push and was once again encased inside a host. He shuddered in relief as the human's body protected him from the elements. A few more moments out in the atmosphere and he would have been dead. Tao began to absorb the base chemicals and nutrients from his new host, careful not to take too much in at once, only replenishing just what he needed to survive. It would take time for this new host's body to adapt to his intrusion.

Roen Tan leaned out the side of the car and took a deep breath. Once he was sure there wasn't going to be projectile vomiting ruining the faux leather interior, he closed the door and sat back up. The chilly night air was soothing, after spending the past three hours in the cramped basement of the nightclub. This was the last time, he told himself, but that was a lie and he knew it.

Every few weeks, out of boredom and loneliness, Roen would come to this dingy club and spend a miserable night standing in the corner before heading home early. He looked at his watch: 1.30. Well, early was a relative term. Roen sighed. He was out another hundred bucks – thirty to get in, and seventy on drinks for himself and the four girls that ditched him the instant they got them.

Checking his face in the mirror, he noticed his bloodshot eyes and puffy cheeks. These late-night outings were a vicious cycle. Roen knew he was drunk, but he'd be damned if he was going to spend another fifteen dollars for a cab. Besides, how would he get his car tomorrow? Spend more money to cab it back? Forget it. What if he got a ticket?

Suddenly, Roen gasped and doubled over, the contents of his stomach crawling up his throat. He threw open the door again and leaned over the edge, pleading with whatever just died in his belly to just get out and end his misery. Funny, he didn't think he'd drunk that much. Maybe his dinner didn't agree with him. Then, as if on command, all the contents in his stomach spilled out of his mouth, in one big disgusting mess, all over the sidewalk.

"Frozen pizza was a bad idea," he grumbled, grimacing in pain. His head pounding and his stomach unsettled, Roen thought he would lose his dinner a few more times. After several seconds, the nausea dissipated and he began to feel better. He leaned back into his car and pulled out of the parking spot, nearly hitting a group of four men wearing what looked like Ghostbuster proton packs sprinting across the street.

Roen decided to not yell at them to be careful and continued on his way. The road blurred a little as he drove. Fortunately, traffic was light and the drive to his apartment – just outside the downtown area – was short. Roen smacked his lips and made a face at the bile still in his mouth. He reached his garage without incident, parked his car, and stumbled toward the elevator. Once the metal doors closed, the nausea kicked in again. Roen focused his attention on the digital display on the wall.

"Fifteen, sixteen, seventeen... a rat cage with a view at least." He scowled, stepping out onto the twentieth floor. He dragged his feet down the hall and wrestled the keys out of his pocket, fiddling a bit with the key until the lock finally opened. Bumping into each wall, he kicked off his shoes and staggered in, not minding the fresh scuff marks on the walls.

Feeling the room spin, Roen made his way into the kitchen for a glass of water. He took a few deep gulps and looked down at the empty bowls on the floor. When was the last time he fed the cat? Poor guy must be starving. Roen filled the bowls with enough food and water to last another week.

He was about to leave when he saw a week-old bag of chips lying opened on the counter. Maybe some salt and carbs would help settle his upset stomach. He grabbed the bag and popped a handful of chips into his mouth. On the way back to his room, he noticed the lights on in the second bedroom. His roommate Antonio must be online again. Roen walked in and leaned over his best friend's shoulder. "The girl at Yale or the hot single mom in California?" he asked.

"Both, and one of the nurses at the cardio ward." Antonio leaned back and winked. "What can I say, once you get an MD attached to your name, they all come out of the woodwork."

Roen shook his head. "Already? Two days in residency and you're already milking it. You're a dog, bro."

Antonio shrugged. "That's Dr Dog to you, good sir. To be honest, I don't like the title. It brings out the wrong sort of interest from girls. I'm going to start telling them I'm a chef instead."

Roen shook his fist in the air. "Oh, why didn't my counselor tell me that doctors get all the women? Damn you, career counselor! Actually, I wish you were a chef. Then I'd get something out of this relationship."

"You don't need a culinary degree to cook frozen food. How was the club?"

"Same old, same old."

"You meet anyone?"

Roen sighed and patted Antonio on the back. "Like I said, same old, same old. I'm off to bed. Have fun, virtual Don Juan. Make sure you're actually talking to women, and not forty year-old perverts."

"Don Juan, MD."

Exhausted, Roen walked into his room and closed the door behind him. All he could think about was sleep. He took off his shirt and pants, and tossed them aside, leaving a trail of clothes on the floor. He plopped onto the bed and stared at the ceiling. Antonio talked to more women in one day – staying in his room on the computer – than Roen did all night at a club.

What was Roen doing wrong? And it's not even like Antonio really tries. Life was so unfair. I shouldn't have flunked chemistry, he thought, I could have been a doctor. But then he remembered that he didn't like the sight of blood. With a deep sigh, Roen turned over, and in seconds was snoring up a small storm.

CHAPTER THREE
THE CALL

Tao watched with interest as his new host milled about in his drunken state. After living through hundreds of lives, he had become quite adept at reading humans. He studied Roen's mannerisms and behaviors, his driving habits, the tidiness of the bedroom, and his interaction with his roommate. He even made a mental note that Roen forgot to brush his teeth.

Waiting until his new host faded into a deep slumber, Tao made his move and suppressed his host's consciousness, and then sat him up. Tao had never been that good at unconscious manipulation to begin with, and already exhausted from the night's ordeal, his control was shaky. He maneuvered Roen like a minivan across the room to the desk and pawed at the football-shaped phone. It took a few tries, but Tao finally dialed the emergency line and waited the established fifteen rings before someone answered.

The other voice said, "Twenty-four-hour wake-up service. We wake up to wake you up. Can I help you?"

"Identification Tao."

"Voice recognition does not match host Edward Blair."

"Host has been terminated."

"Base binary code required."

29

"Binary code one, one, zero, zero, one, zero, one, one, zero, zero, zero, one."

Silence.

"My condolences, Tao. Edward was a good man."

"Thank you, Krys. Register the new host and patch me through to the Keeper."

"Of course. Will it be long before you are active again?" Krys asked.

"I do not know. Depends on the host; you know how it is."

"Aye, I do. Putting you through now. Good luck, Tao."

"Thank you."

Tao felt a sharp pang of regret as he waited. He dreaded this call. It marked the somber finality of losing Edward. He would have to make good on his previous host's last wish soon. That was something he was not looking forward to either, but Kathy deserved better than to be kept in the dark.

A woman's voice came on the line, "Hello, Tao."

"Keeper."

"I am sorry to hear the news. When Edward's tracer stopped moving, we were concerned that you might have been lost to the Eternal Sea."

"Edward made sure I had a chance to find a new host. Did Command receive the upload?"

"Affirmative."

"Is it true?" Tao asked.

"This so-called P1 Penetra program does not seem to be a weapon. Our engineers are analyzing the blueprints now and believe it may be an advanced communication or surveillance array."

Surveillance? With the amount of security surrounding the project, that hardly seemed accurate. The agent they had in the Genjix research division said the project had the highest priority and was carried out with the utmost secrecy. "Did you see the chemical list?" Tao asked.

"We have. It is a mystery. Our people are working on how these chemicals will correlate with such an array."

Tao was silent for a few moments, deep in thought. Finally, he asked the question he was dreading. "Were we able to retrieve his body?"

"I am sorry."

Tao cursed. Kathy would not be able to lay her husband to rest. He had hoped that it was a solace he could provide her. Now, she was robbed of even that. "Marc. He killed Edward. The operation was a double-cross. We need to lock him out of our systems."

"Global security changes have already been initiated. Do not worry about Jeo, Tao. You have more pressing concerns. What is your new situation, and how long can we expect you out?"

Tao pulled out Roen's wallet and recited the information on his driver's license. "New host name: Roen Tan. Age: thirty-one. Height: five-nine. Weight: hmm... someone obviously lied on his license. I believe he is currently north of one hundred twenty kilos. I am still assessing the situation, but I believe I have my hands full with this one. Training time could be significant. Has both mental and physical issues which first will have to be resolved before he can be any use to us."

"Pulling up his complete background now. Nothing overly unusual. No military record. No police record, slightly above average grades in high school, slightly below in college. Hay fever, minor asthma, and some Alzheimer in the family history. Interesting, one of his ancestors a few generations back was a Prophus. Seurot, who is no longer with us, lost during the 228 Massacre."

"I knew Seurot. He was a good Quasing."

The Keeper said, "His records dating back from grade school indicate low self-esteem and social isolation, but a higher than average intelligence and a history of obesity. Initiating host transfer protocols now. Roen Tan will no longer exist in a few minutes. Be sure to make first contact before he tries to pull up his Social Security number or other washed data. Tao, I am going to lay out your situation right now. From his files, this new host of yours is completely inadequate for our needs. Time is short. If he is not flexible for immediate orientation, we will send someone to dispose of him."

"That should not be necessary," Tao cut her off before she could continue. He tried to keep his voice calm, but inside, he fumed. Voluntary transitions were a despicable practice, regardless of how dire the situation was. He had never had to perform one before, and did not intend to start now. "I will attempt to expedite integration. I have already begun his case study..."

"No case studies or gentle awakenings. We cannot afford the luxury of a long honeymoon. I want results in weeks. He needs to be online and ready to work in months, understood?" she said.

"Keeper, please be realistic. He has no military experience. It takes at minimum two years to train an agent, and that is not including his current physical condition. Asking for results in months is an impossible deadline. You might as well send someone in tonight and shoot him." Roen snorted and dropped the phone, mumbling something in his sleep. Tao temporarily lost control and almost fell over. Muttering under his breath, Tao picked up the phone again. "My apologies, Keeper, he is being uncooperative."

There was a pause on the other end. "What if we sent you help to push the host along? There are a few unallocated agents recovering from combat. I can assign one to you."

Tao hated receiving help with the training. He preferred to mold new hosts to his own exacting standards. However, under these circumstances, he had little choice in the matter. "Who is available?"

"Haewon's second year. Eva's fifth. Baji's fourth. Vou's ninth."

"Baji's fourth, is it Dania's daughter?" he asked.

"I thought you would select her. She is in the Philippines right now. I will have her transferred over."

"Yes, perfect. Thank you, Keeper."

"Of course, Tao. Be safe, you were always one of our best."

Roen twisted in his sleep and dropped the phone again. This time, Tao lost his balance and fell over. Near the end of his strength, he gave up and left the body where it lay. The mission, compounded with the strain of a new host, had pushed him to his limits.

Tao needed to rest. For the next few days he would observe his host. Then at the right time, he would introduce himself to Roen Tan, though in reality, there was never a good time for these sorts of introductions.

Usually, he would spend months observing before making contact. But there was much to do and little time to do it. Roen's life was now in Tao's safekeeping. The Keeper had made the consequences perfectly clear. Tao did not intend to lose a second host in such a short period of time. As he retired for the night, he couldn't help but wonder what lay ahead. Chances were he might have lost a generation staying in this host. But what if this Roen Tan could be another Edward, Zhu, or Temujin?

CHAPTER FOUR
THE HUNT

Sean Diamont studied his smartphone, tapping his foot to the beeps of the elevator as it raced up Willis Tower. While everyone else watched the changing numbers like lemmings, he didn't bother. He knew exactly when to get off. To him, every moment in life was part of a chess game. One that he played four steps ahead of everyone else. Events could be measured in patterns and sequences. By recognizing and understanding how and when things happened, Sean found that he could live life very efficiently, exactly how Chiyva wished.

Sean first learned the will of his Holy One when Chiyva found him in the jungles of Vietnam. Back then, he was an undisciplined, delinquent youth whom his parents had shipped off to the army. He was so difficult to train that he was almost dishonorably discharged during boot camp. No one expected Sean to return from the war alive.

Chiyva found the eighteen year-old soldier during an intense firefight that left his platoon dead and Sean captured by the enemy. At first, the boy thought himself mad from captivity when his Holy One first spoke. Then, after many months, he realized God had sent an angel to watch over him. Chiyva taught him how to survive the prison camp, how to read the patterns in the guards' patrols, and how to probe for weaknesses in the prison. Together, they hatched an escape plan. Sean wandered in the jungle for three weeks, surviving off the land, until he eventually made his way to friendly forces. Sean never questioned the Genjix again. He led the rescue party back to the prison camp and received a Congressional Medal of Honor, making him a war hero.

Once back in the States, Sean later obtained a law degree from Northwestern University. He was now a managing partner at one of the largest law firms in the country. Not bad for a young rebel who almost didn't finish high school.

The elevator beeped for the fifty-fourth time and without waiting, Sean exited just as the doors opened. His eyes never left his smartphone as he walked five steps forward, twelve to the left through the glass doors, fifty-three to the right to his corner office. This was Chiyva's way, efficiency without errors. This was how Sean escaped the prison, how he reached the pinnacle of society, and how he became one of the leading senior Genjix in the world.

Sean tore his gaze from his work long enough to wink at his secretary as she handed him a stack of documents, never slowing his pace as he proceeded into his office. She grabbed her notebook and followed. Sean hated pen and paper note-taking. It was slow, clumsy, and inaccurate. Meredith had never made the transition to a computer like the rest of civilization. However, her tenure and loyalty to him were indispensable. It would take years to train a new secretary to her level of knowledge of his work.

She also knew about the Genjix and the true nature of their mission. Sean had a level of trust with her that he could never risk replacing. Therefore, he resigned himself to her slow note-taking. He hung his jacket, sat in his chair, and logged onto his computer, listening to her updates as she rambled down the list.

"...and your 3 o'clock has been pushed back to Tuesday," she was saying. "Your sister's birthday is next week. I went ahead and ordered a bouquet of flowers and a card. Do you want to order new winter tires for her? It's been a brutal winter. Your junior associate needs to meet to discuss the Burton merger due diligence. I blocked Wednesday at 10 o'clock for that. You have a meeting with the CEO of Engras Enterprise at 2 o'clock to discuss the government contract for military equipment. And Devin Watson called and requested you contact him at your convenience."

Sean raised an eyebrow at the last name mentioned. He thought through his responses, giving each their proper due, before turning to Meredith and dictating in rapid succession as she scribbled in her notebook. "Ask the CEO of Engras – Nick, isn't it? – to move our meeting to 7 o'clock over drinks at the Palmer House, and order a bottle of the '93 Cheval Blanc he likes. See if you can get some run-flat tires this time instead of that garbage you ordered two years ago. Also, block out the rest of my afternoon." He hid his rising irritation as she frantically tried to keep up.

"Is there anything else?" she asked when she caught up.

"A cup of coffee in fifteen minutes." And then he waved her off.

Sean waited until she closed the door behind her and then pushed a button under his desk. The room began to hum with a deep resonating modulation. The resonance would block any listening devices aimed toward his office. Sean was sure there were no Prophus spies working at the firm, but one could never be too careful. The humming increased in pitch until eventually, he heard nothing. Satisfied, Sean turned on his video phone and called Devin. After three rings, Devin's face appeared on the screen.

"Brother Sean. Chiyva."

"Father."

Devin Watson was an elderly man with a full head of white hair and a long trimmed beard. His face was weathered and scarred from years of battle and conflict, but his eyes shined with wisdom and fanatical devotion. He was also the hemisphere's senior Councilman and one of Sean's few direct superiors. His Holy One, Zoras, was a dominant Genjix who had occupied some of the most powerful and influential individuals in history. And to the Genjix, that equated to rank and seniority.

"Did we receive a response from the mayor?" Devin lit a cigar and puffed on it.

"I'm afraid so." Sean leaned toward the screen. "He can't convince the city council or the state legislature to allow us to build an offshore platform on Lake Michigan, at least not one with our security requirements. Even with his influence, there are too many questions being raised about the general purpose, and our geological research scenario is being challenged by the environmentalists."

Devin grimaced and took another puff. "This will hinder our manufacturing operations in the Midwest. You need to go back and remind the mayor who put him in office."

Tell him the alternative.

"There may be another solution," Sean suggested carefully. "The mayor has always been a friend and grateful for our contributions. He has offered, as an alternative, the use of land just east of Northerly Island."

Devin frowned, took another puff of the cigar, and looked off the screen, presumably at a map. "Underwater?"

"Exactly, Father," Sean continued. "We take the operation twenty meters underwater off the coast. The mayor has offered the option to build the facility there and connect it to the surface through underground tunnels. Airborne operations can occur at night, and the mayor has assured me that we will not require an audit from the municipal or state government. Basically, everything we need, just not as we had initially planned."

"And the cost?" With Devin, it always came down to cost.

Sean pulled up a file on his computer and scanned through its contents. Satisfied, he turned back toward the screen and smiled. "I just sent you the summary information. The costs are well within the original parameters, maybe two to three per cent higher, due to the need to drill underwater, but not more than five. The short term costs will be higher because of the underwater construction, but we will save in the long run because we will not need to mask the facility from the public."

"Excellent. I'll review these numbers and get back to you. Good work, Sean. I'll expect a project timeline this week. Make sure the critical path does not extend past eighteen months. I expect to go into mass production within eighteen months."

"Of course, Father. Is there anything else?"

Devin took another deep puff. The smoke was so thick that it obscured the screen. Sean wondered if the old man was trying to kill himself with all those cigars. Or was it his Holy One?

Do not think sacrilegiously.

"Apologies, Chiyva, I meant no disrespect."

"Yes." Devin leaned closer to the screen. "What is the status with the break-in at the research base? How does it affect us?"

Sean shrugged. "They know of the program now. As to whether they know what it is designed for? I'm sure they will discern it in time. They were only able to infiltrate our archives. The stolen blueprints were from an earlier failed design; it is a complete dead end, but will occupy them for a year or two before they realize that. We lost one vessel to the Eternal Sea, Yrrika, and we gained a defector. They lost Edward Blair."

"Blair, huh. They must have wanted the blueprints badly to send him. And Tao?"

"Escaped, but we have some strong leads on his new vessel. I have a briefing with the kill team momentarily, as a matter of fact."

Devin scowled. "That's too many resources to expend on a new vessel. You should be focusing your efforts on a Class A target like Haewon operating in your area. Tao's nothing more than a thorn in the side."

"It's Tao," Sean replied flatly. "Chiyva wills it, I obey."

"As you should always obey, Sean." Devin chuckled. "But don't let Chiyva's grudges dictate your priorities, Sean."

"I am only the instrument of the Holy Ones," Sean replied. "Haewon's trail has grown cold anyway. She hasn't been on radar since the Katrina cover-up."

"Haewon should still be the priority if her vessel ever materializes, understand?"

"Of course, Father. The kill team has orders to hunt both."

"Who is leading them?"

"Why, one of their own."

Devin nodded. "Yes, our double-crossing mole who alerted us to their raid. You mentioned the defection in your last report. Who was it, Jeo's vessel? Were we able to acquire any solid information on the Prophus network?"

"Not as much as we would like. He was not privy to higher security systems. However, Jeo assisted in the designing of many of their older networks and we are exploring those options. Who better to hunt Prophus than someone who is familiar with their protocols?"

"Good, good. Keep me informed."

Sean kept watching the screen after it turned black. Regardless of what Devin said, Sean knew where Chiyva's priority lay. His Holy One had made that abundantly clear. Tracking Tao's new host was not going to be easy. The Prophus were slippery with their new hosts. Chances were he had already gone into hiding.

The Genjix were having an increasingly difficult time tracking Prophus movements ever since their last major conflict in Brazil when the Prophus-backed ruling party fell. The Prophus had been on the defensive ever since, the noose tightening around them bit by bit as they lost more and more engagements. They were now more covert than ever.

A renegade Prophus might give the Genjix better prospects, though. It had been over half a century since the last defection, so it was a rare opportunity to utilize someone who had experience with the inner workings of the Prophus.

"Just waiting for you to stick your head out, little rabbit..." Sean's voice trailed off as he drummed his fingers along the desk. "We'll have a net waiting for you." He pushed the button on his intercom. "Meredith, is my 10 o'clock here yet?"

"Yes, Sean. He's been waiting for you."

"Send him in."

Marc walked into his office and sat down in the chair opposite Sean. Looking like he just got out of bed, Marc wore a brown golf shirt and a pair of worn blue jeans. Sean gave him one cursory glance and began typing on his computer.

Fifteen minutes passed before Sean said another word. "I trust your new quarters are to your liking?"

Marc shrugged. "Sure beats the hell out of what I had before."

"And your stipend is adequate."

Marc nodded.

Sean gave Marc a hard look. "Good, then you will wear a suit and be dressed appropriately whenever you are in this office. This is still a law firm, and you're a fool if you think your appearance today didn't raise eyebrows. Do I make myself clear?"

Startled, Marc bowed in response.

Sean went back to his work on the computer. "Now, you have a chance to prove your worth to us. Your standing is low and since you failed to deliver Tao, you're still on shaky ground. This will be your chance to rectify that. Follow me." Sean grabbed his jacket and strolled out of his office, tapping Meredith's desk as he passed by. She followed close behind with pen and paper in hand. Marc, unused to Sean's methods, had to hurry to catch up.

"Are my people in place?" Sean asked.

Meredith nodded. "The personnel you requested were all contacted last night. All flew in this morning, with the exception of two who are still on missions for the Vatican. They will arrive later this week."

"Excellent." Forty steps down this hall, left turn, five steps forward, right turn, nine steps echoed in the back of his mind. Meredith struggled to keep up while reading her notes. "They are waiting in your private meeting room."

Sean walked down the hallway to an elevator and stopped at the door. He stared at the closed doors. It bothered him that the elevator was not waiting for him. It was a small matter which Meredith would have to address. He turned irritably toward her and shook his head. "Fix this." She understood exactly what he meant.

The elevator door opened. Sean and Marc walked in while Meredith stood outside, still scribbling in her notebook. Sean waited for her to catch up before he spoke again. "We need to have our contact in the IRS run those checks on the paper trails. The Prophus are good at hiding their own, and this trail can't be allowed to get cold. I don't care if flags are raised. I want validated information on my desk tonight."

She nodded. "Anything else?"

The nephew and the anniversary.

"Of course, I was wrong to forget, Chiyva."

You must be aware of all things, Sean. Only then can you inspire others through control.

"Apologies, Holy One."

Sean smiled at her and spoke, "I know your nephew is in the hospital for an appendectomy. Be assured that the bill has been seen to. Also, please convey my congratulations on your wedding anniversary. You may leave at 5 o'clock today."

The elevator door closed before she could reply. This time, Sean did not bother counting the beeps as the elevator sped down to the basement to a secret Genjix safe house. A few minutes later, he entered a private room deep underground. The fifteen people waiting for him stood up when he entered. He nodded to a few of them and ignored the rest. They knew who he was, and that was the only thing that mattered.

There were five Genjix among them. Two were newly raised enforcers whom Sean trusted enough for mid-level missions. Three were older Genjix assigned to assist with confirmation of the vessel. While their technology was advanced enough to track Quasing outside a vessel, there was still no reliable method of detecting a Quasing within a vessel other than through physical contact by another vessel. At least, not yet. Standard vessels were too valuable to expend on a surveillance team, but Chiaolar, Heefa, and Iku's vessels were old and no longer fit for active fieldwork. This mission would be a perfect way to utilize these resources. The Genjix did not waste.

Sean nodded to Marc, who took a seat next to him. The rest were humans with ambitions to become vessels, hoping to prove themselves worthy enough to be blessed. This mission would be the perfect test to see which one of them was the most deserving.

"Praise to the Holy Ones," Sean said, taking a seat.

"Praise to the Holy Ones," those in the room intoned.

"Some of you I know, and the rest of you aren't worth knowing until you prove yourself," he started off. "There are two more operatives on their way, once their duties elsewhere are concluded." Sean clicked a button on the table and the room dimmed. A screen on the far wall turned on and an image of Edward appeared.

"This is the Prophus agent Edward Blair, killed last night infiltrating our Hancock research facility. His Prophus, Tao, is a senior player in the conflict. Notable vessels: Genghis Khan, Lafayette, and Sun Yat-sen."

A picture of a dark-skinned woman appeared next to Edward. "This is Stephanie Qu, operating under an unknown alias. Her Prophus, Haewon, is one of their primary rainmakers. Notable vessels: Churchill, Voltaire, and Peter the Apostle.

"We have fresher leads on Tao, so that will be your primary focus. Security forces tracked him to a large male under two meters, heavyset, with dark hair. Possible ethnicities could be Latino, Asian, or he could just be fond of the tanning bed. The target escaped driving a white sedan believed to be American-made, most likely a Ford, a four-seater model made within the past five years. Unfortunately, there were no cameras in the vicinity to record the information.

"Your mission is to track and confirm the new vessel. The Prophus hide their people well. Obviously they have already washed any relevant data in the government systems, so scan for those characteristics. I want passive surveillance until he is located. Then physical confirmation must be made and the vessel captured alive. I don't care if you put him in a coma, as long as he is still breathing. Also, put surveillance on Edward's family. Knowing how sentimental the Prophus are, Tao's new host is bound to pay a visit one of these days."

"White car and a short fat guy? Not much to work with," Marc said.

"If this were easy, I would have just pulled up his address by now and kicked down his door myself," Sean growled.

"What about DMV records?" one of the humans asked. "There can't be that many white sedans in the city."

"The Prophus aren't stupid." Marc shook his head. "Even if you locate the right car, all their records will have been washed, the license plate will lead to a dead end. The Social Security number was probably wiped within an hour of Tao finding a new host. Bank records, medical records, everything would have been altered by now."

"Will we have access to Homeland Security's camera network?" Iku's host asked.

Sean nodded. "You will have complete access to the entire city. I expect active monitoring on the entire grid from 7am to 7pm every day."

"Those cameras are in black and white," someone stated the obvious. "A white car will be difficult to tell apart from other light-colored cars. It'll be a needle in a haystack."

"I didn't say the task was going to be simple. Earning the right to a Holy One requires your diligence. Prove you are worthy," snapped Sean.

"Why not monitor the city around the clock?" Marc asked. "Maybe he works at night. We can put a few resources on the night shift."

Sean shook his head. "We're paying fifty grand an hour for this access. There's a global recession going on here, people. Even we are affected. You'll have access only from seven till seven."

Marc whistled in disbelief at the cost.

"What is the mission timeline?" asked Amber, one of the enforcer vessels.

"As long as it takes. However, I will be displeased if I receive a billion-dollar bill on my desk. See that our quarry is captured sooner rather than later. No doubt the Prophus are hard at work readying this vessel. As you all know, a new vessel is the most vulnerable in the early stages, so time is of the essence. The longer this takes, the more difficult it will be for you to take him down. Furthermore, we're in a major city so the rules of engagement are limited. I want this quiet. We don't need another LA riot to cover up our war. We do not need the heat. Anything else?" No one said a word.

Sean stood up. "You have your orders. All relevant intelligence is being transferred to your accounts right now. Let me remind you of the critical nature of this assignment. Both Hae-won and Tao are considered high-priority targets who are in the upper Prophus echelon. For now, focus on Tao. He is at his weakest right now. We might not have another chance to take him out permanently. Brother Marc will be leading this team. He has intimate knowledge of Prophus protocols and operates with my authority. Do I make myself clear?"

"Yes, Father," the group chorused.

Sean nodded and left the room. He would leave it to Jeo to sort through the details. It'd also be a good test of Jeo's loyalties and competence as well. The two enforcers already had instructions to put a bullet in his head if he did something unacceptable. Marc would accomplish the mission and deliver this Prophus, or die trying. He walked down the hall and pushed the button to activate the elevator, again fuming at the need to wait. Meredith better have this taken care of very soon, anniversary or no anniversary.

CHAPTER FIVE
DAY AFTER

Beep.

Roen woke up groggy, slowly gaining consciousness to the strangest sensation. Something didn't feel right. His bed felt particularly stiff and the view was wrong. Now that he thought about it, it was also cold, and his blanket was nowhere in reach. He paused. Why was he sleeping on the floor?

Groaning, he sat up and stared at his Chicago Bears phone lying off its hook. Oh no, was he drunk-dialing again? He tried in vain to remember the events from the previous night. Roen often worried that he did incredibly stupid things while inebriated, things he didn't remember the next day. Unfortunately, everything past stumbling through the front door was a big haze. Picking himself up, he walked to the bathroom and stared into the mirror. He looked like the walking dead, with bloodshot eyes and a haggard swollen face.

"I think I'm still drunk." He winced, feeling the room sway back and forth. Roen flexed his arms and chest, and sucked in his gut. With a disapproving scowl, he slapped his belly and walked back into his room, surveying the carnage of clothes strewn over the floor. His stomach growled and he wondered why he was suddenly so famished. Well, who was he to argue with his belly? Time to eat.

Beep.

What was that sound? His cell phone! Roen rummaged through a pile of clothes, patting the pockets on each pair of pants. Finally, he found it in a wrinkled pair of khakis discarded in the corner. He sorted through the messages, finding two texts which were sent exactly five minutes apart.

It's 11. Where are you?

I was expecting you in two hours ago.

Roen read the messages again, perplexed. Why would Musday care where he was on a Saturday?

"Crap!" he yelled as he threw on the same pair of khakis and frantically looked for a shirt. Now he remembered why he wanted to make it an early night yesterday. He was supposed to work this morning. As he was about to head out the door, his stomach growled again, and he nearly doubled over in pain.

Roen rubbed his belly and looked up at the clock. He didn't remember ever being so hungry that it hurt. Did he have time to cook a quick breakfast? He was already late. His brain and his stomach had a tug of war for a few seconds on what he should do next; the stomach won and he rushed into the kitchen to make some eggs. It just wouldn't do if he passed out at the office. Half a dozen eggs, two pieces of bacon, and three sausage links later, Roen rushed out the door, still buttoning his shirt just as the clock struck 11.45.

He stepped off the thirty-sixth floor in his office building a few minutes past noon and sneaked toward his cubicle, trying hard not to be seen. He crept down the hallway and turned down one of the aisles. Brushing his shirt to smooth out the creases, he walked by one of the cubicles and smiled at the person sitting there.

"Hey Jill, good afternoon."

Jill Tesser looked up from her work, her thick-rimmed glasses hanging low on her nose; a hint of dimples appeared as she smiled, her face lighting up the room. Roen caught himself staring at her light auburn hair and the faint freckles that accented her bright hazel eyes. He looked away, his face turning bright red.

"Oh, hey, Roen. I see that the slave drivers got you coming in today too, huh?"

"Um, yeah," he stammered. He tried to formulate a clever response. "Yes, they did."

She grinned and went back to work. He stood there awkwardly, trying to think of something to say. She looked back at him. "Oh, I'm sorry. Was there something you needed?"

"Um... no. Just wanted to say hi." Roen waved and then, feeling his ears burn, fled to the end of the aisle across three more rows toward his own cubicle. Trying to appear as casual as possible, he crept to his seat and powered on his laptop. He leaned back and looked around at his disheveled desk that mirrored the state of his bedroom. He was in a six-by-six foot cubicle with blue and red carpeted walls that probably were once popular during the 1960s. Assorted stacks of paper, books, and bags of snacks littered the desk. Roen picked up a half-eaten bag of stale chips and popped one into his mouth.

"I was expecting you in at 9am," a voice said behind him. Roen turned to see his manager standing with his arms crossed. With a carefully combed-over hairdo and a hefty beer belly, Musday had the sort of rotund figure that Roen feared he'd acquire if he spent a few more years at the office. He already wasn't that far off.

"I'm sorry, Mr Musday. I forgot I had to come in this morning."

Mr Musday shook his head. "Everyone else got here on time. You're letting the team down."

"I'll get right on it."

"Good to hear." Mr Musday gave him a plastic smile. "I know we can depend on you." Roen preened and grinned as Musday walked away. When someone asked Roen what he did, he'd explain that he typed incoherent commands that performed virtual tasks to create intangible objects. At the very end of the day, Roen wasn't sure what he did or why he did it – just that every two weeks, he received a paycheck for the hours of his life wasted, building these imaginary things on some server located somewhere. Hours later, after almost everyone had left, Roen struggled to finish his work.

Mr Musday walked by with his briefcase just as the sun was setting. "How's it going?"

"Fine, sir. I'm almost done with our builds. Another hour and they should be ready. I can get started on the backups tomorrow."

"Good, good. We need the backups by tonight though. Make sure they're working before you leave. You'll also need to be at the status meeting tomorrow at 7.30am. Will that be a problem?"

"Of course not. I'd be happy to." Inside, Roen cursed his ill fortune. Work would ruin the rest of his weekend. Roen wilted under his manager's expectant gaze and nodded. He stared as Mr Musday chatted with the few remaining coworkers still milling about, walked into the elevator, and left – probably to enjoy the rest of his weekend while his minions slaved away.

"I hate this job. One of these days, I'm just going to quit. I can't believe Musday asked me to come in again on a Sunday! Sunday's for God and football," Roen muttered out loud. He opened his drawer and ripped open a new bag of chips.

"So?" said Peter, who sat in the cubicle across the aisle.

"It's ridiculous. They don't care about our personal lives."

Peter turned from his monitor and looked at Roen. "Do you care about your personal life?"

"Of course I do."

"Then why didn't you tell Musday you're busy?" Peter asked.

"I can't do that. I'll get a bad review."

"But you just said you hate this job and want to quit."

Roen paused. Peter reminded him of a plaid-wearing Dalai Lama with his rail-thin frame and shaved head. The man looked much older than his forty years. The wisdom he often spouted made painful sense to Roen.

Roen said, "I can't just quit. I have rent, and a cat to support."

"There's your answer, then."

"Doesn't mean I have to like it," Roen said, pouting.

"You're not being paid to like your work."

Roen leaned back in his chair and looked up at the ceiling. "You know, I wasn't always meant to be an engineer. I was pretty good at debating. I bet I could have been a lawyer."

"It's not too late," Peter said. "Go back to school."

"Well, I'm already too busy with this stinking job. I don't have time."

Peter stopped typing and turned to Roen. "You're still young. Study for the LSAT. Go back to school."

"I can't. I have rent and a cat..."

"I know about the cat, Roen. So are you going to do anything about it besides complain?"

Roen sighed. He said, "No, I guess not. Drag my butt into work tomorrow. You have any candy, Pete?"

Peter stood up and walked over to Roen's desk, poured a few M&Ms onto the desk, and petted the large glass figurine of a Japanese lucky cat on Roen's desk. Peter said, "Listen, man, figure out what you want to do and do it, or we're going to have this same conversation when you're fifty and I'm retiring. You'll never be happy if you don't have a passion for what you do." He went back to his desk, and the two sat in silence.

Finally, Roen asked, "Do you have a passion for what you do, Pete?"

Peter gave his wise old man chuckle, causing Roen to visualize the Dalai Lama sitting in a cubicle, being an office monkey. "Honestly, does anyone dream they'll be doing what we do for a living?"

"Then why do you do it?"

Peter turned to him and smiled. "Because I have a wife and two little kids to support, and they're my passion."

Roen hated that pragmatic response, and hated himself even more for not having a similar excuse. He didn't even have a dream; he just existed. Depressed, he looked back at his monitor and slogged away at his work.

It was well past 10pm by the time Roen left the office. Heels dragging, he trudged out of the building and made the lonely walk to the parking garage. The clouds were out in full force tonight, common at this time of year, and a stiff breeze came in from the lake. Roen picked up the pace a bit as he walked the six long blocks to his car. He had the option of parking closer at the Grant Park garage, but parking there cost thirty bucks. That's like two pizzas, so he was resigned to making the long trek to the further away but cheaper garage. He continued south on Wabash and crossed the street, hearing the rumbling of the train as it passed nearby.

Roen's highly attuned sense of self-preservation began to let him know it was unhappy. Something didn't feel right and he fidgeted as his eyes darted up and down the street. It was deserted except for a homeless guy crossing the intersection towards his side. There was no one walking behind Roen either. This part of the Loop was poorly lit and was a bit rougher than the business district just a few blocks north.

Then the homeless guy changed directions and moved onto an intercept course. Roen sighed. He had learned to always keep a few dollar bills on hand to give to beggars. It was the easiest way to get rid of them. Roen handed a buck over before the homeless guy even said a word. "Here you go," Roen said hastily, and tried to pass him.

"Thanks, boss," the homeless guy replied, shifting to his left to block Roen's path. "Look man, I'm hungry. Dollar ain't gonna buy much. Let me get a few more for a meal." He stepped in really close. Roen could smell faint traces of liquor and the stale aroma of unwashed clothing.

"Sorry," Roen mumbled and tried to pass him again. Again, the homeless guy blocked his path, more insistently this time. "Hey, back off," Roen stuttered, trying to keep the homeless guy at arm's length.

The homeless guy pushed him hard, causing Roen to stumble a few steps. "Why you gotta push me? I'm just asking for a couple bucks to eat."

Not one for confrontation, Roen turned into a side alley and immediately regretted his decision. Alleys were where bad things happened and he just did the exact thing the *Idiot's Survival Guide to the City* would tell him not to do. It was a dead end. He turned around and faced the homeless guy, slowly retreating. "All right, how much you need for a meal?"

The homeless guy grinned. "Price just went up, boss. You gone hurt my feelings." Then he became a mugger as he pulled out a knife. "It's going to cost you your cash, your train pass, that bag you carrying, oh hell, everything you got."

Roen fought the rising panic climbing up his throat as he stumbled backwards. How did he get himself into these situations? He thought, Damn you, Musday!

"Look," he stammered, barely getting the words out, "let's talk this over. I can give you my money, but this is my work bag. I need the stuff in it. I'll get in trouble."

"You don't think you're in trouble now? This ain't no negotiation, asshole."

Tell him that he can have the money, but you are keeping your bag.

Roen looked confused. "What did you say?"

"What's wrong with you, boss? God, you dumb. Give me your stuff or I stick you."

Roen retreated until his back bumped against a garbage dumpster. He began to hyperventilate.

What kind of a mugger uses a knife? It is almost insulting. Listen carefully, there are some wine bottles at your feet. Pick them up.

"Who is this? What's going on?" Roen cried.

Your feet. Bottles. Pick. Them. Up. Now!

The mugger advanced. "I'm losing my patience with you, tubby. You're going to be a fat dead man any minute."

Roen looked down at the ground and saw several empty wine bottles. He picked up one in each hand and brandished them in front of him.

Hold them by the neck. The neck. The skinny part.

Roen hastily switched his grip. "Stay back," he warned. The mugger paid him no attention and continued to advance. He was no further than a few feet away now.

Break the bottles and wield them in front of you.

For a split second, Roen saw an image of a black-armored gladiator standing in an arena holding two swords, one held high over his head and the other in front of his chest. He didn't know what was going on or who was talking, but he was so scared right now that he did whatever this voice said. He took the two bottles and smashed them together.

Thunk. They didn't break.

What the...? Roen looked down and tried again.

Thunk. Thunk. The damn bottles wouldn't break.

"Oh, for the love of..." Roen gritted his teeth and tried again.

Thunk. Thunk. They finally shattered into two jagged shards and he waved them in front of him triumphantly, trying to imitate that already fading image of the gladiator.

Good. Say something mean.

"Wha'... what?"

Threaten him.

"You... you give me all your money!" Roen yelled.

That is not what I meant.

The mugger did a double-take. "What? I'm robbing *you*. Give me all your money!"

"Not anymore!" Roen cried. "I'm robbing you."

"You can't rob me. That's not how it works." The mugger no longer seemed so sure of himself and retreated a few steps.

The two stood far apart from each other, both harmlessly waving their respective weapons. Every time Roen advanced, the mugger retreated. And every time the mugger moved forward, Roen scampered backward. They began yelling curses at each other.

"Come on, you fat asshole," the mugger snarled.

"You're a jerk, and you stink," Roen answered.

Attack.

Roen's eyes darted around the alley. "Is my brain trying to get me killed?"

Bullies are cowards. Attack!

Nearly a minute into their standoff, after a lot of bravado on both sides, something in Roen snapped. With a burst of momentary courage and the high-pitched roar of a raging mouse, he swung the broken bottles above his head and charged. The mugger seemed to have enough and fled. Roen chased him for about twenty feet before the physical exertion wore him out. He stopped and bent over, panting.

Let him go. You did well. Go home.

"Who is this?" Roen said, in between gasps.

The voice was silent. Afraid that the mugger would come back, Roen hustled as fast as he could to his car and drove home. He stepped through his front door shortly after 11pm, still shaking. His heart felt like it was going to burst out of his chest. It was too bad Antonio was working at the hospital tonight. He could really use someone to talk to.

Roen plopped himself onto the couch and turned on the television. His stomach growled and he decided that it was time for another dinner. He tossed his shirt onto the floor, popped in a frozen pizza, and proceeded to channel-surf, never staying on one for more than a few seconds. This went on for the better part of an hour as he tried to decide what to watch. It wasn't until after he finished his pizza that he decided there was nothing worth watching.

Roen looked up at the clock; it was just past midnight. With a sigh, he picked himself off the couch, moved to the bedroom, and turned on his computer. He grabbed a bag of chocolate chip cookies lying next to his computer and began to dig through it. For the rest of the night, he played on the computer, immersing himself in a video game – until the clock reminded him that he had to be up in a few hours.

Wearily, he tore himself away from the computer and made his way to bed, idly thinking that he should sign up for a gym sometime this year. He had been saying that since New Year's, and it was already March. Soon, he would do it. Just not this week. Maybe next month. Or maybe when summer started. Definitely sometime before the year ended.

CHAPTER SIX
FIRST CONTACT

Music blared from the radio. Tao woke with a start and listened to the very annoying sound. If pain was a sensation a Quasing could feel, he knew he would be in some right now. The music was so loud he couldn't make out the tune, not that it mattered. Tao was not well versed with most of the musical genres of the past half century. Edward's taste had centered on baroque, which irritated Tao no end. He had more than his fill of baroque music since, well, the baroque era. Musical choice, unfortunately, was never his. Therefore, he took special interest in the musical taste of new hosts, knowing he would be at their mercy for that lifetime.

Getting rid of that alarm clock would be one of the first things he made Roen do after they had officially established contact. That thing just ground on Tao's nerves. Worse yet, Sleeping Beauty here let it blare for up to half an hour sometimes before finally dragging himself out of bed to turn it off.

Tao had bided his time and studied his new host now for nearly two weeks. He almost introduced himself during the attempted mugging, but thought better of it – since at that time, he didn't know enough about Roen to properly make contact with him. Since then, he watched the man live his completely stifling life over and over again, one repetitive day at a time. It was so consistent that Roen even complained about the same things at the same times every day. As far as Tao was concerned, that Peter fellow sitting next to him at work was a saint for putting up with all this. Today would be different, though. Tao was going to start fixing his host and prepare him for what lay ahead.

Roen stirred and turned over, pulling the blanket over his head, muttering something about the television and burying himself deeper under the covers. The radio continued for another twenty minutes before Roen finally did something about it. With an irritated hiss, he rolled out of bed and dragged himself to the desk. He slammed the snooze button and looked at the clock: 7.30am. "I got an hour," he yawned. He lumbered back to bed and collapsed onto the mattress, burrowing a hole under the messy layer of blankets. Ten minutes later, the music came back as loud and annoying as ever.

Tao couldn't think of a more miserable way to start the day. Amazingly, it failed to stir his hibernating host. He waited for Roen to shut it off again, but the man did not stir. How did anyone sleep through this? Tao's patience began to wear thin. While technically time was something he had an infinite supply of, he was not a very patient Quasing. At last, unable to stand the ruckus anymore, Tao ever so casually moved his semi-conscious host's arm and pulled the blanket off his face. Roen rolled over, mumbled something incomprehensible, and pulled the blanket back over his face.

Are you serious? Tao immediately regretted the outburst.

Roen still didn't move. He slept like a rock! This was not a good trait for a soldier. The man was like a hibernating bear and could probably sleep through a firefight. After another ten minutes, Tao had had enough. This wasn't the best way to initiate first contact, but with this host, the sooner the better. Anything else just delayed the inevitable. Roen rolled to his other side, still sound asleep.

Roen Tan!

"Five more minutes," Roen whimpered.

You are going to be late for work.

"Come on, just five more minutes."

Just who do you think you are talking to?

Roen was about to say something else, when he hesitated and opened his eyes. His eyes shifted back and forth and he crawled out of the mess of blankets inch by inch, looking under his pillow and checking under the bed for anything strange. With a perplexed look, he shut off the alarm, yawned, and walked to the bathroom where he splashed water on his face and brushed his teeth. Afterward, he patted his cheeks a few times and studied his reflection in the mirror.

"Hey, what's up? You want some of this?" Roen waved his hands over his head as if he was brandishing the bottles again. This was a daily routine he'd been doing ever since that night. "Yeah, that's what I thought. Give me your money!" He swung his arms in the air. It was a laughable scene, though Tao was pleased that Roen had recovered from the incident enough to be light-hearted about it. He had spent the first week paranoid, frightened, and unsure of his sanity.

But as the week went on, his new host began to enjoy retelling the story to anyone who would listen, embellishing it more and more each time he told it. By yesterday, he took on three men, was bouncing off the walls, and was throwing bottles as if they were shurikens.

At least he had a good attitude about it. One of Tao's old hosts, a certain French general during the American Revolutionary War, used to mope for days after a battle. Tao had trained that out of him real fast.

Another positive from that night was Roen's reaction during the mugging. Even when terrified, he took direction surprisingly well under stress. That was a very important quality that could not always be trained. It was a good trait to have in an agent. And grudgingly, Tao had to admit that Roen was brave as well. Not many people these days would blindly follow orders and charge into battle. That characteristic had good and bad points. Still, it was a trait Tao found useful.

"No voices today, right?" Roen continued his morning re-enactment. "You can't handle this!" He gestured at his large body. After nearly two minutes of dancing in front of the mirror, Roen winked at himself and completed his ritual. Walking back into his room, he looked at the clock and shouted, "Damn that alarm clock! I'm going to be late again!" He hurried to his closet and studied the scattered clothes lying around. Then he looked at the floor and picked up the same pair of pants he wore yesterday. He sniffed them to make sure they passed the smell test and then put them on.

You wore those yesterday. They are dirty. Tao injected that sentence very subtly. Dirty pants were not a great subject for an introduction, but how could Roen even consider walking outside with those on?

Roen stopped, one leg in a pant-leg. He turned to his left and then to his right. He looked up at the ceiling and then back down at his pants. "No voices, no voices," he whispered. Then he looked down at his pants. "Damn, they really are dirty," he muttered. He spit on his hand and rubbed at the stains and wrinkles left from a previous lunch mishap. He was about to throw them into the laundry hamper when he noticed that it had long since overflowed. Roen looked up at the clock again. "Oh, hell with it," he muttered as he snatched the nearest pair of pants in arm's reach and rushed out the door.

Roen rubbed his eyes and tried to stifle the yawn escaping his lips. Three hours at work in the War Room – listening to person after person drone on about statistics this, stress tests that, and control variables something – was more than he could take. Every fifteen minutes, someone would ask him to stop this transaction, start that script, bounce those servers, or check some data. It was unbearable! Most of the requests were met with a sullen "Sure," "OK," or "Whatever."

When he wasn't working, he passed the time doodling in a notebook, drawing little pictures of animals, stars, and smiley faces. Occasionally, Roen would get ambitious and try to draw a symmetrical polygon. After he tired of geometric shapes, he turned the page and settled on a new artistic endeavor. When he finished, he beamed at the picture of a plump donkey wearing a suit and carrying a briefcase. He drew some word balloons over its head and wrote out the caption, "I am what I do."

Then why do you do it?

Roen stopped, the pen falling from his hand. The words bounced around in his head, repeating eerily over and over as they sank into the pit of his stomach.

"Why do I do what?" He said those words very slowly.

Do what you are doing.

Roen leaped out of his chair, knocking his chair over and looking wide-eyed around the room. Everyone stopped what they were doing and stared at him. "Peter, did you say something just now about what I'm doing?" Roen asked, stark panic in his voice.

Peter frowned. "Did I what?"

"I don't know. You tell me."

"I don't know either. You lost me, man," Peter shook his head and gave Roen his Dalai Lama look. "You all right?"

Tell them no and that you are quitting.

"That! Did you just say that?"

Peter's look became one of concern. "You look sick, Roen. Maybe you should get some fresh air."

"I... I..."

...quit. I am walking out of here and never coming back.

"...be right back. I have to step outside for a moment."

Roen practically tripped over himself as he fled and bolted for the restroom. He ran into one of the stalls and locked it. Sitting on the toilet, he took deep breaths and tried to clear his thoughts. The voice was happening again. Was it him saying these things, or was something saying these things to him... from him? What was going on?

"Oh no, not again. I must have done something last night, like I did that other night when it happened. What did I do the same? That's it! I had pizza both nights, and this is some sort of crazy allergic reaction."

Really, Roen Tan? Do you actually think pizza makes you hear voices? Because technically, you had pizza six times in the past two weeks, and I did not talk to you any of those other times. So calm down, and let me explain.

Roen froze. That last bit was definitely not him, or was it? He just didn't know anymore. "I'm going crazy. That, or I have a conscience that has somehow detached itself from my conscious mind, like an active conscious subconscious. That's not good, I think. Well, crazy people don't think they're crazy. So if that's true, and I think I'm crazy, then I must not be going crazy. But if I decide that I'm not crazy, that only enforces the theory that crazy people don't think they're crazy, and I'm actually crazy. So should I think I'm crazy or not?"

Your circular logic is quite dizzying.

Roen stood up and stamped his feet. "What the hell is going on?"

Sit back down. Better yet, leave. I would rather not discuss this in a urinal.

"Who are you? Was that you that other night? Are you that bald guy I saw in my head?" Roen hissed out loud.

No need to speak out loud. I can hear your thoughts just fine.

"OK, who are you?" Roen felt weird thinking to himself like this.

This is a bit complicated. But first, let me assure you that insanity is the least of your concerns. And yes, it was me that night helping with the mugger. That bald man was Oenomaus, a great gladiator that once defeated me. It is complicated. Care to go for a stroll?

"Why?"

Because sitting in a park talking this over is much more pleasant than conversing over a toilet. Besides, I have not seen Millennium Park yet. I hear it is quite lovely.

"But I have to go back to my meeting."

We need to talk about that too. Why are you working at a job you hate?

"I have rent and..."

Yes, yes, and a cat. Listen, Roen Tan, you might be hallucinating and possibly insane. I think right now that meeting is the least of your concerns.

"Didn't you just say I wasn't insane?"

Just putting a little perspective on your priorities.

The voice had a point. Roen opened the stall door a crack and peeked out. He tiptoed out of the restroom, looking both ways as he crept down the hall like he was Jack Maclean robbing the Smithsonian.

That is not necessary. Act natural.

Roen stood up as straight as he could and waddled like a robot toward the elevator.

I said natural.

"I'm trying! Besides, my natural reaction is to run screaming and hide under my desk."

You would not fit under it.

"Hey!"

My apologies. That was not appropriate.

Roen pushed the down button and waited, his foot nervously tapping the floor. When it arrived, he walked in and began pacing in circles as the elevator sped down.

Stop it. Relax.

"I'm sorry. It's a bad habit I have when I get nervous."

There is nothing to be nervous about. Please believe that.

"So, why did you start talking to me that night?"

I saw that you were in trouble and helped you the best I could. Now, go outside and get some fresh air. We have much to discuss.

The elevator reached the ground floor and Roen practically fled the building, running as fast as his stubby legs would go. Feeling faint, he slowed down and made his way across the street toward Grant Park. It was a cloudless, beautiful day, not at all the sort of day he expected to learn that he was clinically insane.

Roen shaded his eyes from the sun as he crossed the intersection. The streets were bustling with people strolling about enjoying the afternoon. Birds chirped and a calm cool breeze brushed against his skin. Roen, stressed and exercise challenged, was wheezing by the time he reached a warm open walkway next to several beds of flowers.

Find a nice bench. Enjoy the day.

Roen avoided the sunny paths, choosing to stay in the shade under the tall trees and thickets. He passed a row of bushes to a quiet part of the park and sat down on a bench. He looked up at the sky and decided to move to the shaded bench on the other side of the path.

You dislike the sun?

"I sweat easily, and it's bad for my skin."

And eating frozen pizzas is good for your complexion? We can get into that later. Let me introduce myself. My name is Tao, and I am from a race of aliens known as the Quasing. I assure you, you are not crazy and not talking to yourself. I am a calm, rational, benevolent being, and I... we need your help.

"My help?"

Yes. My kind has been on this planet for a long time. We have survived for millions of years through the natural inhabitants on this planet. I have chosen you as my new host. This is both a blessing and a curse.

Roen stood up and began to pace again. "Curse? Wait, you're an alien? I think I'd rather just be crazy."

I have been watching you, and I feel that you are a worthy host.

"What? Really? Are you sure you're talking to the right person?"

Pause. *Yes, I am. Sit back down. I can tell you are melting like Frosty without his top hat here. You will probably want to be sitting when I tell you everything anyway.*

Roen moved under a large tree and held his head in his hands. Then he leaned back against the rough bark of the trunk and closed his eyes. This was simply too fantastic. He fought the urge to check himself into a hospital; hospital visits were expensive. Supposedly, people could hallucinate if they had a tumor in their head.

You would rather me be a tumor than an actual alien?

"Neither are exactly great choices. I mean, how did you get here? What're you doing here?"

Our ship was passing near your system when it was caught in a meteor shower. Its cocoon was damaged and unable to regenerate. Dying, the ship steered us toward your planet, hoping to survive long enough to land. However, your atmosphere petrified its outer membrane as we entered Earth's orbit and the ship broke into several pieces. Our kind was scattered all over the planet. The devastation was massive and caused severe climate changes to your environment.

"Wait, you caused the Ice Age?"

Yes, we indirectly killed the dinosaurs.

"That's impossible. That must have happened millions of years ago!"

Roughly sixty-five, give or take a million.

"OK, I'll bite, so how did you survive the crash? Didn't everything die?"

Most of our kind was killed in the crash. Several thousand of us survived the impact in the harder petrified sections of the membranes. We were scattered to the winds. The survivors learned early on that we could survive through the indigenous creatures by inhabiting them, like I am with you. Over the years, we have moved from host to host.

As each host died, we found another, eventually moving from the dinosaurs to the first mammals.

"That's the craziest thing I've ever heard. So you guys were in dinosaurs; then, did you all get together in your dinosaur bodies and build dinosaur cities?"

You are getting a little carried away. We were cut off from each other for the first several million years. The early animals were too primitive for us to communicate with. It was not until the evolution of the primates that communication between survivors was first established.

Over the course of many years, we individually gravitated toward primates, having discovered that they were evolving at a faster rate. That and having opposable thumbs helped a great deal. They were also more easily influenced and less instinctual. Eventually, two Quasing inhabiting primates of the same tribe began to communicate. You will find that many primate rituals were actually ancient Quasing methods of communication. After that, it became a slow process of gathering all the survivors together.

"Oh, this makes perfect sense now. Million year-old geriatric aliens. How do you stay alive for so long? What's your secret?"

Technically, we self-reproduce, similar to how amoebas on your planet reproduce. Over the course of time, we continually regenerate, sustaining ourselves from the nutrients of our hosts.

"So you're a parasite?"

We like to think of it as symbiotic, but we can discuss biology another time.

"Discuss? I feel like a schizophrenic talking to myself. You know, crazy people don't know..."

I have already heard your theory on conscious insanity.

"Fine. Prove that I'm not the mayor of Cuckoo's Nest."

All right. What if I ask you something that you do not know? Would that satisfy you?

Roen nodded.

What is the capital of old Assyria?

Roen frowned. "Is this a Monty Python question?"

No, this is not. What is the capital of old Assyria?

"I must have missed that episode on *Jeopardy*. I didn't know there was an old and new Assyria."

Assur. I was there when it was destroyed. Look that up if you like. And since there is no way you could have known that, how could you know that now unless someone else told you?

"I guess..." Roen sounded anything but sure. "Let's say I'm not crazy and you are whatever you say you are. What if I don't want you here? How do I get rid of you?"

We can only leave a host upon its death.

"What?!"

You have to die for me to get out. Trust me, sometimes we wish we could just leave voluntarily. It would make things a lot easier for us. If it gives you any comfort, I am as stuck with you as you are with me.

"I'm really not comforted here. But, assuming I believe you, which I don't, if your kind has been here for millions of years, what do you want with me?"

We want to go home, Roen.

"Go home? But if what you're saying is true, which I still don't buy, why..."

Can you just take this at face value for a moment?

"Fine. You seem to be very advanced aliens. Why don't you just build another ship? You've had all this time to do it."

We cannot live in your atmosphere. Our way of existence is vastly different from yours. The gases and environment we need to survive are not indigenous to this world. That is why we need hosts. We cannot recreate technology from our home world. In fact, the ships we used to travel through space are bred, not built. That is something we cannot do here. We have to make do with what this planet has to offer.

Our plan is to utilize the intelligent creatures of this planet to one day take us home. When it became apparent that humans were becoming the dominant species, we pinned our hopes on humans to carry us into space. Over the course of centuries, we have guided humans to greatness in order to further advance your evolution. You will find

*that a number of history's greatest figures had a Quasing helping them
along the way.*

"Really? Like who?"

*Socrates, Alexander, Napoleon, Washington, Churchill, Roosevelt,
Einstein, Bill Gates, Steve Jobs – just to name a few. You will find that
more often than not, almost every great figure had our help.*

"You guys were in Jobs?"

*Let us just say that Steve was not as brilliant as everyone made him
out to be.*

"And you're going to make me great as well?"

You will make yourself as great as you want you to be.

A stiff breeze snapped Roen out of their conversation and he
shivered. Looking up, he saw a mass of clouds rolling in from
the east. He must have been sitting here for a while now. Roen
stood up, stretched his legs, and strolled down the walkway.
This was his first time at the park, even though he worked just
across the street.

His mind raced as he tried to digest everything he just heard.
Any one of these people nearby could have an alien in them.
Roen looked around as couples walked by hand-in-hand with
small children running around. They could have been there
all along and he wouldn't know. It could be anyone! He
walked by the giant silver kidney bean sculpture and watched
curiously as his body shape contorted against the reflective
metal. His face appeared as alien as he felt right now.

"This is nuts," he muttered. "I'm just going crazy. It's the
only rational explanation."

I thought we were making headway. What is the problem now?

"The problem is..." Roen said aloud and stopped when an
elderly couple walked past and looked his way.

Remember, inside voice.

He turned away from them and hunched over. "The problem is that I don't believe you. The story you're telling me is
ridiculous. Aliens, millions of years old, in my brain... that's

just crazy. I must be just stressed out from work, or maybe that
pizza gave me food poisoning, or hell, maybe it's residual guilt
from my last breakup eight years ago. Whatever my excuse is,
it's more rational than having some alien living inside me.
Ockham's Razor, man, Ockham's Razor."

Pluralitas non est ponenda sine necessitate.

"Uh... what?"

*Ockham's Razor. That is what it means. William of Ockham was
one of our people. We used its interpretation to hide our existence when
hosts went insane and gave us away.*

Roen threw his hands up. "What the hell! Is everyone in on
this but me? Am I like the last person in the world not to have
my own personal alien?"

Like I said, we tend to occupy positions of influence.

"So what do I get out of this? Can I get superpowers? Will I
fly? Could I climb walls? Do I need a secret identity like Clark
Kent or Peter Parker?"

*Well, as long as I am alive, your memories will be with me. In a
way, you become almost immortal. And as with my previous hosts,
you have all their memories and skills at your disposal.*

"Is that it?"

There was another long silence before Tao finally spoke. *Are
you serious? You mean having an ancient all-wise being at your disposal is not enough? A thousand lifetimes of knowledge and wisdom
is not sufficient to turn you into some semblance of a capable human
being? Have you not ever heard that knowledge is power? You have
in you one of the wisest minds on this planet and that is not enough
for you?*

"Well, since you put it that way," Roen grumbled. "You
didn't have to be mean about it. It would be nice though if I
got some sort of power."

Well, I apologize, but I will not be able to accommodate you.

"You don't have to be sarcastic."

I just think you should be more appreciative.

"You know, for an extraterrestrial, you act awfully human-like."

We were not always this way. When we first arrived, our personalities were very alien compared to how we are now. Our relationship with humans is symbiotic. You influence us just as much as we influence you. Over the course of time, we became more human in our reactions and our thoughts.

"Will I become more alien?"

Hardly. I have interacted with humans for thousands of years. You will have interacted with us for only your lifetime. It is a little different.

"So, that's it, huh? You and I are stuck together, and we have to make like two peas in a pod. Is there anything else?"

There was another pause before Tao spoke. *There is more we need to discuss, but I believe this is sufficient for today. You should get back to your meeting. They will be missing you.*

Roen looked at his watch and cursed. "Crap, I've been gone for an hour! I'm in so much trouble!" He raced back to his office as fast as he could, huffing and puffing by the time he reached the War Room. Trying to act as casual as possible, he sat back into his chair and shrank from the scowls coming his way.

"Where have you been?" Peter hissed, the serene Dalai Lama demeanor shattered. "We could use some help figuring out this java dump."

"I wasn't feeling well," Roen said stiffly.

"Well, get better fast or we'll be here all night." Peter pushed a stack of printouts toward him.

Roen grimaced at the pages of garble and held in a sigh. "Great, I'm going to be here forever."

It is only a java dump. It should not take that long to figure out.

"Well, it's a little hard for me to focus with everything that's happened today."

Flip the page.

"What? You can read code?"

I can do many things. Here, I am already done. Flip the page.

Roen flipped to the next page.

Again. Next page.

"Already?"

Just flip it.

He flipped to the third page. In a matter of minutes, Tao finished going through the large stack of pages. It actually took Roen longer to flip the pages than it did for Tao to finish scanning them. Eventually, Roen just tossed each finished page on the floor to keep up. Several people in the room snickered. Their amusement turned into amazement when he grabbed Peter's keyboard and typed in a few commands.

"Problem fixed." He grinned. He stood up and grabbed his bag. "Call me if you need anything else. Otherwise, have a good night." Without another word, Roen walked out of the War Room, whistling all the way.

CHAPTER SEVEN
GENJIX

Feeling like he just made parole, Roen pranced out of the office and strolled down the street toward the Grant Park North garage. After experiencing the mugging, he decided that the extra cost of parking close to work every day was well worth it. Evening had fallen and the street lamps were blinking on, lighting up the otherwise dark and quiet streets. Thick rolling clouds were moving in from the horizon, covering much of the sky, with barely a star peeking through, as a strong gust blew in from over Lake Michigan.

Roen shivered and pulled his hood over his head, tightening the straps on his down jacket. He felt like the Stay Puft Marshmallow Man. He dug out an old pair of holey gloves which had seen much better days. Springtime in Chicago was unpredictable and sometimes fiercely cold. That still didn't dampen Roen's mood though. He grinned like a mad fool as he kicked up his feet and brushed his hands along a metal grating. It felt good to not be the most clueless person in the room.

"Hey Tao, how did you know what to fix on that java dump?"

We were involved with the birth of the Internet since the mid-Sixties. There are large divisions of Quasing who advance our cause through the development of human technology. Just like your people, we specialize in different tasks. Some work on technology, others diplomacy, and still others military sciences.

"So would I work in technology?"

I am not talking about the host. The host adapts to his Quasing's specialty, which in my case is infiltration and covert operations. While you obviously are not trained for this, I will teach you.

"Well, I for sure am not cut out for that covert stuff."

We will cross that bridge when we get there.

"That still doesn't explain how you can read java code."

When you have lived as long as we do, you learn to accumulate a lot of different skills.

"Sweet!" Roen's grin grew wider as he fantasized about how much easier his life was about to become. With his own smart alien, he could breeze through work. He would definitely have more time on his hands now. Just let Tao do all the work, and they could go home early every day.

I am not here to be your personal assistant.

"Is there a way for me to block my thoughts from you?"

None whatsoever.

"That sucks."

Such is life. Live with it.

"You know, for an all-wise alien, you're quite snarky."

We have personalities like every other living creature. Just because I am an alien does not mean I am a Vulcan or some soulless robot.

Roen rounded the corner toward the garage entrance and went down the stairs, to the sub-level where he parked. There were many cars parked down here. There must be an event going on in the park. Whistling and not paying attention, he dug out his keys and collided with an old man – wearing a black trench coat – who was just getting out of the car adjacent to his. Nearly bowling the man over, Roen dodged to the side at the very last moment and tripped, falling onto the floor. He cursed his clumsiness as he rubbed his skinned knee.

"Sorry about that," he mumbled, embarrassed.

"It's all right, young man. Let me help you up." The old man reached for his hand.

Stop. Do not touch him. Get up and move away.

"Why? What's going on, Tao?"

Still, Roen did as he was told and picked himself up. "I got it," he mumbled. "Are you all right?"

The man smiled. "No problem..." He paused and studied Roen. "What's your name, son?"

Do not tell him!

"Ro..." he began lamely.

That is Omer Singh, host of Chiaolar, a Genjix! I recognize his face. He sensed something when you two collided, but could not identify me yet. He will if he touches your skin!

"What's a Genjix?"

Your sworn enemy. You need to get away now!

Roen froze. "I have a sworn enemy?"

The old man continued smiling. "Nice to meet you, Ro, is it? I didn't quite catch that. Old ears, you know."

Punch him in the face!

"What?! He's as old as my granddad!"

Now! Punch him and get out of here!

Roen knew this was going to end badly. He could see it now as he got hauled to jail for assaulting a senior citizen. Should he plead the insanity defense or the alien-told-me-to-do-it defense? Taking a deep breath and feeling guilty, Roen balled his hand into a fist and swung at Omer. That feeling of guilt faded when Omer calmly sidestepped the punch, grabbed Roen by the coat, and threw him against the wall. His head bounced off the concrete and Roen collapsed onto the floor.

Omer stood over him, still wearing the pleasant smile. "Surveillance cameras in the garage reported a white Ford parking here over the past two weeks. That was half the puzzle. I apologize if it took me so long to follow up on the lead. There are many white cars to track, after all. This morning, the other half of the puzzle materialized in the shape of an obese man leaving that same white car. So, my question for you, son: are you the puzzle piece we've been looking for, and where were you two Fridays ago?"

You need to escape. Omer Singh is an old enforcer. You are no match for him.

Roen turned over, trying to crawl away. Omer chuckled and pinned him down with his boot. "You know, son, you made me late for a very important evening. It's my anniversary, and I spent it sitting in this dank, cold place. My old bones don't handle the chill so well anymore. Hold still for a moment." He grabbed a mass of Roen's hair and pushed down. Roen's forehead bounced off the hard floor once more. "Hello, Tao." Omer smirked. "We've been looking for you."

He is next to you on your right. Turn around, grab his ankle, and roll. On my mark... now!

In an absolute panic, Roen blindly followed Tao's instructions. He turned over as fast as he could, grabbed the first ankle he got his hands on, and kept rolling. Omer squawked in surprise as he lost his footing and fell onto his knees.

Run! Stay low. Weave through the cars.

Roen scrambled to his feet and ran. Omer snarled, and suddenly Roen heard a loud bang, and then a windshield near him exploded into glass shards.

"Jesus, did he just shoot at me?" Roen turned the corner and ran north, passing by several rows of cars. Several more bullets hit cars and shattered more windows. "God, he's trying to kill me!"

Doubtful, he is most likely aiming for a non-vital area.

"Every part of me is vital!"

Focus. Stay very low, turn to your right once you pass this wall. See that minivan near the opposite corner? Make a beeline toward it and hide behind the rear tire. The minivan, not the truck.

"That truck over there is much bigger. Why not that?"

Because if I was Omer, that would be where I look first. Slow your breathing and be quiet.

Roen slowed and began to crawl on all fours, inching next to the minivan and hiding behind one of the tires. He put a hand over his mouth and tried without much success to stay calm.

"How do you know this guy? What's a Genjix?"

I will explain later. And yes, I have dealt with Omer before.

The sound of footsteps grew louder, echoing all over the garage. Omer was whistling as he walked into this section of the garage where Roen was hiding. Roen peered through the minivan's windows and saw Omer's back to him, looking around.

"You must be new," Omer called out. "Do you even know what is going on? What if I told you I could help? I can take that voice out of your head. Why don't you come out? We'll talk." Omer knelt down and scanned the floor. Roen tried to shrink as small as he could behind the tire.

Next time Omer is facing away from you, climb on to the bumper. Put your back to the wall and lift your feet onto the rear bumper. He will be looking for your feet. It is your only chance.

The whistling and footsteps became louder. Ever so slowly, Roen moved into a crouching position and lifted one leg on the rear bumper of the van. It shifted under his weight but did not make any noise. He leaned his back to the wall and lifted his other leg. Immediately, his legs burned from the strain. He groaned and bit his lip. His thighs and calves began to stiffen and ache.

"I can't hold myself up much longer."

Focus through the pain! Steady your breathing.

"Holy crap! My quads, burning like the heat of a thousand suns..."

Take long breaths. Relax your upper body.

There were sounds of another set of footsteps approaching. "Hey, what's going on here? Someone reported loud noises. Has there been an accident, sir? Oh my..."

There was another loud bang and a short painful cry. Roen squeezed his eyes shut and gritted his teeth. This couldn't be happening! Time slowed and he could hear the rapid beating of his heart.

After what felt like an eternity, the footsteps and whistling faded, replaced by the sound of sirens. With a loud gasp, Roen fell to the floor and held his legs gingerly. They were cramped and he was barely able to stand. He leaned against the wall and rested for a few moments. "He just killed someone! What did he mean by helping me?"

I will explain later. The police will be here any moment. You have to get away. Head north and take the stairs at the far end.

"My car..."

Forget your car. It has already been compromised. Run!

"I am not leaving my car here. Do you know how much they charge to keep it here overnight?"

We will deal with that later. Would you rather pay the extra charge or die?

Tao had a point. A cacophony of sirens was playing directly over his head. There would be a lot of questions if they found him here. Roen ran as fast as he could, reaching the stairs and finally reaching Randolph Street. It was packed with people passing through to a concert just down the block. He stood frozen, unsure of what to do next.

Act casual, call a cab.

Roen waved one down and was soon on his way home. "What is going on, Tao? You never said anything about enemies! Are they Quasing too?"

The Genjix are our enemy. I apologize for not speaking of this earlier. I thought it best to tell you about them at a later time. They must have been tracking you. But yes, they are Quasing as well.

"Why are you fighting? Aren't you all trying to get home?"

Starting from the period you refer to as the Dark Ages, our kind split over philosophical differences in our handling of the humans.

Some believed that humans were too unfocused and primitive, and needed conflict as a means for technological evolution. Others wanted to guide humanity toward a more peaceful direction. Eventually, the philosophical rift became too large and we split into two factions, choosing to pursue our means through different methods. The Genjix felt that if we were not with them, we were against them.

"And this was a piece of information you thought I could be told at a later time?"

That is not the last you will see of them. We have to ready you for our war, your war now. We have to prepare you for what lies ahead.

"Are you kidding? Do I look like someone prepared to fight? I just got my ass handed to me by a guy who gets a senior discount at The Pancake House."

We are going to teach you everything you need to know to survive. Like it or not, you are now a soldier. You must learn the craft of war. Most importantly, you must realize that you are fighting for humanity's freedom as well. If the Genjix succeed, humanity will become embroiled in an endless cycle of conflicts.

"Well, what if I don't want to fight your war? If I wanted to risk my life, I would've joined the army. I have a very low pain threshold. I'm an active coward for very specific reasons."

I am sorry, Roen. I know it is not a choice you wished to make, but that choice is no longer yours. I am here and cannot leave until your death. I did not mean to thrust this upon you, but our fates are now intertwined.

Roen buried his head into his hands for several minutes. Finally, he felt brave enough to look up. "What do we do now?"

Go home and get some rest.

Omer hid behind several trees in Millennium Park and watched as the police lights lit up the streets. He took note of every car that pulled out of the garage exit. None of them was a white car. Tao wouldn't be that stupid. There were too many exits to cover though.

He shook his head as he lit a cigarette and walked away from the crime scene. It would have to do. Omer had done his job and identified Tao. Obviously, the boy was untrained, or an old agent such as himself wouldn't have had such an easy time.

Omer exhaled and slowed his heart rate. He had not tasted close combat in a long time. It was too bad his orders were to take the target alive. Otherwise, Omer was sure he could have killed the new vessel even if his eyes weren't what they used to be.

He'd have to report back as soon as possible, while the description of this host was fresh in his memory, which meant it would likely be a few more hours before he got home. No matter, the plans tonight had already been wasted anyhow. This was now his priority. He knew Chiaolar was already displeased for letting the prey escape. Omer had been a faithful vessel since he was a young man and had no intention of risking his standing.

"Forgive me, Chiaolar."

Your failure has already been noted. Contact the kill team at once.

"As you command, Holy One."

Omer took the long route back to his car to avoid the heavy police presence. He opened the door and stared at the bouquet of flowers lying in the passenger seat. His wife would understand. He had more important matters to attend to.

CHAPTER EIGHT
TRAINING

The music started playing.

Please, not again. Roen, wake up.

Roen turned over and mumbled something incomprehensible, pulling the blanket over his face. Taking control of the body, Tao pulled the blanket off and exposed his ears to the full blast of the radio. Roen groaned and grasped for any sort of cover.

Roen, time to train. Get. Up.

Yawning, Roen rolled over and buried his head back into the pillow. "Training for what? God, it's early. What time is it?"

Five.

Roen paused, lifted his head, and blinked at the clock. "Why is my alarm set for 5am?"

I set it while you were asleep. Today is your first day of training. The next time you get assaulted by a senior citizen, I want you to have a fighting chance.

"What do you mean you set my alarm? How?"

We will get to that another time. Right now, you have more important tasks at hand.

"Why are you able to read my thoughts, but I can't read yours? That's hardly fair."

If life was fair, you would already be Special Ops, and I would not have to waste time dragging you out of bed. Now, time for a jog.

"Then, why bother talking to me? Can't you just read my mind?"

The human brain works like a computer. I can extract the information out of you, but it takes some time and much effort. It is faster if we communicate directly.

Roen sighed, shut off the alarm, dragged himself to the bathroom, and brushed his teeth.

"I hate jogging. Can't you just put me on a diet?"

We are doing that too. I threw out all your frozen dinners.

"What?!" Roen protested angrily with the toothbrush still in his mouth. "That's supposed to last me the whole week!"

They are also the reason why you huff and puff walking up stairs.

"Wait, how did you throw my stuff out?"

Quit stalling and get dressed, and bring some cash too.

"Ooh, are we going to breakfast?"

Roen finished washing up and rummaged through his closet for anything resembling workout clothes. He finally found an old pair of basketball shorts and a shirt he hadn't worn in years. They fit him like a bodysuit. Feeling ridiculous, he grabbed a small wad of cash from his desk and left the apartment building. He shivered in the cool wet morning and frowned as he walked down the street. There was a gentle breeze coming from the lake, and the grass was wet from a thick layer of dew. The eerie morning calm was unsettling.

"Where're we going?"

Down this street and make a right. Run until you hit the lake.

"What! The lake? You're crazy."

You are the one talking to yourself.

"Don't make me regret thinking I'm sane."

Hush. Just run.

Roen began jogging at a slow pace down the street. This was the first time in years he remembered voluntarily jogging.

Except for that time he was chased by a rabid dog, the last time he remembered running was back in high school. And since neither the run from the dog nor the one in high school was actually optional, this could be the first time he ever voluntarily ran. Now that he thought about it, this morning jog wasn't much of a choice either.

His chest and legs were burning before he reached the end of the block, and he slowed even more. Roen passed by a café, where the smell of hot coffee and breakfast beckoned. His stomach growled, unused to not being fed first thing in the morning.

"It hurts, Tao. Since this is my first time, can I turn back now?"

You want to quit already?

"Yes. I mean, no. I mean, I'm tired. Besides, this is embarrassing. People are laughing at me."

Forget about them and stop making excuses to fail.

"I'm not. I'm just being practical. Come on, I look idiotic."

I remember you saying that you were disappointed in how your life turned out and that you used to think that you could have made something of yourself.

"Yeah, so?"

Do you know why that never came true?

"Because my parents forced me to study engineering in college and I had a string of bad luck. It's not my fault I'm in a job I can't leave. I have responsibilities now."

You can always leave your job if you choose to. No one forces you to go to work. They do not lock you up at night. Stop blaming your job and your family for your problems. I have looked into your past, Roen. The problem is you do not seize opportunities when they present themselves. You always quit before things get hard.

Roen stopped running halfway across the bridge over the interstate and leaned over the railing's edge, trying to catch his breath. "That's not true! I wasn't given the chance to succeed. If this is supposed to be a pep talk, you suck at it."

It is not supposed to be a pep talk. You have had plenty of opportu-
nities in life. You could have chosen to do anything you wanted in
college, but you chose the safe route. You could have moved out of the
city, but you were afraid of exploring new places. When you hated
your job, you could have chosen other pursuits, but you were too lazy.
You made your own bed, and now curse others for putting you there.

"You don't know me. You don't know what I had to go
through. You go to hell!"

But I do know you. I have searched your thoughts and memories.
Tao's sympathy just infuriated Roen even more. *I know what*
haunts you and what regrets you stow away. I find it very sad that
you have more regrets in life than happy memories.

"Screw you! I didn't ask for this, and I don't need this," Roen
screamed over the noise of the passing cars underneath. "You
asshole! Just get out!" Several runners passing glanced his way,
and then pretended he didn't exist. A few apparently decided
to stay clear of him and crossed the street.

"What are you looking at," he yelled at them. "Never saw a
fat guy run before?"

Get a hold of yourself.

"You know what? You go find yourself a new pet project.
I'm going home." Roen was so angry that he could barely see
through the stinging tears in his eyes. He turned and began to
walk back toward his apartment. "You don't know what it's
like being me."

But I do, Roen. I know what you are feeling. I know about your
childhood, about being the awkward boy that always got picked on.
How you always feel like you are being judged for your weight. Why
you look at the ground so much when you walk down the street,
ashamed to make eye contact.

Roen kept up his angry gait which was almost as fast as his
jogging pace. Perhaps if he ignored this so-called alien's presence, it would just go away. Maybe he should find a priest and
get an exorcism. But then, that would bring back the argument

about whether he was sane or not. No matter what he tried, however, he could not keep Tao's voice out of his head. His frustration mounted.

"I bet you're like everyone else out there. You probably just possess rich or good-looking people or someone with six-pack abs or some football player. I'm nothing. You probably think you got shafted with such a crappy host."

That is not true. You have potential. I know it. Tao chuckled, or what amounted to a chuckle from a Quasing. *You are really no different from several of my early hosts. Their situations were a bit different than yours, but all three of you share similar angst.*

"You mean they were fat with a dead-end job?"

No, they came from wealthy, noble families, but all of you were big babies. The difference is that they learned to overcome their insecurities and grew to be powerful men.

"That's the stupidest comparison I've ever heard." Roen stopped walking and collapsed on a wooden bench. His chest was throbbing, though he wasn't sure whether it was from physical exertion or boiling anger.

You underestimate yourself, as always. As I was saying, Vercinge-torix was once very much like you are now.

"What? Vercinge... is that a person or a medical disorder?"

Have a little respect for a past host. It is their combined experiences and memories that can make you great. Many of my hosts were great figures in history that changed the course of mankind. The very least you could do is be respectful.

"Whatever," Roen grumbled as he leaned back and looked up at the sky. It was getting brighter as the sun appeared on the horizon, bathing the city with a soft yellow glow. He took a few minutes to admire the pretty hues. It wasn't often he got the chance to see the sun rise. After several moments, he finally calmed down, being too tired to stay angry. "So what does this Vercing guy have to do with me?"

He was much like you when I first transitioned with him. He had

*much but was not satisfied. He had principles, but was not strong
enough to follow them, at least at first.*

"So what happened? Did you convince him to listen to you,
and he discovered a cure for the bubonic plague or something?"

*A cure for the Black Death was not discovered until the 1930s.
Vercingetorix was a Gaul who united his people and became king at
the age of seventeen. He rallied them together and was able to give
Caesar one of his rare defeats.*

"Hmm, he does sound an awful lot like me," Roen replied,
his voice dripping with sarcasm. "A kid who becomes king and
defeats the greatest Roman general of all time is so me. And I
suppose he was a coward and a fat-ass as well?"

*Vercingetorix was a fine young man and an inspirational leader, but
he was not born that way. No one is. Great men are forged, not born.
I am not going to insult your intelligence, Roen. You are not great, but
you can be if you try. Is that not worth some sacrifice?*

Roen grimaced. There was no good way to answer that
question. "Fine," he said grudgingly and paused. "What did
this guy do, anyway?"

He led the last great Gaul rebellion against the Roman Empire.

"Why didn't one of your kind just enter Caesar?"

*It is a bit more complicated than that, Roen. We did have someone
in Caesar.*

Roen looked back down at the ground, puzzled. "I don't get
it. Why would you want a host to fight another one of your
own? Was it a Genjix?"

*No, it was one of ours. This was before the split. Times were different
then. Our goals and strategies were different as well. The Roman Empire had grown overly stagnant with its dominance. It was our belief
back then that conflict bred evolution.*

"And then what happened?"

*Well, Vercingetorix lost the Siege of Gergovia, and was locked up
for a few years until Caesar had him strangled in public during the
Festival of Jupiter.*

"What!"

I never said it was a happy ending. It rarely is. But for a brief instant in time, he burned like the sun and changed the world, and is still remembered to this day. Look to your right, Roen. It is the path back home. If you choose, you can take it. It is safe, easy, and comfortable. You do not have to work out or fight or do anything else you do not want to.

Roen looked down the street. By now, the sun was higher and the streets were alive with activity. The streets were filling up with the morning rush hour, and commuter trains passed along the elevated tracks. The sounds of cars honking and people bustling about filled the air. In the distance, a helicopter overhead was most likely reporting the morning traffic.

Or you can keep moving forward. I will not lie to you. I cannot predict what may become of you. It will require a lot of training, hard work, study, and danger. But in the very end, you will know strength. I swear it. You might just become someone who will make a difference in the world.

"You're not much of a salesman, are you, Tao?" Roen chuckled sardonically.

I say it like it is.

"What about that other host you said was a big baby like me?"

Ah... my greatest achievement and failure as a host, Genghis Khan.

"No kidding! The Genghis Khan?"

There is more than one?

"That's awesome. Why do you say he was your greatest failure?"

That is a long story for another time. But I see that potential in you, Roen. I do.

Roen stood up and sighed. "Honestly, I think you're full of crap. But I'm going to give you the chance to prove me wrong. I guess I'd better get started then."

He began to walk toward the lake, slowly picking up speed as he moved deeper and deeper into the city. His face burned as he felt the snickering and judging eyes as he lumbered down the busy streets.

Make it drive you.

Roen huffed and puffed, but kept his face looking forward as he navigated past the stark buildings and down busy walkways. All around him, men and women in suits rushed to work. Cars and buses sat bumper to bumper at intersections, exhaling fumes and noise. Like the blood vessels of the city, the streets pumped them through at a frantic pace. He felt very out of place.

Remember the difference between them and the person you wish to be.

Roen gritted his teeth and pushed forward. The sun was beating down on him by the time he reached Buckingham Fountain. He plopped on one of the benches, gasping for breath. The mist from the water shooting high into the air felt cool to the touch. He rolled unceremoniously off the bench to the grass and lay there for several moments and closed his eyes, feeling the heavy thumping in his chest.

"I think I'm going to have a heart attack. I... I can't breathe."

Well, Roen, would you like to ask the seventy year-old man next to you to give you CPR?

Roen started to laugh, which aggravated his condition. It was another ten minutes before he felt well enough to sit up without feeling faint. He picked himself up and walked to the fountain, scooping water onto his face.

How do you feel?

"Like I want to throw up."

Vomiting is a positive sign for this situation. It will only be a matter of time before this becomes routine to you.

"What? I have to do this again?"

Of course. Tomorrow – in fact, every single day.

"This is going to hurt tomorrow. Shoot, I still have to run back home. I don't think I can make it."

You will be in a lot of pain tomorrow, but that is part of the progress. Do not worry about running back. The jog was enough. You have that cash?

Roen nodded.

Good, go hail a cab. You are late for work.

That night, Roen lay in bed exhausted, but unable to sleep. His body was still throwing a fit about the workout and his knees wobbled every time he walked up stairs. There was just so much to process. What would all this mean for him, and how would his life change? Obviously, it had already changed considering he worked out today. Was he really sure he was sane? He had an imaginary friend as a kid after all, though this new guy definitely was not as nice. Tao was actually kind of a jerk.

Roen?

"Yes, Tao?"

You should sleep. I am going to wake you up very early tomorrow.

"I can't sleep, Tao. Tell me a story."

Once upon a time, there were three bears...

"No, I mean about all those past lives you had. Can you tell me about all those people you inhabited?"

You really want to know?

"Yes. Do you mind?"

Of course not. I am flattered. I can do better than tell you. I can show you while you sleep.

"Is it like when you put those images into my head? They come and go so fast they're almost subliminal. Can you show it to me for longer than a millisecond?"

I could, but you would receive a debilitating headache and get sick. That is why I only flash them momentarily.

"Forget it then. I have a low enough pain threshold as it is. I'd rather you just tell me."

The effect will not be painful while you sleep. You will experience it like a dream.

"Really? That's great. Wait, but if you can do that, why don't you just show me something useful like how to drive a tank or how to build a rocket?"

Chances are, you will never have to drive a tank regardless. The scenes I show you will feel like a dream. You will not grasp everything and they will not be detailed enough for you to learn something technical. However, they will be sufficient for you to learn about my past. It is your past as well, now.

"That's fine. Where are you going to start?"

I am not sure. Maybe the best place to start is with the host that I had my greatest triumphs and failures, a young man named Temujin. Do you know who he is? Roen?

Roen was already sound asleep, his loud snoring echoing through the room.

CHAPTER NINE
SONYA

I traveled in a golden wolf from the savannah of Africa far to the Mongol steppes. I went in the hopes of leaving the chaos of the Roman Empire behind to build a new civilization, one without constant conflict. In this new and beautiful land, I planned a grand experiment, to birth a culture based on peace and enlightenment, to deviate from the Quasing idea that humans can only innovate through war. I placed my hope in a young boy named Temujin, son of a chieftain.

Ray yawned as he sat in the tinted car in the Grant Park North garage. He checked his watch; three more hours until the café upstairs on Michigan Avenue opened. He could get a bagel then.

They'd been sitting in this damn spot for three days now. That new vessel had to come back one of these days for his car. Marc said it was a possibility the mark might return, though Ray was pretty sure the Prophus couldn't possibly be that stupid. But then – if the vessel wasn't aware of the Holy One in him yet – he might. And it was an opportunity the team wasn't going to pass up.

Still, he and Chako had been in this same spot for almost seventy hours now, only switching off to stretch and get food.

Ray was sure the car was getting rather pungent with two un-washed men practically living in it. Another day though and their replacements would come. He'd had similar assignments in the past; uncomfortable, but it was the life he led. A lifetime ago, when he used to work for the DEA, Ray had spent nearly a week observing a Mexican freighter until the drug deal went down. This job at least was close to fresh coffee. In any case, it was better than sleeping on his ex-wife's couch in Detroit.

The garage was mostly empty of cars, except for a dozen or so scattered around the lot. Ray had a direct view of the vessel's car. Ray rubbed his eyes and shook his head, trying to ward off sleep. He'd give Chako another hour before waking him to change shifts. If he was lucky, the vessel would appear and he'd be the one to capture him. Then his ascension to a Holy One would almost be assured. After six years with the Genjix, he might actually become one of them. His life would change then. Ray shifted again in his seat, massaging his numb legs, trying to work some circulation back into them.

A figure wearing a parka came down the stairs and walked toward the vessel's car. Ray took out his binoculars and studied him. He couldn't make out his face, but he was the right size. Ray nudged Chako. "We got a hit."

Chako was instantly alert, peering out the windshield. "A little warm this time of year for a parka, would you say?" he said.

"To the point of it being unusual," Ray replied. "Looks like he's trying to hide his face. We might have our vessel here. Go check it out. I'll cover you." Ray touched his earpiece and re-ported in. "We have a possible hit moving toward the vehicle. Verifying now. Stand by."

Ray pulled out his pistol while Chako got out of the car and sauntered towards the figure. It had to be the mark. Who else would come at four in the morning? The figure by now had reached the Ford and was peeking through the driver's side window. Ray got out of the car and knelt next to the front tires, his gun trained at the possible vessel's shoulder. He had to be careful with his shot. Marc was explicit about taking him alive.

Chako had reached the figure by now and they were exchanging words. Ray was too far away to make out what they were saying. Then suddenly, Chako reached into his pocket and fell. Ray heard the distinct sound of a silenced pistol go off in the otherwise quiet garage. Ray took careful aim and squeezed the trigger, hitting the vessel.

The parka-clad figure collapsed out of view behind another parked car. Ray stayed low and moved to the next aisle, and found Chako lying face down on the floor. Lying next to him was a gray parka. Immediately, Ray ducked behind cover and scanned the area. This vessel was supposed to be new! The Prophus must have gotten to him. He moved behind the vessel's car and looked for any signs of movement.

After several minutes, Ray decided to get out of the open and retreated back to his car. Whoever was here was very quiet; obviously a trained agent. He'd have to drive the car up to Chako, get the body in, and get out of here. Otherwise, he was a sitting duck.

Ray got to the driver's side, opened the door, and slid in. Just as he sat down, a figure appeared from the back seat and slugged him in the side of the face. Ray fell out of the car and onto the floor. Immediately, he got up and reached for his gun. The figure knocked it out of his hand and gave him a sharp blow to the neck. Ray gasped for air as he slammed into the concrete wall.

The dark figure approached. He was short and slim, and wore a hood shadowing his face.

Ray blindly lashed out, swinging with his fists. The first blow caught his assailant in the forehead. He heard a woman's voice as she grunted and blocked the second and third punch. Then she came forward with her right elbow and smashed his nose, breaking it. Blood flowed down his face as he fell back against the wall again. This definitely was not the new vessel. Ray swung a desperate right hook. She danced out of the way and connected with a kick to Ray's midsection, followed by a leg sweep that sent him crashing to the floor.

The figure got on top of him and jammed a gun into his cheek. He could smell the aroma of mint gum as she spoke. "Weeks of surveillance, two agents sitting in a car, Homeland Security access. This is above and beyond your usual hunt orders. Why do the Genjix care so much about this host?" Ray tried to roll over and push her off, but she just pistol-whipped him twice on the face, the second swing cracking his cheek bone. "Unless you guys found a discount broker, Homeland network access can't be cheap," she said. "Answer me, Genjix."

"Go to hell, bitch," Ray snarled, his vision obscured by the blood pouring from his broken nose.

"You first." She pistol-whipped him again. "This is for going against your own species." The Prophus agent pulled the earpiece out of his ear and spoke in it. "You have two dead bodies and two hours before rush hour begins. Clean up your trash." That was the last thing Ray heard before she pulled the trigger.

Sonya drove up to the apartment building and parked on a side street. She took off the bloodstained outfit and changed into her workout clothes. It was some time until dawn and the streets were still quiet.

She checked the mirror and wiped the blood off her face. There was a cut above her eyebrow where the Genjix agent's ring had cut her. She frowned and shook her head in disgust; always the face. Getting caught like that by such an amateur was sloppy work. She went into her first aid kit and applied some hydrogen peroxide on it. Her hands trembled as she dabbed her cut.

Though she'd been with the Prophus for four years, she was still new enough to fieldwork to get the shakes. The old-timers said that'd go away with time. Sonya clenched her fists and took a deep breath. When she felt calmer, she finished up her patch job. She probably wouldn't need stitches. She checked her handiwork in the mirror, grabbed her laptop, and typed up a few notes.

Relay the Homeland expenditures. The Genjix are spending a small fortune on this job. Maybe we can find the source on the inside and cut it off.

Sonya nodded. "If the Genjix have been tracking this new host through Homeland, I want to get a map of all the street cameras. The new host can avoid detection better if he knows where not to walk around with his face exposed."

Good idea. Are you sure you want to start this assignment this morning? You have had very little sleep lately.

Sonya craned her neck and stretched. "I am a little jet-lagged, but it's nothing I haven't done before. I was looking forward to that time off in the Caymans – but it's nice to be back in Chicago. It's been almost two years. Tell Command they still owe me a vacation. A training assignment shouldn't be too tough. I haven't had the chance to read the new host's file. I assume you did during the flight? Why do you think they want this new host so badly?"

I have read the file. This one will be more work than you think. The Quasing is Tao. Several in the Genjix Council have a vested interest in him. They would love to get their claws around that troublemaker.

"Sounds like my kind of Quasing." Sonya got out of the car and walked into the building. Tao sounded familiar, like a name she heard in the distant past. "Did Tao work with Mother before?"

Dania was Tao's previous host's mentor. They worked together for many years. I believe you two met when you were very young.

Sonya chuckled. "And now I get to mentor his new host. How poetic."

Let us just hope things turn out better for both of you than it did for Dania and Edward.

"I've heard of Edward. I think Dania and he did pretty well for themselves in the organization."

I was referring to both of you living a long life.

The elevator dinged and opened onto the twentieth floor. Sonya walked out and looked around. "So what's the scoop on this trainee? We can't just send him to our boot camp? Is he police or National Guard?"

Worse. The Keeper's report says he's a civilian, an unimpressive one at that. Your main focus will be physical readiness at first, followed by hand-to-hand combat, then firearms, then squad tactics. The Keeper stresses that he needs to be up to speed quickly. Someone in the Genjix hierarchy is willing to spend significant resources to find him.

Sonya smiled. "Ooh, nice. A complete build from scratch. I'm going to enjoy this. Will he require a protection detail?"

You are it. This unit on the right.

"Still doesn't seem too bad. He shouldn't take up more than half my time. I guess a vacation in Chicago is as good as any."

Chicago is a hotbed of Genjix activity. There will be more work here, I am sure.

Sonya checked her watch and then knocked on the door. There was a rustling sound on the other side. She waited another second before knocking again. If she had to cancel a two-week beach vacation, the new host would have to deal with waking up early. Finally, the door opened and a tall thin man with brown hair and a pretty face appeared.

"Not our host?"

The roommate. Antonio Desilarez.

"Too bad. He's kind of cute."

"Hi." Sonya smiled. "I'm sorry to bother you at this hour, but..." She stopped. Antonio was gaping at her as if she had suddenly grown elf ears. There were a few uncomfortable seconds before he seemed to finally collect himself. Sonya paused and waited; it was early after all. Maybe he was still getting the cobwebs out of his head. He swung the door open all the way and leaned against it. She saw his eyes check her out, lingering a little longer on her chest than the rest of her.

"I'm sorry, can I help you?" He stuck out his hand. She could swear he lowered his voice. "Hi, I'm Doctor Antonio Desilarez. My friends call me Antonio."

Ooh, a doctor.

"Ooh, a douchebag. I wonder how many times this week he's used that line."

He seems quite practiced at it.

"I'm looking for Roen," Sonya said. "He's not expecting me, but he'll want to see me."

"Of that I have no doubt." Antonio studied her face and pointed at her forehead. "You have a nasty abrasion there. Do you want me to take a look? I'm a doctor."

"I think we already established that," Sonya replied sweetly. "Thanks, but I'll be all right. Is Roen in?"

Antonio stepped aside and magnanimously waved her in. "Of course. How rude of me. Can I get you something to drink? A beer, water? I can make some eggs for you if you like. I'm sorry, you're very distracting. What was your name again?"

"Sonya," she replied. "And just getting Roen will be fine."

Persistent, isn't he?

"I find it quite flattering. Girl likes a little attention once in a while, even if it's from a douchebag."

Doctor Douchebag.

Antonio finally seemed to get the picture and his face fell. "Sure thing," he said. "Roen's still asleep. The last door on the right. Are you sure I can't get you anything?"

"Quite," she said and glided past him to Roen's room. Sonya stopped at the open doorway and looked around. The room was neatly organized, with stacks of paper sorted in bins on the desk. The laundry was in a hamper in the corner sorted by color, and clothes were folded in the open closet divided by seasonal wear and utility. She went to the bookshelf and glanced over the books, which were arranged in alphabetical order. "Tao or the host?"

According to the evaluation, this is all Tao.

"He's left his mark on the new host already then. Roen Tan is that malleable?"

It would seem so.

She walked over to the bed where several blankets were rising up and down. Roen was snoring somewhere in that mound. There was an arm exposed hugging a pillow. She sat down next to him and leaned in close, walking two fingers up the arm. "Wake up, sleepyhead. It's time to lose the donuts," she cooed.

Roen yawned and turned over. Sonya grinned and tapped him harder. "You'll be a fun one to take on field missions. Get up, or I might have to get a little rough."

Roen awoke groggily and turned to face her. His eyes widened; he looked puzzled, as if unsure what was happening. Finally, he whispered, "Are you real?"

Sonya laughed and blew into his face. "Do I feel real? I'm Sonya, and I came to ask you for something."

"Um... huh... ask what?" he stammered.

She chuckled. "Quite the glib tongue you got there. Baji wants to know where those two million rubles Tao owes her are. It's been fifteen years now, and she's adding interest."

CHAPTER TEN
FIRST LESSON

Even at an early age, I sensed greatness in Temujin. He was strong and cunning, able in the ways of war. I was his noble ancestor, and I trained him in the ways of politics and battle. For on the harsh steppes, war must be waged and blood must be shed before there could be peace. And in Temujin, I had the perfect weapon. The question is, can the weapon be sheathed after it has drawn blood?

Roen still couldn't wrap his head around the vision that was hovering over his bed – a pretty girl. She was curvy and muscular, yet slender, with large luminous blue eyes, pale creamy skin, luxurious long black hair, and a whole list of other adjectives that currently escaped him. He gaped, mouth wide open. His brain didn't seem to be working right. The sounds coming out of her mouth sounded like Charlie Brown's teacher in a *Peanuts* special. All he heard was wah, wah, wah.

You sly dog. You never told me about her.

Roen could've sworn he detected amusement in Tao's voice. "You think I would keep HER a secret?"

"Well," the vision of beauty said petulantly. "Where's my money?"

She is such a riot.

"Who?"

Baji. Say hello. I have not seen her host Sonya since she was a little girl.

"Sonya, Baji, hi! It's so good to see you." Roen spoke as if they were old friends, and as he did with old friends, he hugged her. Later on, he would stand by that reasoning and vehemently deny that he hugged her because she was pretty. Sonya laughed and hugged him back, not missing a beat. She smelled very good, he noticed.

Tell her I lost those rubles playing craps. I think the dice were rigged. Roen conveyed the message.

Sonya grinned and stood up. "You're so incorrigible, Tao. Of course they were rigged. Wait until the Keeper finds out how you're using your stipends. Anyway, get up."

"For what?" Roen yawned.

"For your workout. I'm putting you through your paces today."

Roen sat up and stretched, and then plopped back into bed. "Tao and I have an agreement. I'm off on Saturdays."

"That's because your butt is mine on Saturdays from now on." She tapped her wristwatch. "You've got five minutes before I drag you out in your jammies. I mean it."

Roen watched her walk out of his room. Immediately, he hopped out of bed and ran to the bathroom; he took extra time to use mouthwash and comb his hair; he also sprayed on cologne.

You are going to calisthenics, not prom.

"You never told me the other agents were so hot."

The last time I saw Sonya she was ten. Her mother was a host; she and I used to work together. I am glad she had a peaceful transition. Sonya is a fourth-year host, but has known about us since she was a child. She has already spent many years preparing for her ascension with Baji, so she is quite advanced. You would do well learning from her.

Ten minutes later, they were outside jogging down the street. Late April in Chicago was a bit on the soggy side. The ground was wet and a soft layer of mist rested on the city. The sun was just rising from the horizon, and an orange haze bathed the streets in a warm glow. A touch of cool wind blew in from the west that stirred the newly budding leaves.

Roen had lost twenty pounds since Tao had first put the hammer down on his diet and lifestyle a short month ago. Gone were the days of frozen foods, burgers, and chips, replaced by celery, carrots, raw spinach, and pieces of chicken so small he could eat them in one bite.

He hadn't gotten around to purchasing new clothes yet, and his once-tight jogging clothes wore loose on him. Sonya gave him a look and promised to take him shopping.

"Toward the lake?" Roen asked as they warmed up.

"Someplace new," she replied and turned north. Roen shrugged and followed close behind.

"How long have you been at this?" he asked as they jogged through the quiet streets.

"Running? I like to do the marathon here every year if the missions allow for it," she replied. Already, Roen had a difficult time matching her pace.

"No, I meant this Quasing thing." He was already starting to breathe through the mouth. There was no way he could keep this up for long. Thankfully, Sonya noticed and slowed down.

She spoke without any hint of trouble. "I knew about Baji since I was little. Mother used to work closely with Edward. She decided early on to not hide any secrets. By the time I was ten, I knew I wanted to follow in her footsteps and have been training ever since. When she developed cancer a few years ago..." Her voice trailed off. "I had to continue her work."

"I'm sorry," Roen said after a pause. Still uncomfortable with women, he often drew blanks speaking to them. Sonya being attractive did not help matters. "Do you think these Prophus can be trusted?" he asked. "I mean, Tao told me some stories about what they've done, and I can't help but feel like a puppet dancing on their strings."

It is all right. Just pretend I am not here.

She beckoned him to turn off the path onto another street. "It's true that they have influenced our evolution, and as a result terrible things have happened, but there's been good as well. The Prophus might have caused a few wars, but they've been responsible for peace too. Baji once was the Quasing for Franz Ferdinand, the Archduke of Austria-Este. He was in the process of trying to reform and stabilize Austria-Este with all its ethnic groups when he was assassinated. Sadly, had he lived, the First World War might have been avoided. It's difficult to determine where humanity would be without Quasing influence. For all we know, if it wasn't for them, Neanderthals could be ruling the world."

"Didn't Franz Ferdinand cause World War I?"

"His assassination did, courtesy of the Genjix. They wanted the ethnic tensions to continue in the region and were in control of the monarchy. It goes in hand with their belief that conflict breeds innovation. Look at the unmitigated disaster that followed his death."

"I guess." Roen was not convinced. "Where're we going, by the way?" This was obviously not a random jog.

"We're close." She pointed ahead. "Just down the block right off Lake Street." They stopped in front of a rundown warehouse with a Morimoto Chocolates sign at the front, and she led him to a side door down a small alley. Roen studied the building; it didn't look like any chocolate place he'd ever seen, though he kept his hopes up. The window panes were darkened and smudged, but looked to be in good condition. The door was rusty and weeds grew from between the cracks on the sidewalk. Above them, the elevated train tracks rumbled as a train passed by overhead.

"Come on, what are you standing out there for?" Sonya

called from inside. "We have a lot to do; my report says you needed to be field ready yesterday."

"Report? What report? Who are you reporting me to, Tao?"

Your mother asked me to keep tabs on you.

"That's a very mature thing to say."

Stop taking yourself so seriously, Roen.

He followed her into a small dark room. How much did she know about him? The small room was the size of a walk-in closet. There was a large metal circular door that looked like a bank vault on the far wall. Roen studied the shiny steel surface of the hatch and then the rusted surroundings. Something wasn't right. Sonya fiddled with several buttons on a small panel and then the hatch rumbled and hissed open.

"Safe house CW12," she stated as she walked in and turned on the lights, "your new training center."

Roen followed her and looked around in amazement. The interior looked nothing like the exterior. They stood on the upper floor of a two-level warehouse that seemed impossibly larger inside than it appeared from the outside. There was a running track along the edge of the upper floor that opened to a workout area on the lower level; assorted weight lifting machines littered the main gym floor with rows of dumbbells stacked on one side; there was a boxing ring in the center and a firing range on the far side. The near corner had what seemed like living quarters, including a kitchen with a television. There was also a bank of computers next to it. Everything seemed state of the art.

"What is all this?" he asked in a small voice.

Start memorizing these locations. They could save your life one day.

"It's one of our safe houses. We have a few in every major city; completely self-sufficient and always stocked with supplies. This particular facility is masked as a storage warehouse for cake mix. Passcode: 93276 and your voice imprint." Sonya walked to the weight station. She turned to him and patted the bench. "You ready?"

Roen's eyes grew wide. "Ready for what? Lifting? I don't think I have ever touched weights before."

"I can tell. You've lost a fair amount of weight already, but unless you plan to run away from every Genjix you meet, you'd best pack on some muscle and learn a stiff jab." She pointed a finger at him and beckoned him closer. "Don't worry, I'll spot you."

"Are you sure?" he asked. "I mean, you look tough and all, but you're a little thing."

"Oh?" There was a glimmer of a challenge in her voice. "Care for a little wager? We'll start light, twenty-fives on a side. Loser pays for dinner."

Roen lay down on the bench and looked at the bar over his head. "Dinner? Sure!" Truth be told, he was willing to pay her just to have dinner with him, but at least this didn't sound so desperate. "Here goes nothing," he muttered.

Do not make me look bad in front of Baji.

Roen lifted the bar and steadied it. This wasn't too tough, at least not as bad as he feared. He lowered the bar to his chest, surprised at the ease. When he tried to lift the bar back up though, it wouldn't budge. Roen strained harder. He pushed. He grunted. He yelled. His arms responded by collapsing, bouncing the bar once off his chest.

"Errr... gr... arghh," he groaned, squirming and straining. "It's on my chest," was all he could gasp.

Come on, you can do it!

"My, we do have our work cut out for us," she murmured. "Baji thought you were further along than this." She lifted the bar off him and put it back onto the stand.

Stop making me look bad then.

"Piss off, Tao," Roen growled in between deep breaths.

"Sorry? What did you say?" Sonya's upside-down face came into view as she leaned forward. Roen had to take a moment to admire her perfect complexion.

"Um... nothing," he replied lamely.

They spent the rest of the morning working on different weights and machines. Since Roen was new to weight lifting, Sonya took the time to teach him the proper techniques and, as she claimed, was able to out-lift him on every apparatus. He marveled at how someone with such a small frame could be so strong. By mid-morning, Roen lay on the floor exhausted as his muscles ached and begged for mercy.

She knelt next to him and handed him a cup of water. "Not bad for your first time. Don't worry about the low weights. You were game to try and that's really all that matters. The rest will come."

"Are we done?" he begged, bone-tired.

"One more thing," she said, walking over to the wall and picking out two pairs of boxing gloves. "Put these on." She tossed a pair to him. Roen fumbled the catch and the gloves bounced off his chest. He stared at them as if they were spiders.

"I don't like to fight," he said.

Oh, come on, Roen. What are you going to do next time a Genjix wants to kill you, beg him to death?

"What're you going to do when a Genjix tries to kill you?" Sonya asked, giving him a stern look.

Roen shook his head. "Seems both you and Tao are preoccupied about me getting killed."

"You should be too." Sonya climbed through the ropes and waited. "Get used to it. You are what you are now. The sooner you embrace it, the better off you'll be. Come on, get into the ring."

Sighing, he climbed in and put on the gloves. They squared off in the center of the ring. Roen had no idea what he was doing. He planted his feet on the canvas and held his hands up like he remembered in those Samurai Sunday movies he watched as a kid. Sonya promptly batted them away with her left fist and smashed him in the cheek with her right, knocking him down to the canvas.

This is serious business, Roen.

"Ow!" Roen lay on the floor and looked at the ceiling. That girl could hit! Her face appeared over him again, and she offered her hand.

"If you're going to treat this lightly, you're in for a long three minutes, because I'm going to knock you silly." All of a sudden, she didn't look so sweet or cute anymore. He grabbed her hand and got up, this time far more wary of her as she closed in again.

Watch her range. Use your reach. Move your feet. Do not let her just walk in on you.

Sonya grinned and circled like a shark coming in for the kill. She moved in and threw three quick punches. The first connected with his face before he was able to back up and avoid the others. He lunged, batting his hands and striking only air as his momentum carried him forward.

Do not overcommit. Watch your center of gravity, and keep your guard up!

Sonya sidestepped his clumsy wide swings and popped him once in the face with a left followed by a hard right that sent him sprawling back down to the floor. With a loud frustrated growl, Roen punched the canvas, jumped to his feet, and bullrushed her like a crazed gorilla. She dodged his attacks with ease, dancing around his slow combinations and giving him another peck on the cheek with her fist. Roen snarled and lunged again, throwing a wild punch that popped her in the ear. Immediately, Sonya cried in pain and clutched the side of her head, going down on one knee.

"Oh my God, are you all right?" Horrified, Roen ran over to her and put his hands on her shoulders. "I didn't mean to hit you that hard. I'm sorry!"

Roen, no! An image of a nude woman covered in blood wielding an ax flashed in his head.

"That was dumb," was all Sonya said before her uppercut caught him flush on the chin, snapping his head back and flooring him for a third time.

Idiot! How can you fall for that?

Roen groaned as bursts of bright stars obscured his vision and a single tear ran down his face. His jaw went numb and he couldn't quite feel all his fingers and toes. His hearing became muffled as if he was at the bottom of a swimming pool. In the distance, he heard the muffled roar of a waterfall. Suddenly, everything popped and his vision cleared.

"Ow... I always wondered what a concussion felt like," Roen finally managed to say. He sat up and looked around. Sonya had already taken off both their gloves and was handing him a cup of water.

"Don't fall victim to the helpless woman crap," she said, grabbing him by the hand and pulling him to his feet. "It's insulting. We can pull the trigger as well as any guy."

"You could have taught me that lesson in a less painful way." He grimaced.

"But it wouldn't be as much fun." She grinned. "Now the lesson is ingrained in you. Better that lesson from me than from a Genjix. I think that's enough for this morning."

"You're a dark, dark woman," Roen groused. "I think my brain moved in my skull." He looked up at the clock. "Oh, wow, it's almost noon. Time really flies when you're having fun." He chuckled sarcastically as he climbed out of the ring, his weary muscles protesting. Sonya leaped out of the ring – like a dancer or a ninja would – and followed, locking the main door behind her as they stepped outside. The warm morning had lost its chilliness, making way for a beautiful day.

"Do you think we can take a cab back?" Roen asked as they walked to the corner. "I'm pretty beat."

"Tired?" She grinned. "We're not done yet. Let's go to lunch – on you, of course. I haven't had a man buy me a meal in months. I feel like Thai. Afterward, we need to get some paperwork done." She gave him a sharp slap on the butt and jogged him down the street.

CHAPTER ELEVEN
JOINING THE NETWORK

My dreams were nearly realized when Temujin, now known as Genghis Khan, had united all the tribes. He was my greatest achievement, the human host who would change history and reshape the world. It was then that I faltered. I should have ordered Temujin to build that new world with what he already owned. Instead, he wanted more, and I did not stop him. I was greedy as well. Together, we had built the greatest army the world has ever seen, and we could not stop ourselves from using it.

Roen and Sonya had a quick lunch at a local diner down the street. He was positively giddy spending time with who he considered the most beautiful girl he'd ever met. Even better, Sonya was so easy to get along with. He peppered her with questions about the Prophus and the war, and she gave him honest answers, never making him feel foolish for asking. Throughout the entire meal, he couldn't help but grin like a puppy. They returned to the safe house and relaxed on the couch in the living area.

Roen's stomach was gratified after many weeks of eating Tao's prescribed rabbit food diet. Tao had objected to almost all the dishes Roen wanted. Thankfully, Sonya gave him a pass and he pigged out. He knew that Tao would make him pay for this dietary indiscretion later on, but for now, he just burped contently like a sloth and began to doze off.

"Not nappy time yet, buddy." Sonya nudged him as she took out a manila envelope. "We have some super-secret agent stuff to talk about."

Roen perked up. He liked the sound of that. This whole alien-in-his-body was starting to sound better and better. First, he got to hang out with a hot girl, and now he was going to be James Bond.

He would have to go shopping for a new wardrobe to fit his new role. Roen imagined a long trench coat like Neo, with cool sunglasses and a big gun hanging at his waist. Maybe he could have a secret weapons locker built in his closet or by the laundry hamper. Or better yet, it could be a compartment that opens once he turned some hidden lever. Turn the faucet left two turns, pull *Brave New World* on the shelf, tap the alarm clock twice; bam, machine gun! Would he need to learn to tango for infiltrating enemy galas?

You are an idiot sometimes. Do you know that? This is not a Hollywood movie and we are not taking direction from CIA for Dummies. And being an agent is not the same as being a spy. You have no idea what clandestine work is like. You might not be suited for it.

"Why not? You won't know until I try."

First of all, it is tedious, and you have the attention span of a fruit fly.

Roen was about to protest and then shrugged. A guy couldn't argue with the truth.

Second of all, a good spy is a good actor and liar. You are terrible at both.

"I am not that bad!"

Look, Roen, I have seen you play poker and lie to your friends. You are bad at both. You start breathing heavily, you avoid eye contact, and you fidget. Trust me. Everyone picks up on that. Why do you think you always come out of those games broke? For now, focus on your physical deficiencies and the technical knowledge necessary to be an agent. The rest will come in time. We can worry about the finer points of subterfuge later.

"So." Sonya curtsied flamboyantly. "Welcome to Sonya's Crash Course School of Secret Agents. Congratulations, you survived your first morning. Here is your merit badge and cookie. Tell him, Bob, what does he win?"

"Tao, I think I love her. She's hot *and* a geek."

She is so far out of your league that you are not even playing the same sport.

"Can I ask her out? Is there some rule about agents dating other agents?"

You have had many bad ideas over the past month. That one is the worst of all.

She handed him the envelope – and the small black box – with a flourish. "Welcome to the network."

Roen took the items and looked them over. This must be one of those secret agent box-that-wasn't-a-box things. On the top was a white button with large lettering on top saying You Break It You Buy It. He had a sudden urge to push the button, but stopped himself. "What does it mean?" he asked.

"It means," Sonya said, "you are officially a novice agent and will be on active duty. You didn't think the Prophus were in the business of handing out free personal training, did you?"

"What? Tao, you never told me this. What happened to no strings attached?"

I never said that. I did tell you though, that you would be called to duty very soon. You have to earn your keep somehow.

Roen's heart began to hammer in his chest, his feel-good warm fuzzies disappearing in a puff of smoke. His hands shook as he held up the envelope and tried to see through it. "What's in it?" he gulped. "Do I have to kill somebody or something?"

Sonya walked up and gave him a hug. Roen inhaled her sweet scent of apricots and citrus. She pulled back, took out her pistol, placed it in his lap, and smiled, none too sweetly. "This evening actually. You need to assassinate the President of the Philippines."

She laughed at the wide-eyed look of panic on his face and shook her head. "Gullible, aren't you?" She took back the pistol and winked. "I wouldn't worry too much. First missions are softballs, and in your case, I made sure you're playing t-ball. Why don't you read through the briefing? When you're done, we can go over it. And do hurry; it's time-sensitive."

"Time-sensitive? You mean this stuff will be out of date if I read too slowly?"

She rolled her eyes. "It means the packet combusts into a little ball of fire in four hours or when you press that button, so you better start reading."

He dropped the envelope as if it had bitten him. "You gave me a bomb?"

"It's a fail-safe, Roen." She shrugged. "Just open it."

How is that for James Bond-like? This message will self-destruct in ten...

"Shut up, Tao. And that's *Inspector Gadget*, anyway."

Touchy right now, hmm?

Roen wasn't sure what made him more apprehensive; that he was now involved in this crazy world of danger, or that this packet could blow up in his hands. His once safe – albeit boring – life had just crashed around him, and all the warmth and appreciation he had for Tao for helping him with his health disappeared.

But this was what he was training for, right? This was what the Prophus wanted him to do, to complete their objectives. They didn't give him access to this incredible gym just so he could turn his life around and look for his inner six-pack abs. Sonya wasn't here for his personal betterment, nor was she here to make him feel better about himself. This was all done so he could become one of them, a Prophus agent.

What did Tao say that night when the Genjix jerk jumped him? The Prophus are waging a war for humanity's sake. Roen Tan had become a soldier in that war. His life would no longer be a wasted one, sitting in a cubicle, working at a job he hated. Before Tao, the world didn't care if Roen existed or not. He didn't matter. And now that the chance to make a difference was lying in an envelope in front of him, his new reality hit him like a bucket of cold water.

"I can make a difference," he said under his breath. He stared at the packet and picked it up. Roen took a deep breath and ripped the corner off. "So be it, let's get started." There was no use in shirking his responsibilities. He might as well just face them head on.

Sonya stared at him, a small smile on her face. She walked over to the cabinet, grabbed two lowball glasses, poured some scotch in each glass, and handed one to him. Roen clinked glasses with her and downed the drink in one gulp as he went over the contents.

The documents reminded him of the welcome packet he received when he first started his desk job. Besides a rather generic letter welcoming him to the network, there were several pages of security guidelines that he had to read through. Another document had his network email address, ID and password, and several security codes he had to memorize. There was also a passport and driver's license for a Hamilton Lee, a smartphone, and a map of Chicago with several red circles drawn all over it.

That is your fake identity in case you are wondering.

"This is so cool."

You are easily amused. Memorize all of this by tonight.

"What? All of it?"

Of course. You need to start using an undetectable alias.

"Gahh... it's like homework."

You think the life of an agent is all fun and games?

Roen finished reading the first set of documents and picked up the second, which was only a page long. It was his first mission. The details were sparse. It instructed him to reconnoiter an area off the coast of Lake Michigan for five nights. He flipped the page over and looked up. "That's it? This is my mission, to stare at a patch of pond for a week? What kind of assignment is this?"

Sonya chuckled. "Like I said, t-ball. It's a good way to get your feet wet, no pun intended. Do you have any questions?"

Roen put down the papers and stared at the scattered items on the coffee table. "I don't know. This is so much so soon. I feel rushed. Is this how fast the Prophus always move?"

Sonya shook her head. "You're a bit of a unique case." She knelt down in front of him and held his hands. "I know this is all very overwhelming, but you joined us at a particularly important time within the war. You have to understand, the Prophus have a small army of agents and all those agents would give up an arm to be a host. Some of our people have spent years fighting for the cause, hoping one day to earn a Quasing. They usually choose crème dc la crème for that privilege, hand-picking from the best military, scientific, and political minds. You're very lucky to have Tao, but you're behind the curve, so we need to get you up to speed."

Roen nodded solemnly. "I'll do my best."

Sonya patted him on the arm. "I know you will. Just try not to get killed until your best is good enough." She stood up and made another exaggerated curtsey. "There's one more thing. And Bob, what else does Roen Tan win? A new car!" She tossed him a set of keys.

Roen couldn't help it – and Tao would most likely never let him live it down as long as they were together – but he jumped up and down, and screamed like a little girl who just got a pony for her birthday. Ever since that night with Omer, Roen had abandoned his car. Tao had informed him later on that a Prophus cleanup crew had picked it up and sold it at an auction. Since then, he had been taking the bus and train around the city. Roen hated public transportation. Now, he got a new car!

"Call it an initiation present." Sonya grinned. "You want to see it? It's been sitting in the garage all morning."

Images of James Bond's Aston Martin flashed through his head as he scampered – faster than he ever jogged – toward the garage. Maybe it was a Porsche. Or a convertible Mercedes or BMW with built-in machine guns. And flamethrowers. And oil slicks like in *Spy Hunter*. He ran to the loading dock with Sonya close behind, swung the door open, and gaped. He turned to Sonya, paused, and then looked back at the car.

"You got me a brown Fiat hatchback?" he stammered. "My old car was worth twice that! I didn't even know they made Fiats in this country."

The Prophus own quite a few shares of Fiat. We can get them at cost.

"Color not to your liking?" She was having way too much fun at his expense.

"Yeah, poop brown sucks for a car color. I thought I'd get something nicer now that I'm an agent."

Sonya shrugged. "Sorry, budget constraints. Besides, the point of a secret agent is to blend in with your surroundings. Driving around in a Ferrari would make you stand out like a sore thumb. Besides, can you even drive stick?" That shut him up.

She gave him one more pat on the butt as she put on her jacket and walked toward the door. Before she left, Sonya turned and grinned again. "One more thing, just a little piece of advice. Make sure you have all that information memorized before you push that button. And when you do push it, don't be near anything flammable. Well, enjoy your ride and good luck on your mission tomorrow. Try not to die." And then she was gone.

CHAPTER TWELVE
THE TRUTH

I did not say no when he invaded the southern Chinese kingdoms. I did not say no when he moved his armies west. By the time I ordered Temujin to stop warring, it was too late. I did the unforgivable thing and lost control of my host. Like many others before us, we both became victims of our success. By this time, Temujin knew nothing but war. The Mongol civilization knew nothing else as well. I had created the one civilization that I had hoped to destroy.

"So, what's all this about?" Antonio demanded as Roen came home and kicked off his shoes.

"I don't know what you're talking about," he replied innocently.

"Don't be a smart ass. Something is going on. You're out every morning jogging these days. This is coming from a dude who would rather break a leg than break a sweat. I haven't heard you bitch about work in a while. You're working out with a sizzling hot girl, and you're not playing video games anymore."

Roen tried to appear nonchalant as he walked to his room to change. "Priorities, my good man. It's just time to do more with my life."

Antonio followed. "That's a bunch of bull; you're different. You're not the fat bastard I know and love. Are you doing drugs? Are you on cocaine? You can tell me. I'm a doctor and your best friend."

Roen smirked. "You make it sound like my lifestyle change is bad."

"Not bad, but still alarming."

Roen hesitated. He'd been dying to tell someone about this. If he couldn't tell his best friend, who could he tell? He finished changing and walked into the kitchen.

Antonio trailed after him, opening the fridge and pointing inside. "Look at what you're eating now too. I came in last week to grab a pot pie, and there weren't any! In the three years that we've lived together, there hasn't been one moment where we didn't have enough sodas and pot pies to last through a nuclear winter. I used to be comforted by the fact that if we were ever trapped in our apartment, all we needed was the food in the freezer and an oven to survive. Now, all we have is a bunch of raw veggies and brown rice! Where's the frozen pizza? Where's the ice cream?"

Roen sighed. A pizza would really hit the spot right about now. He'd been behaving well this past month. Was it wrong to treat himself?

Stay on the bandwagon. Avoid temptation.

"But... it's been so long! Don't I get a reward for being good?"

Fitness is its own reward.

"That's easy for you to say. Argh! Now I can't stop thinking about pizza."

Tao and the lack of pizza had been gnawing at Roen for weeks now. His alien secret and his angry neglected stomach were itches that just wouldn't stop. He decided then and there to scratch both itches at the same time. He had behaved well, and by golly, he was going to eat that well-deserved pizza, Tao be damned! Besides, it was good to bond with his roommate. He'd been so busy that the two had barely spoken.

"All right, let's go to Lou's for dinner and grab some deep dish. We can talk about it then." Roen closed the fridge.

Wait... talk about what? About me? This is a bad idea, Roen.

"That's what I'm talking about." Antonio whooped. "Hang on. Let me get my jacket. I'll drive, then?"

Roen twirled his keys around his fingers. "Look who got a new car!" Antonio grinned and ran into his room.

Do not say anything to your friend!

After knowing he was getting deep dish pizza, Roen became more and more excited. His taste buds sprang to life and his mouth watered at the very thought of cheese, pepperoni, and butter crust. The two almost raced down to the garage in glee and moments later were driving downtown to their favorite pizza joint for some Chicago deep dish. Soon, they were waiting for their order in one of the booths, the aroma of marinara and pepperoni filling their nostrils. Roen had to keep reminding himself that this was only for a special occasion.

"First of all, what's the deal with Sonya? I mean, come on, buddy, I didn't know you had it in you." Antonio squinted at Roen. "Wait, she's not a professional, is she?"

"Professional what?"

Antonio laughed. "Get your mind out of the gutter. Professional trainer, dummy. Well, if she is, I don't blame you. You look like half of you already. Literally. So if she is, she's worth it." He paused. "Is she?"

"No."

"Then who is she and how did this miraculous transformation come about?" Antonio made circular gestures at Roen's slimmer body.

Roen did not feel comfortable talking about Tao, having promised to never reveal their secret. But Sonya's mother had told Sonya, and it wasn't like Antonio would ever betray him.

They were best friends! There was no harm telling one person, was there? It might even help put things in perspective. Finally he decided to just spill it and see what happened.

Do not go down this path. It is dangerous for you and your friend. If the Genjix ever find out where you live, they could get to you through Antonio. And I promise you it will not be pleasant for him. For both your sakes, do not tell him anything.

"Tao, I know what I'm doing. He won't give me away. Besides, I need to tell someone. Even Bruce Wayne had Alfred to cover for him. I need an Alfred."

You need to shut your mouth if you know what is good for you.

"Antonio, do you believe in aliens?" he said in a low voice.

Damn you, Roen.

Antonio's brow bunched up. "Aliens: like the movie *Aliens*, *Star Trek* aliens, *Invasion of the Body Snatchers* aliens, or do you mean illegal aliens?"

"The *Body Snatcher* variety," Roen replied.

"Good movie and no, I don't believe in aliens, especially those that come all the way over here from another galaxy to take over someone, unless they're here to steal our women. That I'd understand, and even then I think they'd have hotter women over there anyway. There's no need to steal ours." Antonio laughed half-heartedly. His laughter died when he noticed Roen's face darken. "Are you implying you're acting weird because you were body-snatched and you're not the real Roen, but a fake clone Roen, and the real Roen is in a cocoon on some mother ship where they plan to suck his blood?"

Roen shook his head. "You're getting *Invasion of the Body Snatchers* mixed up with *Killer Klowns from Outer Space*. They're the ones that wrap you up in cotton candy and drink your blood."

"Close enough. So what about them? You saying you have some alien in you?"

Roen looked both ways over his shoulder and leaned in, his

voice reduced to a whisper. "What if I told you that for the past few months, I've had an alien life force living in me named Tao?"

You just do not know when to shut up.

"Tao is a Quasing," he continued. "His kind is involved in some civil war. These aliens are powerless to do anything on Earth due to our atmosphere, but they can inhabit humans and speak to us. Tao came to me when his previous host died on a mission. He's a being that's been around for millions of years. He's inhabited all sorts of people and used to be in Lafayette and San-Feng."

"What the heck is a San-Feng?"

"Beats me. Someone important, I guess."

"Hmm." Antonio looked worried. "And what does Tao want with you?"

Roen sighed. "He wants to train me to be a field operative so I can carry out Prophus missions. That's why I've been getting in shape. I'm being deployed in the field soon."

Antonio frowned. "You know, I'd swear you're trying to pull a fast one on me if I didn't know your lousy poker face. Is Tao with us right now?"

"He's always with me."

"Can I say hi?"

Roen shrugged. "I guess. He can hear everything we say."

Antonio leaned forward and raised his voice. "Hi, Mr Tao. How are you? How does it feel being in Roen? I bet you're not used to that much space."

"Not funny." Roen scowled. "Come on, I'm serious."

"You want me to take you seriously?" Antonio looked exasperated. "All right, I'm sorry. Does Tao want to say hi to me?"

"Do you have anything to say, Tao?"

Go to hell, Roen.

"Tao says hi," Roen replied.

Antonio leaned back and took a sip of his drink. The waiter brought the pizza and the two took a break from their discussion to help themselves to a few slices. Roen passed Antonio the grated cheese and grabbed the crushed pepper. His stomach groaned with anticipation at the piping hot pizza with the generous heaping of marinara sauce spread over the thick crust. Each slice was two inches thick stuffed with pepperoni, olives, spinach, and onions. Roen cut the cheese strings that stuck to his slice and took a large bite. It tasted like heaven.

"So is Sonya one of them body snatchers?" Antonio asked, his voice muffled by the food in his mouth.

Roen nodded.

Antonio shook his head. "I don't know, buddy. Look, you're my boy, but this is nuts. I think you're going crazy."

Roen scowled again. "I'm not crazy, Antonio; don't say that. It took me a long time to come to grips with this."

Antonio shook his head. "Different strokes for different folks, I guess. Some need a heart attack to decide to hit the gym, while others just wake up one day and think it's time. Maybe your motivation is interstellar war, but I think your type of motivation is borderline schizophrenic."

Roen slammed a fist onto the table, earning him looks from those around them. "Look, for the last time, I'm not crazy; this is serious! You wanted to know, and I trust you enough to tell you. You have to promise to keep this a secret."

For the first time, Antonio looked uncomfortable. "Who am I going to tell? What am I going to tell them? My roommate thinks he's possessed by an alien that's training him to be James Bond?"

Roen shook his head. "Tao was right. This was a mistake. You know, forget it."

"Come on, Roen, what did you expect me to think? I mean, show me some proof. Show me some alien technology or superpowers or something. Bend metal or fly or grow a tentacle. You can't expect me to believe you on blind faith."

"I have no powers. It doesn't work that way. The Prophus can only act through their hosts."

"Right. That's awfully convenient," Antonio didn't bother hiding his disbelief. "Like Kyle Reese not being able to bring a weapon back from the future."

"But in *Terminator*, he was right. They should have believed him," Roen countered.

Antonio shook his head. "That's why it's a movie." He stood up and put some money on the table. "Look, I'm going. You should think about getting help. It's cool that you're losing weight and working out, but it's not healthy how you're going about doing it." He patted Roen on the shoulder and left him sitting alone at the booth.

Roen brooded for several minutes. Antonio's words stung, and at the same time, made sense. Could he be using this story of aliens and wars as a way to subconsciously force himself out of his rut? He could imagine doing something like that. The idea of being a cog in something important appealed to his ego. His own unhappiness might not be enough to make him want to change, but a covert war with the balance of humanity at stake certainly would.

Great, are we back to this again? Talk about two steps forward and ten steps back. Is your sense of self so weak that anyone can convince you of anything? If you were ever captured, you would crack under interrogation before they even ask the questions.

"Well, he does make a valid point. What if you're my subconscious trying to motivate me after everything else has failed?"

What do you want? Proof? Is Sonya not enough proof? What about the Genjix that tried to kill you? Do beautiful strange women come knocking on your door in the morning to go running with you?

"Good point," Roen conceded. "I didn't think of that."

And that is the crux of your problem. You do not think. I warned you. No good could have come from telling your friend. Do not bring

*it up again. It will pass, and if we are lucky, he will forget all about
it. We have bigger things to worry about, anyway.*

·"Like what?"

*Like converting you to the metric system and figuring out what to
do with your infant-like hand-eye coordination.*

CHAPTER THIRTEEN
TRAINING WHEELS

Temujin was an old man when I finally gave up on him. Our last words together were not pleasant. He accused me of betrayal. And in a way, he was right. I had betrayed us many years ago by being weak. One day, I stopped speaking to him. The next, he died in a skirmish. He was my greatest triumph and my greatest failure. At that moment in time, the potential for a great civilization was within his grasp, and it slipped through his fingers, and I was to blame.

Roen's glorious career as a Prophus agent began rather ingloriously, scouting the harbor before settling down on a spot next to the Adler Planetarium, where for the next several nights, he watched birds splash around a patch of black waters off the coast of Lake Michigan with a pair of night vision goggles he purchased at a sports store. It was like watching television static for the first four days.

Roen realized during those long, dull hours what Tao meant about the drudgery of covert work. By the third night, he wanted to cut himself to stop the numbness. It didn't help that there was literally nothing there, not a person, a boat, not even stinking fish. Still, he tried to do the job diligently, though he felt free to complain to Tao every step of the way.

"This is a complete waste of time, Tao. I'm observing open water, for God's sake. Can't we just put a satellite here instead of me wasting precious sleep twiddling my thumbs? If I wanted to be bored out of my mind, I'd just go to work, which I have to be at in four hours, I might add."

Satellites are expensive to use. You are much cheaper. I tried to warn you. Agent work is all boredom mixed with a few seconds of excitement that makes you wish you were bored. You will learn to appreciate this peace. Excitement in this line of work usually means someone is trying to put a bullet in you.

"I'm so cheap I'm working for free. I even had to pay for my own stuff here."

The fifth night, a small craft appeared and several dark forms jumped into the water. Roen took a few pictures of the boat and recorded the longitude and latitude using a GPS, before calling the mission a success. He never found out what any of it meant.

Over the course of the next few weeks, he received a dozen more assignments through his new network email. The first few were more reconnaissance missions: a house on South Cicero Avenue near the airport, a diner in Little Italy, a coffee shop in the Lincoln Park area, a public mailbox – yes, a stinking mailbox! – on Diversey and Clark.

Most of those experiences were even worse than the first assignment. And all these were done as he worked around his regular job. Roen ended up taking more vacation and sick days over the next month than he had over the past five years. Once, he had to call in sick two days in a row while sitting in a van for thirty hours. Any excitement of being a bona fide secret agent evaporated along with his dreams of becoming Dirk Pitt or James Bond.

He began dreading the emails that popped up in his inbox. It became so bad that he actually started looking forward to the days at the office. But no matter how mundane and boring those assignments were, he carried them out the best he could.

The only saving grace was the time he spent with Tao. During those long stretches of boredom, Tao would go over the dreams he imprinted into Roen, explaining the reasoning behind many of his decisions. Roen always awoke from those dreams seeking explanations. He remembered fragments, but had difficulties understanding the complete picture. Between the dreams, Tao's stories, and the images that Tao flashed into his head, he began to grasp the magnitude of the Quasing and how much they influenced human history.

Tao's lives soon became one of Roen's favorite pastimes. He learned about all the previous hosts that Tao inhabited, and began to respect the wisdom of his Quasing. Tao told stories of his previous hosts, starting from his time as a Babylonian to the many Romans he inhabited, then to the Gauls and the Egyptians, and then to the Far East as a golden wolf to Genghis Khan; how he invented t'ai chi in China, how he started the White Lotus society, and then how he started the Ming Dynasty. While Roen had always known Tao had survived through thousands of years of humans, listening to the breadth and depth of each host's experience was overwhelming and humbling.

It was then that he realized a few things. First of all, those previous hosts started out just like himself, initially scared and unsure of the Quasing. Many of them became great and capable men that changed the face of the world, others tried to follow Tao's guidance, and a few outright rebelled against him. The second thing he realized about Tao's hosts was that from the African warlord to the Chinese emperor to the Spanish assassin and many others, they all lived dangerous, violent lives. He wondered if he would become like them, and the possibility disturbed him.

"So, if you kept trying to create these civilizations and kept failing, why didn't you just find a genius pacifist who couldn't be coaxed to violence?"

It is not like pacifism is in their DNA. You never know what the nature of a host will be. Part of it is nurture, yes, but you have to realize that the world was less civilized back then.

"I don't know, Tao. Seems to me all your hosts were pretty violent. The only common denominator I see is you."

I will not apologize for my hand in guiding humanity. I do what I believe is right.

Slowly, his view on life changed as he settled into his new role. Roen couldn't quite put his finger on it. His priorities were shifting and all the annoyances that used to drive him into conniptions didn't seem to matter anymore. The four-dollar coffees, crowded lunch lines, and long red lights all became background noise. When he just missed the bus or forgot his wallet, he just shrugged it off. The changes were apparent that things felt different and it bothered him. He was settling into this new foreign life, and he wasn't sure he wanted to.

When he was not running asinine missions or working, he trained with Sonya. His usual daily schedule consisted of: getting up in the morning, training with Sonya, going to work, training with Sonya again, doing an asinine mission, and then getting a few hours of rest. The few nights he was not on assignment, Sonya added in extra workouts.

By the time June rolled around, Roen saw real progress in his fitness. He was now in the best shape of his life, though that historically didn't amount to much, but the hard work was paying off. He even swore he saw a stomach muscle somewhere in his belly region. His stamina had improved by leaps and bounds as well. Sonya and he often went on long ten-kilometer jogs (she always measured in metrics, which was fine by him since it was shorter) that were impossible for him just two months ago.

With Roen becoming more autonomous with his physical conditioning, Sonya shifted the direction of their training from basic conditioning to combat exercises. And while Roen took to fitness training and even grew to enjoy it, hand-to-hand combat became his new arch-nemesis. Though Tao and Sonya spent a fair portion of his training on it, they were having little success.

He was hopelessly uncoordinated. His reflexes were still poor, his fighting instincts were non-existent, and he had a laughably low pain tolerance. Though he outweighed her by nearly double, Sonya was able to hit harder and faster, and manhandled him in every sparring session. And on one beautiful but terrible morning, his training really took a turn for the worse. They started fighting with weapons.

Tao's groan inside Roen's head matched his own out loud as the staff struck him across the face. He grunted in pain, dropped his own staff, and turned away. That was a mistake as another blow caught him in the gut, doubling him over, followed by a sweep that took out his legs. Roen crumpled to the floor in a heap. Tao's groan, however, was not from pain; but one born from frustration. At this point, Roen couldn't care less how frustrated Tao was as he lay on the floor rubbing his chin. It wasn't like the Prophus could feel pain anyway.

How many times do I have to tell you not to bite on every feint? Look how far away she was! Two quick flashes popped inside Roen's head, both of Sonya executing similar attacks. *Learn to recognize it!*

"Easy for you to say. You're not the one getting whacked silly."

Baji must be mocking me.

"Are you all right, Roen?" Sonya picked up the staff and handed it back to him as he scrambled to his knees. "You need to gauge distance better. You're falling for the same trick every time."

I rest my case.

"That explains why you managed to hit me in the same place four times now." He grimaced.

"Maybe you shouldn't leave that opening for me." She blew

a strand of hair from her face and waved him back. "Let's try this again, and try to hang on to the staff."

He could tell her patience was wearing thin as well. The two squared off in the ring and began anew. Roen had finally overcome his self-consciousness and was wearing only a pair of shorts. It had taken him a while to feel comfortable enough to go shirtless. Sonya, as usual, wore a dark blue close-fitting shirt and pants, garments that covered most of her body.

They circled and stalked each other, both looking for an opening. Sonya shuffled her feet, feinted high and then slashed low. Roen managed to block her quick swing as the two shafts clacked with a loud thunk. Sensing an opening, Roen stabbed at her face with the butt end. Sonya moved fluidly and parried, guiding his thrust away from her body. Then she pivoted forward and twirled the staff, striking him on the side of the head. He staggered backward.

Turn right! Roll with the blow. Keep the guard up. An image of a monk blocking a sword flashed in his head.

By this time, Roen was used to following Tao's running commentary and tried his best to follow the instructions. He felt his back to the rope as he retreated. Sonya gave him no quarter, however, and charged again. He barely dodged another blow as he fell back, hopelessly off balance. She pressed the attack, pouncing on top of him and spearing him in the stomach. She ended the melee just short of a killing blow. Roen groaned and Tao muttered something he couldn't make out.

Sonya shook her head and offered her hand. "I think that's enough for the day. You need to get ready for work, anyhow."

Roen couldn't agree more. He could see the disappointment in her eyes. The past couple weeks of workouts had been painful. Getting beaten up twice a day was starting to take a physical and mental toll on him. He was becoming discouraged and started dreading these workouts. Sighing, he picked himself up and hopped in the shower. By the time he got out,

Sonya had already left. Roen walked up to the mirror and felt his tender ribs. A splotch a nice shade of purple was already appearing. There was a nasty looking welt appearing just above his temple as well. He looked as if he'd just gone five rounds with Mike Tyson.

"No male modeling for me," he sighed as he got dressed for work.

An hour later, Roen dragged his tired, sore body to work. His coworkers had already gotten over their initial concerns with his bruised and often-cut face. Maybe they thought he had joined a fight club or something. He had become used to it and barely noticed the worried looks on their faces.

Fatigue had become an issue though. Both Tao and Sonya pushed him so hard; he always felt exhausted. Roen desperately wanted to call in sick today after the morning workout, but willed himself to go in. He was determined to finish as much work as possible before the weekend. He sat at his desk and stared at the list of jobs slated for the day: a few script adjustments, some applications to deploy, and several diagrams to update; all in all, a typical monotonous day.

"The world spins despite me, not because of me," he muttered. Last week, one of his coworkers died after twenty-five years of service. There was an email and eulogy sent by one of the managers – and then a mad scramble by everyone else to loot his office supplies. Roen picked up his stapler and held it over his head, exclaiming loudly. "This is all I'll amount to. This is my stapler. There are many like it, but this one is mine. My stapler is my best..."

It is not even really yours. If you quit your job, they keep the stapler.

"Hush, Tao. You're ruining my moment with myself."

Your moment of self-pity? And yet you cannot bear to quit the job that makes you feel this way.

"Well, when can I quit and get on the Prophus payroll?"

When we can trust you enough to do more than stalk a mailbox.

Roen sighed. "You know, I bet the Prophus have pretty deep pockets. Why don't you put me on retainer now? My development would be so much faster if my only responsibility was to train."

Throwing money at you just because you do not like your lot in life? No thanks. We are not your sugar daddy.

"You'd get better results out of me that way."

Your progress has been commendable enough... wait... scroll back up. I see the problem. Comment that code out and change the global variables.

Roen complied and did as he was told.

Anyway, as I was saying, I am pleased with your progress, maybe even proud.

"Does this bruised and battered face look like something anyone should be proud of?"

I had my doubts at first. You were an out-of-shape man with low self-esteem and underdeveloped social skills. Now you are an in-shape man with low self-esteem and underdeveloped social skills.

"Thanks... I think."

There has been a marked improvement. Your reaction time has improved somewhat as of late. Now, if you can only stop fighting like a girl.

"What do you expect? You got a girl to train me."

I take that back. Saying you fight like a girl is an insult to girls everywhere. I bet you would not dare say that in front of Sonya.

"Damn straight I wouldn't. I still have nightmares about her right hook."

That is because you never see it coming. You have to read her telegraphs when she feints to your right. It is her MO.

"Oh, I see it coming. I just can't react fast enough."

This is serious. If we do not resolve this problem, you will never survive in the field.

Roen finished deploying his applications and crossed them

off his to-do list. He opened one of his diagrams and began to make changes. With Tao's help, his productivity had doubled and the quality of his work had improved tenfold.

By noon, he had finished almost everything, something that used to take him all day to do. Whistling, he locked his computer and grabbed his workout bag. The one redeeming value of the company was the gym located in the basement. While it was unsettling to see his overweight coworkers sweating in shorts, it served as a grim reminder that he used to be one of them.

As he often did, Roen took a detour to the elevator and walked a few aisles out of his way. Sometimes, he almost wished Jill wouldn't be at her desk. She had been traveling for work this past month, so he hadn't seen much of her lately. His heartbeat quickened and his palms began to sweat.

Oh come on. You treat her like a Greek goddess and act like a lap dog around her. It is embarrassing.

Today, he was in luck, or not in luck, depending on who you asked. Jill was busy typing on her laptop. Her auburn hair was tied in a bun, and she wore a sharp gray business suit, along with her cute nerdy glasses. Roen sucked in his breath and felt his heart skip a beat. He slowed down and stood there silently, not sure what to do now that she was there.

Can you just say something to her? This silly ritual is more than a bit creepy. If only you could tail targets as well as you tail her. Make up your mind and say something, or stop stalking her.

"Um, hi, Jill."

I meant something charming.

Jill looked up, her eyes widening as she saw him. "Oh, hey, Roen. Wow, did you lose weight? You look great!"

"Um... uh..."

Why do I bother? Here, repeat these words verbatim. Thanks, Jill, you look pretty good yourself.

"Thanks, Jill, you look pretty good yourself," he repeated dutifully.

"Aw, you're sweet," she said. "No, I'm serious though. Have you been working out?"

Just a little bit. I am trying to be healthier these days. But I am serious too. You also look great.

Roen again repeated what Tao said.

Jill frowned. "No way. I've been traveling so much that I haven't been to the gym in weeks. All that eating out every night. I have a triathlon coming up and have hardly trained."

There, you have something in common. Ask her to exercise with you.

Roen went out on a limb and added his own bit. "Why would you need to work out? It's not like you're..." He caught himself at the last second.

Stick to my script! If I wanted you to improvise, I would have told you!

She chuckled and then frowned at him, a mischievous twinkle in her eye. "You're being awfully nice to me today. Are you looking for candy?"

He laughed nervously. "Of course not. Anyway, I have to go... I'm running to lunch... to the gym. I mean... to jog on the treadmill, uh, not to eat, I mean. Well, OK... bye." He turned and fled.

Jill looked a bit confused. "...all right, Roen. I'll see you later."

Ask her out, dummy.

"No way!"

Stop walking now!

"No!"

Now, Roen Tan!

He stopped. It was Tao's authoritative voice.

Turn around and ask her.

Roen planted his feet and shook his head.

Ask, blast it!

With an overwhelming sense of dread, he tiptoed back to her desk. "Hey Jill, I've been meaning to ask you. You... hmm... want to grab dinner this weekend?" His voice cracked just a little as he spoke.

She looked up again, surprised, but not in a deer-in-headlights sort of way that he had expected. She shook her head. "Sorry, I'm heading back to Frankfurt Friday. You know how that Tillian project is."

Roen was crushed. Shoulders slumped, he turned and walked away.

Stop, fool! She did not say no.

"Roen, wait," she called out. "I need to stay with the project until the second stage is completed. Rain check for when I get back?"

Stunned, all he could do was nod dumbly.

Say something! Thank her and tell her you will call her when she gets back.

"You serious?" was all he could muster.

No, dummy!

Jill giggled. "Of course. I'll get you the dates and we'll plan something."

"Great!" He turned to leave again.

How are you going to call her? Get her number!

"Oh!" He turned back again. "Let me get your number. I mean, could I get your number?"

She grinned impishly and jotted it down on a piece of paper. "First Friday back, OK?"

He nodded and practically skipped down the aisle, the butterflies in his stomach bubbling up in joy. "She underlined her number twice on the Post-it. That means she likes me, right?"

Stop grinning like a mad fool and get to the gym, you big peacock.

CHAPTER FOURTEEN
RECONNECT

Through the next century, I drifted, moving from animal to animal, observing and learning about man. My thoughts often returned to Temujin and the mistakes I made. I had tried to build peace through war. I would not make that error again. Undeterred in my ambition for a new enlightened world, I traveled from the Mongolian steppes to the kingdoms of the south and was spoken of as a mythological creature among the Chinese people there. Those who profess to enlightenment called me the Ho Lung, the Fire Dragon.

That night, Sonya came over to watch a boxing match, much to Roen and Antonio's delight. The fact that she enjoyed sports was just another added bonus for them to have an even bigger crush on her. Antonio fawned over her every request, much to her evident amusement.

Having been knocked out several times by her, Roen was no longer as susceptible to her charms. To his surprise, she was the one to suggest staying over. The plan was to wake up at sunrise for a training session. The Chicago summer was in full swing and they planned to take full advantage of it by running along the lake. Afterward, she said she wanted to lay out at Oak Street Beach, lamenting how Lake

Michigan was a poor substitute for the Caribbean, but it'd have to do.

Sonya also finagled the use of his bed, leaving him the living room couch. Roen wasn't sure how she pulled it off, but at the end of the night, he found himself holding a pillow and blanket staring at the lumpy old taupe-colored couch his parents had donated from their basement. Falling asleep was never a problem though. Grumbling aside, he was asleep the instant he laid his head on the pillow, his shallow snoring resonating across the entire apartment.

A few minutes past midnight, once he knew that Roen was hibernating like a bear, Tao got up and walked his body toward his bedroom. There were still sounds coming out of Antonio's room, which was expected as Roen's roommate kept odd hours. Antonio saw Tao walk by and waved. "Where're you going?" he asked.

"To my room," Tao replied, eager to brush him off.

Antonio smirked and winked. "You mean to Sonya's room? Sly dog. You could have told me you wanted to call dibs. I won't try to compete with you if you like her. You're my boy. I'll let you have her."

Let him have her? Tao couldn't help himself. "You know what, buddy? You think you can beat me for her? You go ahead. Want to make a little friendly wager?"

Antonio looked up from the computer and raised an eyebrow. "Hmm? I see your newfound weight loss is accompanied by brain loss. What's the bet?"

"Hundred dollars on her affections."

Antonio whistled. "Not so friendly after all. Sure?"

Tao nodded.

"What if she doesn't like either of us?"

Tao smiled. He said, "If she does not like either of us, then you win as well, yeah?"

Antonio grinned and walked up to Tao, extending his hand. "Deal. Honestly, if you find a girl who likes you, I'm happy for you, man. It's win-win for me." He grinned and pointed at his face, "But you're not going to beat this."

Tao winked and shook Antonio's hand, and then walked over to his room and tapped on the closed door. Not waiting for an answer, he opened it and walked in, locking it behind him. The light was on and Sonya was sitting on the bed waiting for him.

"Hello, Tao. It has been a while."

"It is good to speak with you again, Baji. How are things with Sonya progressing?"

"Very well. Her talent is unmatched; without a doubt the strongest host I have had in a thousand years, even more than her mother. You?"

"It has been a long time since I had a host this raw. I have to admit, Edward spoiled me. He was a joy to work with. I still have to settle with his family."

"Shame on you, Tao. You should have seen to that already."

"Unfortunately, Edward did not have a contingency plan with his family. He never wanted to think about it. Right now, Roen is too delicate to handle the trauma of condolences."

"The young man is not doing too badly, Tao. He did start late but has progressed well. How long has he been with you?"

"Just under three months."

"A pittance, Tao. He will be competent soon enough."

Tao sighed and sat down next to her on the bed. "Time is a luxury I do not have. The Keeper has made it very clear Roen needs to be up to speed soon. He begins actual combat missions in two months and he hasn't even held, much less fired a gun yet. The Keeper is correct, though. I need to be back in the field as soon as possible. With the current debacle in the Middle East with Israel and Iran, and the loss of influence in two South American countries, we are being pushed back on our heels. To make matters worse, China is poised to be the new powerhouse in the world, and the Genjix has made sure we have no foothold in their government. We are dangerously out of position in the world."

Baji shook her head. "How were we supposed to predict the rapid ascension of the communists? Aligning with nationalists was a losing position, but the right thing to do. We were in too deep regardless."

"Have we made any headway with the Vatican?"

Baji grimaced. "We have lost ground. Our bought neutrality is over. With Jerrix as the new pope, expect a cleansing from within that will push us out entirely. It will become as bad for us as during the Dark Ages." She grabbed a stack of papers on the desk and handed it to him. "The last few months of intelligence reports you have missed; fun reading."

Tao took the stack and skimmed through them. "Like watching someone slowly suffocate," he muttered.

"It is worse than you think. There is a proposal on the table to build a safe haven in the event we need to go dormant. Some believe this generation is lost."

Tao looked up from the papers. "Really, that bad? Where?"

"Greenland."

"Figures." Tao scowled. "Too unrealistic to hope for a nice isolated tropical island?"

"Completely." Baji chuckled. "Real estate is too expensive."

"How are our financial figures looking at least?"

"That is our lone bright point. Tresk was spot-on in predicting the right revenue-generating models. Thank goodness for our cosmetic pharmaceutical division."

"Indeed," Tao replied. "Such an irony that our quest for mankind's greater good required an appeal to their shallow nature."

"No one wants to pay for a cure for cancer, but Heaven forbid a man lose his hair or an erection." Baji hesitated. "There is one more thing, Tao. A Decennial has been called, and the Genjix have agreed. They are working on a date now. Initial date proposed is sometime middle of next year, possibly in Spain or Singapore."

Tao scowled. "We called it? Why? The last one set off the Korean War. What good does the two sides talking ever achieve?"

"The technological curve on this planet is increasing exponentially. Both sides have adjusted their timelines; the Genjix by as little as two hundred by their plan; ours by seven. We have reports that the Genjix have begun prototyping this Penetra scanner. Code name: Longbow. Our people are focusing on disrupting the supply lines for its parts. The design list requires very specific pieces of technology. The manufacturing plant is the underwater facility off the coast here. It is impossible to infiltrate. Intel has also confirmed that there is a massive three-phase program in the works, with the Penetra program being the first phase."

"Longbow, huh. It must be a game changer to carry such a lofty name," Tao murmured. "We are losing this fight one step at a time. The planet is following the Genjix timeline."

"And now Command is scrambling for reconciliation," Baji said. "They fear total capitulation."

Tao spat. "Fools. We have been on the brink of capitulation for five hundred years. Already, we see the effects of their industrial push. If the Genjix have their way, the planet will be barren and stripped of all resources in order to achieve the expedition of the return."

"Acceptable losses by the Genjix." Baji shrugged. "Be sure to burn these documents when you have finished with them. No need to put your boy in a panic yet. When do you think he will be ready to take the field?"

Tao shook his head. "Not sure. Definitely not until we overcome his physical deficiencies. He could be destined for a desk job."

"Hardly, Tao," Baji snorted. "You were always one of our best field agents. You coaxed the most out of even the most helpless ones. Look at what you did with Genghis and Shamshi-Adad. If my memory serves me, Shamshi-Adad wanted nothing more than to breed horses and children, especially after his father gave the kingdom to his brother. It took an inordinate amount of prodding from you to get him off his rump to go conquer his own kingdom. He did much more than that. Assyria was a bona fide empire back in the day."

Tao laughed. "I did set that one right. Shamshi-Adad – that man was quite the rascal. I am quite proud of that one."

"Just do the same for Roen. He will come around. As for teaching him how to fight, what about that ever-so-modest and humble fighting style of yours you created in China during the fourteenth century, the one you claimed you discovered when you saw the bird and the rat fight? What did you call it, the Grand Supreme Fist? I am surprised you did not call it Tao Fist. It is no wonder Napoleon and Lafayette could not stand each other. There was too much ego in the room."

"It was a magpie and a snake, and I swear I was not the one that came up with the name. San-Feng came up with that on his own." Tao paused thoughtfully. "You know, I thought the Grand Supreme Fist might have been too difficult for him, but it actually might be a good fit. Learning it requires unlearning everything about body movement, and Roen never had any to begin with."

She said, "Well, Dania and Sonya never understood your Supreme Fist, but Roen might. He just needs to apply himself."

"The problem with Roen is not his desire. It is his self-doubt and awkwardness. He is also very stubborn. Trying to convert him to the metric system is trying to teach a Gaul haiku."

"It just takes practice. You will think of something. You always do. You invented half a dozen martial arts. If you could do that, I am sure you could train him in one of those to some degree of aptitude."

"That is a bit of an exaggeration. If you looked at all those martial arts, they were all similar, just different means to an end."

Baji threw a playful jab at Tao, which he blocked. "Rubbish, Tao. All combat ends at the same place. It is the training that is important. Just figure out what style of combat Roen takes to and run with it."

"Perhaps," Tao replied.

The two spent the rest of the night reminiscing over better times and chatted about the future. All in all, it was nice to enjoy each other's company without having to deal with hosts. The sun was just appearing over the horizon by the time they decided to turn in. The effort required to control their hosts was quite draining.

"We should speak again soon," Baji said as she escorted him to the door.

Tao nodded. "I look forward to it." As he turned to leave, he stopped and grinned. "One more thing; humor me with this one. Not if, but when Antonio decides to make his move on Sonya, have her tell him that she is flattered – but her heart is set on Roen."

Baji laughed. "Sure thing, Tao."

He winked and hurried off to bed before Roen woke. As he laid his host back on the couch, Tao thought back to the time he spent in China after Temujin. His mind wandered to the years after he left the Mongols and moved south to the Yuan Dynasty where he met San-Feng and created the Grand Supreme Fist.

As he often did when he thought about the past, Tao reminisced over the many mistakes he made. A few key moments could have changed the world for the better or hindered the Genjix's rise to dominance.

Tao mulled over his conversation with Baji until sunrise lit the apartment. The problems of the Prophus weighed down on him. It bothered him that he was on the sidelines during such a critical time. If a Decennial was scheduled, he needed to be there. With Roen's current progression, his attendance was in doubt. While Tao did not value those old fools meeting under a banner of truce, it was still an important event.

At this rate though, his host was ill-prepared for such an intense encounter with so many Quasing in one place. The man might crack under the pressure and get himself killed. But Tao could not even consider putting Roen into a combat situation until Roen could handle himself in a fight. There had to be something he could do to accelerate Roen's training. Training with Sonya had taken him far, but Tao needed to change his approach somehow.

The magpie and the snake. Tao searched his memories of that one vivid moment in history. While events of that fight were not in any history books, it launched a thousand schools of study.

San-Feng had stumbled upon the two animals fighting. The magpie was trying to eat the snake. However, each time the magpie attacked, the snake would evade the magpie with its loose and supple body, always staying out of range of the magpie's sharp beak. And then just as the magpie missed, the snake would strike, springing like a tightly wound coil releasing itself. The magpie then used its wings to evade the snake's attack by striking at odd angles to trap and peck it. The snake would always recoil from harm's way and strike back with lightning speed. Again and again, the two fought their dance of death.

Finally, after a fierce fight, the magpie took off into the sky, seeking easier prey. Tao, having inhabited birds and snakes before, knew exactly how they fought. He had envisioned the instincts he had when he occupied those animals. It was that

moment of revelation that led him to teach San-Feng the
Grand Supreme Fist.

*Damn it. If I can create the all-powerful Grand Supreme Fist, I can
teach this lug how to fight. Roen, wake up!*

CHAPTER FIFTEEN
LIN

It was there that I met Chang San-Feng and created the Grand Supreme Fist. It was also there that I joined with a man with great potential, much like Temujin, but tempered with humility and wisdom. His name was Zhu Yuanzhang. Born in poverty, Zhu had lived as a monk, a beggar, a rebel – and later as a leader of the Red Turban sect during a tumultuous time. Zhu Yuanzhang was quick to accept me, believing that the Ho Lung had come to him in his people's time of need.

I said, wake up, Roen!

"Whuu... What?" Roen woke with a start. "What's going on? Why am I on the couch? Oh yeah." He sat up and yawned. "What time is it?"

Get your workout in and then take the rest of the day off. We have much to do.

Roen blinked several times and buried his head in the pillow again. "Why am I so tired? I feel like I didn't sleep a wink last night."

Wake Sonya and start your morning jog.

"I feel exhausted. You know the body's defense system is weak when it's tired. I might catch a cold. Maybe I should take the day off." Roen pulled his blanket over his head.

No excuses today.

"Why are you so crabby?"

Go. Now!

Roen knew better than to argue when Tao was in such a mood. Complaining every step of the way, he rolled off the couch and knocked on Sonya's door. Coincidently, she was just as tired as he was. Their workout was very half-hearted as they both struggled to get through all the exercises. They cut the session short, and Sonya left to take care of her tan. Tao made Roen clear his schedule and had him drive away from the city to the suburb of Skokie to a plain unadorned building off the side of an alley.

"What is this? Another Prophus safe house?" Roen mused.

You will see.

"Not used very often, huh?" Roen kicked aside some garbage that littered the ground as he approached a rusty metal door. It squeaked as it opened as if it hadn't been used in ages, revealing another vault-like door similar to the safe house that Sonya and he trained in. Roen punched in his code and watched a layer of dust fall from the ceiling as the vault door rumbled open.

Like the safe house at Lake Street, the interior looked nothing like it did on the outside. However, instead of training equipment, this building looked like someone's home – with the exception of a large circular mat in the center of the room. Against one wall were dozens of assorted potted plants; on the opposite wall were a row of pinball machines and electronic equipment. An antique table, rocking chair, and couch were the only other furniture in sight. An old pudgy Chinese man with short black hair was sitting in the rocking chair reading a book. He did not seem to notice Roen walk in.

"This is something you don't see every day. What is this place?"

Go greet Sifu Wei Cheng Lin. Sifu means master in Mandarin. With respect, mind you, and take your shoes off, for God's sake.

"What's he a master of? Is that an Atari next to the television?"

Pay attention. Bow when you first speak to him and tell him Ho Lung greets him.

"What? What's a Ho Lung?"

Just say it.

Grumbling about bacteria and dirt, Roen took off his shoes and placed them next to the door. He strolled up to the man. "Um... Hi, Master Wei Cheng Lin. I was, uh... sent here by Ho Lung."

That is not what I told you to say.

The wizened old man, eyes still fixed on the book, spoke in a soft voice. "You are trespassing. Leave now." He pointed to the door, not bothering to even glance Roen's way. Roen shrugged, turned, and began to walk away.

Stop.

"What? What do I do now? I don't get it."

You really should follow directions better.

"You didn't say anything about verbatim."

Roen turned around again. Lin leaped from the chair at a blinding speed. His hands flashed forward and struck the air where Roen's head had been moments before. The punch was so fast Roen thought he heard the air pop. Stumbling backward, he covered up and retreated.

"What the hell? I don't want to beat on an old guy."

You have a bad track record with old men. You should worry more about your own safety right now.

Roen raised his guard just as Lin closed in waving his hands all crazy-like. Those strange gestures befuddled Roen. The old guy's palms were open and his arms outstretched as if he was trying to slap Roen. Both arms were waving in small circular patterns, moving back and forth like pieces of string blowing in the wind. However, when Roen blocked the slaps, it sent a shock through his body, unlike anything he had ever felt before.

"Ow! That hurt. That really, really hurt."

Punches are supposed to hurt.

"He hits like a Mack truck!"

Immediately, Lin moved to Roen's side and struck again. Roen barely blocked the attack as it came dangerously close to his face. The force of the blow pushed him backward. Roen retreated, shaking his hands in pain – as Lin continued stalking him, and whose hands still waved in the air as if they were live snakes.

Roen knew he had to keep his guard up, but the nerves in his arms refused to comply, and he found himself suddenly defenseless. He looked at the supposedly old and wizened man – who no longer seemed that old or wizened. Roen tried to move to the side, but was cut off as Lin pressed the attack.

After another punch that nearly took his head off, Roen decided that he had had enough. If the old fogey felt he had the right to knock Roen silly, then well, Roen was going to hit him right back! Roen stepped in and threw a hard right cross at Lin's chubby cheeks, just like during his fighting sessions with Sonya. The punch flew well short of its target.

Come on, that was embarrassing.

He followed through with a high kick. Lin stepped past his kick and karate-chopped his shins. Roen staggered and his knees buckled. Determined not to fall, he retreated again, trying to shake off the numbness in his legs. Lin pressed forward, darting in from side to side. Roen threw a few jabs, trying to keep him at bay, but his arms felt like lead weights. Lin smashed his defenses and, before Roen realized what had happened, flipped him onto his back.

The geezer who just beat the snot out of him stood over Roen and shook his head. Then he extended a hand, helping Roen stand up. "I hope you're a new host in need of training and not a live operative. You move like a pregnant cow."

"I'm a new host in need of training," stammered Roen. His

entire body hurt in so many places that his brain couldn't process all of it.

"It's good to know Command isn't completely bottom feeding." The old man nodded. "Who did you say sent you again?"

"Ho Lung greets you, Sifu Wei Cheng Lin," Roen managed to say through gritted teeth.

Wei Cheng Lin brightened up. "Oh, Sifu Tao, yes, it is so good to see you again. I see you picked a fixer-upper as your next host. I grieve with you for Edward."

"Tao, did you used to be a Ho Lung?"

Yes. I am quite a legend in Chinese mythology, you know.

"You'll have to tell me about that sometime."

Roen bowed. "Thank you, Sifu Lin. To be honest, I'm not sure why Tao sent me here."

Lin chuckled. "Isn't it obvious? You were sent here to be trained."

"But I'm already being trained," Roen protested.

Lin gave a snort.

Roen looked around the room. "This is what you do here? Train agents?"

Lin nodded. "I was once an agent, but one particular mission made me too visible in the world, so I went underground, and now I train."

"What mission was that, Sifu Lin?" Roen asked.

Lin gave him a blank stare. Finally, he replied, "It is of little matter. I am content serving any way they require. I have seen your abilities. We have much work to do."

"Is that why you attacked me?" Roen asked.

"How else could I gauge your real skill if you didn't think you were fighting for your life?" Lin smiled. "Do not worry; you are in good hands. Sifu Tao would not do otherwise."

"Sifu Tao?" Roen asked.

"Just as I train his students, he was once my master," Lin said. "In fact, you can say he was a master to all of us in our art."

"And what art would that be, Sifu Lin?"

Lin put his hands together and bowed. "Why, the Grand Supreme Fist of course, or what you might know as t'ai chi."

Sonya adjusted her sunglasses before putting them on. She lay out on her beach towel and enjoyed the weather as she tanned in her two-piece swimming suit, soaking up as much rays as possible. She tapped a hidden button on the side of the sunglasses. Several small screens turned on in her lenses. Now she had a three-sixty view of the area.

She sighed in contentment and relaxed. "This is the life. It isn't the Caymans, but it'll do." Oak Street Beach during the summer was packed with beachgoers. After the harsh Chicago winters, the people congregated on the beach with enthusiasm like a colony of ants. The crowd was loud as the hordes of humanity crowded the small beach as if it was the last strip of sand in the Midwest. Actually, that might not be that far off, Sonya thought.

Just remember you are still working.

"I'm never not working. The camera facing east is a little fuzzy."

It will have to do. I doubt our contact is coming in from the lake anyway.

"Well, Gaston better get here soon. I have plans with Roen today."

You are spending far too much time training him.

"He needs the work. Besides, he's like the puppy I always wanted."

Do not get too attached. Command is putting him in the field soon.

Sonya sat up. "What? It's too soon. He's not ready."

He will have to be. This is a bad time for Tao to take the year off. You need to get back to Europe.

Sonya shook her head and laid back down, pretending to doze off, while keeping an eye out for the signal. "I'll talk to the Keeper. It's only been a few months. He'll just get killed."

Nonsense. Soldiers in the United States go to war after basic and advanced training after five months; other countries, far less. Roen's had much more intense training from you.

"He wouldn't have even gotten into the army the state he was in when Tao found him."

Sonya's thoughts stayed on Roen. If that was the case, his training would have to be stepped up. She'd have to cut short the hand-to-hand combat and move to firearms and squad tactics. She was concerned he might be getting overwhelmed. She waited for another thirty minutes before turning over onto her stomach. As soon as she flipped over, the south camera picked up a flash, and then two more quick flashes. "We're a go," Sonya murmured. It was too bad. Now she'd have an uneven tan.

I was beginning to wonder. After the past two months, I was afraid something might have happened to Gaston.

Sonya packed her bag and headed south, making her way through the mass of humanity to the even more crowded beach bar. She ordered a cocktail and made eye contact with an older white-haired German man who looked out of place with the current crowd. They made eye contact and then he looked to his left. Sonya looked back and studied her drink. "Necklace, earrings in both ears, ring on right forefinger, book in his left hand."

Six-minute wait. Head west.

"The underground tunnel then."

When she looked back at where Gaston was standing before, he was gone. Sonya stayed at the bar for five minutes, before making her way from the bar toward the tunnel under Lakeshore Drive. The dark tunnel that connected the uptown neighborhood to the beach was a dark, dank contrast to the sunny beach seconds earlier. Sonya slowed her pace as she entered. She could feel the vibration of the cars passing overhead.

Gaston was a very high maintenance mole. Recently, he had gotten increasingly paranoid about these meetings and demanded more intricate methods of establishing contact. As of right now, Sonya was one of four agents rotating as handlers in order to throw off any possible surveillance. Still, it had taken six years for him to infiltrate the Genjix research division – and the Prophus were happy to oblige him as much as possible.

A figure hidden in a side crevice spoke. "A monkey, after getting drunk on brandy, would never touch it again."

"And thus, is much wiser than most men," Sonya answered.

Gaston grabbed her wrist and pulled her close. His face had already turned red from the few minutes he spent at the beach. Sonya wondered how much sun the man actually got. He seemed more nervous than usual. Sonya began to worry. "Is everything all right?" she asked. "You've missed the rendezvous three straight times now."

He began to whisper in quick bursts. "I cracked the security of the P1 logistics last night. The Genjix are building a scanner that can detect Quasing in hosts."

Those idiots!

Sonya was shocked. If this was true, it not only was a powerful weapon for the Genjix, it could change the entire dynamic of the Quasings on Earth if humanity ever got a hold of it. "Are you sure?" she asked. "Our own scientists think it's some sort of short-range sensor."

Gaston shook his head. "The blueprints Edward obtained from the archives were dead-end designs."

Damn. We have a small army of scientists trying to make heads or tails of those blueprints.

"Can you steal the real ones?" Sonya looked over her shoulder. "Do you know what the later phases are?"

Gaston shook his head. "They have me studying Quasing physiology relative to earth compounds. Penetra is only the tip of the iceberg. P1 is only the beginning that will lead to something even bigger. P3 is supposed to have planet-level ramifications. I'm not sure how everything is related. Here." He handed her a piece of paper. "This is the best I can do. The Genjix are at the prototyping stage of P1 development. Here's the material manifest for the next few months. The two critical ones are coming from Canada via Wisconsin by freight and Utah by air."

Sonya took the paper and put it away. It was something at least. "We'll have teams ready for intercept."

He grabbed her by the arm. "Look, when I broke into their system last night, I tripped several security protocols trying to access the later phases. I covered my tracks the best I could, but they're going to figure out there's a mole in their midst soon. I need to get out."

Sonya nodded. "I'll talk to Command and see what we can do."

Gaston kept his grip on her arm and pressed his face close to hers. "You don't understand. Sean's moving the entire research division to the underwater facility as we speak. It'll be impossible to leave. They have a team going over the security breach right now. When they add all the bits and pieces left from my countermeasures, they'll realize it's me. And by that time, I'll be trapped down there."

Sonya's hair rose on the back of her neck. Was Gaston asking to be pulled out right now? He couldn't be serious! "I can't authorize this," she hissed. "We need to talk to Command. Can you wait until tonight? I can have a team ready by then."

Gaston squeezed her arm harder. "I'm saying it needs to be authorized right now! By you. I need to disappear. If not, I'm a dead man."

Sonya, you are not equipped to extract him. If what he is saying is true, you can be sure the tracers are on. If you pull him out now, you are endangering both of you. You have to get confirmation and back up from Command.

"But what if he's right, Baji? If I don't bring him back, he might not survive long enough for us to ever extract him."

Gaston has been with the Genjix for six years. He should be able to survive three hours. We do not have an extraction team ready, nor do we have the procedures in place to smuggle him out of the country. When the Genjix realize he is gone, you will not be ready to protect or hide him. The odds of the two of you reaching a safe house right now are small; it would be extremely difficult.

Sonya's mind raced as she tried to consider her options. Her instincts told her Gaston should leave with her now, but her experience told her it was a suicidal move. Even if they got to a safe house, the Genjix could just descend on it before they got a jammer. If they could assemble a team in place, there might be a chance.

"Baji, can we get a team to meet us at a safe house?"

Rapid response at best will be ninety minutes.

"Ninety minutes! How can it be this slow?"

We do not have a large presence in the Midwest. The budget does not allow for it. It is not like Western Europe where we can drop an army at a minute's notice.

"That's a long time to hold down the fort on my own."

It is suicide.

"Gaston," Sonya tried to keep her voice level. "It's not a good idea. I don't have the tracer jammer with me. They'll know immediately if we go on the move. I'm unarmed, and frankly, I'm wearing sandals. We're not going to get very far. At the very least, give me three hours. I promise you, I will be back with a team. We can jam the tracer and you can disappear."

Gaston was squeezing her arm so hard it began to hurt. She could see the tightness around his eyes as he weighed his options. "Three hours, no more," he said. "Theater on the Lake." He slowly released his grip.

Sonya gave him a reassuring look and nodded. "Stay low, use protocol three contact handshake." She turned around and walked as fast as she dared out of the tunnel toward the nearest safe house. She was on the phone with the Keeper within seconds of her arrival there. Within an hour, she was armed and ready to go. Within another hour, a squad of four other agents was assembled.

By two and half hours, they were heading to the rendezvous point. The sun was starting to set by the time they reached Theater on the Lake. It was an old building in a forested area just north of the beach. The area was quiet, with only the sound of cars from the highway behind her.

Sonya's squad fanned out to establish a perimeter. She knelt down and made a fist with her hand. The squad settled in and waited. At the three-hour mark, all was still quiet. Sonya motioned for cover and moved up to the front door. It wasn't locked.

She pointed at two of the agents to follow her in and they searched the small theater. Most of the interior was caked with dust, except for a portion near the entranceway; that area was spotless. She motioned to the other agents to search the area. Sonya bent down and sniffed the floor. There was a faint aroma of bleach.

A few minutes later, one of the agents called her into the restroom. He pointed at a soft portion of the concrete wall that was still damp. Sonya drew her knife and cut into the wall. It was patched recently. Embedded into the concrete, she found a bullet.

"Definitely a .45 ACP by the looks of it," Sonya said. "There's been cleaners here." She dug out the bullet and rolled it between her thumb and index finger. Sonya shook her head and buried her face in her hands. If she had only listened to him. At least Gaston might have had a chance then.

You cannot blame yourself for this.

"Of course I can, Baji. I followed orders and protocol when I should have followed my gut. Damn it!"

She checked her watch and looked at the rest of her team. "Wrap it up." There was nothing else they could do here tonight. Hopefully, she was wrong and Gaston could somehow get in touch with them soon, but she feared the Prophus would never hear from him again.

CHAPTER SIXTEEN
TRAINING WHEELS OFF

Zhu Yuanzhang was quick to accept me, believing that the Ho Lung had come to him in his people's time of need. The people of the Han were currently in the oppressive grip of my own creation, as the ruling Yuan Dynasty were the descendants of Genghis Khan. As the leader of the Red Turban sect, Zhu preached a peaceful resolution with the foreign dynasty, balking when all others cried for war. Together, we planned to build a new world through peaceful means. Then one night, I received a visit from the Council.

Roen caught a glint of black hair fifty meters in front of him. It was on the other side of the street approaching the intersection. He kept his face looking forward, only glancing at his mark every few seconds. He nearly tripped on a fire hydrant as he hastened along.

You are too stiff. A good tail is always relaxed and blends in with the environment. Just pretend you are shopping like everyone else down the street. She just turned down Oak. Go!

Roen started sprinting, crossing in the middle of the street, causing a few cars to angrily honk at him.

Stop causing a scene. Blend, I said! That is important even when your mark is out of sight.

"If I don't hurry, I'm going to lose her."

Do not forget to report to your team.

"Oh yeah. Sorry. Sky Eagle, this is Training Wheels. I have eyes on the mark. Mark has just turned down Oak and proceeding... um... east, no, west. Mark is heading west. Did you really have to call me Training Wheels?"

This is Sky Eagle. West on Oak is dark. No agents in vicinity. Reestablish visual. And yes, "Training Wheels" is an apt code name for you.

Roen turned onto Oak and his heart sank. There were a hundred people walking along both sides of the street. His mark was nowhere in sight. He looked around wildly, running around and peering into store windows.

Training Wheels, what is your status?

"Uh... I do not have eyes. Crap, I think I lost... there she is!" Roen slowed down to a trot and closed in on the mark again.

Update the team. Always keep your team in the loop.

"Sorry. Sky Eagle, visual has been reestablished. Mark is continuing west down Oak crossing Rush. Wait, she stopped at the intersection."

Roen immediately stopped walking and pretended to be very busy looking at purses in the corner window. He kept tabs on her as the mark stopped to get a newspaper out of the bin. She then proceeded to head south-east on Rush Street.

Roen crossed the street and kept a safe distance behind her, trying to match her steps. His heart began to beat faster. He looked down at his watch: twenty-two minutes. Things were looking good. Then the mark stopped again, looked up at the street sign, and then looked back – directly at Roen. He stopped again and looked at the window display, this time a shop selling lifelike dolls that could be custom made to look like the little girl who owned it.

No, Roen! What is the second rule of tailing a mark?

"Do not react to your mark's movements."

And what part of not reacting means coming to an abrupt stop every time your mark does?

"What should I have done then?"

You should have kept walking forward as if her stopping meant nothing to you. Pass her if you have to and then backtrack.

It seemed that Tao wasn't the only one who noticed Roen's jerky movements. The mark gave him one suspicious look and then immediately took off, running at full speed across the street and through the park. Roen immediately gave chase. She was fast, weaving through people and trees, turning abruptly several times, trying to throw him off. He kept his head up and tried to keep track of her, running parallel to her when he could, hoping she would get disoriented with his position.

Update your team!

"Sky Eagle, target has taken off on foot, heading south and west through um... trees and grass... some park, just passing Delaware."

Trees and grass? That was useful.

Roen stopped at the intersection and looked around wildly. At this point, he didn't care if people thought he was acting strange. Out of the corner of his eye, he saw a flutter of black hair down a side street and took off after it. He was starting to close in on the mark again, when she made a quick right into the alley. Roen sprinted as hard as he could, his heart pounding out of his chest.

He looked down at his watch: twenty-eight minutes. Almost a new record. Then as he turned the corner into an alley, an arm appeared at his neck level and clotheslined him. He flipped backwards and did a somersault onto his face.

Roen groaned and rolled over as Sonya squatted over him, making a gun shape with her fingers. "Bang, you're dead," she said, and winked. He could only try to blink the stars out of his eyes and clutch at his throat as she helped him sit up.

"What did I tell you about rounding corners blind like that?" she scolded.

"Twenty-eight minutes," he moaned. "I was so close to finishing."

"You know what you did wrong back there, right? The mistake that allowed me to run?"

"Stopping when you did?" he said weakly.

She nodded. "The double-stop. Once is forgivable. Two means you have an amateur tail on you. Stop using bad spy movies as training material, Roen." She helped him to his feet. "Come on, that's enough for today. Let's get some real work in."

That training run was a shining example of how Roen's July went. Having graduated from stalking inanimate objects to live target reconnaissance, he had been struggling to adapt to dealing with so many moving variables. To his surprise, tailing an individual was really hard! He lost three of his first five tails. One called the police on him and he ended up spending a night in jail, and one ended up somehow tailing him. Finally, Tao enlisted Sonya to help out. It took a month of constant practice before he improved to a level that Tao deemed as passable in the fine art of stalking. Still, it was obvious he had a long way to go.

With Lin doing the bulk of the hand-to-hand training, Sonya shifted her focus to firearms. As with hand-to-hand combat, Roen was a less than stellar gunman. When not being followed by Roen, Sonya worked on teaching him how to shoot a gun, starting with firearm safety and maintenance, and eventually moving to proper shooting techniques and squad drills.

She also made him spend hours upon hours repeating the most simplest of tasks: taking the safety off, taking the clip out, putting a new one in. He wasn't sure why he had to keep practicing that over and over again, but Sonya insisted that the repetition was important.

There was no way to say it nicely; Roen was a terrible shot. At first, he tended to miss the target sheet entirely. But he kept at it though, running Sonya's instructions through his head as he emptied clip after clip of ammunition at the little red dot at the center of the target sheet. He began to hate that damn red dot. After nearly three weeks of non-stop target practice, his arms felt like noodles with anchors attached to them. Slowly though, his aim improved and he was starting to hit the red center with regular frequency. By August, he had improved enough that Sonya referred to him as a you-don't-quite-suck-anymore shooter.

"You know you can't use a .22 in a gunfight against Kevlar," she said after he proudly showed her his first perfect round of target shots. "The recoil is small, which helps your accuracy, but it has the stopping power of a BB gun. It won't even slow an armored opponent."

Might as well be firing paintballs.

"Hey, I'm working on it."

Well, we will have to graduate you to a .45 soon. That peashooter will not do.

"It's my first time working with these weapons. You and Tao are both on my case. Man, give me a break," he complained. "What do you use?"

Sonya pulled out one of the guns from the rack. "I'm partial to the MK23 myself." She pulled out her handgun, pointed it at the thirty-meter target, and hit just left of the bullseye by a scant two centimeters.

"Showoff," he grumbled. Roen stared at her much larger pistol and then back at his own small one. It looked like a toy gun by comparison. "I just need some time to get used to it," he grumbled, his face turning red.

"No rush. Baby steps. You're still a man," she said encouragingly. "You'll get there. You just have to remember to keep your hands steady and not squeeze that trigger so hard. Come on, let's move on to rifles."

Thankfully, he was a much better shot with the rifle. A straight week of practicing nearly dislocated his shoulder, but Roen took to it more naturally than the pistol. Along with the rifle shooting, she began to teach him the basics of squad work, including the signals and formations utilized by Prophus teams. This part he actually enjoyed. The two made a small obstacle course where Roen could pretend to break into buildings and clear out rooms. In a way, it was a lot like playing a video game. By the end of the month, after almost fifty hours spent at the range, she had officially declared that he was ready for actual fieldwork. And it wasn't a day too soon.

No sooner had Sonya reported that Roen completed his rifle and squad training, he was called up from the minors and sent on his first team mission. According to Command, his training was complete and he was being moved to active duty.

Sonya and Tao protested his elevation through every channel possible, but on one cloudy August afternoon, just as the hot summer was giving way to cooler winds, Roen found himself driving his Fiat hatchback through fields of dairy cows towards his first real assignment – raiding a Genjix warehouse. He felt a mixture of fear and excitement, but his main concerns were to not die, to make his mentors proud, and to not make a fool of himself, in that order of importance.

He remembered sitting in the safe house, listening as Sonya yelled at whoever was on the other line about not putting him on the assignment, but it was out of her hands. Roen promised himself that all their work would not go to waste. The drive north up into Wisconsin gave him a lot of time to reflect on what lay ahead.

"Do you think the Prophus will reimburse me for gas?"

I am glad you have your head in the game.

"I've been in the car for almost two hours now. There's only so many ways I can imagine getting killed. Now I want to think of happier thoughts."

Like gas reimbursement? May I remind you that we gave you this car?

"May I remind you, sir, that I would still have my old car if those crazy maniacs weren't trying to kill me?"

Touché. Make a right turn here. The base of operations is that farm.

Roen pulled in to what seemed like a deserted farm and parked in the gravel driveway. He got out and looked around. There wasn't a soul in sight. He climbed up the wooden stairs to the main house and knocked on the door. With a shrug, he walked to the end of the porch and looked out at the two silos, the fields of corn, the barn, and the large pole barn at the back.

Out of the corner of his eye, he saw a flash of crimson light and then a small red dot climbed up his shirt. Roen paused, at first wondering where he got the stain from, and tried to brush it off. Then he realized what it was and tensed.

"If you knock loud enough at the gate," a voice said from somewhere inside the house.

"You are sure to wake up somebody," Roen answered.

The red dot disappeared and a man in full riot gear came out, with a rifle swung over his shoulder. "You one of our replacements?" he asked, extending his hand.

Roen shook it and nodded. "Roen Tan."

The agent came to attention and saluted. "Commander Tan, it's a pleasure to meet you. Agent Charles, sir. Please, come in." Taken aback by the sudden display of respect, Roen followed him through the house, out the back door, and toward the warehouse. "I have to tell you, sir," the agent continued. "We didn't expect one of you to be on the ground with us."

Roen could only nod, dumbfounded and unsure how to respond.

"That was unexpected. When did I get promoted?"

All Prophus hosts are raised to commander ranks. It allows our people to assume control of any situation if the need arises.

They walked into the large pole barn which was a hive of

activity. Roen counted roughly twenty agents in full armored gear getting ready for the raid. There were half a dozen large trucks with assorted logos like Mick's Plumbing, Real Haul, and Great Bedding Supplies on the sides. The agent led him to the center of the room where six men were huddling around a table. The agent walked up to an older square-jawed man barking orders to the others and whispered into his ear. The man looked up from the table and came forward, giving Roen a crisp salute.

"Commander Tan, it's a pleasure. Commander Wuehler." Roen shook his hand. "Thank you, sir, for helping us out on such short notice. Half our team seemed to have contracted food poisoning over the last few days and we're a bit short-handed. The men were pretty excited about your arrival when they heard a host was going to be running this shindig with us."

"I'll help however I can," Roen said gruffly.

"I assume you want your own squad?"

Trying his best to hide his uneasiness, Roen shook his head. "No, no, that will be quite all right. I'll attach to one."

Wuehler stopped, looking perplexed. "I read through your file, sir," he said, "and to be honest, there wasn't much in it. I'm assuming black ops then? CIA? NSA? Not MI6 with that accent."

Roen's face turned a slight shade of red. "Um... well, Commander Wuehler," he stammered. "Not exactly. I don't have a military background. I kind of fell into being a host by mistake. I actually just finished my training," he finished lamely. "This is my first combat mission."

No need to be ashamed. You did not have to volunteer so much information, though.

The disappointment in Wuehler's face couldn't be more obvious. "I see. Well, that explains why on the notation, I was instructed under no circumstances to allocate grenades to you."

"I just learned how to shoot a gun this month," Roen mumbled.

Again, that complete and total honesty. Really unnecessary.

Wuehler shook his head. "An accidental transition. I understand." He turned to one of the squads in the back. "Faust, come here!"

A gruff Middle-Eastern agent – with a goatee Roen would kill for – walked up and saluted. "Sir?"

Wuehler gestured at Roen. "This is Commander Tan, Prophus host. He's joining your team, taking the rear observer position. Get him up to speed on your squad's objectives, and above all, keep him safe."

"Yes, sir!" Faust saluted Roen and led him toward the squad he was attaching to. "So you're not here to evaluate a potential host from the team?" Faust asked.

Roen shook his head. "I'm just a rookie learning the ropes."

The look of disappointment on Faust's face was no less soul-crushing than the one on Wuehler's. "You're a lucky man, Commander. Some of the guys have been waiting ten years to become a host. They thought with you coming, maybe Wuehler or one of them was finally getting his just due and being evaluated for a Quasing."

Roen wanted to go hide in a corner somewhere. After quick introductions to the team, Faust ran him through the squad's objectives for the mission and before he knew it, they were all loaded into their separate trucks, speeding down the highway toward the Genjix warehouse. Roen's squad of four was tucked in a hidden compartment in one of the trucks marked as a laundry delivery service. His squad's objective was to clear the eastern section of the warehouse through the loading dock.

It was an hour-long drive to the warehouse, disguised as an automotive repair depot somewhere in the outskirts of Madison, Wisconsin. Roen tried to relax as the truck jostled them around in its bed. Faust was going over the blueprints while two of the other agents were exchanging words, occasionally looking his way. The last agent, an older looking man, was taking a nap.

Roen tried to get some sleep as well, but every little bump on the road startled him. Finally, he gave up and began to recite all the squad signals in his head. At best, if he messed them up, it'd be embarrassing. At worst, someone could die.

The truck rumbled to a stop and Roen could hear voices outside as the driver spoke with someone. Then he heard a gate grind open. The truck continued on for a few more minutes before stopping again. Then the engine turned off.

Roen heard several footsteps near the rear of the truck and the back door opening with a loud clang. The team froze and waited. Roen held his breath and closed his eyes, trying his best to stay still. They were well hidden in the secret compartment, under stacks of folded sheets, and would only be discovered if someone removed several of the bins.

An eternity later, the voices trailed off and then they heard the signal. The driver banged on the side of the van twice, paused, and then three times more. Then it was several minutes of silence. Faust shook the sleeping agent and the older man woke suddenly alert and ready.

That is something we have to work on. Waking you up is like trying to wake a hibernating bear.

"What can I say? I need my beauty rest."

You must be not getting enough sleep then.

"Touché."

Faust made a circular motion with his hand and the team leaped into action. Faust turned a latch on the floor and pushed down. The bottom swung outward. Dipping down head first, he scanned the area before dropping to the floor. He signaled for the others to follow, and one by one, they lowered themselves under the truck.

The cool air felt good after hiding in the stuffy truck. Roen took a deep breath and moved near one of the rear tires. The agent to climb out last pushed a small button and retracted the secret door.

When the coast was clear, they scrambled from cover and assembled in the shadow of the truck. They were in a large garage with an elevated platform on one end and large gray gates on the other. Faust motioned to one of the agents and pointed at the far corner of the ceiling. That agent took one glance at the small camera rotating back and forth and then scrambled behind a large crate. He pulled out a pistol with a silencer, took quick aim, and destroyed it with one shot.

"Won't they notice the broken feed?" Roen asked.

Faust nodded. "Intel indicated a rotating feed on only two monitors. They'll notice it, but it'll take them a while to figure out which camera the white noise is coming from." He signaled to another agent, who started working on the keypad. The team held their position and waited.

Then the agent working on the keypad raised a fist in the air. Roen heard footsteps approaching the door from the other side. Faust made a quick motion with his hand and the team melted into the background, hiding behind whatever cover they could find. Moments later, two custodians in white walked out through the double doors, chatting while pushing a cart. Roen watched them from behind several metal drums, training his sights on them as they loaded supplies onto a second cart. He was sure everyone else on the team had their guns trained on these poor unsuspecting souls as well.

Easy there. Do not get trigger-happy.

"That's one thing you don't have to worry about."

Several minutes passed by as the two men continued loading their supplies. When finished, they went back to the door and one of them punched in the code on the keypad. The doors unlocked and they passed through. Faust signaled furiously at the closing doors. The nearest agent leaped out of his hiding place and dove forward, managing to stick his hand in just before it closed. Roen helped him up and the rest of the squad filed through.

The warehouse was a large cavernous room with crates stacked on top of each other. Roen could hear talking somewhere north of their position. Faust was whispering into his communicator and signaled for the team to hold their position. Several more minutes passed. Roen's heart was hammering in his chest and sweat poured down his face. He began to breathe in short gasps. This was the real thing! Then Faust signaled to the team and counted down from five.

On the north end of the warehouse, someone screamed. Then there were several loud bangs as a cloud of smoke filled the room. Roen's squad split into pairs and proceeded to move forward. Roen was assigned to Faust and watched as he began to move forward. His brain told him to stay close behind Faust, but his legs wouldn't move.

Roen, move. You have to back him up.

Faust turned and looked back, gesturing for him to follow. Roen wanted nothing more than to run back through the door, back to the loading dock. But then he thought about leaving Faust by himself. He couldn't abandon his squad-mate like that. Roen willed himself to put one foot in front of the other. Each step was excruciating, but he kept going. When he reached Faust, the man put a hand on his shoulder and whispered. "Stay close, sir. I got your back."

Listen carefully to my voice. I will guide you. Step, step, step. Stay lower.

Roen nodded and followed Faust, staying a few meters behind him, with Tao literally directing his steps. Between Sonya's training and Tao's constant instructions, he managed to continue moving forward as they cleared through the maze of crates. This was like a video game, he reminded himself. I'm just playing a game.

They made a few turns as his squad began to close in from the east side of the docks. Every time they reached an intersection, his heart beat even harder. Was the enemy on the other side? His hands were shaking so badly he almost dropped the rifle. Faust gave him a worried look.

"Do you need to head back to the dock?" he leaned over and asked.

It took Roen a lot of effort to shake his head. Of course he wanted to, but the shame of doing so was even greater than his fear of the Genjix. Faust looked him over once more before nodding. He looked around the corner and then gestured for Roen to follow.

Control your breathing. Deep breaths. You can do this!

There was an intense firefight going on at the north end. Roen's natural urge was to run away, but he gritted his teeth and kept moving closer to the battle. He just about reached the center of the warehouse when Faust stood up, using a crate for cover, and opened fire. Roen slid in next to him and peeked over the top. In the haze, he could see flashes from the muzzles of the rifles, and shadows of figures running back and forth. He couldn't tell who was friendly and who was the enemy! He just stood there, moving his gun back and forth, unable to pull the trigger.

"This is nothing like a video game! Tao, what do I do?"

Exactly what you are doing now. Only pull the trigger when you are sure of your target.

Faust ducked back behind the crate and pulled Roen with him. "I'm going to move to a forward position. Cover me."

"Should I follow?" Roen asked.

Faust shook his head. "Just give me suppression fire." Then he ducked and slipped around the crate.

Roen had the urge to disobey orders and follow. Part of it was because he didn't want to seem like a coward staying back, but mostly because he didn't want to be left alone. It took him a few seconds to calm his nerves as he aimed his rifle up at an angle toward the ceiling to make sure no one would get hit, and then he emptied his clip, waving his gun back and forth. When he had emptied his rounds, Roen reached into his belt for another clip. He was shaking so badly though that he fumbled and dropped it.

Now he understood why Sonya drilled him again and again in reloading clips. In a live situation, his hands seemed completely paralyzed and disconnected from his brain. As he bent down to pick it up, he saw a dark figure sneaking up behind Faust. There was no time to warn him. Roen swung his rifle up and fired. Unfortunately, he never got the gun clip in. He heard the empty click-click as he pulled the trigger and realized his mistake. He had to do something! In desperation, Roen hurled his rifle at the Genjix agent. It bounced off his arm harmlessly and fell to the floor. The Genjix agent turned his rifle toward Roen instead. Now unarmed, Roen panicked.

Duck! An image of a soldier diving into a trench just as a grenade exploded flashed into his head.

Roen screamed and dove to the side, right as a spray of bullets punctured the crate he was leaning on moments before. He slid onto the floor and twisted onto his back, trying in vain to pull out his pistol. He saw the Genjix agent adjust his aim and knew he'd be too late. Then the Genjix agent went limp and fell to the floor.

Faust appeared a second later and checked the body. He picked up Roen's rifle, helped him up, and handed it back to him. "I owe you one, sir," Faust said, and grinned.

He gestured for Roen to follow and they continued inching closer toward the main fight. Two other Genjix agents appeared along the way, and both times, Faust took them out before Roen could even aim his rifle. Roen realized that without Faust, he'd be a dead man by now many times over, though technically, it'd be true the other way around as well. He gritted his teeth and stayed close.

They engaged two other small groups and pinned down a third before backup flanked them. In every exchange, Roen was fairly confident he didn't hit a soul. By the time they reached the north end of the warehouse, the sounds of the battle were dying. The other Prophus agents were already securing the rest of the warehouse when they joined the main group.

Wuehler appeared through the haze and walked up to Faust, asking for a status. The mission had gone off without a hitch. There were three casualties on the Prophus side and fifteen on the Genjix side.

"Well done, team," Wuehler said. "Get the trucks back here and start loading."

"I didn't do anything," Roen muttered. "I just laid suppression fire and shot at the ceiling."

"Nonsense," said Faust. "You saved my life back there. You followed orders; you didn't run away; and you lived. That's all anyone can ask of a squad-mate." Faust stuck out his hand.

He is right. You did well.

Roen shook his hand, feeling anything but brave. He stood next to Faust and Wuehler as they directed the rest of the team to load the crates onto the trucks. "What are we after anyway?" he asked Wuehler.

"Not for me to ask, I just follow orders," he replied. "These all seem like advanced electronic parts. Seems the Genjix are building something new. There's a refrigeration unit with several drums of chemicals, some of them toxic by the skull and crossbones. My boys aren't equipped to touch the stuff. We're calling in specialists now. Whatever these Genjix are building, our job is to make sure they don't finish it."

Roen nodded and looked around. "What about this mess? How do we hide what just happened?"

"Our cleaners are good." Faust grinned. "We've gotten pretty good at keeping a low profile." He paused. "You really are new at this, aren't you?"

Roen nodded.

Faust put one hand on his shoulder. "You did a good job, sir. Whoever trained you would be proud."

I know I am.

And for some reason, that meant more to Roen than anything else in the world.

CHAPTER SEVENTEEN
FREEDOM

The visit from the Council came from Zoras in the guise of a Westerner. I was being commended for my work with the Mongols, he said. The conflict created by Genghis's war engine was more than they could have hoped for, he said. It was a stab in the heart to hear those words. Then he gave me even worse news. The Council had ordered me to replicate my achievements with these people as I did with the Mongols. Here was the second time I faltered. I did not say no. Back then, a Quasing did not say no to the Council.

Roen barely had time to get back to Chicago and shower before going into work late. He strolled into the office just after 10am, aware but apathetic to the raised eyebrows that followed him to his desk. Thanks to Tao, work was now a breeze, and as long as he finished his projects, why should anyone care when he came in? Besides, he'd just returned from a firefight. After that, being a little late hardly seemed a big deal. What could possibly faze him here?

There was a Post-it note on his monitor: See me at once! Mr Musday.

What kind of person signs his signature with Mister? Roen crumpled the Post-it note and tossed it into the garbage. He took an apple out of his bag and cut it in half, taking a bite as he opened his email and checked his messages.

Peter looked over. "Where were you this morning? Musday's looking for you. He wasn't happy you weren't in yet."

"I had a very long night." Roen shrugged. In the past, a summons from Musday would leave him full of anxiety. Now, he just let work roll off his shoulder. When thrust into a five-hundred-year war with the fate of humanity on the line, pleasing the boss at work no longer seemed like a big deal anymore.

"Well, you should go see him soon," Peter said.

"I will, after I finish my apple." Roen took another satisfying bite.

Ten minutes later, he stood outside Musday's door and tried to whistle Adagio in G Minor while the man pompously checked his email and pretended to be too busy to notice him. He surprisingly didn't feel the same apprehension he usually felt standing outside his manager's door.

Listen, Roen, whatever you choose to say, just do not forget about you.

"What does that mean?"

It means whatever you think it means. Just remember who you are and have confidence in yourself.

Roen spent the next few minutes contemplating those words until Musday finally beckoned him in. "Sorry to make you wait. Have a seat."

Roen sat down and leaned back. "You wanted to see me, Tom?"

Musday shot him a grim look and pointed at the clock. "I need you to be on time. You're part of the team, and we need to be able to depend on you."

Roen tried his best to respond in a calm voice. "I don't see a problem. I had something important come up last night, and I did work late the previous night, not to mention I stayed over on Sunday to help Peter with the Kol project. Also, I delivered all the Claims projects a month early. Everything else on my plate is on time and my development teams love me." In the past, being defensive was his first response to any form of criticism. Now, he just wanted to get his point across.

Roen, whatever you are getting at here...

Musday's voice rose. "You came in late. What if we needed you? We have strict rules about our hours. If everyone ignored them, our team couldn't function properly. It's like stealing from the company."

"I'm working overtime with no extra pay," Roen countered. "You could argue that the company is stealing from me."

...keep it up.

"The overtime is built into your salary." Musday tapped his finger on the table for emphasis.

"Where does it say that in my contract?" Roen reminded himself to stay in control. He wasn't here to pick a fight.

"Look, Roen." Musday leaned forward as if divulging a secret. "We're a team, and we have to function as one. I'm telling you what is best for your career. This is a warning."

"For what? Talk to me if my projects are running behind; talk to me if I'm not getting the job done; otherwise, I believe I can manage my own time." Roen was surprised at how composed he was.

Musday became angry. "Fine, you're not doing your job."

"Then fire me." Roen stood up and turned to leave.

Musday scowled as if he had something to say and then stopped. Finally, he spoke in a measured tone. "Just make sure your projects don't fall behind."

Roen smiled and nodded. "Of course, Tom."

When he left Musday's office, he threw his hands up in elation.

That was good.

"That felt liberating."

Do you know why?

"Because he's been a total ass and had it coming to him?"

Possibly, but the real reason is because you are not afraid of your job anymore. You have more confidence now. You believe in yourself more.

Roen stopped walking and looked out the window. It had rained the past few days, but the sun was out now, a beautiful yellow ball of warmth shining in the sky. From his building, he could see Lake Michigan stretch out for several miles. He remembered to convert that to kilometers. Roen was starting to think in metric, but sometimes he slipped and reverted back to his old habits. Tao still continued to badger him about that.

Across the street were Buckingham Fountain and Millennium Park. He remembered all the days he wistfully thought about going for a walk while still stuck in this prison. Then Roen realized that Tao was right. He spent all those years living to work and not working to live, always afraid of losing a job he hated; therefore, he accepted anything they asked of him. He had become so used to this monotonous life that maintaining the status quo became more important than his own happiness. Standing up to Musday was the first step to reestablishing his freedom. Smiling, he decided to take the scenic route back to his cubicle.

When he sat down, he received another pleasant surprise. An appointment he had made quite some time ago appeared on his schedule. Jill was flying in today.

Roen's stomach was in twisted knots when he pulled into the driveway of her high-rise. He stopped at her front door and waited, fingers tapping the steering wheel as he tried to calm his jitters.

If you keep this up, you are going to start sweating. And really, it will go downhill from there.

"I feel like throwing up." His nervousness increased when a few minutes later, Jill came out of the building and waved. He got out of the car and opened the door for her. She gave him a hug and got in.

"I'm so glad we're going out tonight." She smiled as they pulled out of the driveway. Roen beamed. She looked great, exactly as he remembered. Her hair was trimmed a little shorter than the last time he saw her, and she seemed to have lost a little weight.

"Did you lose weight?" he blurted out, instantly regretting his words.

Idiot!

"What's that supposed to mean?" Jill asked, giving him an inquisitive look.

"Um... Uh... I didn't... I mean..." he stuttered. Thirty seconds in and he already had a misstep.

"Hah, I'm just kidding. I did lose a few pounds overseas. German food is so heavy it's hard to stomach sometimes. I also got my butt off the couch and started training for that race I signed up for."

At least think before you speak. Better yet, do not say anything else without my express approval if you want to get anywhere.

"Yeah, too much sauerkraut... ha, ha..." Roen struggled mightily for a witty response. Upon failing to think of one, he settled for, "So, how's the weather? There, I mean, in Frankfurt. Not here. Obviously we know how the weather is here." He gave a nervous chuckle.

Stop talking. I am serious.

Jill took it all in her stride. "It's a fun city, and the culture there is fabulous. It's such an old place with so much history, I spent days just walking around being the silly tourist. I did miss home though. How are things here?"

"Much better now that you're back," he blurted out.

There was a moment of silence.

You did not just say that.

Finally, she smiled. "Aw, that's sweet, Roen. I'm happy to be back."

Listen; let me drive from this point on.

"Um... yes please help, Tao!"

This is what you are going to say.

"So what's the big surprise tonight?" she said. "Why were you so mysterious about it?"

"I wanted to take you to someplace different instead of a dinner and a movie," Roen repeated Tao's words verbatim. He headed north along Lakeshore Drive and exited the highway onto Addison Street and headed toward the large ballpark. "So, we're going to a Cubs game!"

Jill gasped, "Really? That sounds great! I'm not really a sports fan, and I know nothing about baseball, but I always wanted to check it out."

Roen shrugged and tried to appear cool. "I figured it'd be something new and I wanted our first date to be memorable. Besides, you can't live in Chicago and never go to a Cubs game!"

They parked in one of the side lots and followed the throng of people moving toward Wrigley Field. The air was electric as they joined in the festive atmosphere. He handed the attendant their tickets, and they strolled into the complex and into the hallways decorated with rich baseball history. Roen pointed out the different portraits of players that lined the walls, as they stopped by one of the booths to buy hot dogs and beer, before making their way to the bleachers to find their seats.

"You know a lot about baseball," she marveled as they sat down. "I never had you pegged as a sports buff."

"I'm not," he admitted, "just something I've gotten into lately."

In reality, he knew nothing about the game except for the lines Tao fed him. Roen had to admit that Tao was one smooth cat. He had a knack of saying the right charming lines. During the course of the game, they had a good time as the Cubs played the Mets in an exciting game. Roen made sure to keep the beers and food coming, joking that she'd always remember their first meal together as beers in plastic cups and pretzels.

Jill laughed, exclaiming that dressing up for sushi and a silly movie easily took a back seat to a lively game. By the seventh inning stretch, the two were feeling pretty good as they cheered and booed each spectacular hit and botched catch. The atmosphere inside Wrigley Field was vibrant, and the two rode the euphoric mood alongside those around them. By the time the game ended, neither was paying much attention to the score. It didn't matter that the Cubs were crushed in the game, just that they had a good time.

"I have to say, you're not a boring date." Jill chuckled, wrapping an arm around his as they joined the crowd streaming out of the ballpark.

"I aim to please," Roen said, and grinned. "I'm glad you're having a good time."

He caught himself with his improvising. "Oops, sorry, Tao. I forgot about listening to your lines."

Actually, Roen, I have not given you one for the past hour. It has all been you.

Roen suddenly felt something catch in his throat and a wave of emotion washed over him. He thought about the many hours that Tao, Sonya, and now Lin were putting into him and how grateful he was to all of them. There was no way he could have done any of this without their continuous support.

"Hey Tao, thanks."

For the perfect date? I like her. She seems like a keeper. I do not think auburn is her natural hair color, but hey, no one is perfect.

"No, I mean thanks for everything. Before I met you, I was an out-of-shape fat slob who hated my life. Now, I feel like I'm finally going somewhere with my life."

What is good for the goose is good for the gander. We are in this together. Remember, what is the capital of old Assyria?

Roen chuckled.

"What's so funny, Roen?" Jill said, touching him on the shoulder.

"Nothing," he replied. "Just thinking about how fortunate I am."

"That's sweet." She melted a little, leaning on him, and holding his hand.

Roen opened the door for her and she got into the car. The next stop he planned was a quaint little wine bar in the Bucktown neighborhood. They spent the rest of the night in a dark romantic booth, sharing a bottle of red wine. While the ballgame was a nice event to break the ice, the intimate atmosphere of the booth was the perfect opportunity for Roen to confirm a second date. The end of the night finished with a small kiss on the cheek.

Watching in admiration as she walked into her high-rise, he grinned from ear to ear as he pulled out of her driveway onto the street. His cell phone rang as he sped onto the highway. Roen pulled it out of his pocket and held it to his ear.

"Yeeelllo?" he chimed.

"You sound chipper," Antonio said on the line. "I guess the date went well."

"Yes sir, yes sir," Roen said, still grinning. "It was good times. We have a second date already planned for next week."

"That's awesome, buddy. Glad to know you closed the deal. So that means you'll come out? I know clubbing was contingent on a good date. Now that you've had a good time, it's time to celebrate! Besides, I need a wingman when I talk to the ladies."

Roen knew from past experience that clubbing rarely ended well. But he had promised Antonio he would go if things went well, and a promise was a promise. "All right, I'm in," he answered. Roen turned his car around and sped off back toward the city.

CHAPTER EIGHTEEN

DISCOVERY

Through Zhu, I followed my orders better than any on the Council could hope for. They called me the Empire Builder. Under my direction, Zhu led a rebellion against the Yuan and pushed them back north to the steppes. It was to my shame that I turned Zhu from a peaceful man to one who would claim the Mandate of Heaven, and who became the dictatorial Hongwu, Emperor of the Ming Dynasty.

I had sold him the dream that with this power, we could peacefully enforce the enlightenment we had always dreamed about. And there, I repeated the same mistake I made a century earlier. Enlightenment and peace can never be achieved by force.

Sean tapped his temple with his fingers, his eyes moving between the assorted pieces laid out before him. He glanced up at his opponent and then at the clock. Four minutes on his side, six on the other; plenty of time. Then his frown broke into a sly grin as he moved one of the pieces and tapped the chess clock. It would be checkmate in six. Sean studied his grandson's face, which fell into a grimace as Jacob realized that the trap he had so painstakingly set up had just been broken.

Still, Sean's chest swelled with pride at the cleverness of young Jacob's strategy. It was elegant and subtle and would have perhaps worked on a lesser opponent, but not someone who had played the game since he was the Shah of Persia two thousand years ago. Still, he had great hopes for the boy. Jacob would make a fine vessel one day.

"You overextended your bishop," was all Sean said, as he leaned back to take a sip of his tea. He waited in anticipation for Jacob to make the only logical move, if he was clever enough to see it. Sean was disappointed when the boy moved another piece, trying to salvage the game. If he had the foresight, he would have conceded on the spot. Instead, he would waste time fighting a lost cause. Still, Sean resisted the temptation to correct Jacob's mistake. Let him learn.

Suddenly, his cell phone vibrated toward the edge of the table. Sean's eyes flashed in anger. Meredith knew better than to bother him at this time of the day. Even those on the Council would be put on hold until his time with Jacob was done. He considered not picking it up and letting the fool thing fall off the table. However, with each successive buzz, his eyes wandered more and more to the errant phone. What if it was important? Obviously it must be if Meredith allowed it through. Well, curiosity killed the cat and Stonewall Jackson, and it was killing Sean right now. With a harrumph of resignation, he moved another piece, hit the chess clock again, and picked up the phone.

He said, "This had better be good."

Meredith's words came tumbling out as she apologized. "I'm sorry, Sean. I know this time is off limits, but Mr Kenton was very insistent and said it was absolutely critical that he get a hold of you no matter what and..."

Sean bristled, but kept his voice deadpan. Meredith's stark terror was punishment enough. "Patch him through," he said.

"Right away."

There was a click as Marc's voice, oblivious to the pain he just put Meredith through, came on. "We got a hit, Father."

Sean perked up and leaned forward. "Where?"

"We received a hit last night from a speeding ticket on a brown Fiat. The image was a close enough match to our target to trigger an alert on one Hamilton Lee. Lee's information was a dead end, obviously washed. Tonight, that same Fiat was spotted by a camera at an intersection pulling into a parking lot of a local nightclub. We believe he might be there."

A nightclub? Limited exits. Multiple civilians. It violated the agreement they had with the Prophus, but Sean never put much stock in collateral damage anyway. If a public relations nightmare ensued, that was what the mayor was for. "When can you get your team there?" Sean asked.

"A team of ten has been assembled, Father. Waiting for your go-ahead."

Sean's mind raced as he formulated a plan. After a couple of deaths on the team, this was their first lead in months. The bills from Homeland were astronomical. They might not get a better chance. "Capture Tao alive."

"As you wish, Father."

Sean put down the phone and studied the board again. Strange, the boy only moved a pawn forward, an unexpected and useless move. Why had Jacob done that? The boy smirked as he leaned back, looking as if he just made a masterful play. Sean looked at the chess clock and realized he just ran out of time. The boy had made the move with the sole purpose of burning out Sean's time. Conniving. Manipulative. Brilliant. "The day is yours," said Sean beaming, and standing to shake Jacob's hand.

Jacob blushed, the faint words of praise a rarity from his grandfather's lips. "Was that Genjix business, Grandfather?" he asked.

Sean nodded. "We have a Prophus quarry that we've been tracking for quite some time now. We have a strong lead."

"Really? Was he anyone famous?"

Sean shrugged. "Genghis and some Chinese emperor were

his crowning achievement. Other than that, a string of incon-sequentials and several mishaps. I believe he shot President McKinley. Otherwise, a minor player, but one I would love to talk to in person."

Jacob shook his head. "Those Prophus are such bad people. I can't wait until I can help you root them out. Dad says they're all made up and that you're just a crazy old man."

Sean smiled. "Did he now? Remember, Jacob, your father is a fool, but even fools can be dangerous. Your mother is the one you should be listening to. Our blood runs deep with the Holy Ones. One day, you'll have one of your own; perhaps even Chiyva if you're so blessed."

The boy looked at Sean with adoring eyes. Chiyva often said that the boy reminded him of Francisco Cisneros's protégé. Young Paneese died far too soon.

Between Sean's rapid rise and Jacob's potential as a vessel, Chiyva had a real chance to reclaim his rightful spot back on the Council. But for now, the boy needed training. The Adonis program did not usually accept twelve year-olds, but older youths had been sent to the Hatchery before. Chiyva had enough authority to make it so if he chose the boy to be his. The boy's parents would object sending the boy away, the weak father most of all; but it wouldn't be their choice if Sean and Jacob wished it to happen. His mother would grieve, but she would understand the great opportunity presented her son.

"Tell me a story about Chiyva, Grandfather, please?" Jacob pressed.

"Why don't we play another game, Jacob?" Sean patted his grandson's hair. "And I'll tell you a story from a long time ago, about the evils of those Prophus..."

CHAPTER NINETEEN
ENCOUNTER

For the first few years, the Ming Dynasty was prosperous. Zhu was a strict but fair emperor. He codified the Da Ming lu, the Code of the Great Ming, to establish equal rights among the masses, something which humanity had never seen before. He fostered an agrarian society and suppressed violence. And even though he was a tyrant, he was beloved by his people. I saw the advantages of what Zhu's absolute power could do. We could finally implement our enlightened theories. But once again, the Council had other plans. Zoras appeared to give me new orders.

The bouncer gave Roen a dismissive look. "Thirty bucks."

Roen took his ID back, pulled out his wallet, and peeled off two bills.

Did he just say thirty dollars? To get into the club?

"Yep."

That is outrageous!

"You're telling me. And I used to go out three times a week every week for three years."

No wonder you still rent.

The noise level at the club was ear-shattering as he walked into a packed room with a ceiling that rose three stories above

182

him. The sound of a booming deep bass shook the walls in a repetitive rhythm that Roen could feel in the pit of his stomach. A dizzying array of bright, colorful lights sprayed the room, overwhelming the eyes.

It is loud in here.

"That's one way to put it. Try actually talking to someone in one of these places."

Roen left the main dance floor and went down a spiral staircase to the basement, where there was another dance floor. The atmosphere of the room was less spastic, with slower music. It was also better lit and without annoying pulsating lights. There, he found Antonio and some friends sitting in a booth against the wall.

After initial greetings were exchanged, Roen turned his attention to getting a drink. Buying drinks from the bar was like playing roulette; sometimes you got lucky, sometimes you didn't. Patrons leaned against the bar, waving their money and hoping the bartender acknowledged their existence. Only at these places would the words "I know the bartender" have any pull. It took Roen fifteen minutes to get a beer.

Explain to me how this is fun: thirty minutes in line, thirty dollars to get in, ten minutes to work your way down here, ten more saying hi to people I can tell you barely know, and now fifteen minutes ordering a beer that costs twice what it should. You just lost an hour of your life.

"Why do you think I always swear to never come back?"

And yet you still do like an addict.

"More like a lemming."

That works too.

Antonio walked to Roen and put his arm around him. "So your date went well?"

Roen nodded.

"Well, that's a reason to celebrate. Cheers." The two clinked their bottles together. "And you're going to see her again?"

Roen nodded again.

"Another reason to celebrate." The bottles clinked again. Antonio was hammered; his voice slurred and he leaned on Roen more for support than friendship.

"So, get this," Antonio continued. "While you were pulling one of your disappearing acts the past few days, Sonya stopped by to drop off some books she wanted you to read. I made my move and asked her out, and guess what? She said I was sweet and she liked being friends, but she likes you! You! Over me! Actually, she didn't say she liked you, she said she was, and I'll quote, 'totally in love with you.' Imagine that! My boy here doesn't get a date for like ten years and now, not one, but two hot chicks are madly in love with you. I have no idea what self-help book she's having you read, but I want it."

Roen was speechless. "Wait, what?!" The words came tumbling out of his mouth as he stood there in shock. "Sonya's in love with me? Are you kidding?" Suddenly, he felt conflicted. She liked him? A flood of questions poured through his mind as he struggled with this new dilemma. Who was the better match for him? Who had the better personality? Who had a better figure? Who would his parents like more?

Do not get ahead of yourself.

Antonio laughed at the expression on his face. "You mean you didn't know? The way she gushed about you, I thought your morning workout sessions were more like make-out sessions. Oh, here's your money for the bet. You deserve it." Antonio handed him a wad of cash. "You better be buying the drinks tonight, you sly dog."

Roen held the wad in his hands and stared at it. "Wait, what bet? What is this money for?"

Put the money away and nod. Trust me on this one.

"Don't rub it in, man," Antonio grinned. "But seriously, what's your secret?"

"Um... it's my personal alien I was telling you about. He's been giving me dating tips." Roen smiled weakly.

I pat myself on my metaphorical back.

Before Roen could say another word, Antonio was off again, mingling with the crowd. Roen just watched as his roommate glided from group to group, talking to friends and strangers alike. He always admired how easily Antonio got along with just about everyone. Even strangers treated him like they were best friends after only a few minutes.

"So what's this money for? What bet is he talking about?"

You do not remember that bet you two made?

"No, what bet?"

You have a rotten memory.

"I'd remember if I made a hundred-dollar bet. Heck, I get nervous making twenty-dollar bets."

Well, stop thinking about it and use your newfound earnings to buy another drink.

Having finished his beer, Roen braved the packed crowd on the dance floor and worked his way back toward the bar. He waited another twenty minutes before the bartender noticed him. Not wanting to make the journey again, he ordered two scotches and double-fisted them back to the booth. There, he spent the rest of the evening drinking alone and watching the crowd.

Like ants over cake at a picnic.

"And you want to use us to take the Quasing home? Good luck."

It was either you or the Neanderthals. There is still debate whether or not we made the right choice. Good thing dolphins do not have hands or you would all be extinct by now.

Roen raised his cup in the air to no one in particular. "Here's to dolphins and their flippers."

Indeed.

"I always heard dolphins were smart."

They make humans look like chimps in any pattern recognition test.

"Pattern recognition test?"

Fundamentals of logical deduction, my friend.

"Good thing we have thumbs to offset our lack of intellect." He raised the cup again. "Here's to thumbs."

The party was still in full swing when Antonio staggered back to the booth a while later. Under each arm was an attractive girl. "Ladies," he said with a thick slur, "this is my buddy. Say hi." The two smiled and waved. Antonio moved his arms away from their waists and patted Roen on the back. "This over here," he gestured to his right, "is Laura. And this," he gestured to his left, "is... what's your name again?"

The pretty blond frowned and slapped Antonio on the chest. "Jerk," she berated him playfully. The blond leaned forward and stuck her hand out, and said, "Hi, I'm Amber, you must be Roen." Roen leaned forward and shook her hand.

"Tao," she hissed.

Roen! Genjix!

Suddenly, Amber leaned forward and punched him in the face. Roen's head snapped back and he fell back into the booth. Antonio looked bewildered. Before Antonio could say another word, Laura chopped him at the base of his neck and he fell forward.

Roen was used to being beaten in the face and quickly recovered from the blow. He focused on Laura while she was busy with Antonio. Still lying on his back, Roen kicked out and caught her on the side, sending her tumbling into the crowd.

Immediately, Amber lifted her leg and hammered it down on his stomach. Her stiletto heel dug into his midsection. He howled in pain and sat up. Grabbing her ankle, Roen pulled her leg and swung a hard right hook that caught her squarely in the face, knocking Amber over to the adjacent booth.

Get out of here. There might be more.

Roen climbed out of the booth, clutching his stomach. He turned toward the stairs just as Laura crashed into his back, slamming him against the wall. Roen fell forward, cutting his face on the hard brick surface. His arm banged against a large hanging mirror, causing it to crash to the floor. Glass shattered and spilled across the floor.

The crowd around them stopped dancing and stared at the chaos unfolding. Roen turned around just in time to catch another blow to the face. He reeled backward and hit his head on the wall again. Stunned, Roen fell to one knee as a rain of punches and kicks landed on him. While none of the strikes were particularly hard, the sheer intensity of the attack was overwhelming.

Roen, they are going to kill you. Laura is close by; stop covering up and take her out!

Peering through his spread fingers, he saw that Laura was standing just a foot away, launching kick after kick at his head. Ignoring the blows, he wrapped his arms around both her knees and squeezed. She gawked in surprise as he lifted her up and slammed her to the floor. The crowd collectively gasped until Amber jumped over the booth and elbowed him in the side of the head. A burly older man joined in the melee. Roen blocked a punch and ducked another – before a hard kick to the chest sent him stumbling back.

They are closing off your escape. Get upstairs!

Roen glanced at the stairs and took off. His chest burned and he had trouble catching his breath; that last blow had knocked the wind out of him. The burly man moved to intercept him but was a second too late as Roen reached the stairs first.

By this time, the music had stopped and the bouncers were converging on the fight. One bouncer grabbed one of the girls by the waist and tried to restrain her until she kicked his shins and elbowed him in the face. Another bouncer suddenly collapsed face first, dropped by an unknown attacker. Several others were barreling through the crowds, knocking people over as they tried to reach Roen.

There must be at least a dozen of them.

Roen continued climbing up the stairs. When he reached the top, he bumped into the chest of a large man blocking his path. The man was bald and very muscular – and he had several scars on his face. He gripped his massive hand around Roen's throat and pinned him against the railing.

Marc! Be wary of him. Watch out for his elbow strikes. He is also very strong.

"My God! His grip... is like steel. He's... choking me."

"Hello, Tao," Marc growled. "Where do you think you're going?" He pulled a fist back, ready to pummel Roen. Suddenly two bouncers from the club jumped on top of Marc, trying to wrestle him down. With a snarl, Marc grabbed one bouncer with his free hand and threw him over the railing. The man screamed as he flipped over to the floor below. Marc turned his attention to the other bouncer and head-butted him. The bouncer staggered backward, and Marc finished him off with a kick that sent the bouncer tumbling down the stairs.

Roen took advantage of the distraction, slipped out of Marc's grip, and threw several punch combinations. It felt like striking thick slabs of meat. Roen retreated, holding his wrist.

"Ow, my hand! What is this guy made of?"

Tougher stuff than you. Feint high, strike low. An image of Sonya performing one of her attacks popped into his mind.

Marc turned to him and snarled. Roen threw a left jab and a right hook, followed by a low kick, hoping to take the man's legs from under him.

"A man who cannot stand cannot fight," Sifu Lin often quoted.

Marc moved surprisingly quickly for such a large man, blocking the jab and dodging the right hook. The kick struck his shin though with a satisfying crunch. The only effect, however, was a barely noticeable stumble in Marc's step. He retaliated. Roen dodged the first few, but subsequently collapsed under the barrage of punches. The man hit like a tank.

"I had expected more from you, Tao," Marc said, standing over him. "Your new host is no Blair." He raised his fist to finish Roen off just as a beer bottle flew through the air and struck Marc in the face, exploding into small fragments. He snarled in pain and staggered backward, blood dripping down the side of his face.

"Roen! Get out of here!" Antonio yelled, struggling with the crowds trying to escape the riot.

The room downstairs had degenerated into a full-blown riot. The Genjix were busy fighting several bouncers and club patrons at the same time – and winning. Bodies lay all over the floor as the dozen or so Genjix laid a path of destruction through the packed room.

Roen saw Laura strike one of the bouncers in the neck. The man collapsed, holding his throat and gasping for air. One of the Genjix swung a barstool in wide arcs, hitting anyone unfortunate enough to be in his way. Then he caught sight of Amber making a beeline toward him.

That was when Roen decided that enough was enough. He hated leaving Antonio down there, but he had to escape. He ran up the stairs as fast as he could. Most of the club patrons on the main floor were unaware of the riot below. Roen made his way toward the main door, pushing people out of his way as he approached the exit.

At the door, a bouncer with a headset stopped him. "Hey, you're not going anywhere. We have the cops coming right now."

Take him down!

Without hesitation, Roen threw a punch at the bouncer's face. When the man tried to block the punch, Roen grabbed his forearm, pulling him off balance just enough for Roen to connect with a left hook into the bouncer's ribs, followed by an uppercut that connected to his chin. The man dropped like a rock.

Good work. I see Lin's training did not go to waste.

"He wasn't an agent, just an average Joe."

That had a size and reach advantage over you.

"I'm not that short."

You are not that tall.

Roen burst out the door and scanned the streets. People milled around, some in line waiting to go into the club, while others waited for the valet. The cool night air was a shocking contrast to the humidity inside. Several people nearby pointed at his cuts and bloodstained clothing. In the distance, the sound of sirens became louder.

Time to make yourself scarce.

"Don't have to tell me twice."

Roen took off running, ignoring the people yelling at him to stop. He presumed that they were bouncers or worse, the Genjix. He rounded the corner on West Superior Street and headed east toward his car. As he turned, he glanced back at the club – just in time to see a small group of people run out. One of them saw him in the distance and they took off after him.

"Crap, they saw me."

All that running and you cannot run any faster?

Roen ran faster than he had ever run in his life. Sheer panic gave him an unexpected rush of adrenaline, so that he no longer felt the aches and pains from the melee. It was impossible to get into the car and drive away before they reached him. He sped past it to the State Street intersection with the Genjix closing fast. He'd have to find a place to hide.

Ignoring the red light, Roen ran through the busy intersection and turned south onto the densely populated main street. While it was late, Chicago still teemed with night life. Patrons were streaming out of bars and clubs, trying to make their way home or elsewhere. This time, he did not bother looking back and instead tried to blend in with the crowds.

What are you planning to do?

"I might as well lead them on a wild goose chase and head back to my car after I lose them."

Too risky. They might have someone watching it. You better leave it there.

"The Prophus must go through a lot of cars."

Roen turned at every other corner and moved through different crowds, trying to make his movements as random as possible. He reached Michigan Avenue and headed south. It was nearly two in the morning, and the crowds had thinned out. He was tired and desperate to get home, yet the fear of the Genjix kept him moving.

"What should I do, Tao?"

Well, you are the mark, and the only way for you to know if you are still being followed is to know where the trackers are at. Protocol is to stop moving and try to locate them.

"Stop moving? I don't want to do that."

I sort of figured. Resort to plan B.

"What's plan B?"

Text message 227 to the number 64732 and head for the safe house.

"Go to the safe house. Gotcha. What's the text message for?"

It alerts Command of an incident and they can home in on your location through your phone.

Roen dug out his phone and texted the message. "Now to the safe house? It's not that close."

Time to put all that running to use. Get going.

Roen took off in a sprint, running south on Michigan Avenue and turning west onto Lake Street. Behind him, he heard the distinctive sounds of rifle shots. Who was shooting at whom? He didn't stay to find out. He ran as hard as he could, changing direction every few blocks in order to throw off any possible pursuit. He was near the safe house when Tao ordered him to stop running.

Hide behind these bushes and wait. See if anyone is still on your trail. It will not do you much good if you lead them to the safe house.

Roen crept into a row of bushes and tried to make himself as small as possible, while still able to see the streets east and north of his location. His reconnaissance training from the past several months kicked in. He steadied his breathing and focused on his surroundings and the likely entry points his pursuers would come from. He became very still, moving elsewhere only when necessary when a young couple walked dangerously close. Now that this was a real life-threatening situation, he was thankful for all the monotonous training he had to endure.

Watch for oncoming cars turning. Their headlights will pass right by your location.

Roen remained still, checking his watch at set intervals. Finally, after thirty minutes, he felt safe enough from pursuit to climb out of his hiding spot and head toward the safe house. Just to be safe, he went a longer route and circled to it from the west.

That was very well done. You utilized your training very well.

"I'm glad you approve. You think I can move on to something more interesting like clandestine work?"

You are not ready for that sort of espionage yet. There is a difference between that and just field surveillance. One step at a time. Remember, I have been busy trying to help you see your toes when you stand.

"I wasn't that big," Roen grumbled aloud.

You looked like an offensive lineman.

A train passed by overhead on the elevated tracks, temporarily overwhelming his hearing. Roen stopped, leaned against a wall, and waited. It was only after the rumbling faded into the distance that he felt safe enough to continue. Roen walked to the safe house and punched in the entrance code. Staying alert, he didn't relax until the metal door closed behind him and locked with a loud click and a hiss.

The safe house was dark, as usual. He walked over to the control panel and flicked the lights on, only to come face to face with the muzzle of a pistol. The panic came back in a rush. The Genjix must have compromised this safe house! Instinctively he froze and threw his hands into the air.

Your first instinct is to surrender? We are going to have to work on that.

"Oh, it's you, Roen. Thank God you're all right." Sonya's voice almost stopped his heart. Roen nearly collapsed in relief. She turned on the light and hugged him. "I got the text that something happened. The GPS had you in this area, so I came to the safe house, assuming you would make your way here."

She smelled like cucumber and citrus, and her skin felt very soft. Roen held her tightly as the shock of the night finally settled in. He almost didn't make it! Roen suddenly became very aware of the dried blood all over his body. As much as he did not want to, he let go of her and went to the sink to wash up.

"You're bleeding. Is it serious?" she asked, moving to one of the cabinets and pulling out a tube of antibiotic ointment and some bandages.

"Nothing sleep and a bottle of Macallan won't cure," he joked. Now that she pointed out his wounds, the pain that had been dulled by adrenaline came screaming back. He walked up to a mirror and studied the Genjix's handiwork. "They did quite a number on me," Roen muttered. His face was a mess of black and blue welts, and he was cut in several places. He grabbed his shirt and took it off, wincing as he pulled it over his head, revealing more bruises and gashes along his chest and back when he looked in the mirror.

Sonya whistled as she walked up to him and studied the cuts. "I don't think any of them will require stitches. Did you break any bones?" He shook his head and sat down in the chair. Roen watched her as she meticulously cleaned the wounds. She took out several rolls of bandages and wrapped some of the larger cuts. Sonya then began to dab the ointment on his body. It stung, making him recoil from her touch. "Stay still, you big baby," she murmured.

"You're very good at this," he remarked.

"Something Mom taught me," she replied. "There were a few times when she came home from a mission with bullet wounds or worse. I learned to be a pretty good nurse that way." She caressed his cheeks, checking over her handiwork; their eyes locked briefly. Their faces were nearly touching. On impulse, Roen leaned forward and kissed her.

What are you doing?!

He waited for the uppercut that would floor him at any moment. That would hurt, he thought, but it would be worth it. Instead, he was pleasantly surprised that she kissed him back. Not a big kiss, but a light, gentle one. Roen stood up and wrapped his hands around her waist. She pulled back and looked to the side. The two stood there uncomfortably.

"I'm... I'm sorry," he apologized. "I don't know what came over me."

Stupidity obviously came over you.

"No, I'm sorry," she replied. "We shouldn't be doing this." She was still leaning on him though. Not sure if he should let go, Roen decided to finish what he set out to do and kept holding her. She did not try to pull away again. They just looked at each other. Roen noticed that her breath smelled good too.

"You're going to get us in trouble," she whispered.

"With whom?" he asked.

"Baji," she murmured. "She's screaming at me right now, asking me what the hell I think I'm doing."

"That's funny. Tao isn't saying anything."

Like hell! You two work together. Do not jeopardize your professional relationship because you have pubescent hormones.

"He just said that I'm confusing our professional relationship with affection."

Sonya leaned close to him again. Roen leaned forward as well. She moved past his lips and kissed him on the cheek. "I think you are, too. Let's not do something we're both going to regret. I like you and you're my friend, a good friend, but we work together, and something like this could cloud our judgment and get us killed. You should get some sleep. You must be exhausted." She put her hands on his forearms and then moved away. Turning, she walked to the kitchen and poured herself a glass of water. "You want some?"

"Is that you or Baji talking?" he asked.

"I'll take that as a yes." She picked up two glasses and handed one to him.

"Is that you or Baji talking?" Roen repeated.

"A bit of both," she replied. "Are you going home in the morning?" Her sudden change of topic had a tone of finality to it that told him the discussion was over. Reluctantly, he nodded.

"I'll go with you," Sonya said. "There might be trouble at your place. No matter what, don't call your roommate. He might be compromised." She pointed at the glass in his hand. "And don't think for a minute that I'm your maid. Wash the glass before you go to bed."

And before Roen could utter another word, she went into one of the bedrooms, shutting off the light – and left him standing there in the dark.

Sonya's angry face came very close to Roen's as she reached over and pulled him up by the front of his shirt. "Damn it, Tao, what was that all about?" Sonya growled.

Twenty minutes ago, Roen had fallen asleep on the couch at the safe house while Sonya took the lone bedroom. Now Baji, controlling Sonya, hovered over him and looked like she was about to take a swing at him.

Tao, controlling a sleeping Roen, feigned confusion. "You mean the ambush tonight?" he asked innocently.

"No, I mean your host trying to stick his tongue down Sonya's throat!"

"I'm sorry, Baji. I did not know he was going to do it."

"Well, she is confused now. She has spent so much of her life preparing for her role that she has not experienced much of a social life."

"That is your fault, not mine. You should have made her a more balanced individual."

Baji replied, "All your hosts seem to share the same womanizing traits."

"Why are you so upset? Do you mean she likes him?"

"No, I mean she's not focused on the task at hand. Get your playboy under control, Tao, or I will put him in his place."

"Easy there, Baji – you sound like a disapproving mother."

"You are damn right I am disapproving. Sonya has been groomed for great things. She has more potential than any other host I have had in centuries. Do not ruin her, or I swear..."

"You really should let her live a more balanced life," he said.

That probably wasn't the right thing to say. She glared at him and snapped. "Shut up. You take care of your host, and I will take care of mine. I never intruded on Edward's training."

"I let Edward marry and live a semblance of a normal life."

"That is a tragedy in itself when you consider the usual fate of our hosts."

"What about Dania? Do you regret her having a family?" Tao asked.

"What I regret is her marrying another host. Jordan's death broke her will. I will not let the same thing happen to Sonya."

"By not ever letting her discover love? Sorry, Baji, but I do not have as much control over my host as you have over yours. I will work on getting rid of his free will right away."

She said, "Do not turn this around on me."

"I suggest you just let them be for now and worry about it

later. We have a little crisis on our hands. Have you notified Intelligence?" Tao asked.

As Baji finally began to calm down, Tao pulled her clenched fist away from his shirt.

She scowled and slumped into the recliner next to the couch. "This is not over yet, Tao. We are going to finish this conversation later. And yes, Intelligence found a hit on Hamilton Lee getting a speeding ticket off of Highway 80 last night. With all of Roen's information washed, it must have tripped an alarm when his identification hit a dead end. That means the Genjix are actively monitoring for him and parsing through negative hits as well. Tell your boy to be more careful. They must want you badly."

"What can I say? I do good work. At least one good thing came out of all this."

Baji shook her head. "What good can possibly come from this? Roen's risk levels now are exponentially higher. I would almost call in bodyguards if I thought they would be of any use."

Tao grinned. "No, bodyguards would just attract more attention. I think tonight's little encounter should prove to the Keeper that Roen is ready. Even with only a few months of training, he performed admirably." Tao stood up and walked over to one of the computers. "You should get some sleep. They are getting up in three hours. This might not be over yet."

"You are not going to bed?" Baji asked.

"Not yet. I need to expand Roen's data wipe. From now on, he will only be Roen to those around him. Once that name enters a government system or credit agency, he will become Ron Tam."

"Cute, just enough to cry user error."

"I thought so too. Goodnight, Baji."

Baji stood up and walked toward the bedroom. She glared at Tao one more time before going in. She said, "Hey Tao, we

did well with Roen. You should be proud. But regardless, tell
Roen to keep his mitts off Sonya or I will kill him myself."

"He loves you too."

CHAPTER TWENTY
AFTERMATH

After driving back the Yuan, the Ming were the dominant power in the region and had few enemies. So without an outside enemy, the Council ordered that I oppress the people, to drive them into rebellion in order to create more conflict. At that time, I was on the cusp of a cultural revolution. I was close to fulfilling my dream. So again, I tried to refuse. And again, I was weak and failed my host.

"So how's t'ai chi with Lin going?" Sonya asked as the two stood in the elevator at his apartment building, watching the numbers climb.

"Great," Roen replied. "It's working well for me. Why didn't you ever study with him?"

Sonya shook her head. "I tried a few years back. T'ai chi isn't my thing. It's too slow-paced and I couldn't grasp all that internal stuff. I'm more suited to Savate and Krav Maga."

There were a few more moments of awkward silence as they stood on opposite sides of the elevator. She had let him sleep in until noon. Roen was grateful for that, considering the previous night's events. The two had had a quick lunch in silence and then headed toward his place shortly afterward. Sonya's question to him just now was the first words they'd spoken all day.

Roen was equipped with a pistol, a machete, and a pair of knives. He wore a thin Kevlar suit underneath the rest of his clothing and had the gun cleverly hidden in his thin leather jacket. The machete sheath was strapped to his back – and the knives were inside his boots – in case the fighting got close and ugly.

Sonya, on the other hand, was armed to the teeth. Besides a small rack of throwing knives strapped to her back, she carried three pistols hidden somewhere within her bodice. Her Kevlar outfit covered her torso, and the weapons were neatly concealed so that she looked like she was wearing a business suit.

Roen desperately wanted to talk about last night with her, but was actually relieved that she didn't bring it up. He didn't know how she felt about him. In fact, Roen perceived a subtle coldness that wasn't there before. He wasn't sure what to make of it. Should he tell her how he felt? How did he feel? Was he being impulsive or did he really have feelings for her?

Maybe Tao was right; maybe it was all in his head. Roen just didn't know. And then there was Jill. What about her? He cursed himself for putting himself in such an awkward situation. For years he'd had no love interest. Now he had two.

A little focus, please?

Tao was right. None of this would matter if he didn't get through the next ten minutes alive. Roen pushed those thoughts into the back of his mind and concentrated on their plan. They could be walking into a trap.

"Why do they want me so bad?" he sighed.

"Tao's a valuable capture," Sonya answered. "According to Baji, he's upset many in the Genjix hierarchy and is considered a top-twenty target. He must be on someone's grudge list, because I don't think Baji even makes the top hundred."

That is because Baji is a slacker.

"What a dubious honor to be proud of," Roen muttered.

Hey, it took a lot of work to make that list.

"I'm sure you're very proud of yourself."

Quite, thank you very much.

The elevator doors opened with a soft hiss. The two stepped out and crept toward his apartment. As they neared it, they heard a click and froze. It was all Roen could do to keep his gun in its holster and not fire at the first thing that moved. Mrs Fitzgerald, his elderly next door neighbor, came out with her little dog Mocha.

"Good morning, Mrs Fitzgerald." He waved with a plastic grin.

"Hi, Roen. I see you have a friend." She smiled at them both. "She's so pretty. My, did you lose weight?" Mocha jumped and barked at them. Roen bent down to pet the dog and moved aside to let her pass.

"What are you two up to?" the elderly lady asked.

"We're pretending to be secret agents," Sonya said, and winked.

Mrs Fitzgerald laughed. "You kids have fun. Come on, Mocha. Let's go for a walk."

The two waited until she walked into the elevator before they moved again. Standing on both sides of his front door, Sonya drew her gun and waited for Roen to unlock it. As soon as he opened the door, she moved inside to sweep the entranceway.

"Clear," she whispered.

Roen drew his gun and went in after her. They searched the apartment, one in front of the other, positioning themselves against walls and behind furniture as they swept each room. Both the bedroom doors were closed. The living room and kitchen were exactly as he had left them the night before. There was no one in the hall bathroom either.

"Your room," she whispered and pointed. Sonya turned the doorknob and moved in. Roen stayed by the door until she waved him in. She waved her gun toward his bathroom. It was clear as well. It seemed the Genjix didn't know about his place after all. Then they heard a loud thump coming from Antonio's room. The two immediately raised their guns again and moved to his door.

"On three," she whispered as she kicked the door open. Antonio was sprawled on the floor in his boxers. Sonya holstered her gun and put a finger under Antonio's nose.

"He's breathing," she said, "and he smells like a wino."

"He's snoring too." Roen added, "I think he just fell off the bed."

"Antonio, you all right?" She patted him on the cheek. "Wake up. You alive and kicking?"

It took a few seconds before Antonio opened his eyes. He looked at them standing over him and yawned. "Water," he croaked. "I have a horrible hangover."

Roen went to the kitchen and took a couple bottles of water from the fridge. He brought one to Antonio, who sat up and winced. He downed the bottle and looked back and forth at them. "Why are you guys so dressed up? Damn, your face, Roen. Who were those chicks that wanted to kick your ass?"

Roen shrugged. "Um... Beats me. Just some girls that thought I was someone else."

Antonio stood up and stretched, a little unsteady on his feet. "Well, they tore the place up. By the time the cops came, they had bolted out of the club. Most of the bouncers had to go to the hospital. The cops are writing it down as gang violence. Ha, ha. They think you're in a gang. Anyway, that was an eventful night. I think it was the first time I ever got beat up by a girl."

"It's all right." Sonya smiled. "Roen's used to that."

Antonio grinned and checked himself in the mirror. "God, I look like Frankenstein." He made a face. "So what do you two lovebirds have planned for today?"

Roen almost choked on his water, but Sonya took it in her stride and shrugged. She said, "Not much, holding hands at

the beach, seeing a movie, making out, lifting weights together, you know... the usual stuff."

"Wearing all black leather? Not sure what sorts of workout
you two have in mind." Antonio snickered. "Unless you're off
saving the world with your aliens."

Sonya threw Roen a sharp look. He felt his face turn hot and
shrugged apologetically.

"Oh, didn't Roen tell you about his alien-saving-the-world
story?" Antonio chuckled.

She laughed it off. "Well, he does have quite the imagination.
I'm going to have to hear about it sometime. Come on, Roen,
we're going to be late." She turned abruptly and left the room.

"You all right there, buddy?" Roen asked, patting him on
the shoulder.

Antonio nodded. "Not the first bar fight I've ever been in. If
anything, I should be asking you that. You look like a hot
mess. How does it feel, getting into your first riot?"

Roen grunted. "It's an experience I can do without."

Antonio laughed, winced, and rubbed his head. "I need a
shower," he sniffed. "Well, don't tell her you got your rear
handed to you by two girls half your size. Last night was crazy!"

"Roen, you coming?" Sonya's voice came from the front door.

"I have to go. I'll see you later?" Roen said solemnly. In truth,
he'd been afraid he'd find his roommate hurt or dead. The relief
of finding Antonio all right nearly brought him to tears.

*That is why for the good of both of you, it is best to keep what we
do quiet.*

"I understand now. I'm sorry, Tao."

"No problem." Antonio grinned. "You'll be back in time for
dinner? We'll go grab some pizza or something. You've been
hanging out with Sonya so much I'm starting to get jealous."

"Sounds like a plan." Roen smiled and left the room. Sonya
was waiting for him outside. He could tell she was furious. He
felt his stomach twist into a knot as he walked into the elevator.

"Is something the matter?" he asked innocently as the door closed.

She grabbed him by the shoulder and shoved him hard against the wall. "What the hell were you thinking telling him about us? You're going to blow our cover!"

"What?" he stammered. "Antonio thinks it's a stupid joke! He doesn't take it seriously!"

Her nostrils flared as her face came very close to his. "If the Genjix ever catch wind of you, don't think for a moment they won't torture the information out of him. And don't think for a moment he won't tell them everything he knows. If they ask the right questions, Antonio will lead them to me as well! How could you be so stupid?"

"I didn't realize at the time," he stammered. "I felt like I had to tell someone."

"Don't you realize that our lives require utmost secrecy? This isn't a game we're playing. Your friend's life depends on what you don't tell him."

"I'm... I'm sorry."

"Who else did you tell?"

He shook his head. "No one. I swear."

Sonya's face stayed hard for several seconds before it finally softened and she let go of his shirt. "Did you tell Antonio about the safe house or where I live?"

Roen shook his head. "I don't know where you live. You never invited me over."

"Good, and it's going to stay that way, big mouth." She added, "If I have to move out of my loft because you've compromised me, I'm going to kill you, Roen!"

And she means it too. Her mother was wealthy. Sonya probably has a very nice place.

Marc walked into Sean's office and bowed. "Forgive me; I have failed."

Sean didn't bother looking up from the deposition he was reading. He had been notified within minutes of the boy's escape. The basement had only one main exit. They had laid the perfect trap and the fool had let him escape. Still, after looking at Heefa's report, Marc made all the right calls. Sean himself would have planned the attack the exact same way, except that he would not have failed. Marc stood at attention, awaiting the consequences of his failure.

"That's twice now," Sean finally remarked. "Has our prey suddenly developed skills, or are you that incompetent?"

Marc replied, eyes downcast. "His physical appearance is different from Omer's original report as well. The Prophus have trained him well."

"Of course he has been trained," Sean snarled. "It took you almost six months to find him. Did you think he was just sitting idle this entire time? On your knees!"

Punishing every subordinate who had ever failed him would leave him with no subordinates. However, allowing such a golden opportunity to go to waste was inexcusable. Who knows if the Genjix would ever get the chance to capture another highly sought Prophus again? Marc was lucky the two enforcers had vouched that the failed capture was due to incompetence and not the work of a double agent.

Sean considered suitable punishments for the failure. Marc was not a man without usefulness. To incarcerate him only weakened the Genjix, and a physical punishment was barbaric and ineffectual. However, strict discipline must be maintained even among those counted as blessed. A lack of consequence for failures only encouraged complacency.

Sean stood up purposefully and towered over the cowering Marc. "Your standing has been lowered. You will learn that the Genjix are neither as soft nor as forgiving as your old comrades. Any more failures and you will be ordered to release Jeo to a vessel more deserving of a Holy One."

Marc's body stiffened and he involuntarily looked up at Sean, his face turning pale. Jeo wouldn't be pleased if that order was given, though it didn't matter to Chiyva what Jeo thought. Any decree from a Genjix of his rank was as good as law. Sean was sure the man had already learned his lesson and knew that Marc would be haunted until the day he could reclaim his place.

Tao is a great prize. Redouble your efforts.

Chiyva's remarks puzzled Sean. Apparently, this went deeper than he thought. "He's just one Prophus, Chiyva. I know you have history with him, but why is he so important?"

Your only concern is to execute my command.

Sean could feel the Genjix seething, which was unusual. Chiyva was always in control, but Genjix grudges always ran deep, tempered over the years of war. Well, if his Holy One wished it so, it was Sean's sacred duty to see it done. He looked Marc in the eyes. "Do you believe your team can pick up his tracks again?"

Marc nodded. "It will be more difficult, but the question is whether he is worth tracking at this point. Even though he is still raw, he was able to elude capture. The Prophus have already altered all his records, and Tao has already trained his new vessel. He will be ready in the future. Is it still worth expending resources?"

"It is if I say it is. It is not for you to decide," Sean growled. "Your access to Homeland Security's network is now gone. You will have to focus your surveillance on high probability areas with the resources you have. You are now forbidden to make contact without my express authority. Keep your team ready to move at any moment."

Marc bowed. "I am here to serve."

"Serve better. Now, get out of my sight." Sean picked up the deposition transcript and began reading where he had left off, already oblivious to the other man's existence. Marc bowed and hastily retreated. Sean focused on his document, but his thoughts raced. Once a Prophus entered their defensive net-work, he would be difficult to corral, and the cost to continue this manhunt was extraordinary. There were better uses for their resources.

He had known Chiyva long enough to know something was amiss. Chiyva was extraordinarily meticulous and logical; to display anger and emotion was out of his character. Despite what Marc said, Sean also had doubts that his team could track him down again.

You have doubts about my judgment?

"Never, Chiyva. I live but to serve the Genjix."

You question my motives then?

Sean hesitated. "I fail to understand the significance of this Prophus."

One of Tao's previous vessels was Rianno Cisneros.

The reason for Chiyva's insistence became clear. Sean pulled out a small glass figurine of a turtle and caressed it in his hand. "Say no more, Chiyva. I will bear all the strength at my dis-posal to see that your directives are carried out."

CHAPTER TWENTY-ONE
TAILING

The Council must have anticipated my possible disobedience. Zoras revealed to me that Europe in its current state had already been abandoned due to a period of stagnation, and that the Council planned to wipe the slate clean in order to rebuild from the ruins of a broken world. They called forth a world-killer, now known as the Black Death. I was given a choice. The Council had sent a ship laden with plague rats just off the shores of my lands. If I disobeyed, the Ming would suffer just like those halfway across the world. I told myself that I had no choice. Looking back, there was always a choice.

Sonya watched Roen leave his office building and wait in front of the coffee shop. Like clockwork, he left work no later than he had to. He checked his reflection in the window and fiddled around with his shirt. What was Roen up to? Then he walked out onto the street, stopped and then went back to the window to check his hair. He seemed a little nervous.

Sonya chuckled. "I love his awkward mannerisms. They're so endearing. He'll make the perfect spy one day."

If he does not pass that test tonight, he might not ever become one.

"I think these written tests you're making him take are a little harsh. I never had to take them."

You and Roen are not even the same species in my book. If Roen Tan was the first Cro-Magnon we had encountered, we might have put all our eggs into the Neanderthals.

"Now you're just being mean. You still haven't forgiven him for that night at the safe house. It's been three weeks."

Moments later, an auburn-haired woman came up to him and they embraced. Then holding hands, they walked into the coffee shop. Sonya shook her head. "Well, this is interesting. Our Roen has a love interest. He's all grown up now."

Do I detect a hint of jealousy?

"No. I don't think so. I look at him like my little older brother. I'm happy for him." She kept her eyes on the door. Then her eyes wandered to the dozens of people standing on the street. Did anyone take notice of them? Had anyone nearby made a move to keep him within sight?

I do admit that I am protective of you. You are Dania's daughter after all. In a way, you are mine as well.

Sonya sipped her tea as she looked back down at the magazine she was reading. Ever since the night at the club, she had made a point to tail him on his way to and from work. She was worried that the Genjix were starting to triangulate his whereabouts. Already twice in the past month, Sonya found two other Genjix agents lurking in the South Loop area.

She finished her tea as she watched Roen and his mysterious date come out and walk down the street. They turned and disappeared around the corner. Sonya surveyed the surrounding area for any sign of possible tails. Sure enough, moments later, a man who was waiting at the bus stop turned and began to follow Roen.

The man with the gray coat and brown sunglasses?

"I see him; the one at the bus stop. That's the second tail on this block that's caught wind of Roen this month."

We need to get him out of this area. They are closing in on his waypoints. It is only a matter of time before we miss a tail.

Sonya stood up and began to follow Roen's tail. The man wasn't half bad. He kept a safe distance from Roen and didn't react strongly in any way when Roen and his friend changed directions. Sonya continued walking as she didn't have a care in the world, keeping tabs on both the tail and Roen.

The three parties involved kept about a block apart. Roen and his girl, oblivious to what was happening behind them, continued on their merry way. The two walked into Grant Park and seemed to enjoy each other's company. Sonya kept an eye on them and the tail as she trailed behind far enough to remain undetected, but close enough to act if the tail made a move.

"They seem very happy, and Roen's a sweet guy. Why were you so angry with the kiss?"

You are meant for someone else. I do not want your future husband to be involved in all this.

Sonya chuckled. "That basically narrows my dating pool to nil. My entire life is this war."

That is not true. What about that dentist who was completely infatuated with you?

"Oh, Baji, Darren was nice, but way too domesticated. Movie night? Poker with his friends? Ugh. I know you want me to meet a civilian, but that sort of life isn't for me."

Your mother never recovered from Jordan's death. I am trying to spare you that pain.

"I felt Daddy's death as well. It hurt me just as much."

And I do not wish for you to go through that again.

Roen and the girl sat down in front of Buckingham Fountain and were talking intimately. The tail had swerved to the side and had planted himself near a food stand. Sonya sat down at a bench in between the two and took out her magazine. For the next ten minutes, she learned more about road bikes than she ever wanted to know. The tail was sitting at a small table eating a hot dog. Roen and his date were still talking. Then they kissed.

"I wonder if they were dating before he kissed me."

If they were, Tao and I will have some serious words.

"Baji, relax. It was just a kiss."

Tao is a bad influence on humans. Edward was such a gentleman before Tao got his claws in him. He once tried to date your mother before she met Jordan. A scene of a young Edward flirting popped into Sonya's head. It was followed by laughter and a hand, which Sonya assumed was her mother's, pinching his cheeks.

"Wasn't Mother much older than him?"

By about ten years.

"I don't blame him. Mother was very beautiful." Another image flashed of Dania looking into the mirror. It was one that Baji often showed her. Sonya smiled; it was one of her favorite memories of her mother. "Hey, I want to hear what they're saying." Sonya moved closer and sat down about twenty meters away. Then she pulled out a small listening device and aimed it at the couple.

This is very inappropriate.

"I know, but so much fun."

Roen was saying, "You're right. I was going to make it a surprise, but you forced my hand. I've already booked a ski trip for your birthday. Thanks for ruining your gift."

"Really?" Roen's girlfriend sounded skeptical. "When's my birthday?"

There was a pause. "December twelfth," he answered finally.

You know Tao is feeding him all that information.

The girl laughed. Something about her voice irritated Sonya. The girl said, "I thought I had you there for a second. I'm impressed, Roen Tan. I didn't think you remembered what month it was, let alone the day."

Sonya smiled. "Seems you're not the only one who thinks that, Baji."

He has the memory capacity of a gerbil.

"You kidding?" Roen was saying. "Spent an entire night

repeating your birthday over and over again just to make sure I wouldn't forget."

"I bet you did," she teased. "You have the worst memory, I swear. So where are we going?"

There was another pause. "Galena." Pause. "It's in Illinois." Pause. "West of Chicago."

She leaned back, impressed. "Well, look at you. Aren't you suddenly the romantic one?"

Their conversation went on and on. Sonya turned off the listener and went back to her magazine. Any more of that conversation and she thought she might get sick. She still kept an eye on the tail, who must be on his third hot dog now. They were in a far too populated area for anyone to act, so the only thing she could do was wait them out.

Are you unhappy, Sonya?

"Not unhappy per se. It's just nice to have someone sometimes. My life right now is mission after mission. And it's not that I regret it. This is all I ever wanted to do, but listening to them makes me a little wistful."

I am sorry you feel this way. I am to blame. Tao said I should provide a more balanced life for you. Perhaps he is right.

"Baji, I appreciate everything you've done for my family. You have nothing to say sorry for. Wait, Roen and girlie are moving."

Sonya kept her face down as Roen and his girl got up and walked back the way they came. Out of the corner of her eye, she saw the tail move as well. She saw his lips move as he strolled after them.

"We need to move fast. He could be calling in a kill team."

Take him out at the first isolated spot you can find.

The stalking continued. The tail was a third of a block behind Roen while Sonya kept half a block behind him. They ventured west to Michigan Avenue and then turned north.

Somewhere along the way though, Roen's tail must have detected something. Maybe Sonya got too close, maybe she had a miscue in her reaction, but whatever she did, the tail was suddenly aware that something was wrong. This began a new game.

The tail broke off from Roen and walked into a store. Moments later, he came out and changed directions. He then turned west onto Madison Street and then right on Dearborn Street. He was moving in random directions in an attempt to identify *his* tail. Unfortunately for him, Sonya was very good at this game.

She timed her steps with his and the two crossed paths just as they passed by an alley. In a split second, she rammed her fist in his gut and pushed him into the alley. The tail wasn't completely unprepared. He took her initial hit well and retreated behind a dumpster.

"Hmm... he seems like he knows what he's doing. Is he gun worthy?"

Not if you can avoid it. It will cause too much attention in this populated area. Watch for his, though.

The tail tried to pull out his pistol. Sonya dove forward and grabbed his wrist. Then she hit him on the chin with her forehead. Sonya wrestled the gun away and threw it to the side. The tail shoved her away from him, and the two squared off, sizing each other up. Sonya was careful to cut off his exit. He was younger than she thought, but he looked and moved like an experienced agent. The way he held his hands and moved his feet told her the tail had Mossad training.

Watch his left. He is a southpaw.

"Just out of professional curiosity," Sonya asked, "what gave me away?"

The tail smirked. "You're good, girl. I give you that. You don't think you were the only one listening in on Mr Tan, do you? I picked up your interference. Our toys are better than your toys."

"That is true," she conceded.

"What about me?" he asked. "What gave me away? It'd be good to fix for next time."

Sonya shrugged. "You just weren't that good."

It was a brief and ugly exchange, and was over in moments.

When it was over, Sonya stepped out alone from the alley, dusting off some grime that got onto her clothes when she threw his body into the dumpster.

"I think it's time Roen quit his job. Going to work is getting way too dangerous for him. And me."

I agree. We will arrange to have him laid off. At least then he gets severance.

CHAPTER TWENTY-TWO
T'AI CHI

And for the third and last time, I faltered. My sin against Zhu was great. In order to save what we had built, I destroyed it from within – through him. I betrayed his trust and twisted him into everything he wasn't. This was done in order to save his people, I told myself. His peaceful reign became one of suspicion and terror. I conceived the birth of the infamous secret police which terrorized his people. I sent his armies forth to suppress all dissension. I destroyed my own dream.

"Relax your breathing. Feel the chi flow through your arms. Push with your entire body, not just your arms."

Roen let Sifu Lin drone on in the background as he focused on the Chen-style form. It always surprised him how much he sweated practicing t'ai chi. It was even more surprising how hard it was to move at a slow and controlled pace. He originally thought moving at a snail's pace would be much easier than moving fast, but that wasn't the case. It forced him to pay attention to his body in a completely different manner.

"I said, not your muscles!" Lin admonished.

Roen felt a sharp rap on his shoulder from Lin's stick.

Roen had avoided sports as a youth and had never developed any athleticism. Sonya's training improved his conditioning and strength, but she wasn't able to improve his coordination. She explained that physical coordination required years of practice to obtain muscle memory. Since Roen started training his body later in life, it was a harder lesson for his body to grasp.

Lin's teaching was the complete opposite. In fact, the pudgy short t'ai chi master taught him to stop thinking about using muscles altogether. Roen realized then that he had a natural affinity for t'ai chi and his progress had been quick. Lin often commented that it was because Roen was a totally empty canvas with nothing to unlearn.

"The muscle is only a small part of the body," Lin continued. "When you punch with muscle, you are using a fraction of the power one can generate; the arm, forearm, or parts of the upper chest, but not all of you."

Focus on relaxing. Worry about what to eat for dinner later.

Tao's ever-present advice sped up Roen's development as well. It helped that he had two very demanding teachers. While Sifu Lin constantly berated Roen for every small mistake, Tao was even harder on him, scolding him not only for mistakes he made but for times when his mind wandered. While frustrating, it was one of the few times he heard Tao become so passionate.

"I am, Tao. Leave me alone. You're screwing up my concentration."

Maybe if you stopped thinking about food every five minutes.

"I can't help it. This everlasting diet is killing me. I want some steak and potatoes so badly."

Your "Buddha pounds the mortar" looks pitiful.

"Well, maybe if you..."

Another sharp rap on the shoulder from Sifu Lin's long stick caught Roen's attention. "Stop wasting my time and listen to Tao," Lin said.

"Wha'...? How did you know what Tao was saying?" Roen asked.

"I know exactly what he said, considering your terrible posture and the lazy Buddha-pounds-mortar. Looks more like grandma-slaps-baby's-butt. And your silk-reeling looks like fairy dancing." Lin gave him another poke in the ribs for good measure. "Again!"

Roen gritted his teeth and began anew, working through the form. He reached the same segment he was previously at when he felt the sting of the stick again.

"Gah!" he yelled in annoyance.

"Your silk-reeling is awful." Lin scowled. "Your right arm should move like this. Your left hand should move like that, and it should all flow." Lin demonstrated the move more fluidly than Roen could ever hope to do.

He is right, you know. You are making San-Feng roll in his grave right now.

"The move doesn't seem to have any purpose, Sifu Lin. I feel like I'm just waving my hands in the air," Roen protested.

Now you asked for it. Why would I invent a move that has no purpose?

"You think 'silk-reeling' is frivolous?" Lin sounded like a four year-old discovering the truth about Santa. "Here, grab my wrist."

Facing him, Roen grabbed Lin's right wrist. Then, before he could react, Lin performed the same smooth silk-reeling motion and suddenly, a sharp pain shot up Roen's arm as Lin escaped Roen's clutch and reversed the hold. "I can also do this to your fingers." Lin demonstrated that. "And your shoulders." He slipped his right hand under Roen's armpit and flipped him onto his back. "And if I get my hands on your head, well, it might snap off. The only reason you cannot make it work is because you are doing it wrong. Don't presume these moves are worthless because you're too incompetent."

Someone started clapping. Roen looked up from the floor and saw Sonya smirking as she walked up and embraced the wizened old man. Roen's face turned a slight shade of red, and he picked himself up from the floor.

"What brings you here today, child?" Lin said warmly.

"I have the intelligence reports from the Tibetan underground you requested. I told them I'd deliver it personally. I have a date with Roen after you're through with him. We're going to learn to block throwing knives. How is his training coming along?" she asked.

"Block knives?" Lin chuckled. "His brain talks too slow to his hands to block knives. He's a clumsy oaf. He forgets things right after I tell him and whines like a little girl, but he's much further along than I expected." It must have hurt Lin to say that. It almost sounded like a compliment. If Roen didn't know better, his master almost sounded proud. "He could be adequate one day, once he stops being such a slow-witted buffoon." Lin smiled at Sonya. "Why, child, are you afraid he'll one day surpass you? Are you ready to try t'ai chi again?"

Sonya shook her head. "I tried it three times already, Master. It's just not for me. Besides, I've never met a t'ai chi practitioner besides you that could take me on."

"Really?" Lin grinned, with a conniving look on his face. "That sounds like a direct challenge... to Roen."

"What?" Roen said, startled. "No it didn't!"

Sure sounded like one.

"Shut up, Tao! You just like seeing me get beat up."

I admit I find a perverse enjoyment in that.

"Show some respect to your family art, boy, and defend its honor," Lin growled. Sonya grinned, took off her jacket, and cracked her knuckles.

Roen sighed and met her in the center of the circle. He'd thought his days of physical abuse by her were over.

The two bowed and circled each other. Roen had sparred with Sonya dozens of times now and was familiar with her techniques. She utilized Krav Maga's aggressive style to batter through her opponent's defenses. She was also fast and had few real weaknesses. She utilized angles, her legs were quick, and she did not have a dominant hand she relied on.

Roen thought the only real weakness she had was her defense. Sonya did not like to retreat. The few times he was able to set her back on her heels, she would disengage to look for a new angle.

Not a bad analysis. Utilize your superior weight. Watch her kick to your chin. She is flexible and likes to sneak it high once in a while, which you often fall for, I might add. Remember that she likes to go forward, sometimes a bit too much. Take advantage of that. And watch out for that right hook!

Roen measured her footsteps as she moved, feinting to the left and right, until she suddenly leaped toward him, throwing a jab as she closed in. Roen twisted and countered, throwing a combination of his own. She blocked his attack and kneed him in the stomach. He grunted and retreated, managing a grazing punch to her chin as he moved backward.

If she had any reaction from his blow, she didn't show it. Immediately, she went on the offensive again. Roen rolled with the punches, squatting low and dodging, keeping his elbows tight to his ribs. Then – right as she overextended herself just a smidgeon – he launched himself toward her. The attack caught her off guard and he slammed into her, knocking her off her feet.

You took too many hits setting that up. That only works on smaller opponents anyway, and you will not be engaging many her size.

Sonya picked herself up and looked impressed. "Very well done, good sir. I see you have learned something, though you had to block several of my punches with your head for that."

Roen gingerly touched his eye and blinked. There would be a beautiful black eye in the morning. "Part of my master plan." He grinned. It hurt a little to smile.

She put on her game face and launched at him again, initiating the attack with a left-right combination. Instead of blocking, Roen spun to his left and her blow just missed him. He kept spinning until he made a full turn and was now behind her. She was precariously out of position, and he went to work. He grabbed her in a bear hug. Sonya grunted in surprise as he lifted her up. Even sweating, she smelled good.

He grinned triumphantly. "I got you this time. You can't get out of this. Give up and..." She kicked back and caught him in the knee. His legs buckled; she threw her head back, striking him in the forehead. "Ahhh," Roen cried, dazed, but he held on.

On the side, Lin laughed. "I didn't teach you t'ai chi so you could become a professional wrestler, stupid boy."

That looked painful.

"Thanks for the useless observation, Tao."

Sonya took the opening to squirm out of his bear hug and kick him in the face. Roen's head snapped back, and he crumpled to the floor. She stood over him, panting and grinning. "Not bad. This was your best effort yet. You move like a t'ai chi practitioner already. You don't hit like one, but you're starting to move like one." She offered her hand.

"I think I need to lie here for a few minutes." He grimaced. "I'm feeling light-headed."

"Come on, you big baby." She grabbed his hands and pulled him to his feet, ignoring his groans. Roen leaned on her as they walked back to Lin. She felt very soft.

"You did not win, but I was not disappointed." Lin nodded.

Roen wasn't sure, but that could've been the second almost compliment he had ever received from Lin. Twice in one day. What was this world coming to?

"Well, this was fun, but we have to get going," Sonya said as she wiped her face and grabbed her jacket. "Get dressed, Roen. I'm taking you out to dinner, my apology in advance for what I'm about to put you through tonight."

CHAPTER TWENTY-THREE
AWAY GAME

To make matters worse, the plague found its way to these lands anyway. The turmoil I had created set the tone for the next three hundred years until the dynasty fell. When Zhu died, I had my fill of empires and dreams, and decided to return west. This part of the world deserved to be free of me, for I had brought nothing to the people here except death and tyranny.

Exactly seven months into his life as a host, Roen was laid off from his job when his company found contractors in India who did the same work for a quarter of the price. It was a mixed blessing of sorts. Tao had no choice then but to put him on a Prophus stipend, meaning his official job from that point on was to not screw up his missions too badly. The stipend, though, was pitifully small.

"No wonder Marc defected," he said, gaping at the first check that came in.

You start at the bottom of the totem pole like every other rookie. Why do you think I told you to keep your job?

"How can I afford anything with this? I get more collecting unemployment!"

Bullets are expensive. Learn to shoot better.

"Do I ever get more?"

You mean like a raise? Sure, start killing Genjix or better yet, invent Quasing membrane reproduction in this atmosphere. Command would probably buy you a tropical island then.

"I'd like Moorea please."

You will have to get in line for that one.

Much to his chagrin, Roen immediately began to miss his old job. It was one of the last pieces of his normal, prior life he had left. A year ago, he would have rejoiced at being laid off and becoming a full-time agent. Now, it made him sad. He spent his first few unemployed days waking up early and staring from his balcony at the hundreds of people bustling off to work.

"I used to be one of them. I don't know if I like the new me."

There is a period of adjustment, Roen. You are simply maturing into your new role.

"Period of adjustment? Is that what you call it? I don't know who I am anymore."

Since Roen no longer had disposable income to do much else, he found himself spending more time training with Sifu Lin. Lin seemed to have finally warmed up to Roen, which wasn't saying much. The stick was still there, as were the constant verbal punishments, but more and more, Lin spent his time teaching rather than punishing.

November 15th became a day that Roen considered as important as his birthday, or whenever Jill's birthday was. That day was the first time he successfully landed a blow on Lin. Roen didn't know which of them was more shocked.

The strike resulted from a complex series of feints and side-steps – that started with Roen getting punched four times – before he caught Lin out of position, and popped him on his chubby cheeks. It was a satisfying punch. Very satisfying. Lin blinked once in surprise before he howled with laughter, and with what Roen could only presume was pride. Then Lin actually stopped training early to sit and enjoy several bottles of Lin's favorite beverage: Taiwan Beer.

Roen should have known it was a trap. After he had gotten drunk, Lin insisted on continuing their lesson. What happened afterward wasn't pretty.

The new year rolled around and Roen had just returned from a six-week-long string of assignments, culminating in a security detail escorting a prominent host. He was in Iowa as part of the protection detail for a Prophus presidential nominee. While the Secret Service officially managed the nominee's security, a dozen Prophus agents worked around the clock to ensure her safety from the real threat of Genjix assassination.

Intelligence had found a Genjix sniper team on top of a building outside the nominee's hotel. The Prophus came down in full force on the sniper team and neutralized them just before the nominee left her car. During the exchange, Roen startled a sniper trying to escape, and the sniper tripped and fell off the side of the building. The rest of the team thought enough of Roen to give him credit for the kill. Their nominee lost the Iowa primary by thirty points.

"We really know how to pick them, don't we?" he muttered as he drove back home.

We knew she was a long shot, but we had to try. Getting one of us in the White House is a real game changer.

"Still, thirty points? Stalin could run in the Iowa primaries and do better than thirty points."

Regardless, there was an attempt on her life, and we stopped it. I consider that a job well done.

"I guess. I think the Genjix could've just waited until after the primaries and saved themselves some bullets."

Roen stepped into his apartment, exhausted from the constant travel. Antonio, as usual, was working the night shift at the hospital and wouldn't be home until tomorrow morning.

It was too bad. The two hadn't spent much time together recently and Roen missed him. Roen turned on the television and surfed through the channels, pausing on CNN and ESPN. It was the usual news: the Bears weren't going into the playoffs, the Bulls' offseason was terrible, and there was an SEC investigation at two firms for securities fraud.

He tuned out the rambling commentary as he logged onto his network system and perused through Prophus news. He didn't anticipate another job for at least a week or two. Still, he diligently checked his messages and was about to log off when a new message popped up. Roen sighed and opened it, skimming over the background and going straight for his actionable items and timelines. He had thought he'd have a few days of rest at least.

Roen leaned back onto the couch and picked up his cat. The poor creature had been feeling neglected for months now and hissed as he tried to escape. He held on to the tabby as he squirmed and dug his claws into his arm. "Now, now, pussycat," he murmured.

Have you decided on giving him a real name yet?

"Nah... Meow Meow's a fine name."

No, it is not. That is like calling a dog Bark Bark.

"Actually, it would be more like Woof Woof, but I think Meow Meow sounds cuter."

Your naming habits will get your kids beat up in the schoolyard.

"Well, Roen's a pretty good name then. I got beat up quite a bit in grade school. In fact, I think I will go Freudian and blame my problems on my childhood. Was Freud a Quasing?"

No, just a con man. You should get some sleep. The briefing for the mission is tomorrow morning at the safe house.

Roen frowned as he finished reading the email, dropping Meow Meow unceremoniously off his lap. This seemed to be a more complicated mission, not like the typical low-level work he'd been doing the past year. He must be moving on up the ranks. He shrugged, went to the bathroom and stared at the mirror. His once chubby face had been replaced with a gaunt one, with dark bags under the eyes, and sunken cheeks. His hair had been cropped short months ago to keep it out of his eyes. Roen was unshaven, but not in the 5 o'clock-sexy way. He barely recognized himself. "What happened to me?" he muttered. "I don't look so good. I go from cute and fat to ugly and skinny. Why can't I just have the best of both worlds?"

You were not that good looking to begin with. Think of it as growing more distinguished with age.

With a sad little shake of his head, Roen finished cleaning up and went to bed.

The next morning, Roen walked into the safe house and looked around. He thought there would be others to meet him. The room was dark and no one was around. Immediately, he sensed that something was wrong. Over the past year, he'd learned to appreciate his spider senses when they were tingling. Now they were sending shivers up and down his spine. Roen pawed for the light switch. He caught a faint scent of citrus before someone else turned on the lights. Then he felt a soft breeze tickle his ear.

"Boo!"

Roen tried to draw his pistol but found his holster empty. He spun around, ready to fight, but instead came face to face with a grinning Sonya, now spinning his pistol around her finger.

"Sonya!" he cried, nearly fainting with relief.

She shook her other index finger at him and returned his pistol. "Tsk, tsk, Roen. I had you there. You have to be more careful in the future."

"What're you doing here?" he asked.

She walked over to a chair and sat down, putting her feet up on the table. "I am the tactical lead for your new mission, Mr Roen Tan. For the next week, you'll be reporting to me.

Command has deemed you ready for international man-of-mystery work, instead of just trolling around the Midwest."

Roen looked skeptical. "Really? Command said that?"

"Well, I had to vouch for you," she admitted. "This one is delicate. The Keeper has asked for Yol's release."

Out of the question. Tell her Yol's release is not an option.

Tao's quick retort startled Roen. "What? What does Yol's release mean?"

"Tao can fill you in," she said. "He's been hiding a Quasing from us for years now, and it's time Yol returns to us. I'm sorry, Tao, but recently, there's been a rise in network attacks on our older legacy systems. There's very few active Prophus who can manage those systems. Yol and Jeo designed most of them, and since Jeo's playing for the other team, we need Yol."

"But I thought Quasing couldn't leave hosts unless the host dies." Roen frowned.

"And who says you don't have a sharp wit?" Sonya turned, walked to her bag, pulled out a manila packet, and handed it to him. "We leave for Dublin at 1500 hours."

"Why me? Can't we use our agents in Europe?" he asked.

Sonya shook her head. "We need you on this one. More specifically, we need Tao. Unfortunately for you, you're him."

Tao was being strangely quiet about the situation. Usually, he would at least give Roen a few comforting words or berate him for whining. The silence was awkward as Roen waited for some guidance.

"Tao, speak to me. What's going on?"

There was a long pause before Tao finally spoke. By now, Roen had been with him long enough to know something was wrong. *The briefing will tell you everything you need to know. You might as well open it and find out. Sonya said something about legacy systems being compromised. If that is true, then it is serious.*

"What are these systems?"

Like most large companies, the Prophus invested heavily for several decades in mainframe and older technology. Updating those systems is quite an expensive and time-consuming endeavor, so we never did.

"What do you mean updating? Like we're not Y2K compliant?"

Please. We're infinitely old. We number our system with six digit dates. Y2K was a joke.

"How did we not protect ourselves from this sort of stuff?"

We are fallible like everyone else. Besides, the first thing to go during cuts is always the IT budget. We had a defection some time back: a Quasing named Jeo, a technical operations specialist. You met his host, Marc, at the club. We tried to eliminate his clearance after his defection, but he must have been planning this for a long time.

If there are still intrusions, then he has created a back door. Our network integrity could be compromised. If they can hit critical systems, it could be catastrophic. But we are getting ahead of ourselves. See if the documents in the packet shed any light on the situation.

Roen opened the contents and began to sift through the papers. He picked up several stacks of bound foreign currencies and put them to the side. He rifled through a thick stack of papers and sorted them into different piles. There were two packets labeled Biographies and a map of Dublin with specific areas marked in red. A separate clear bag contained several passports, plane tickets, and several false identifications.

Roen sat down and began reading through the biographies, hoping to glean the nature of his mission. Actually, he had no idea what he was looking for. The first biography recorded the background of a Gregory Blair, listing his education, accolades, and accomplishments. They were quite impressive: graduated from Oxford, three years as an officer and pilot in the Air Force, four as an Area 51 scientist, never married, honorably discharged, and a Prophus agent up until three years ago. His historical background ended abruptly with his current whereabouts unknown.

"What happened to him?"

Read on.

Roen pulled out the next biography about a Prophus named Yol. The biography dated back thousands of years to the beginning of recorded history, when Yol first joined the Quasing collective. Then it skipped a period during the Babylonian Empire where he was a minor official in the imperial court, and proceeded to run through his various hosts. Roen didn't recognize most of the names, though a few did stand out.

"Wow, Yol was Galileo and Duke Ellington? That's pretty cool. Why couldn't you be anyone like that?"

What? Are you serious? You do not think Genghis Khan or inventing t'ai chi is significant?

"I guess so, but Galileo discovered that the Earth rotated around the sun. That was pretty revolutionary back in the day."

That is such a load of crap! Galileo discovered that the Earth rotated around the sun because Yol told him! We are a spacefaring race. It is not a discovery if someone tells you! Yol's hosts are always taking credit where credit is not due. Did you know that he once claimed to discover spaghetti?

"Well, did he?"

Of course not. The Chinese did. It is called noodles.

"Whatever. You sound jealous."

Skipping the sections he thought irrelevant, Roen learned that Yol was a technology operations specialist. He had some tactical experience as a general in Napoleon's Russian campaigns and as a Japanese colonel during World War II, but otherwise he primarily occupied hosts who were artists, philosophers, and scientists.

"Talk about always picking the losing side. No wonder he decided to stick to geeking. So what is this all about? Is this Gregory person Yol as well? What does all this mean?"

Read the blue sheet.

Roen picked up a blue document which bore an official-looking seal and a signature at the bottom. "By the order of

Keeper of the Prophus Command, Tao is to provide the immediate release of Yol from his host Gregory Blair and to assist
with the integration of Lieutenant Paula Kim and Yol." Roen
frowned and leaned back in his chair. The orders were straight-
forward enough. He didn't quite understand why he or Tao
had to be involved. Couldn't any of their other agents overseas
do it? Something didn't smell right here.

Sonya came up from behind, leaned on his back, and looked
over his shoulder. "Any questions?"

He handed the paper to her. "I don't get it. Why do I have
to be the one to kill this Gregory?"

"Not you," she said, "but Tao needs to free Yol."

"Because?" Roen was getting a headache.

"Because we don't know where he is," she snapped. "Tao's
been hiding him from us for years now and with things this bad,
we need him back. Edward and Tao have refused to disclose
Yol's location, and now the Keeper is forcing matters. Look, Tao,
you've made your point, and we respect that. But more ur-
gently, a systematic controlled lockdown was initiated on a
quarter of our European safe houses. Half of our monitoring
system went down, and we lost contact with at least a dozen
field agents."

"So they want me to hack in? I don't know anything about
hacking."

"You're not going to do it," she said. "Neither is Tao. He's
passable, but not exactly a qualified expert. That's why you're
going to Dublin first. We need Yol."

"And Yol's in Dublin? Why can't he just log in and take care
of everything?" Roen threw his arms in the air. None of this
made any sense. It had never even occurred to him that there
were disagreements between the Prophus. "Well, how does
Tao hide someone anyway?"

He is in a mental institution.

"What?!" Roen exclaimed aloud.

Sonya picked up a red document. "Three years ago, Gregory was injured on a mission with Edward. Gregory was pronounced brain dead and disappeared soon after."

Roen frowned. "So Tao kidnapped a brain-damaged Gregory. Why would he do that?"

I refuse to kill an injured host simply because his usefulness is at an end. Would you like us to kill you if I ever decided you were no longer of use?

"Good point. Forget I asked."

Roen leaned back and scratched his head. "I still don't get why he would hide Gregory from the other Prophus."

Look at Gregory's last name again.

Roen looked at Sonya, horrified. "That's Edward's brother, and you want to kill him! And you're forcing Tao to do it!"

"We need Yol." Sonya sat down in front of him and clasped his hands. "Tao needs to understand that. Our ranks are thin, and Yol's a high-value operative. Command isn't oblivious to his situation. That's why they didn't force the issue earlier, but Tao, it needs to be done."

There was a long silence before Tao spoke. Roen could tell these were words he didn't want to say. *I will visit Gregory, but no promises.*

Roen relayed the message.

"Thank you," she said, and gave his hands a small squeeze. "Baji says she knows you'll do the right thing."

"So, that's the mission then?" Roen asked. "You want to take Gregory out?"

"That's the bulk of it," Sonya continued. "There are two parts to this mission. After you establish contact, assuming we have no choice but to eliminate Gregory, we'll need to move Yol to the new host. Paula Kim is already standing by in Dublin. We'll get the details once Tao lets us in on them. It could be as simple as walking in and checking Gregory out, or it could require a complicated infiltrate and eliminate scenario."

"Infiltrate and eliminate?" Roen clicked his tongue.

Infiltration is one of my specialties.

"Is that a fancy word for breaking and entering?"

Semantics, but if this mission is to go through, there are a few things we need to do. We have some loose ends to tie up.

"When do we leave?" Roen asked.

"When you get your butt to the airport," Sonya replied. "The rest of the team is already on their way there."

Tell her I need some time to take care of an important matter.

Sonya frowned and checked her watch when he told her Tao's request. "Don't bail on us, Tao. I know you're thinking about it. 1500 hours at the airport. You better be there."

Roen nodded and turned to leave. "What do we have to do, Tao?"

You will see. Prepare yourself, Roen. This is not going to be pleasant.

CHAPTER TWENTY-FOUR
LOOSE ENDS

I made my way to Spain. By then, the Black Death had passed, and a rebirth, a Renaissance, was sweeping over Europe. I ran into an old Quasing friend, Chiyva, who I thought shared my ideals. Together, we searched the land and found Rianno and Francisco Cisneros, two brothers who would be suitable hosts. The four of us were close, and it was here that I connected with other dissident Quasing, disillusioned with the decisions of the Council. It was time for a change in our approach toward humans. We began to nurture the seeds of that change.

Roen left the safe house shortly after and made the long walk back to his apartment to clear his thoughts about ending Gregory's life. In a strange way, it felt like fratricide. His head ached and it was difficult to keep his emotions in control. He just didn't know what to think.

Neither Tao nor he exchanged words as he went home. Roen spent the rest of the morning taking care of personal business. He told Jill that he was being sent to training for work by his new job and would be back in two weeks, declining her offer to pick him up at the airport. He felt guilty for giving her such short notice. She herself was only back for a month before having to head back to Frankfurt in February. Now, the few precious weeks he had planned to spend with her were cut in half. As always, Jill was understanding and supportive. Roen called his parents that he was going on a last-minute vacation with a few friends. Once he had everything packed, he stopped by Antonio's room to give him the rent check and to tell him to pick up the mail.

Antonio raised an eyebrow at Roen's explanation when Roen told him about traveling for work. "Again? You were just gone for almost two months. How can you be home only a few days before you have to leave again? These Bynum people seemed to be working you to the bone."

"It's a new job," Roen mumbled, his eyes wandering as he looked at everything but Antonio. "I want to start with a good impression."

Antonio scrunched his face as he studied Roen. Finally, he leaned back and shook his head. "You got a flush and you're trying to sell me deuces. You're bluffing about this trip."

Guy reads you like a book.

Roen didn't respond. He knew Antonio was onto him.

Antonio grinned. "You're trying to think of an excuse to lie to me right now, aren't you? I can tell. You freeze up like that every time. So spit it out, what's the deal? Where have you been traveling to?"

"Oh hell Tao, I'm just going to tell him."

We do not have time for this.

"It's Tao and the Prophus," Roen blurted out.

That is it! You are never getting sent out as a covert operative. Your weak mental fortitude will crack under pressure the moment something happens. I can see it now. Border guard: Identification please, Mr Edwardson. Roen: All right! I am a spy! Arrest me now!

"The... aliens again?" Antonio looked taken aback.

Seriously, if you cannot lie your way past your roommate, what chance do you have outside?

"I'm being sent on a mission," Roen finished lamely. "I have to go."

"You're trying to save the world because the aliens told you to?" The disbelief in Antonio's voice was painful.

I mean, can you stop telling the truth every time someone asks? Or at the very least, just tell him it is none of his business.

"I can't, Tao. He's my best friend."

"Just tell anyone who asks that I'll be back soon and that I'll call them," Roen replied aloud.

Antonio shrugged. "It's your life, buddy. But do me a favor and just be careful, wherever the hell you're off to. And if it is some girl, I am not covering for you with Jill. I like her more than I like you."

"Traitor." Roen shook his head and grinned. He turned to leave and then stopped. "Antonio, if for some reason, I don't make it back..."

Tao groaned, inwardly.

"I can have your stuff?" Antonio said cheerfully.

"Of course." Roen grinned. "But if I don't, tell everyone I'm sorry."

Antonio nodded. Roen left his apartment and felt very alone in the elevator as it sped down to the garage. The Prophus had replaced his car yet again with a busted-up black Hyundai. He wasn't sure who was responsible for picking his rides, but he was sure they were getting a good laugh at his expense. He got into his car and pulled out of the garage.

That was a little histrionic. Are you all right?

"I'll be fine, Tao. To the airport now?"

Not yet. We have an errand before we head out. Drive west toward the suburbs first. We have to make a stop in Naperville and talk to Edward's wife.

"What? Why?"

Because I owe it to Edward. Better late than never.

Roen said nothing more as he drove along Highway 88. He

occupied his mind by weaving in and out of traffic. Driving in Chicago was bad all year round, and today was no exception.

Tao spent most of the trip prepping Roen on what he needed to tell Kathy. It was still going to be a lie, but at the very least, it might give her closure. An hour later, Roen exited toward a suburban neighborhood, wrinkling his nose in disapproval at the single family homes with their freshly cut lawns.

Not your kind of place?

"I'm a city boy."

You will sing a different tune maybe when you have children one day.

"If I live that long."

Such a pessimist. Turn in here and go up three houses.

Roen pulled up next to a large blue house with an enormous yard. He got out and looked around, whistling at the large houses that dotted the block. It was a very nice neighborhood. Everywhere he looked were watered lawns, neatly trimmed bushes, and large trees not found in the city. A group of kids were playing across the street, and birds flitted among the trees. "This place is nice, if you like that kind of stuff," he said reluctantly.

One day, my friend, one day.

Roen walked up to the door and rang the buzzer. He felt uneasy and anxious, though he wasn't sure why. What did Tao need to talk to Mrs Blair for? Surely it had nothing to do with him? He heard footsteps on the other side of the door.

"Who is it?" a voice said.

"It's um... Roen. Roen Tan," he answered.

The door opened, and an attractive woman in her mid-forties appeared. She had blond hair and still looked youthful, though Roen noticed there was a touch of weariness about her, despite her friendly smile. She was dressed in jeans and a blue flannel shirt.

"I'm sorry, I don't recognize that name," she continued. "Is there something I can help you with?"

"Mrs Blair, I'm here to talk about Edward," he said.

The smile disappeared, and she gave him what he could only describe as a stink-eye. "Who are you?"

"A friend," Roen stammered. He began to recite the story they had agreed on.

Her stare intensified and she cut him off. "Edward and I were married for fifteen years. I know all of his friends and you, Mr Tan, are not one of them."

"Tao, this isn't working out very well. Did she have any idea about you?"

No. Edward was very careful about keeping his Prophus operations hidden from her. She thought he just traveled a lot.

"I... I know... Edward and I worked together," Roen stammered.

"Really? Doing what?"

"Business consulting," he said.

"What's the name of the company?" she asked.

"Bynum Consulting," he replied promptly. They were getting back on script. "I wanted to offer my condolences, and that..."

"You're a little late, Roen. My husband died ten months ago."

"I know it has been a while. I'm sorry that it took so long..."

"So do you still work at Bynum?"

"Yes. Yes, I do. I was a colleague of his for only a short time, but..."

"That's interesting." She smiled.

She is on to you.

"On to me what? I have no idea what I'm talking about."

"It's interesting," she said, "because after Edward disappeared, I tried to contact Bynum to find anything that might help me find him. Imagine my surprise when I discovered that Bynum was some dummy corporation in Brooklyn."

"Um... well, it's complicated, Mrs Blair," Roen replied.

"Complicated? Maybe you should have been the one to talk to those men from the FBI. The ones who came to my home to ask about the guns they found in his deserted car." Roen felt like a deer in headlights. This was way off script. "Or maybe you can tell me why I couldn't even pull up his information when I looked up his Social Security number!" He gulped anxiously, wilting under her gaze as she stuck her finger in his face.

"So what exactly do you do then, Mr Tan, that you worked with my husband on? Consulting? Or did you two rob banks together?" she asked.

Edward was not a criminal!

"Edward was not a..." he stammered. "It's not like that, Mrs Blair. It's not what you think."

"Frankly, I don't care anymore," she hissed, closing the door.

Roen stuck his hand through the opening as it closed. He began to talk quickly, repeating Tao's words. "I know a lot about you. I know you and Edward met shortly after West Point. I know that you wish you had a green thumb, but you've never been able to keep a plant alive for more than a month. And I know that you pretend to be a terrible cook to your in-laws because you worry his mother would try to compete with you. I know you have a bottle of Mouton-Rothschild '82 that you were saving for your twenty-year anniversary."

The door stopped just short of crushing his fingers and opened. Kathy, her eyes watering, stared at Roen in disbelief. "How did you know that?" Her voice came out a hoarse whisper.

"Mrs Blair, it's a long difficult story, one I need to explain. But the first thing I want you to know is that your husband was a great man. He died fighting for a good cause."

"He... fought? Was he in the CIA?"

"Something like that, but even more covert," Roen replied. "I can't get into details, but that's the first thing you should know. That's why he had to use Bynum as a cover. Please, I know I have a lot of explaining to do. May I come in?"

She hesitated, and then beckoned him in. He thanked her and followed, feeling very uneasy as she motioned for him to take a seat in the living room. "Please excuse the mess," she said, "I wasn't expecting company. Is there anything I can get you?"

Roen smiled. "Edward joked that you would always apologize for a messy house even though you always kept it immaculate." She looked at him in shock. Roen sat down and said solemnly, "Mrs Blair, did Edward ever talk to you about Tao?"

"Edward used to talk about Tao in his sleep. What is Tao?"

"I think you better sit down," he replied.

Then Roen told her everything; Tao felt that he owed that to Kathy. Full disclosure was something Tao rarely did, but Kathy would see through any deception, especially with a poor liar like Roen. He skipped over much of the history of the Prophus, but went into detail on Edward's life, using specifics that no one else could have possibly known. "So, this spirit... Tao, was with Edward when he died?" she asked through moist eyes.

Roen nodded.

Kathy wiped the tears that were streaming down her face and shook her head. "How did he die?"

"Please don't. It won't do any good. He was a hero and missed by all of us. You were his last thought. He told Tao to tell you that he loved you and that he was sorry." Roen paused. "Tao misses him too."

She blew her nose on a handkerchief and dabbed her eyes. "I think this story you're telling me is too fantastic to be true, but it does explain a few things. No wonder Edward knew so much about history. I always thought it was unusual for a meathead majoring in political science to know more about the French Revolution than I did."

Kathy is a history professor.

She looked Roen up and down and laughed dryly. "And it explained how he always came home from his business trips looking like he got into a fist fight. Whatever you do with these aliens, Roen, you seem to have the same problem he had. To be honest, I don't know what to believe anymore, and I really don't care. I just miss him."

Roen said, "I'm sorry you had to find out this way."

"I'm still receiving checks from Bynum. Who is sending them?"

"Our organization," Roen replied. "You'll continue receiving them for two more years. The Prophus try to take care of their own."

There was a rustling at the door, and a boy of about five walked in. He was a solemn boy with brown hair and hazel eyes. He carried a brown stuffed dinosaur in one arm. The boy studied Roen for a few seconds, and then offered his dinosaur to him. Kathy walked over and gave him a hug. "Roen, this is Tyler. Honey, this is Roen Tan. He's a friend of your daddy's."

Roen's heart sank. Edward had a son? His stomach churned at the thought of the boy having to grow up without a father. He thought back to his own family and what would happen to them if he didn't make it back. Who would tell them? Would it happen like this? One day, years after he died, some stranger would walk up to their door and try to explain how he passed away?

He stood up and went to Tyler. "It's an honor to shake your hand, young man. Your father was a dear friend of mine and a great person."

Tyler shook his hand timidly and then hugged his mother. They stood there for a few awkward moments before Tyler spoke. "Are we eating soon, Mom?"

She patted him on the head. "In a moment, dear. Would you like to stay for lunch, Roen?"

He shook his head. "I'm sorry, Mrs Blair. I can't. I have a flight to catch." She nodded and walked him to his car. As he stepped outside, he turned and offered his hand. "Thank you for your hospitality, Mrs Blair."

"Call me Kathy," she replied, giving him a warm hug. "Listen, Roen, I don't know if what you said was true. But if it is, remember those around you who love you. Make sure whatever sacrifices you make are worth it." As she spoke, more tears began to well up in her eyes.

He hugged her back and got into the car. As he drove off, Roen looked in his rear-view mirror and saw her sobbing on the driveway. He thought about his own family again. What would his parents do? He never took into consideration the consequences of his actions and how it would affect the ones he cared about. It was selfish of him.

"Tao? If something ever happens to me, you will tell my family, right?"

Of course.

"Do me a favor, tell them immediately after... after my death? Don't make them wait."

I will.

"Thanks. Where do we go now?"

Head toward O'Hare. The jet is waiting for us.

CHAPTER TWENTY-FIVE
ON THE RADAR

The Council did not tolerate our dissension, and in retaliation, called for a cleansing. The Spanish Inquisition spread across Europe, a cover for the Council to rid itself of the hosts of renegade Quasing. They called us Prophus, betrayers. They referred to themselves as Genjix, the old order. From that moment, all Quasing were forced to choose sides. It was at this moment that the war to control humanity's destiny had begun. To this day, we proudly bear the name Prophus.

Sean stood on the balcony above the docking bay floor and watched as the small army of scientists packaged the various prototypes for transportation. He brushed his hands across the railing and wrinkled his nose at the layer of dust there.

The underwater facility was not finished yet; construction was three months behind schedule and the builders were starting to cut corners in order to make up for the lost time. It was obvious to him where they were being sloppy. Sean made a mental note to remind the foreman that this was a research manufacturing facility and not some lumber store. This disgusting display of filth was unacceptable. If the prototype's electronics failed because of dust in the systems, Sean would have his head.

"Status," he said to no one in particular.

A beady-eyed project manager walked up next to Sean and bowed. "Father, the Chinook will be arriving within the hour to make the delivery to the air base. The Newfoundland base has reported that the freighter is standing by and ready to transport. Capulet's Ski Lodge is expecting us. However, there is a delay in the vat decontamination. Cleaning crews anticipate a detoxification period of four weeks before they're deemed safe for disassembly."

"And the scientists and engineers?"

"They will join the prototypes within two weeks."

"Another delay." Sean ground his teeth. This month was already a wash. Two more weeks before the team could continue on the Penetra, and a bloody month before they could even take apart the damn vat. Who knew how much longer it would require for transport and reassembly, not to mention rebuilding the control mixtures. Further and further back.

The mayor had delivered the permits as promised, but the delay in completing the production facility had hindered the research and construction of the prototypes, and the program as a whole. Add in the frequent raids from the Prophus on their supply lines, and the schedule had been falling behind. Now, with the discovery of a mole – their chief biologist no less – their entire operation was compromised, and the only option now was to move the project to southern Europe. Sean hadn't thought the Prophus had such a large presence in the Midwest. It was one of the reasons he had chosen this location.

"Unacceptable," he snapped, causing the five people around him to jump.

Your control has been disappointing. I expected better.

"No one is punishing me more than I am, Chiyva. I am shamed before the Holy Ones. I swear I will raise myself in your eyes."

Sean turned to the project manager and grabbed him by the tie. "I expect the cargo loaded and the Chinook up in the air within twenty minutes of it reaching the platform. Cancel the scientists and engineers' leave. No one is allowed out of this facility. They are to go directly to Capulet's Ski Lodge as soon as they are packed. Do you understand, Mr Cuinn?"

"Father," Cuinn stammered, "half of them are contract civilians. They'll be gone for a year. This will be the last time they can see their families."

There is a time for a whip, and there are men who respond to whips. You are misjudging those you lead.

Sean scowled, barely suppressing his rage. "You have my orders," he snarled. "And you tell those contractors working on this facility that if they don't make the next deliverable, I am docking one percent a day off their pay." He turned and stormed off. "And if they object, shoot them."

The weight of the Genjix is heavy on you, my son. Perhaps it has been too great.

"Chiyva, my purpose is to serve. I will not tolerate these failures."

When the P1 project to develop the Penetra scanner was first conceived, Sean had been honored to be the vessel given the task. When the initial theoretical designs were approved, he thought his rise to the head of the Council was all but assured. But the project had been plagued by delays.

To make matters worse, when Devin saw the bill for the Homeland surveillance of Tao, Devin nearly came down to Chicago to shoot Sean himself. Add that to Marc's complete failure to capture Roen, and it had been a very bad several months.

Control. Always be in control. Remember where I came from.

"Apologies, Holy One."

Chiyva was right. Chiyva was always right. Sean closed his eyes and took a deep breath, bringing forth the dreams his Holy One had shown him. He thought back to the hundred years Chiyva lived in the dark in captivity. He remembered his own capture with the Vietcong. This delay was nothing.

He opened his eyes and exhaled. The project was still on course, if not slightly delayed. A few months in Quasing time was insignificant. It was better to get the project right. His place on the Council would be assured, regardless of how late the project was, as long as he delivered. He was the blessed one; it was up to him to show the humans he was their better.

Sean turned and walked back to Cuinn. "Let the scientists and engineers have their leave, Mr Cuinn. Give them an extra week. It has been a difficult few months for everyone. The time off will be good for them. Let everyone know that their work is appreciated and to come back refreshed, but remind them that the next delivery date cannot be missed. Understood?"

Cuinn nodded and bowed. "They will appreciate it, Father."

Sean's phone rang. He excused himself and answered it.

Marc was on the line. "Father, the surveillance team at Kathy Blair's house picked up Roen Tan. He stayed for an hour and then left toward O'Hare Airport. Our agents followed him to a Gulfstream heading east."

Sean's mind raced. How could he take advantage of this information? "Were you able to get a satellite on it?"

"Even better. One of the surveillance team tagged it. We're tracking the plane now. It's currently across the Atlantic heading northeast. It appears he's headed to England."

England? What could Roen Tan be doing there? "How far are you behind him?" Sean asked.

"I can be on a jet by tonight. However, we might lose him if his trail is not picked up when he lands."

Sean formulated a plan in seconds. The opportunity was far too great for them to let it slip through their fingers again. Tao would be away from his safety net. If they could manage to keep tabs on him, an assault team could take him when he least expected it. "Contact the European Council; calculate the trajectory of the plane and have a surveillance team ready at whatever airport they are landing at. When can your team be ready?"

"Tomorrow at the earliest."

"You will lead the attack personally."

"As you wish, Father."

Sean hung up and smiled. Things were starting to look up.

CHAPTER TWENTY-SIX
PREPARATION

When the Genjix first struck with the Inquisition, the Prophus were unprepared for their brutal onslaught. It was swift and deadly. Many of our hosts were imprisoned and put to the question and then murdered. Those Prophus survived in rodents for years until they could make their way to other human hosts. The Genjix, who controlled the papacy and Spanish crown, waged a cleansing across all of Europe. It was a dark time. One that would set the stage for the next five hundred years.

"A beverage, sir? Coffee? Wine?"

Roen looked up at the flight attendant and smiled. He could really get used to this sort of luxury. They were in a jet that was just large enough to seat fifteen, yet an attendant was present to serve drinks. "Scotch with a touch of water, please," he responded. The flight attendant smiled and returned with a glass.

He took a small sip and looked over at the other passengers. Sonya sat next to him, and two other men took the seats across from them. Earlier that afternoon, the small group had met at O'Hare and, without a word, boarded a private Swiss chartered jet specializing in confidential travel.

Roen could hardly contain his excitement. He was playing a major role in the mission, and this flight on a private jet was what he had in mind when he first signed on as an agent. This was a far cry from the boring reconnaissance and security details he had been doing for the past year. Even his compatriots looked like they were personalities out of the movies. He half expected secret compartments to pop out any second with the nuclear launch codes at his disposal.

After drinks were served, Sonya motioned for them to gather around. As the tactical lead, she was second in command to Stephen, a senior officer from Command. The lowest man on the totem pole, Roen found it peculiar that they operated with a cross matrix hierarchy. This was Sonya's first time in this role, and he could tell she was a little nervous as well.

"Now that we're in the air and the pleasantries are over," she said, and then introduced everyone formally.

The highest-ranking Prophus here, Stephen was a dangerous looking man. With a suave, self-assured demeanor that oozed dangerous and cool, he reminded Roen of a sixty year-old Texan James Bond. He wore a sharp black suit, complete with tie, and looked more like a CEO than an agent.

Stephen patted Roen on the shoulder. "You have big shoes to fill, son."

"So I've heard," he replied dryly.

Dylan, a giant ugly mass of a man with half his face burned, chuckled. "I don't remember your mother being so serious all the time, Sonya. Now that I think about it, with you and Tao's new boy here, I suddenly feel like I'm too old for this. Maybe it's time for a desk job." The man was dressed in a pair of jeans and a brown bomber jacket. He slouched in his seat with a highball of liquor in his hand, which he had refilled liberally.

"It was time for a desk job the moment you finished your training." Stephen grinned. "But we must be too old if we're taking orders from someone we both used to baby-sit. I remember having to spank her once when she tried to lasso her dog." The two men laughed uproariously.

Sonya blushed, looking chagrined. "Stephen, Dylan, you're both my uncles and I love you, but I'm leading a team here." She gave them both a look Roen was very familiar with. She was all business right now.

Dylan held up his hands. "I'm sorry, Sonya. It's been years since we last saw you, and you've grown so much. Dania would be proud."

"You're right, though," Stephen added. "Back to business. You're in charge of this soirée. What's the plan?"

Sonya quickly took control of the meeting, speaking in a more formal manner than usual. "The mission is threefold. First, we locate Gregory and bring him to a safe house. We know he's in a hospital in Dublin, just not which one. Roen should be able to sign him out with the forged next-of-kin documents without any problems. We'll evaluate the situation from there. An agent, Paula Kim, is assigned to assist Roen with the extraction. Since he's never been out of the United States, she'll help deal with the natives."

"We're going to Ireland, not Egypt." Roen frowned. "It's not like they're speaking a foreign language. I hardly need a babysitter."

Stephen grinned. "You've obviously never tried to talk to someone with a thick Irish accent. It might as well be Egyptian. Besides, have you ever driven a car with the steering wheel on the right side? We'll be down one agent by car accident."

"It's just a precaution," Sonya assured him. "Besides, nothing personal, but no one here trusts you to navigate Dublin by yourself. We'd rather not lose you to bad map reading. Just think of her as your tour guide."

"Why do we have to bring him back to the safe house just to kill him?" Roen asked. "Why don't we just do it at the hospital?"

Stephen shook his head. "We don't do that to our own. As important as this mission is, our man's getting full honors from us. None of us would expect anything less when it's our time."

Dylan and Sonya both agreed. They saw Gregory as a comrade first and a Prophus second. He felt ashamed of his words. He didn't know the history that these people shared with the man that they were about to kill. This was as deeply personal for them as it was for Tao. As far as they were concerned, Roen was the stranger to their tightly knit family.

Roen was a little disappointed by the straightforwardness of the plan. He had imagined having to infiltrate the hospital under the cover of darkness, and then fight his way with the team up to Gregory's room to whisk him away. Walking through the front door and signing him out was decidedly unglamorous. He might as well be visiting his grandmother at the retirement home. They weren't even going to give him a gun. He had to insist on one before they relented.

Better than having to stake out a mailbox for sixteen hours. Even I wanted to poke out my eyes when we did that.

"You have eyes?"

Fine then. Poke your eyes out.

The flight attendant served dinner as they ran through the logistics of the mission and pored over the map of Dublin. One of the primary rules of engagement for both the Prophus and the Genjix, second to self-preservation, was remaining undetected in human society. It was one of the few agreements both factions strictly enforced. "Tell us about Yol's new host?" Dylan asked.

Sonya pulled a file from an envelope and laid it over the map. She pointed at the picture of a young woman. "Lieutenant Paula Kim: background in electronic counter-espionage, risk assessment specialty, and decorated field agent for Her Majesty's Secret Service. She's been an operative of ours for years. European Command feels she'll be ideal."

"Are we expecting resistance of any sort?" Stephen asked.

Sonya shook her head. "There should be no Genjix whatso-ever – a stroll in the park."

Dylan picked up the files and browsed through them. "So Paula and Roen sign Gregory out, and the rest of us will just hang out at the pool until they get back? Sounds straightfor-ward enough; best mission I've been on in years."

"Well, you insisted on volunteering," Sonya replied. "Com-mand thought this should only be a three-person operation. You two are just support."

Dylan's jolly face became serious. "Look, Gregory and I go way back. I think a forcible transfer stinks as much as the next guy, but I owe it to him." He brightened. "Besides, it's an all-expense-paid vacation. With our budgets as tight as they are these days, I'll take every perk I can get."

"So I guess the only piece of the puzzle left is which hospital Gregory is in?" Stephen said. All three looked at Roen.

Roen blinked and shrugged. "I don't know. Tao never told me."

Sonya rolled her eyes. "Would you please coax that very im-portant piece of information out of him? It is a rather crucial bit."

"Well, Tao? You heard her."

Premeditated murder on a loyal injured agent is unforgivable. There will be words with the Keeper when this is all done. Tell them these are my conditions. If Yol has to be released, it will be only by my hand. And if he is responsive at all, then the mission is off.

Roen gave Tao's terms.

Sonya bristled. "No conditions for Gregory, Tao – this isn't debatable. If there was any hope for him, he'd have come to years ago."

"His call or the mission's off," Roen snapped. "Listen, I know how important this mission is to the Prophus, but think about what you're asking. You want Tao to kill Edward's brother. And the rest of you fought alongside him. If any part of him is still in there, we abort."

Sonya began to give an angry response and stopped short. She glanced over at Dylan and Stephen. Both nodded slowly and looked away. "It'll be Tao's hand and his choice," she relented.

Thanks for supporting me.

"Bah, Tao. What are hosts for? You get my back, I get yours, right?"

You are a good man, Roen.

"Besides, if you didn't get your way, I'm sure I'll be hearing about it until the day I die, which these days, could be at any moment."

Quiet, you. The only way you can die on this mission is if you trip on the sidewalk and bang your head. Gregory is at Blackmoore War Hospital.

"Tao thanks you," Roen said sincerely. "The mark is at the Blackmoore War Hospital."

"Send a query to Intel to see if they can pull up a layout for us." Sonya looked at Dylan.

"Tao knows the layout of the facility. He's been there many times," Roen added.

"I'll pull it up anyway," said Dylan, "every little bit helps."

"Pass the information along to Paula as well," Stephen added. "Now that we have that information, when are we going in?"

Sonya looked at her watch. "We land at 0400 local time. Paula and Roen will head out first thing in the morning after visitor hours start. I suggest you all get some sleep."

CHAPTER TWENTY-SEVEN
PRELUDE

All had seemed lost. It was too dangerous to stay in Spain, for inquisitors were constantly searching for us. Our only hope was to try to survive the century and regroup. When we heard that Zoras, who was now a Grand Inquisitor, was leading an army to capture one of the last Prophus strongholds in Spain, we did the only thing we could do. Rianno and Francisco Cisneros led their small party of Prophus to a cove in the southern coast of Andalusia; we went to where a ship waited to take us across the Mediterranean Sea to the land of the Moors. We were then betrayed.

Paula Kim met them at the airport and after quick introductions, drove them to their base of operations. They settled down at a safe house disguised as an old bed and breakfast in a quaint residential part of town.

Roen marveled at the resources that the Prophus had on hand to acquire such detailed information so quickly. They pulled up doctor rotations, delivery schedules, even the vacation days that were being taken by the staff. After the meeting, the group broke apart for final preparations. Everyone went about their downtime a bit differently.

Sonya was busy poring over the maps again with Paula.

Stephen and Dylan were at a table playing cards and swapping stories. Roen sat in the corner away from the others, meticulously wiping down his FN Five-seven pistol and studying its every detail. This was the first mission that he actually felt the part of a spy instead of a glorified bodyguard. His initial excitement on the plane had long faded, replaced with doubts. The idea of what they were about to do left him with a bad taste in his mouth. He kept himself preoccupied by working on the gun.

An hour later, his gun was spotless, but Roen kept taking it apart, cleaning the parts, and putting it back together. Besides the gun, he was allowed to carry a knife in his boot and a few flash bangs. He felt almost silly walking into a hospital so heavily armed, but it was better to be prepared just in case. This was his life as a Prophus agent – possible danger at every corner, always looking over his shoulder. It was still a strange feeling, one that he couldn't quite get used to.

Stephen came over and sat next to him. "If I polished my gun as much as you are right now, my wife would get jealous. Something on your mind, son?"

Roen shook his head. "No, sir. Well, to be honest, I have some doubts. It's one thing to fight an enemy trying to kill me. It's another to take out an innocent person, an ally no less, just to free his Quasing. Before I never had to question myself if what I'm doing is right. But now..."

"You can't take deeds at face value, son," Stephen said. "Sometimes, what seems evil may prove to do good down the road. It's a brutal world we live in. It's never black and white. You have to learn to see how pushing over one domino affects the rest of the puzzle."

"I think no matter how you try to justify the good of this mission, it just feels wrong," Roen said.

Stephen scratched his chin. "I don't know about that, Roen. One of the agents we lost because of these safe house lockouts was a buddy of mine. Jack and I went back thirty years. Good man. I wouldn't be standing here if it wasn't for him on more than one occasion. I wasn't there for him when he was caught out in the open in Austria; I'd like to think that I'm doing everything in my power to make up for it. Gregory and I go back a ways; he was my friend. I know he'd think the same thing."

He paused. "I checked your files. This is your first high-level field mission?" Roen nodded. "And you have credit for a past kill?"

Roen shook his head. "Guy had two left feet and tripped off a building. I never actually shot anyone."

"Not a bad thing," Stephen said. "Just remember to respect the gun. Remember what it can do."

Roen nodded. "I really don't want to kill people."

Stephen shook his head. "Sane men never do. That makes you human. Folks who have no regard for life are the ones you have to worry about. The day you find yourself not caring if someone lives or dies is the day you should hang up your spurs and quit this line of work. It means you're losing your humanity, and that humanity is what the Prophus are fighting for." Stephen stood up and patted him on the back. "Just remember, son, always look for a reason not to shoot. You remember that and you'll be fine."

Roen watched Stephen rejoin Dylan and continue their card game. Why would Stephen tell him to not shoot? Wasn't that the reason they were here? To shoot and kill the enemy? The thought of killing someone made Roen nauseous. He just didn't want taking someone's life on his conscience. He didn't know if he could live with himself.

"Tao, I don't think I'm in the right line of work."

Roen, what you are thinking is perfectly natural. In fact, I am glad you feel this way. A natural killer who shows no remorse is not the kind of host I want to have, and not one that the Prophus needs when

life and death is on the line. Duty and responsibility are heavy things,
and not something you should treat lightly. If it is not a burden to you,
then you are *in the wrong line of work.*

Sonya came by later. She sat down next to him and grabbed
his gun, putting it aside. "Hey you, how's it going?" She put
her hand in his and he felt the small calluses on her trigger
finger.

"I was kind of hoping our first trip together would be to the
Bahamas or Vegas. This wasn't high on my list of vacation des-
tinations."

This is the part where I interrupt. You have other things to worry
about than flirting with your commander.

She chuckled. "Baji warned me about Tao and his hosts. You
need to focus on the mission."

"Warned you?" he mused. "I'm hardly a danger to anyone."

"You underestimate yourself, Roen Tan," she murmured.
"It's late. You should get some sleep."

"Aye, aye, ma'am." He saluted.

She waved him off. "Military protocol sounds silly coming
from you for some reason. Just remember; we're not in the
gym anymore." She put her hands on his shoulder and leaned
over. "You leave in four hours."

Sleep did not come easily that night. Restless with anticipation, Roen spent the quiet hours tossing around in bed. He
envied the two older men sharing a room with him as they
slept, seemingly oblivious to their surroundings. It figured that
the only time he actually needed to sleep, he couldn't.

Relax. You are as jumpy as a kid on prom night.

"I never went to prom."

You know what I mean. Settle down a bit. Take a deep breath.

"How do they sleep so well?"

Experience, many years of it. One day, you will be like them too.

"If I live that long."

Hush, sunshine.

Roen sat up in his cot and started counting seconds of the clock. His lack of sleep just exacerbated his mood. Not a good way to start his budding career as a real spy.

He lay back down and stared at the ceiling, his mind wandering randomly. Would his parents understand? Would his dad be proud? Would they get some kind of severance if he died? Kathy seemed to be getting something. Should he give some to Jill? If something happened to him, would she think he just blew her off?

What about Antonio? After all, he does pay half the rent. What about his cat? Roen had heard about people who put their pets in their will. Maybe he should have a will drawn up. Maybe he should become an organ donor, but who would want organs riddled with bullet holes?

Roen.

"Yes, Tao?"

Go to sleep.

CHAPTER TWENTY-EIGHT
GREGORY

There, in a quiet cove on an icy winter day – with a ship anchored just off the shore – Francisco Cisneros betrayed us and slew Rianno, declaring himself a Genjix. Just as I had committed the ultimate betrayal of my hosts, my friend and brother Chiyva had done the same to me. Grieving for a lost host and friend, I fled into the forest and was fortunate to find a deer. For the next few decades, I plotted my revenge.

Roen struggled against fatigue the next morning. What passed for coffee at the safe house didn't help, and the food stored there was the kind that belonged in nuclear bomb shelters. How this place passed for a bed and breakfast was beyond him.

The one thing that was well stocked here was their selection of teas. He had always thought the British obsession with tea was a stereotype in campy movies. Not so. The sheer combination of tea blends and mixtures and condiments required a series of alchemical decisions that would have befuddled his chemistry professor. When he finally settled on drinking his tea plain, Paula shook her head in amusement, muttering something about primitive Americans under her breath.

Roen and Paula left for the hospital right after breakfast. The car ride was quiet; hardly a word was spoken between them.

He spent the time looking out the window and studying his guide. Paula was a somber looking woman in her early thirties with a slender but muscular build. She had a handsome face with sharp Asian features, and the look of someone who was always in control. Roen didn't want to admit it, but he was totally intimidated by her. She approached her assignment chaperoning him as seriously as if she was about to assassinate the pope.

The car rumbled down the cobbled street with a low growl as the engine struggled to navigate the hilly incline near the outskirts of town. Blackmoore War Hospital was a long-term care facility that treated all sorts of illnesses ranging from cancer to leprosy.

The Prophus as well as the Genjix had long used facilities like these all over the world to house their people. Schizophrenia and other mental illnesses were common among their hosts. According to their research, two per cent of documented schizophrenic patients were hosts overburdened by the strain of their Quasing.

Roen realized that no matter what type of fieldwork he did, there was lots of waiting. After an hour-long car ride through morning traffic, they reached the hospital only to wait another thirty minutes before the dour-faced woman at the front desk called his name. There, they were escorted to the psychiatric ward holding room by a bored orderly, where they waited another twenty minutes before a young nurse in pink scrubs finally took them to Gregory's room.

"Is this it?" Paula asked as they moved to the room labeled 3005.

Roen nodded. He moved his hand to the handle and slowly turned it. However, something stopped him from opening it. He froze, a wave of intense dread sweeping over him. Roen stood there immobile for several seconds. "I don't know if I can do this."

I am not sure if I can either.

Paula put her hand on his arm. "You all right?"

He didn't answer. He kept on staring. This opened the way into a part of Tao's past that he wasn't ready to confront.

"Do what you have to do, Roen. I'll stand watch outside."

He glanced at her worried face once and then back at the door. Summoning what seemed an unnecessarily exorbitant amount of strength to finish turning the handle, he finally went inside and closed the door behind him.

Roen stood in a barren room barely larger than his closet at home. There was a small table and chair against a wall and a bed on the far end. An old looking man in a common green hospital gown sat in a wheelchair facing the wall. This must be Gregory. He made no sign that he heard Roen enter. Roen stood at the door, unsure if he should announce himself.

Moments passed; Gregory didn't even twitch a finger. Roen had never seen a picture of him, but somehow felt an immediate kinship with him. Gregory had a faraway empty look as he stared forward. Roen grabbed the chair and scooted it closer to Gregory. The metal chair made a fingernail-to-chalkboard screeching noise as he dragged it along the tiles.

"Hello, brother," Tao whispered in a hushed tone through Roen as he sat down.

Gregory didn't respond.

Roen leaned over and caressed the other man on his forehead. He repeated Tao's words the best he could, though much of it was so painful for him to say. "I'm sorry I haven't been able to visit as much as I liked. I see that the years haven't been kind to you. You lost all your hair and you stopped working out." He tried to chuckle as he spoke, but it came out as a sob. Gregory continued staring forward, still showing no signs of life. Roen bit his lips and continued. "You might not recognize me, but it's Edward. Well, it's not really Edward anymore, but it's Tao. Can you hear me?"

Gregory gave no answer. A bubbling despair began to boil from Roen's stomach and stopped short at his throat. While the man sitting before him was technically not his brother, the emotions he felt from Tao nearly overwhelmed him. A tear escaped his eye, and he found himself shaking. This was the man he was supposed to kill today. He was a Prophus agent. And now that Gregory was no longer of use to them, they wanted Roen to kill him. One day in the future, it could very well be Roen sitting here in a plain room of a psychiatric ward.

"I... I know what you're thinking," he managed. "I say I'm Tao, but I don't look like Edward. Well, I have some bad news; Edward's dead. I'm Tao's new host. You know how it goes. The body dies, but the spirit lives on. Who would've thought that you'd live longer than Edward, huh? The world's a crazy place. I'm Roen. I guess this makes us half-brothers in a way."

Roen couldn't stand sitting there any longer. He stood up and exhaled. Grabbing Gregory's hand, Roen started shaking it desperately for any signs of life. The reality of the second part of the mission came crashing down on him as hard as any punch from Lin or Sonya. The very thought of euthanizing Gregory, even in this state, made Roen nauseous.

Tao sorted through his memories with Gregory and Edward. "Do you remember what happened when you felt Yol's presence? You said it was like you just met your soul mate. Remember when I teased you about that? How I said now that you found your soul mate, you never had to leave the house again? I was proud when you joined the Prophus family. I hate what's happened to you. That's why I'm here, brother. The Prophus need Yol back badly. You need to wake up right now."

His earpiece crackled and Sonya's voice came over their secured frequency. "Paula, Roen, we need to bring you in right away! Intelligence just reported that one of the Genjix satellites altered course last night and moved over Ireland. It's on a trajectory toward Dublin. You've been compromised. Secure

Gregory and take him to the delta spot. Switch cars before you bring him back."

Paula opened the door and ran in. "Did you get that, lad? Time's up."

Roen opened his mouth, dumbstruck. His memories of the Genjix from the night club returned as if it were yesterday. He stared at her, unsure of what to do. Paula drew her pistol. "Take the wheelchair," she commanded. "We're getting out of here now."

"But I still need to check him out," Roen protested. "They'll think we've kidnapped him."

"No time. If the Genjix have tracked us, they can take out both Yol and Tao in one attempt. We can't let that happen. Take Gregory to the back entrance. I'll get the car and rendezvous with you there. If anyone stops you along your way, take them out."

Roen released the safety on his gun as Paula left the room. He put it in his jacket pocket. Nervously, he gripped the handle of the wheelchair and felt his heart racing. Roen tried to block out his fear as he pushed Gregory out the door and wheeled him down the hallway. The fact that Gregory's life was in his hands gave him that extra amount of courage to focus on the task at hand.

The back ramp can take you to the first floor. Do not take the elevator; it might be watched.

"Was it the third or fourth door? I don't remember. What if someone tries to stop me?"

The security guards here are armed. Talk your way through or knock them unconscious. Do not draw unless they fire first.

"Shouldn't I shoot them before they get a chance to shoot me?"

Guards will not shoot on sight. Genjix will.

"Well, getting shot at first is a lousy way to find out."

Shooting an innocent guard is even worse. Turn right here and take the third door on your left. Take the ramp down. There should be a double door at the far end.

Roen obeyed and pushed Gregory down the hall as fast as he could, almost tipping the wheelchair over a few times in his haste. He burst through the double doors, looking frantically for the car. They were in a large gravel lot with only a few parked cars, nowhere near enough cover. Paula was nowhere to be seen.

Gritting his teeth, he rounded the corner and came face to face with a menacing-looking man in black. Roen immediately knew it must be a Genjix agent, not so much because the man dressed like he was a card-carrying member of the assassins' guild, but because the man was pointing an assault rifle at his face.

Roen blinked, frozen in surprise for a split second, and then dived to the side, tipping the wheelchair over and dragging Gregory down too. Bullets flew overhead, hitting the wall just behind them. Panicking, he tugged at his gun in his jacket, only to fumble as it came out. He stared in horror as the assassin lowered the rifle straight at his head.

Cut the knee. Use the gravel. An image of a gladiator fight appeared in his head. Whoever he was at the time grabbed a handful of sand.

Roen's training kicked in every time Tao gave orders. He grabbed a fistful of gravel and threw it into the face of the Genjix agent. Then as the man was distracted, Roen kicked out and swept him at the ankle. The Genjix agent tumbled to the ground. Roen picked up his FN Five-seven and put two slugs into the man's chest. Hands shaking, Roen let his pistol slip from his grasp and crawled over to the fallen man. His eyes were wide open and lifeless. Roen reeled backward in shock, falling onto his butt. He couldn't tear his eyes from that blank dead stare.

Get a hold of yourself, Roen!

He stared at the small pool of blood expanding from the body, staining the gravel with red.

Snap out of it! We have to get out of here.

Roen put his hand on his forehead, shaking uncontrollably. Whatever shock he thought he would feel for his first kill was nothing compared to the avalanche of sudden remorse that seized him. Another man wearing the same black uniform appeared around the corner and pointed a rifle at him. Roen could do nothing but stare at the gun muzzle. The man mouthed something silently and gestured with his rifle in slow motion. Roen could not hear a thing. His eyes wandered between the man and the dead body lying before him.

Listen to me! Listen to my voice!

He couldn't make out that incessant buzzing in his ear. What was that from? The man cautiously approached Roen, still waving the rifle threateningly. Then his body suddenly stiffened and he slumped over. Paula hopped out of a car and ran to Roen. She knelt down and shook him.

"Get up, Roen! Damn it, get up!" she yelled.

He looked up at her with a puzzled expression. He could hear the words, but wasn't quite sure what they meant. Paula leaned back, gave him one measured look, and then slapped him hard. Time sped up again.

"What? What are you doing? You hit me!" He blinked.

"I'm trying to keep your bloody arse alive. That is what I'm doing. You have your wits about you, man?" she snapped. "How's Gregory? Are either of you injured?"

"He's... I don't know."

In that moment of near death, he had forgotten about his ward. Some protector he turned out to be. He found Gregory face down on the gravel. Roen checked him for any injuries. He seemed unharmed. Then, Roen turned back to Paula just in time to see three more Genjix agents appear around the corner. Instinctively, Roen barreled into her and pushed her to safety. He felt the zing of bullets fly past overhead as they both crashed into the ground. He landed hard and had to reorient himself. Paula, on the other hand, had already taken out one of the Genjix with a headshot and was exchanging fire with the others.

Careful. Marc is one of those three.

Roen recognized the large dark man as the same Genjix who led the attack at the club. His threat advisory level jumped from red to stark terror. He had to keep it together for Paula and Gregory's sakes. The Genjix agents spread out as Paula desperately tried to keep them at bay. She dove behind the driver's side door and yelled, "Get in!"

Still too frazzled to think, Roen dumbly did as he was told. He wrapped his arms around Gregory's waist and dragged him toward the car as Paula laid down heavy suppression fire. The Genjix agents returned fire, kicking up the ground near Roen's feet. Then just as Roen was about to throw Gregory into the back seat, a concussive explosion knocked him off his feet. Grimacing in pain, he checked his body for the gunshot wound, only to find none. Horrified, he looked over and saw blood dripping down Gregory's chest. Roen hefted Gregory up and threw him in the car.

"Let's go!" he yelled as he jumped inside the back. Paula shot off one final burst before getting in and driving away. As they pulled away from the hospital, Roen looked into the rear mirror and saw Marc gesturing at two gray cars that pulled in next to him. He got in one and was soon giving chase.

"What's the situation?" she shouted as they sped off.

He looked up, still a little in shock.

Snap out of it. People are depending on you.

"How many do we have behind us?" she yelled.

He looked behind them. "One... no, two cars," he answered.

Tell her the type, number of agents, and armaments you see if possible. Give her as much information as you can.

"Sorry, Tao." He told her everything he saw before they turned the corner.

"Paula, Roen, I need a status," Sonya's voice crackled over the comm. "Is the package secure?"

"The package is secure, but damaged," Paula confirmed. "We have two incoming: gray four-door sedans, eight agents, at least one Genjix."

"How badly damaged?"

"Stomach wound. High possibility of bleeding out."

"Get to the delta and switch cars. Stephen and Dylan are already on their way to intercept. You are to proceed back to the nest immediately. Do not deviate."

"Roger."

Paula looked over at Roen. "Get some pressure on the wound."

"I'm sorry," Roen mumbled as he pressed down on Gregory's bloodstained shirt.

"You did fine," Paula exclaimed. "No time for apologies now."

"I didn't mean to freeze up."

"Don't worry about it." She turned to look at him sympathetically. "It happens to the best of us. Now, keep a lookout in the back and be my eyes for the tails."

Paula weaved recklessly through traffic, but the two cars gained on them bit by bit. Every time Roen thought they had lost them, the gray sedans would appear around the corner. They inched closer and closer until they were only a few car lengths behind. Then suddenly, a white van came out from the corner of Roen's eyes and rammed into the side of the lead gray sedan.

"Dylan just initiated contact," Sonya's voice crackled over the comm. "Get the package back home safely."

As the second sedan swerved to avoid Dylan, a jeep came from behind and slammed into its rear. The gray sedan swung sideways and flipped into the air. "We got you covered,

Paula," Stephen's voice popped up on the earpiece. "Get our boys home."

Paula sped away from the accident. They switched cars at the delta location and drove through several additional back streets before finally arriving at the safe house. Roen bolted for the bathroom and threw up. It was a good thing he hadn't eaten much that morning. He hung over the toilet and closed his eyes, the images of Gregory and the assassin's blank face haunting him.

Roen sat on the tiled floor for a good twenty minutes before he felt well enough to come out. Whatever he thought he knew about being a secret agent was completely different than what it really was. One thing for sure... one damn thing for sure; whoever glamorized this in the movies had some serious issues.

CHAPTER TWENTY-NINE
SAFE HOUSE

Over the next forty years, Francisco Cisneros became the most powerful man in Spain. A cardinal and a regent, he wielded power second to only the pope. Chiyva's rise coincided with his host. He was now one of the most powerful Genjix on the Council. Together, they hunted the Prophus and sowed chaos amongst the humans. Francisco lived until he was eighty-one. Chiyva had planned his succession carefully, and groomed an heir for his transition so work would continue uninterrupted for another generation. That is, until I got my revenge.

The room was eerily quiet as the others stood by the windows and checked for signs of a possible attack. Dylan had returned before Paula and Roen and looked none the worse for wear except for a bruised cheek and a gash along his arm. Stephen came a bit later, favoring his left leg.

Everyone geared up and manned a defensive perimeter inside the house. Dylan was up front, Sonya in the rear, and Stephen somewhere in the attic with what they referred to as a pulse automatic Gatling gun. Roen had no idea what that was, but it sounded ominous. It definitely was not in any of the manuals he read. He was too shaken up to care, though. Paula was bandaging Gregory's wound. All Roen could do was sit in one of the chairs and stare as she frantically tried to staunch the bleeding.

Now that he was officially a killer, he realized that he no longer wanted this life. "Get it together," he muttered, rocking back and forth.

They kept watch for another hour before Sonya walked into the room and laid her rifle on the table. "I think we're clear. I don't think they found the safe house. Intel has a satellite on the location anyway. They'll keep us in the loop. We're in too heavily populated of an area for them to make a daytime assault, anyway. We need to see to Gregory and make a decision." She moved over to him, still staring blankly at the wall, and took his hand. "Hello, Gregory," she said. "This is Baji. I'm Dania's daughter, Sonya. It's an honor to meet you. Yol, I can tell you're in there. Can you take control and say anything?"

Gregory remained expressionless. The others gathered around. Everyone laid a hand on him and closed their eyes. It reminded Roen of one of those healing prayer circles he attended in college church. No one ever got healed, but it was a good way for him to get close to some girls. Right now though, Roen screamed inside for Gregory or Yol or God or anyone to say anything. The silence was deafening.

"If a Quasing can control us when we're unconscious, doesn't it mean that Yol's not inside?" Roen said desperately, grasping at straws.

Stephen, who had a hand on Gregory's shoulder, shook his head. "Camr says he can feel Yol in there. There's no doubt about that."

"Then it proves that Gregory's still there. That's why Yol can't take control!"

"I'm sorry, son," Stephen said sadly. "Gregory's brain damage is likely permanent and he's no longer there. Quasing control their hosts through the brain functions. If the brain functions are gone, then there is no way to establish any sort of control." He turned to Paula. "Are you ready?"

She nodded solemnly.

I am afraid he is right. When I first brought him to the hospital, Yol was able to perform basic rudimentary movements: shake his head, nod, move his lips. The doctors performed three surgeries and I had hoped he just needed time to recover. We have to assume the worst.

Sonya handed him a small syringe. "I'm sorry. Time's up." Roen stared at it dumbly. "It's up to you." She patted him gently on the back. "It'll take about ten minutes to take effect."

Roen removed the cap of the syringe and looked at the sharp needle. He pursed his lips and shook his head. This was not what he signed up for. Suddenly dizzy, he felt the need to sit down again. He placed the syringe on the table and looked down at Gregory. "I don't know if I can do this."

I know how you feel, but I think our answer is clear. Gregory is never coming back. And if anyone is going to do it, it should be us.

Fighting back tears, Roen picked up the syringe, and with shaking hands, inserted it into Gregory's vein. For the next few minutes, nothing happened. He had half expected convulsions or thrashing or some violent reaction to whatever poison was in there. Then just as Roen began to think that it didn't work, Gregory's eyes widened and he inhaled sharply. His body relaxed and slumped over. His face now had the look of someone who was sleeping and finally at peace.

Stephen and Dylan put their hands on Gregory's forehead and murmured in unison, "Return to the Eternal Sea. Your soul will live always."

Behind them, Paula gasped and fell to her knees. Sonya and Roen turned and ran to her side. "Yol?" Sonya asked.

Paula nodded, her eyes squeezed shut as she dry-heaved. She stayed on her knees for several moments as if trying to catch her breath. Finally, she looked up with watery eyes and whispered. "Gregory thanks you. Yol does too."

Dylan knelt down and helped Paula to her feet. "Paula, just be Yol's mouth and repeat his words for us. How are you doing, old friend?"

Paula looked at him, eyes groggy. "God, what happened to your face?"

Dylan grinned. "Sure sounds like Yol. Welcome back. I'm sorry about Gregory."

She turned to Stephen and managed a weak smile. "Still a stiff with a suit after all these years?"

Stephen chuckled and patted her on the back. "That's Yol all right."

Paula looked up at Sonya. "So this is Dania's little girl and Baji's new host. I haven't seen you since you were very young, Sonya. I'm sorry about your mother." She turned to Roen with a touch of sadness. "How did Gregory outlive Edward?"

Roen opened his mouth, but no words came out. He had heard the story about Edward's death many times, but now he couldn't bring himself to say the words. His eyes filled with tears. He mumbled, "Sorry," and turned away.

Paula gave him a sympathetic look and nodded. "I need to see what the damage is. Roen, could you be a dear and get me a cup of tea?" He nodded. "Earl Grey tea steeped for precisely three minutes, with a splash of non-fat milk afterward, and two spoonsful of sugar; brown please. Thanks, dear," she added. Roen shook his head as he tried to memorize the concoction as he went to the kitchen.

Fifteen minutes later, the group huddled around Paula as she worked on the servers and firewalls. It was a dizzying array of systems, subsystems, and assembly code which made Roen's head spin. She typed at a blinding pace, fingers blurring on the keyboard as she moved back and forth between programming languages and scripts as she navigated through multiple windows all at once.

"Damn, I'm bloody good," she crowed as she leaned back

and stretched, admiring her handiwork. Roen couldn't quite put his finger on it, but there was a new element of histrionics in her actions that was noticeably absent from her mannerisms before. Paula turned and presented the screen with a flourish.

Dylan chuckled. "I guess we're getting somewhere. It's quite eerie how fast Yol's personality infects his hosts."

"What did you do?" Stephen asked. "Has the back door been closed?"

She nodded. Paula added, "The Genjix connection has been severed."

"That was quick," Dylan said. "How did you do it?"

"Root password propagated through single sign on." She grinned. "Simple as that."

"I thought Jeo changed all that," Sonya said.

"He had what we call sudo root control, not *root* root. No one knows *that* root except for yours truly."

"So," Stephen asked. "Why was this root access not logged into our central archives?"

"Because of situations exactly like this." Paula smirked.

"What if we had lost you to the Eternal Sea?" Sonya asked.

Paula shrugged. "You weigh your risks. If Jeo had full root access, all we could do is pull the plug on the actual boxes and pray. Every creator of our systems makes his own back door. It's a security loophole we leave for ourselves. Since I designed most of the security systems, I made my own back door. It's not like you were missing it. You didn't even know it existed. And no, I won't give it out."

"We can talk about protocol later," Stephen said briskly. "What's the damage?"

"Let me check," Paula said, sitting down and typing furiously. The screen moved at a blinding pace again as she navigated through a series of complex windows and maps.

Roen had no idea what he was seeing, let alone make sense of the complexity of the system. Several minutes passed by as she pulled up map after map of Europe and Russia. She paused every few seconds to scribble something on a piece of paper and then continued to type.

Feeling useless and sick, he left the room and went to the kitchen. There, he poured himself a scotch and waited, running the recent events over and over in his head. Looking down at the dried blood still on his hands, he got up and washed them at the sink. In all his life, Roen had never thought he'd end up where he was at right now. He was a guy who got squeamish watching horror movies. How did his life get this way?

"Tao," he muttered. "Tao got me this way."

I know you are upset. We can talk this over.

"Talk it over?" Roen bit his lip. "What's there to talk about? We just had a shootout at a hospital, and I killed someone."

You saved Paula's life today and performed your duties admirably.

"They're really not my duties, Tao. I'm doing your job. You know, I've been working so hard to become what you all wanted. I thought this was what I wanted as well. But now, I don't like who I've become. This isn't me."

Roen, no one should have to do this, but we have no choice. You do this not only for me, but for your species. We are in this together.

Roen shook his head in disgust and downed his scotch. "Stop fooling yourself. We're not in this together. I'm an unwilling participant." He sat back down at the chair and poured himself another drink, swirling the scotch in the cup.

I am sorry you feel this way. I truly am, but what options do we have? Do we just let the Genjix win?

Roen grimaced and closed his eyes. "Perhaps. Perhaps you can't, but I still can. This isn't the life for me."

Sonya walked into the room and looked disapprovingly at the half-empty bottle of scotch. "Paula's done," she said. "I thought maybe you'd be interested in seeing what your hard work has accomplished." At this point, Roen couldn't care less what Paula had found, but he followed Sonya back into the living room.

Paula had a look of satisfaction when they rejoined the group. "I got some good news and some bad news. Which one first?"

"The bad," Sonya, Dylan, and Stephen all said at once. Roen shook his head. What a bunch of pessimists.

"The Genjix got into the network through UDP subnet traffic, getting past our firewalls through a hidden account that Marc hid in the systems. He must have planned his defection for months. We had half a dozen minor systems compromised."

"So what's the good news?" Sonya asked.

"The good news is that it's only half a dozen minor systems. Marc isn't as good as I thought he was, or it could have been much worse. By the way, the most recent Genjix activity was yesterday. They located the stockpile in northern Africa and managed to disable the security. You can bet they're moving on it within the week."

Stephen turned a slight shade of green and cursed. "That's twenty percent of our global armaments! Who do we have defending it?"

"The security detail says less than two dozen non-Prophus guards," Paula replied.

"That's the good news?" Sonya demanded.

"That doesn't sound like good news at all," Dylan added. "Sounds like pretty horrible news if you ask me."

Paula shrugged. "It's actually better than I thought it'd be. We lost a lot of redundant systems and have a couple dozen or so safe houses compromised. If we move quickly, we can relocate the stockpile before the Genjix get their hands on it. It could've been much, much worse. I don't know why you guys didn't update these systems like Yol told you to years ago." Sonya and Dylan looked at Stephen, who managed to look a little embarrassed.

Stephen is on the finance committee.

Stephen raised his hands defensively. "Do you know how much it costs to update all those systems? We have a war to pay for, and munitions and medical bills aren't cheap."

Sonya looked at Dylan accusingly. "Yeah, stop getting shot so much!"

"And you stop shooting so much!" he shot back.

Paula handed Stephen the piece of paper she'd been writing on. "Here's the compiled list of all the compromised safe houses and systems. Get that out to Command."

Stephen nodded and took the paper. "Good job, Yol. I'll get this to Abrams and the fleet immediately. Now, if you will excuse me, I need to order a force to the stockpile. Clean up and close shop. I want us to be ready to leave within the hour. Good work, everyone."

Roen looked up, startled. "Wait, did he say fleet? Tao, we have a fleet?"

It is not large; nothing to write home about, but sizable enough for an amphibious land invasion if necessary.

"Where the hell do they moor it? I mean, do other countries lease out docks for warships?"

Depends on the country. The Genjix pay pretty exorbitant sums to Sweden to house theirs. We pay much less hiding ours off the Ivory Coast. We are organized much like any other government with different departments, governing bodies, and fiscal budgets to manage. The only difference is we do not have a country of our own.

Sonya took charge as soon as Stephen left the room, ordering the others to start packing. "Stephen's calling in a strike. We leave for Africa in the morning."

The thought of going to another firefight gripped Roen with dread, not because he was frightened, but because the thought of possibly killing another person made him ill. He wavered on his feet before he sat down on the couch. He watched the others pack for a few minutes before walking back into the kitchen and pouring another scotch.

Tomorrow, they would land somewhere in Africa and do it all over again. They would shoot at the Genjix, and the Genjix would shoot back. At the end of the day, everyone would rest so they could do it all over again the next day. It was like they were in Valhalla or something, except it was real. For Roen, this was hell. He felt trapped.

Roen, it is understandable...

"Shut up, Tao. I don't want to hear it."

Stephen came in and looked at the bottle. He looked as if he were about to say something and then stopped. Then he took out a glass from the cupboard and sat down next to Roen, pouring himself some scotch. Stephen lifted it up to Roen and downed the drink with one gulp. "Let me guess: you hate yourself, you hate Tao, you probably hate me, and you just want to go drown yourself in a bottle somewhere as far away as possible, right?"

"Well," Roen said grudgingly, "I don't hate you, I think. You just about nailed everything else though." He paused. "How did you know?"

Stephen emptied the rest of the scotch into both their glasses and then threw the bottle into the garbage. "It's all over your face, son. I know exactly what you're going through. I went through the same thing."

"But you're one of the leaders of the Prophus," Roen stammered. "How can you be as pathetic as me?"

Stephen shrugged. "I was a line cook in New Mexico when Camr's old host stumbled into the restaurant, bleeding out of his head. Guy died right in front of me. Jim was his name." Stephen lifted the glass up in a salute. "I was a damn good cook too, a white boy who cooked Mexican food in a part of the country that was half Mexican. You have to be good to survive those critics. I was younger than you, maybe twenty or so when he transitioned into me. By the time I was twenty-two, I was off on my first mission. By the time I was twenty-four, I told Camr to kiss my ass and left. Didn't talk to the jerk for five years."

"You left the Prophus? Why?"

Stephen grinned. "Everyone leaves the Prophus at one point in their life. Hell, it's practically a rule, kind of like how every little girl runs away from home at least once in her life. Every agent who's been drafted tries to get away at least once too, or in Dylan's case, four times."

"How'd they drag you back?" Roen asked.

Stephen chuckled. "Drag me back? I begged to come back once a couple of things changed my mind about them. First of all, I found out the Genjix got Mondale on the Democratic ticket. I knew they were up to no good then. Second of all, once you open Pandora's Box, you can't put that stuff back in. Do you think you can sit on the sidelines knowing everything you know now?"

"I don't know."

Stephen held the glass up to Roen and they touched glasses. Then he waited until Roen finished the entire drink before he put his own down, untouched. He stood up and patted Roen on the back. "Well, I'm giving you time to find out and sending you home. You think things over and come back when you're ready. To be honest, I never agreed with the way the Keeper pushed your training, Tao or no Tao. The Quasings are important, but it's the humans who support them who do all the hard lifting. If she has a problem with it, she can take it up with me. This would be a lot to take for anyone with a civilian background."

"Home? What about Africa?"

Stephen shook his head. "Not with where your head's at. You have some thinking to do."

"What if I'm never ready?" Roen said in a small voice.

Stephen turned and walked toward the door. "Then count yourself blessed and don't come back."

• • • •

Sean stared impassively at the screen at a chastised Marc. This was the last straw. Could he be so incompetent? The assessment on Jeo showed anything but incompetence. Unimaginative, yes; but an unmitigated failure, no. Still, two botched ambushes.

It could be that Tao's host was now fully trained and had become the second coming of Miyamoto Musashi, but Sean doubted that as well. All reports indicated a long-term project. He should have been ripe for the picking after only a year of training. Sean knew Tao was good, but could he be that good? The responsibility ultimately fell on Sean; he accepted that. Now, he was going to correct his mistake.

"You imbecile," Sean snarled. "How the Holy Ones could have blessed you with one of their own is beyond me. That boy was never even in the Boy Scouts, let alone military training, and you lost him twice now!"

"Father," Marc began, "I have found a solid lead on another senior..."

"Utter another word and I will order you to draw your pistol, put it in your mouth, and pull the trigger," Sean growled. "I'm tired of your empty promises. Your standing is nothing now. I am removing you from the Tao mission. Your place is now at my side on security detail and filling my wine glass and doing my laundry until such time that I feel like you can handle tasks that do not require an apron!"

"But–" Marc stammered.

"Agent Sandis," Sean barked at Iku's vessel. "You are in charge of the team now. If that moron standing next to you utters another word, shoot him in the head." Sandis, looking grim, drew his gun and pointed at Marc's head.

"Anything else to say?" Sean snarled. "You are damn lucky your security exploit resulted in some benefits for us. Otherwise, I would be more than content to extract Jeo from that sham of a host and give him to someone who deserves a Holy One. Now get out of my sight." Sean turned the screen off and stared at it for a few moments longer. Nothing more could be done about these recent failures. At the very least, on the bright side, he now had a new butler.

"Third time's a charm, Tao," he muttered. "I still owe you."

CHAPTER THIRTY

BACK HOME

On his deathbed, Francisco Cisneros brought Paneese, his protégé, into his chambers and together, they prayed and waited for Francisco to die. Chiyva hoped for a smooth transition to continue his work and assure his place on the Council.

Since Rianno's death, I had prepared for my vengeance. On the day of Francisco's death, I struck. Disguised as a priest, I walked into Francisco's room, closed all the windows, and slew Paneese before the transition could be made. Then I revealed myself to Francisco and slew him as well. I took out a small baby turtle and placed it next to Francisco's bed. Chiyva had no choice but to join with it instead. Then for the next hundred years, I imprisoned him.

Roen went home the next morning, feeling relieved and ashamed. He couldn't look the others in the eye as he said his goodbyes. They all gave him sympathetic looks and told him to get some rest. He wished them luck and took the lonely flight back to the States by commercial airline.

Sitting in coach on the way back was a far cry from the private plane he flew out to Europe, underscoring just how his status had fallen. Roen returned to Chicago and promptly withdrew from everyone. The few times Tao tried to speak with him, Roen ignored him. Roen spent the first few days sitting on his balcony drinking and watching the clouds pass by. He often woke up in the middle of the night with Gregory's eyes haunting his dreams.

It didn't help his mood when he learned that the Prophus failed to secure the base in Africa. The Genjix had successfully raided the stockpile and removed the majority of the armaments before the Prophus even got there. By the time the Prophus assaulted the base, the Genjix were thoroughly entrenched and repelled them during two frantic days of battles. The news went downhill from there. Both Paula and Sonya were injured before the Prophus finally ordered a withdrawal.

The ensuing fight was a disaster for the Prophus; they also lost a warship and over thirty agents, three of them hosts. Could he have made a difference? Probably not. Could he have saved Sonya and Paula from getting injured? Possibly. Regardless of the scenarios that could have happened, he was never going to find out, because when push came to shove, he gave up and went home. Yes, Stephen had ordered him to, but Roen didn't contest it. Instead, he accepted it. In fact, he was downright relieved.

He struggled with his decision to leave, wondering if it meant that he was a coward. Then again, when had he ever been brave? It seemed a year of training hadn't improved his courage. Or maybe it was something deeper? Was it not so much his courage, but his objection to a life of killing and war? Or was he simply hiding his fear behind some facade of morality? Roen didn't know the answers.

At first, he thought Tao would try to guide him out of whatever was happening with him, but Tao was uncharacteristically silent. It felt strange to have that voice missing in his head. Roen didn't want to admit it, but he missed Tao. It was as if a part of him had just disappeared. And with Tao's absence, Roen again lost any semblance of purpose in his life.

"Tao, am I a coward?"

Oh? Are you speaking with me again?

"Forget it."

There was a pause before Tao finally spoke in a calm, soothing tone, as if speaking to a child. *No, Roen, you are not a coward. You are no more a coward or fearful than any of my other hosts.*

"You mean Genghis had bouts like this?"

No. Genghis was stupidly brave. That trait had nothing to do with my influence.

"Then what's wrong with me?"

I would tell you what I told Edward when he threw his first tantrum. You are causeless.

"What does that mean?"

Find yourself and maybe you will understand.

Roen wasn't sure how to go about finding himself. Luckily, he had plenty of free time to figure it out. He was still receiving assignments from Command, albeit less frequently than before. He used to receive a steady stream of assignments at least once a week. Now, he'd only heard from them once in the last month.

The quality of his assignments declined as well. Most of them were back to the boring observation details. Roen was playing in the minor leagues again, receiving rudimentary missions of very little importance. That suited him fine. He just didn't care anymore.

Somehow, he had come full circle and was back working at a job that had no meaning to him. He might as well be back at his old company. When he was on an assignment, he did just the bare minimum to get by. Roen didn't know how it could be possible, given the events of the last year, but he was back to a meandering existence. Life as an agent now felt as pointless as being a computer engineer.

He spent the next few months wandering alone in the city when he wasn't on assignment, seeking to discover some semblance of who he used to be. Sadly, the old Roen didn't exist anymore, and whoever Roen was now didn't belong in the ordinary slow-paced world. All that was left of his life was influenced by the Quasing, and there was no way he could escape it.

At first, Roen thought if he just pretended Tao didn't exist anymore, he could blend back into society. Even that was impossible. The things he knew now – and the ignorance that everyone else had regarding the world – followed him everywhere he went. Every event, accident, or military coup Roen saw on the news made him wonder which faction was involved. Every new technology introduced or regime change made him suspect Quasing conspiracy.

Jill was the lone bright spot in his life and he cherished her more than anything else in the world. She was the only thing he could think of that made sense, and when he was with her Roen felt as if he still had some purpose. She was worth fighting for. He was painfully aware that she could not understand the depth of what was bothering him and that eventually, left unchecked, it would push her away.

So Roen was grateful that she still traveled frequently and didn't see him wallow in this sad state. He tried to put up a happy front when they were together, but Jill saw through him and did more than he ever could have expected to support him. She patiently hung around when he putzed around listlessly in his apartment and nurtured him even when he was insufferable, and he loved her the more for it.

Roen retreated deeper and deeper into himself and became a recluse. His days blurred together and soon, he stopped caring altogether what happened outside of his apartment, leaving only to work out or shop for food. He watched copious amounts of television. So much so that Antonio joked that he worked for Nielsen. It was ironic though, that in his absence to the outside world, Roen learned more about the world than at any other time in his life.

He was strangely glued to world events as if subconsciously he was keeping tabs on the war. Occasionally, he logged into the network to correlate his conspiracy theories with the events of the day. Slowly, he began to see the broader picture of how the Quasing affected the world.

The Prophus kept a detailed database to record all their activities and aggregated them to create a visualization of events that affected the planet. Situations as small as a lumber shortage in Idaho could be traced to the degradation of the Amazon rain forest, and could again be traced to the pirates off the Somali coast. Roen was starting to realize what a complex web the world was, and how the pull of even a single thread could cause ripples on the other side of the planet.

For instance, the Prophus had developed a new form of processing oil that resulted in greater energy output with less environmental pollution. It was their hope that this process would help stem the world's thirst for oil. It was also very profitable.

The Genjix stalled approval of the process through Congress and lowered the price of coal from their subsidiaries while ordering OPEC to raise oil prices. The Prophus had no choice but to increase oil production from their offshore oil platforms. The Genjix responded by sabotaging the platforms to cause a spill while crying foul on the environmental consequences, simultaneously increasing all their orders of oil in China to offset the surplus. The Prophus retaliated by canceling business contracts and exports to China in order to undercut the demand.

Usually, these tit-for-tat maneuvers went on back and forth a dozen times until eventually armed conflict broke out. It was a cycle that occurred over and over again. As he delved deeper, Roen began to recognize this same pattern as he peeled through the many layers of Quasing history. Cause and effect. The Prophus and Genjix were knee-deep in controlling specific outcomes of human history.

"How many of these were you responsible for, Tao?" Roen murmured to himself as he pored over the numbers for all of history's pandemics.

Do you really want to know?

"I wasn't being serious. Wait, were you responsible for any of these?"

The Italian plague of 1629. I had a hand in it.

Hearing that made Roen even more depressed. The Prophus was just as bad as the Genjix. "And you wonder why I'm so disillusioned."

Do not judge me in hindsight. The Italian city-states, under the control of the Genjix, were about to join in the Thirty Years War. If that had happened, we would be calling it the Fifty Years War today. It was the only way at the time to prevent Europe from being ripped apart. There is more to a tree than what is above ground. Look past the surface.

Roen felt a little embarrassed. Obviously, there was much more to these things than he realized. Still, was it justifiable to kill hundreds of thousands of people to prevent a war? To him, it seemed like both sides had committed unforgivable atrocities. "You both have a pretty high tally, Tao. I'm sure both factions aren't getting gifts from Santa for the next million years. The end doesn't always justify the means."

You are partially correct and completely wrong. It is not the action you have to consider; it is the intent. The Thirty Years War killed an estimated seven to twelve million people. No war can last thirty years unless new nations are brought in every few years to stoke the fires. The Genjix did just that. They had two objectives: to maintain Catholic control over Europe and to advance the uses of the gunpowder. They did not care who won as long as they achieved their objectives.

If we had not prevented the Italian city-states from joining the war, I believe it could have lasted at least another fifteen years, with the casualties numbering in the tens of millions. We had to do what we did to save lives and to preserve human society. Look past the what and see the why. Then you might understand.

Roen was still dubious about that line of logic. But he had never thought about the reasons for people's actions until now. "Can you explain to me how you know the things you do will save lives?"

Unfortunately, we do not know for certain. We just have to believe it will. We know our enemy, and we know what they are capable of. Did I ever tell you about the bubonic plague?

Roen nodded.

And the Spanish Inquisition? And the Thirty Years War? And both world wars?

Roen nodded each time.

They were all products of Genjix plans, part of their doctrine about conflict and human evolution. What we strive for is to stop the Genjix from starting the next world war or the next pandemic outbreak. You are unhappy with the things we make you do. Be angry if you like, but I will not apologize for who we are and what our mission is on behalf of your species.

You think you are doing us a favor? Let me clarify something. The Prophus are outcasts because we defended you. Our lives would have been easier if we simply said nothing. I sympathize with you for the loss of the innocent, but I have seen more evil done on behalf of our return than you can ever imagine. Grief is a luxury I cannot afford.

"How do you know the Genjix aren't right? I mean, we're a pretty dumb bunch. Look at the race to the moon. I read that the Genjix goaded both the US and USSR toward the Cold War and the space race. If there wasn't that conflict, would there have been a race at all?"

It is true the Cold War was a milestone in human space travel and brought us much closer to returning home, but who is to say that the progress might not have been faster if both nations had put aside their differences and worked together toward that common goal?

"I never thought of it that way."

It is a lot to take in. Conflict does breed innovation, but so does

*diversity and cultural development. Bringing people together to share
ideas is just as powerful a catalyst.*

And then finally, after six months of not speaking to each
other, Roen opened up just a sliver. In reality, it was a long
time coming. Roen missed Tao like he would an old friend he
had lost.

"Tao, I forgive you."

Wait, I am the one being forgiven?

"Let's say there should be apologies on both sides."

Fair enough.

"Humor me while I have another moment with myself with
you. I've been angry for a while now. I didn't want to see a truth
that I didn't like and while this whole thing is still very depressing, I get it. I don't agree with everything you preach, but now
I know where you're coming from."

There was a long pause before Tao finally spoke.

*This game we play to control humanity is not a pretty one. I regret
having to play it at all. Roen, I am grateful to you for what you sacrifice on behalf of the Prophus. I do not always show it, but I am. When
you are ready to continue with this war, we will do it together. And if
you are not, then I am content to wait.*

Roen shook his head. "I do need to get back in the game despite my injured sensibilities. This isn't the time to stay on the
sidelines."

The two talked late into the evening, well after the scotch
was gone and the television aired only infomercials. There was
a feeling of forgiveness in Roen that warmed him from deep
inside, and suddenly he felt a semblance of his old self again.
It was that or too much scotch. Regardless, it gave him peace.
He knew now that running a mission was not enough. He also
had to know its purpose, and that made all the difference.

*Hey Roen, thank you for forgiving me, and I do apologize for putting
you into this situation. You should get some sleep though. You have a
big day tomorrow.*

"I do?"

Seriously, I do not know how you survived your entire life without me. You have dinner with Jill's parents tomorrow.

Roen froze and looked at the calendar. In his wallowing, it had slipped his mind! Jill had made the reservations two months ago. "Thanks. I guess I owe you another one."

This one is a freebie. I believe I also owe you thanks as well. So many times, I put heavy expectations on my hosts and forget that their sacrifice is even greater than mine. You are my partner, Roen, and for that, you have my gratitude.

Roen grinned. "What's the capital of old Assyria?"

Cute. Now, off to bed, young man. Take a shower and get a haircut tomorrow morning. You look like as bad as you have been feeling the past few months. Jill's parents will take exception to their daughter dating a vagrant.

CHAPTER THIRTY-ONE
THE PARENTS

The Genjix's newest conflict, the one you now refer to as the Thirty Years War, was just starting to take a hold of Europe. Our own war with the Genjix had been escalating as well. During those years, a myth sprouted among the Catholic clergy about the mystical Chest of the Menagerie. It was said that this chest had godly or devilish powers. In either case, the church wanted to find this chest badly. Just as the violence broke out, a French cardinal, Armand Jean du Plessis de Richelieu, was notified of the Chest of the Menagerie's location. Zoras, his Genjix, rushed to action.

Roen was more afraid of meeting Jill's parents than of being shot at by the Genjix. It didn't help that Jill was just as nervous. The two had decided to go all out, making reservations at the famous Alinea restaurant just north of downtown Chicago. This time, none of Tao's soothing words or encouraging pep talks made any difference.

After a lifetime of the fast-paced whirlwind of the Big Apple, Louis and Lee Ann Tesser were now living out their golden years in San Diego. Louis was a retired stockbroker, and Lee Ann used to be a general counsel for a hedge fund. Roen never felt so under a microscope in his entire life. They studied him with bemused expressions, as if he was an orangutan throwing feces at the keepers.

Jill wasn't much help. She was a bundle of nerves and gaped in shock when she first saw his ragged appearance. He had shaved, gotten a haircut, and wore freshly laundered clothes, but there was no hiding his gaunt face, tired eyes, and pale skin. The ladies at the salon could only do so much. The two of them stood just outside of the restaurant like disciplined children with her parents. Immediately, Roen knew he was being appraised like a side of beef. The question was whether they were appraising him for steak or for dog food.

"So, you two work together?" was the first thing Lee Ann said. "Are you an attorney as well?"

"Actually, I was let go earlier this year," Roen admitted, turning a slight shade of red.

Ah yes. Roen's famous truthful stupidity rears its ugly head again.

"Well, isn't that important in a relationship, Tao?"

Not to the parents!

"So what are you doing now?" Louis asked as they walked into the restaurant and sat down at their table.

Keep to the script. Do not undersell yourself.

Roen told them the rehearsed tale he told all his friends and family – that he worked for Bynum Consulting doing technical strategy. Her parents asked polite softball questions up until around the time the appetizers came, then the conversation ever-so-subtly became an interrogation. As a former lawyer, Lee Ann had a way of asking seemingly innocuous questions that had far more layers than they seemed. Questions that started innocently – like how many days a week he traveled – morphed into how little time they could possibly spend with each other into how he could take care of her if he was never around. Other questions like him renting and having a roommate turned into how he expected to start a family.

Thankfully, Roen received a slight reprieve when Lee Ann

and Jill gave each other a knowing look and excused them-selves, walking away to talk in private. Unfortunately, it left him alone with Louis.

"Look, Roen," Louis began, "let's get a few things clear. This is the second time that Jill has introduced us to one of her boyfriends, so it's a big deal. Now, I might've been a big-city stockbroker, but I'm just a country boy from the swamps of Alabama, so I'm going to tell you some of my country-boy sex-ist philosophies, and you're gonna listen." Suddenly, his proper New York accent changed into a Southern twang.

Roen gulped and nodded. This was going to be bad. His mind raced as he tried to mask his terror.

"I like you," Louis said. "You seem smart, but not too smart. You're attentive, polite, and you're scared of me. That's a good thing; that's how you should be. So here's my philosophy on life and women, and I want you to listen good. I've always viewed God as very fair. Girls in their twenties – the world's their oyster. They're beautiful. Older men want to date them. Guys pay for everything, and everyone desires them. Men on the other hand, when we're in our twenties, we're dumb, we're poor, and women our age want nothing to do with us. You follow?"

"Um... Tao? What the hell is he talking about?"

I like this guy. He is quite the philosopher.

"But like I said," Louis continued. "Our Lord is a fair and good God. How things even out is that women might shine bright, but they burn out fast. Their lives are over by thirty. What do you geeks call it? Half-life? Shelf life? Whatever. It's shorter than for us men. They have to find the right guy right away or it be-comes a game of settling. That's why Jill's mother and I got married at an early age. She found the best guy she could pos-sibly find at her peak. Guys are like wine. We get finer with time. We start earning money. We become more confident. We become more distinguished with age, and younger girls will still date us. You get me?"

Roen nodded, though he wasn't sure at all where this was going. "I think so," he mumbled politely.

"So," Louis continued, "Jill's shelf life is almost over and she has to find a quality man soon, and by the way I figure it, she's been spending the best years of her life with you. And while you're getting better, it's no big deal if you move on later because you're still aging well, like a good bottle of cab. You know where I'm going with this?"

Roen shook his head.

I never had it figured that Louis was such a philosopher. In another time with the right Quasing, he could have been a Nietzsche or a Voltaire!

"If I find out that you wasted the best years of my little girl's life because of your fine-wine-aging process, I'm going to kill you. Because if she thinks you're the best she can do, and she loves you, hell, I'll buy it. I might even call you son one day, as long as you know how to hunt and fish. But if you're anything other than what she thinks you are, I'll turn your fine-wine-aging ass to vinegar so fast you better hope you can get FedExed to Africa, because I will hunt you until the ends of the green Earth, so help you God." Louis bared his teeth and then finished his beer with one big chug. "We clear, son?"

"Crystal." Roen felt what little blood was left in his face drain to his feet. "I just want..."

Louis laughed. "I'm kidding. Actually, I'm not, but I'm glad you know where we stand. So what're you drinking?" He gestured toward the waitress.

"Scotch," Roen replied quietly.

"Ahh, a man with hair on his back." Louis ordered two scotches.

Jill and Lee Ann came back a few minutes later with martinis in hand. Jill gave him a small worried smile. Her parents continued his interrogation through seven more courses of dinner until they seemed to know more about Roen than his own parents did. By the end of the night, Louis offered to pay for dinner and insisted when Roen tried to pick up the tab anyway. Her parents gave him a very neutral-sounding goodbye, saying that it was nice to meet him and that they hoped he would find a job that didn't require so much traveling. Jill and Roen beat a hasty retreat to compare notes.

"Dad paid for the bill," Jill said, "that means he approves."

"From where I come from," Roen said, "when someone pays the bill, that means it's business and not friendly."

She smiled. "That's not my dad. If he doesn't like you and you're paying, he'll order a thousand-dollar bottle of wine – and spill it just to see the look on your face."

"Does that mean I pass the test?"

"And they want you to get a job that doesn't require so much traveling. That means they want us to spend more time together," Jill added.

"I don't know how you can see all that meaning into that," he said, and shook his head. "All I got was a death threat if I don't treat you right."

She leaned over and kissed him. "Well, that's one thing I agree with Dad on." Her voice changed. "Hey, listen, thanks for meeting them. It's important to me. I'm going to Frankfurt again for the next few months. It's important to me to have this meeting before I leave. It's good for a girl to know she's got someone to come back to."

Roen felt a soft lump in his throat as he pulled her close. "I'll always be waiting for you," he said. In his head, he knew that he shouldn't make promises like that with his line of work. Would Tao's next host end up paying Jill a visit like he had with Kathy? The very thought made him shudder.

Roen, do not assume such things. Your life can be a full one. It is still your right to find love and happiness.

"But at what cost? That I leave her a widow?"

You do want to marry her then?

Roen stopped. He never even thought of it until now.

One step at a time, my friend.

"He tell you his stupid wine metaphor?" Jill was saying.

Roen nodded.

She rolled her eyes and laughed. "I don't know how many times I've had to hear that. That's a good thing though. He's taking you seriously."

"It's so backward, yet true," he mused.

"Whatever," she murmured as she took his hand and led him out of the restaurant. She flashed him one of her bright dimpled smiles and said, "I'm still getting better with time. You'll just have to see and find out!"

Roen looked at her and his heart suddenly swelled to the point his eyes filled with tears. Yes, he was pretty sure. He did want to marry her.

CHAPTER THIRTY-TWO

BACK INTO THE FOLD

The Chest of the Menagerie at the time was hidden well in Prophus'
hands. When the fighting first broke out in the lands once known as
the Holy Roman Empire, the decision was made to move the chest to
England where it would remain secure during the conflict. I am not
sure how the Genjix came across this information. Were we betrayed?
Did their spies find the chest? We will never know. But within hours,
Armand – that is, Zoras – had assembled a small army and attacked
the escort. The capture of the Chest of the Menagerie changed the dy-
namic of the war forever.

Roen fidgeted in a booth at the Salt and Pepper Diner, in the
Lakeview neighborhood of Chicago, as he watched the people
come in and out. It was late September and he had just returned
home after a two-week assignment – his most important and
morally challenging assignment to date – and received new orders to come to the diner. It was an unusual order, almost like
some sort of covert operation.

After that long talk with Tao, he had begun to take his job
as an agent more seriously. This time though, Roen was not
satisfied with just being a good soldier. He also began to care
why his assignments had to be carried out. That made all the

difference in the world. Slowly, Roen had earned the respect of those he worked with and regained some of the trust he had lost with Command. It also gave him purpose.

In his most recent mission, he had joined a small task force that broke out a number of Canadian dissidents, who were about to be extradited back to Canada, from a prison in northern Minnesota. He didn't even know Canada had dissidents. After all, wasn't Canada one of the happiest countries in the world?

But now, he knew better than to take his assignments and the Prophus objectives at surface value. Beside the fact that several of the dissidents were Prophus agents, it seemed Canada was a hotbed of Genjix activity and they were exploiting much of the natural resources there to fund Russian production of military arms, which, in turn, was being used to supply North Korea with weapons.

The Genjix were attempting to destabilize the region with their long-term objective of increasing China's influence – a government which the Genjix controlled – in order to expand the Chinese naval sphere of dominance over more of the Pacific. The dissidents were sabotaging the Genjix operations before they were chased over the border and captured by the US border patrol. Roen might have missed a few points when he read over the report, but that seemed to be the general gist of the operation.

He had at first balked at firing at American troops. It was his government after all, and he felt like a traitor. He grieved privately about some of the things he had to do. He knew he had shot a few of the guards as they had made their escape. He prayed that they recovered from their injuries. He only hoped that the ends justified their means.

Roen knew he wasn't that sort of agent, so he was feeling apprehensive as he waited at a booth in the corner over a burger and fries. He really missed fries a lot. Potatoes bathed in hot oil were rarely on his menu these days. He was pleasantly surprised when Stephen and Paula appeared and sat down opposite him.

"You did good work on the Happy Mounty operation," Stephen began after the three exchanged pleasantries. "I know your moral principles must have balked at the orders."

Roen nodded. "Yeah, at first, but I get it now. I know why it had to be done."

Stephen grinned. "That's good to hear. You're probably wondering why we're here. Well, I wanted to check up on you and see how you're doing. I've read the reports and wonder if you're ready to continue your development." He leaned forward. "Do you know why you're a Prophus agent?" Stephen had an intense look in his eyes as he asked the question. Paula was just as intent as they both studied him.

Roen squirmed as he thought it over. He was about to talk about his past few missions and then stopped. This was obviously some sort of test. Those missions were effects of a cause from the Quasing conflict. He moved up a level and thought about the eighteen months he'd spent with Tao, and all the training and work they put in. But again, his training was nothing more than a tool, an effect to further a greater cause. That cycle continued until he thought about why he now existed and why the war was fought.

"I want the Quasing to return home without destroying the human race in the process," he finally said. "I want humanity to evolve naturally and work in a partnership with the Quasing, not to be subjugated and manipulated by them."

Paula smiled and turned to Stephen. "I'd give that answer a B-plus. It's not the most chipper way to go about it, but he does have Tao in him, after all."

Stephen nodded. "Tao's always been a hard-ass. I wanted to speak with you personally and look you in the eyes before I do this." He pulled a manila envelope with the now familiar black box from his leather satchel, laid them on the table, and slid them forward. "You're going to the Monaco Decennial. You leave in four days. I wanted to personally convey my congratulations."

It is well deserved, my friend. I am proud of you. This is really like a true diploma from Command.

Roen had trouble processing this at first. He'd heard about the Decennial here and there over the past year, but never thought much of it. In fact, every time he brought it up, Tao told him that there was no way he'd be ready to attend.

Paula grinned. "Good work, Roen. You've finally been invited to the adult table."

"Thank you both." He felt a little embarrassed with all the sudden praise. "I don't know what to say."

Stephen shook his head. "Don't thank us yet. It's a dangerous assignment, so you'll need all your wits about you. Everything you need to know will be in the mission briefs. You are strictly an observer this time around, but it's a big step. Now, what's good at this place?"

The three of them stayed for dinner and moved next door to a local bar for drinks afterward. Roen had many questions about the assignment but restrained himself rather than look like the rookie. Was it that important that Stephen had come personally to speak with him? Why was Paula here?

Nevertheless, he pushed those thoughts out of his mind and enjoyed their company. They were the closest thing he had to friends within the Prophus network. Stephen managed a large operation out of the east coast while Paula now ran a special ops team out of London. The three ended up barhopping through several Chicago bars that night. Roen learned that drinking with Stephen and Paula was no joke. In fact, he probably was in more danger drinking with them than fighting the Genjix. Stephen was a jovial drinker while Paula took it as if she were personally propping up Diageo stock. Several hours later, they stumbled out of the last bar and said their goodbyes. As Roen headed out, Paula called him over.

"Roen." She smiled. "I'm proud of you for coming, lad. For keeping up with the drinks I mean, not the whole Decennial thing." She broke into a grin. "I'm just kidding. I have a favor to ask."

"Sure," he answered, "anything."

"Can I stay with you tonight?"

Now, Roen knew he'd had a few too many drinks, but he swore he heard that correctly. It took him more than a few moments to regain his composure. "I have a..." he began.

"It's OK, you're not my type." Paula chuckled. "Yol wants to catch up with Tao."

"What type would that be?" he asked, slightly offended.

"Men without aliens in them." She smiled. "Come, Yol would like to know where the mighty Tao is holding court." The two hailed a taxi and were soon off to his apartment. Right when they walked through the front door, Paula, without bothering to change out of her clothes, had found his room and passed out on his bed.

Roen stared longingly as she lay sprawled out on his comforter. "Why do they always get my bed?"

You are a gentleman and I am sure they appreciate the gesture.

"I enjoy sleeping in my bed. Do you think she'd mind if I scooched up next to her on the other side?"

Jill has a key to your apartment. Imagine how fun it would be if she decided to stop by.

"She's in Frankfurt."

That is not the point. Here is a word of advice. Do not put yourself in a situation where Jill is justified in throwing a pan at you, regardless of whether she is nearby or not.

With a sigh, Roen gave his bed one last yearning look, before he grabbed a spare blanket and walked out to the living room.

• • • •

Tao waited until Roen was asleep before he took control of the body. It took quite a bit longer than usual. Tao had trained Roen the past few months to become a light sleeper. That was good for missions. Tao could now wake Roen at a moment's notice and not after five minutes of prodding. However, it was bad for a Quasing who wished to take control of his sleeping host.

Tao waited a little while longer to make sure Roen was sound asleep. When Tao was sure, he got up and moved him into the bedroom. Yol was already up waiting for him.

"How are things with Paula?" Tao asked as they sat down on the bed. "Are you two getting along?"

Yol smiled. "She is smart, competent, and very dry, but also very accommodating. I am fortunate to not have to housebreak her too much, though her politeness is rubbing off on me. The other day, we stopped by a burger joint, and she told the server that she would prefer a number four. Who talks like that?"

"No one does polite like the English, except for the Japanese, maybe. It is good for you though; keeps you in check. Are you satisfied with the Keeper's selection then?"

"We make a good team. She is very methodical and tempers my impulsiveness. How are things with Roen? First time I saw him, he seemed ready to jump out of his skin. I know he struggled with this calling. Paula has been keeping up on his assignments. He seems to have come around."

Tao nodded. "He has finally realized the meaning of our work. His heart and head are in the right place. That is all I can ask for. I believe he will be a credit to my previous hosts." Tao paused as he thought about what he was going to say next. "About the past couple of years..."

Yol shook her head, then raised a hand. "You did the right thing. I could only imagine the pressure the others must have put on you. Gregory was lost, but you gave him a chance at least."

"When did you know he was truly gone? Did his mind suffer?" Tao asked.

Paula's face was lost in thought for a few seconds before Yol responded. "Humans are peculiar. Unlike us, their minds can die but the body lives like an automaton. During the first year, he was sometimes coherent, and I could speak with him. But those moments became rarer as time progressed. Eventually, I was left alone with his shell. He was a body without a soul. I begrudge you nothing. When I lost all access to his senses, I knew he was gone."

"Edward had planned on visiting that year he died. Unfortunately, he was not able to make it, and then I was preoccupied with Roen. I am sorry."

Yol put her hand over Tao's. "It is the past. How did Kathy take it?"

"I was not able to speak with her until this year. She knows now."

Yol nodded. "She deserved the truth. Is Roen's relationship serious?"

"It is. He worries his line of work will cause Jill grief. After what happened to Edward, I do not blame him. Little good comes from all this."

The two spoke for several more hours. They had begun working together soon after the fall of Rome and the rise of the Italian city-states, and while they had lost touch during the Inquisition, they had resumed their friendship in the New World and worked closely together ever since. There was a lot of catching up to do. It was very therapeutic for Tao.

Brotherhood was something Tao understood, both in a human and Quasing sense. While he had known many other Quasing, Yol was his brother in every way through all those centuries. They had a unique relationship. The last Quasing he had this sort of close bond with was Chiyva. Tao felt a twinge of rage at that name. It was comforting that he knew where Yol stood. The two separated just before daybreak. Tao wanted to make sure that Roen had enough sleep before the mission.

"Listen, Yol, I need a favor," Tao asked before he left.

"Anything," Yol said.

"If anything happens to Roen or me, and I am returned to the Eternal Sea, please speak to them regarding his sacrifice. I promised him."

"Of course. It is something we should all do right away. One more thing, Tao, lighten up a bit. You have an obsessive and depressing effect on your hosts."

Tao turned to Yol before he left the room. "I will lighten up when I remove Jeo and Chiyva from this world."

CHAPTER THIRTY-THREE
MONACO DECENNIAL

Inside the Chest of the Menagerie, Zoras found hundreds of small animals, each with a Genjix prisoner inside. It was there that he freed Chiyva. Enraged at the imprisonment of the Genjix, Zoras decided to teach the Prophus a hard lesson. And what happened next was a crime among the Quasing that echoes to this day.

Prior to the incident with the Chest of the Menagerie, we were content to wage war in a manner that delayed and inconvenienced the other side. Killing a Quasing's host was enough to set that Quasing back for years. In an act of unspeakable horror, Zoras raised the stakes.

Roen was as nervous as a teenager about to ask a girl to prom as he stepped off the plane and blinked into the very bright sun that beat down on him. There was a different feel to attending the Decennial than any other mission. It felt significant. Like Stephen and Paula had said, being allowed to attend meant he was considered an agent worthy of a Quasing. It was almost like his Quasing bar mitzvah.

Being in Monte Carlo didn't hurt either. It was the perfect blend of tropical weather, gorgeous old-world Europe, and glitzy Las Vegas, all wrapped up in a few square kilometers.

But the conference wasn't the reason he was nervous – what made him nervous was waiting at the bottom of the stairs.

Sonya waved enthusiastically as she barreled into him with an embrace that nearly knocked him off his feet. They hadn't seen each other since the Dublin assignment and he missed her like crazy. Command had pulled her off his training after the Yol assignment and had kept her in England to deal with the Labour Party's precarious position. The last he heard of Sonya, she had just been promoted to command the Prophus security detail for the Decennial.

Roen often saw her name in the communiqués from Command. She was climbing fast through the ranks and becoming a star in the organization. He received an occasional email from her – with a reminder to stay in shape, and study up on this weapon or that world event – but nothing ever remotely personal. He had begun to think that all that time they spent together was nothing but business to her, a mission for her to complete and then forget.

For Roen, her absence had been a painful void in his life that slowly faded as the months passed. He had nearly stopped thinking about her, until Sonya emailed him telling him she'd pick him up. Their embrace was held a bit tighter and longer than appropriate. Roen felt a twinge of guilt about Jill.

He studied Sonya as they walked through the airport terminal. She looked a little tired and had a few gray strands in her otherwise luxurious black hair, but still looked gorgeous. Roen had to keep himself from gawking. Sonya would never be a Bond girl. She would just make James Bond look bad; could definitely kick his ass too.

The two walked very close and chatted as if no time had lapsed. Roen felt ashamed, but he missed being so close to her. As much as he didn't like to admit it, his infatuation with her returned as strong as ever. Though they were and always would be good friends, there was something about that first crush, especially with someone who taught you how to shoot a target a hundred meters away at a full sprint. The window for anything past friendship had long passed, and he couldn't help but feel regret for that lost possibility.

Hello? Jill? The girl you are ring-shopping for?

"I know! I'm just regretting. Can't a guy do that?"

Depends on who you ask; I am sure Jill will say otherwise.

"Listen, Thought Police, I'm only reminiscing."

Reminiscing is when one is thinking about the past. What you are dreaming about never happened. The word for that is fantasizing.

"Well, good thing you can't tell on me."

Technically, I could.

"Traitor. So what's the history with this shindig, anyway? The briefs were vague on the history of this soiree. How did this Quasing convention come to be?"

As the name implied, it began in the 1800s, after the second American war, and was meant to be held every ten years. Our conflict with the Genjix changed from a war of control, to one of outright revenge. Entire host families were being massacred, and the violence spiraled out of control to humans not involved with the Quasing. It culminated with a group of Prophus causing the Boston Broad Street Riot in the 1830s, just to cover their escape from an attack on a Genjix safe house.

From that time on, both factions decided to sit down every ten years and hammer out rules of engagement. Guidelines, if you will. Thus, we now have the Peace Accords, a toothless yet constricting document that tells us how to not annihilate each other. However, ever since the 1871 Decennial, which caused the Chicago fire, they have been held only when both sides agreed to meet.

"So Mrs O'Leary's cow didn't kick over the lantern, huh. And isn't not annihilating each other a good thing?"

Depends on which way you look at it.

Roen and Sonya got into the car and sped off toward the Metropole, their hotel. She wanted to know everything that had happened to him since Dublin. He was surprised to find out that she had kept detailed tabs on all his missions. And when he told her about his conflicts with being an agent, she admitted to him her own struggles with being one as well.

"Then why didn't you call or visit?" he asked, a bit subdued. Her doubts would surely have helped give him perspective.

Sonya paused, and then looked away. "Stephen told me not to. After Dublin, he said you needed space to find yourself. I was told to keep my distance to see if you'd come back on your own. I'm sorry."

Roen was speechless. It made sense, he supposed, but still, that's why they lost touch? He knew he shouldn't care; they were just friends, but he did care, and it made him furious. The two sat in silence until they reached the Metropole.

The Metropole was owned by Vinnick, a powerful Genjix on the Council that the Prophus trusted to be honorable. During the four-day conference, the two factions operated under a strict banner of truce. The regular staff was replaced by non-combat personnel from both factions and strict rules were put in place to deter violence. All agents were forbidden from open conflict under the penalty of being sent to the Eternal Sea.

Covert work, however, was still tolerated as long as no one was caught. This made the Decennial dangerous, and the friendly daytime meetings sometimes degenerated into assassination attempts at night. These conference protections only extended to the four walls of the hotel, so it became open game once anyone stepped off the grounds.

As a precaution, they formed a joint task force consisting of members from both sides assigned specifically to keep the peace. Roen marveled at the first three checkpoints on the way in, and they were still on the driveway leading to the hotel. Once he got out with his bags, he had to join another line to the fourth checkpoint, where security searched through his luggage. They confiscated his pistol, knife, even his flashbangs.

"Man, Tao. It's worse than airport security here."

You should have seen it before these rules were set up. We almost started World War III one year when they snuck in a biological weapon.

"What?!"

It is all right. We brought incendiaries that year, so it kind of evened out.

"Why do I feel like coming here was a very bad idea?"

Why do you think I was originally against you coming? I did not think you would be ready by the time the Decennial was held. You have proved me wrong though.

Roen checked into his room and went over the conference itinerary. Tao did not have any issues to bring up, but wanted to keep up to date with current events. In the past, his previous hosts had always played a contentious role in these negotiations, but Tao did not think Roen was ready for that sort of limelight.

Next Decennial, perhaps?

"I get stage fright."

Roen pulled out a map of the resort and looked at the layout for all the emergency exits, committing them to memory. The Metropole was divided into two large wings connected by a central area that housed the lobby, restaurants, and stores. There were large circles on the map, around all the connecting points between the exits, and a big red square around the eastern wing. The Prophus had the western one.

"Guess I'm not supposed to go to that wing," Roen muttered.

Most of the action will occur in the central lobby or pool area during the night. It is not unheard of for teams to make incursions as well. Just stay in your room.

"What if I need to go down to buy toothpaste or a magazine?"

Then you deserve to die for your stupidity.

"You're in a bad mood, aren't you? I guess a night out on the town is not going to be on the cards tonight, huh?"

Only if you want to get assassinated on the way back. This is serious, Roen. The most peaceful Decennial we ever had involved four deaths across both factions, and that was a hundred years ago.

"Jesus. Why do we bother coming?"

I agree with you there, but even warring countries need to communicate sometimes. Think of it as a United Nations with only two countries.

"Not a big believer in email, huh?"

Roen spent the afternoon unpacking, taking the opportunity to shower and nap before meeting up with Sonya and Paula for dinner. Stephen and Dylan joined them for drinks afterward at the bar.

You can relax tonight. The night before the conference is called the Homestead Reunion. It was the one time when all Quasing put aside our differences.

Roen watched Genjix and Prophus interact as if there wasn't a five-hundred year-old war going on. Many old friends torn apart by the conflict reconnected here. Even the others sitting with him were frequently greeted by many of the agents from the other faction. No one greeted Roen, though.

"Tao, I have no Genjix friends, and it's your fault. Sonya and Paula both have a line of people waiting to talk to them. Heck, even Dylan and Stephen got a few."

I find this reunion experience preposterous. If you are at war, be at war. This is not halftime at a ball game. Timeouts should not be allowed.

"Really? I find it quite civilized."

There is nothing civilized about war, Roen. Do not be fooled by this charade. These same Genjix buying you drinks tonight were trying to kill you yesterday. And they will try to kill you tomorrow.

"No one is buying me drinks, thanks to you."

Some friends you can do without.

It was obvious most of the other Quasing did not share the same views as Tao. The bar was becoming crowded as the revelry grew into a full-blown party, though Roen did notice a few scowling faces of Genjix sitting at the far end. Obviously, Tao's views were shared by some on the other team as well.

Tao wanted him to have a clear head for the next four days and forbade him to drink. That suited Roen fine, since no good ever came from drinking with Stephen and Dylan anyway. His "Tao won't let me" excuse worked for the most part, though Dylan called Tao "Mother Hen" for the rest of the night. As the night wore on, the others dispersed to mingle with the crowd until he found himself alone.

After sitting by himself for an hour and experiencing a pre-agent life flashback of loneliness, he decided to stop looking like such a loser and went for a walk. Roen was pretty sure no one would miss him anyway. He left the main building and went to a small outdoor café on the balcony. He ordered a latte and sat back, admiring the city lights.

"Hello, Roen, is this seat taken?"

Roen turned and looked at a distinguished looking gentleman standing before him.

Chiyva!

Roen had never heard Tao snarl before, if a Quasing could even snarl. He jumped out of his chair, eyeing Sean warily. Roen didn't know much about the man, except that Sean was a high-ranking Genjix, heading up much of their American operations, and that Tao hated Chiyva's guts. Their paths had crossed often and Chiyva had been responsible for the deaths of Tao's hosts on more than one occasion.

Tao made another snarling, strangled sound when Roen noticed Marc standing just behind Sean. Marc's look expressed pure hatred. Roen's hands tightened into fists as he returned the glare. He briefly considered throwing his beverage at Marc until he remembered where he was.

Sean rolled his eyes. "Oh, sit down, Roen. We're not going ten rounds right now. Ruining Homestead Reunion would be bad form, and I just got my suit back from the cleaners. Besides, are you sure you want to go toe to toe with me? You might have escaped from old Omer and a few incompetent troops, but you'll find me a bit more challenging. Please, sit. I trust you've met Mr Kenton?"

"I'm not such an easy target anymore," Roen hissed, before hesitantly sitting back down.

Sean smirked at the guards eyeing them warily and followed suit. Behind him, Marc stayed standing. Sean ordered a coffee and took a long exaggerated sip when it came. He then put the cup down on the table, crossed his legs, and leaned back. Neither Roen nor Sean said a word as they studied each other.

Sean said, "You've never been an easy target, even since the beginning. You've avoided the mental midget here a few times now." Sean gestured back at Marc. "And you're looking well, like you almost fit your role with Tao. Almost." Sean wiggled a finger at Roen's chest. "There's a whole lot less of you now than initially reported. That or our operatives need new glasses."

"You should have made your move a year ago when I wasn't ready," Roen said haughtily.

"Well, there are ten million people in Chicago." Sean shrugged. "Like finding a needle in a haystack. Trust me, if we could have found you sooner, we would have. Oh well, there's always next time." He chuckled. "That's the thing about us blessed ones. There is always tomorrow, if not this lifetime, then the next."

Roen did not know what to make of this stern, coldly polite man. He was actually let down by Sean's appearance. He looked normal, even handsome. There was a touch of gray in his neatly trimmed black hair that made him look like a statesman. Otherwise, he had just a normal face with a slightly longer chin. Then Roen realized: it was his eyes. Sean's gaze was one of complete confidence, as if he knew something no one else did. This was a man so sure of himself that nothing else mattered. It was all Roen could do to rein in his emotions and not flee the table. Sean seemed relaxed and smiled humorously as Roen squirmed in his seat.

Sean picked up his coffee and took another sip. "I'm sorry, how rude of me. Would you like another drink?" He signaled for the waitress. Roen shook his head emphatically.

"Can I get either of you anything?" she asked, pulling out a notepad.

"I'm fine, miss," Sean said. "But my young friend would like a drink."

"No, I'm fine, really," Roen started and then looked at the waitress. Oh, what the heck, he might as well order as long as Sean was paying. "I'll have a venti mocha latte with skim milk, extra dry with a dash of nutmeg, and a half shot of hazelnut."

"Got it. I'll be right back," she answered and left.

"That's quite a tall order you have there." Sean chuckled. "Whatever happened to just coffee?"

"I like to have it my way." Roen shrugged.

"Yes, yes," Sean said, taking another sip. "For me, the world's complicated enough as it is. Why does one's drink have to be? But then, that's always been the Prophus way, hasn't it? To make things far more complicated than they should be. You muddle things up so badly that it's difficult to know what's right from wrong, unlike our clarity and single vision."

You mean simple-minded vision? Roen snarled Tao's response in the same tone.

Sean laughed. "Possibly. Tao might call us simple-minded for not taking into consideration all the factors that might contribute to the issue, but we Genjix think that it's more about staying on course with our end goals. We believe the Prophus have lost that perspective. You've lost sight of what's important and have become too concerned with humans this and social issues that."

"We just do not believe in destroying and enslaving humanity just to get home," Roen said, repeating Tao's words.

Sean's calm expression altered, and for a second, Roen thought he was going to spit out his coffee. Sean stared at him for several seconds before breaking into laughter, a deep, loud uproarious outburst that was the last thing Roen thought would come out of the man. It was an awkward moment and he retraced their conversation trying to figure out where the comedy in the whole matter was.

And just as quickly as it began, Sean's fit of joviality ended. Moments later, he looked calm and composed again as he shook his head. "I must say," he began, "I'm surprised. You still think we care about going home."

What?!

Roen was stunned. Obviously, so was Tao. What was the whole point of all this then?

Before he could ask, a tall young man – dark-haired, with a thin chiseled face – appeared next to Sean and whispered into his ear. For a brief moment, Roen thought he saw a flash of uncertainty in Sean's eyes. Then he politely excused himself and walked off with the young man as they whispered together off to the side.

There was something very unsettling about that young man. For one thing, Roen couldn't tear his eyes off him. For another thing, the young man made the statue of David look like a sumo wrestler. He had muscle in places Roen didn't even know had muscles. His physique could put an underwear model to shame. And to make matters worse, he was handsome beyond belief. Roen hated to say it, but he could very well be staring at the most perfect looking human being he'd ever see. It made him feel more than a bit jealous. But there was also an inhuman quality about him as well; something impossibly cold in the young man's eyes and an arrogance that turned Roen's blood to ice.

Snap out of it before you become a groupie.

"I can't help it. That is one good-looking dude. Is he even human?"

An Adonis Vessel, the Genjix practice of eugenics. These unnatural beings are chosen at birth for their genes, and trained since infancy for the only purpose of being a replacement vessel for senior Genjix. They are travesties of nature.

"Travesty or not, I feel totally inadequate around him. He's built like a superhero or something. Now I know how normal chicks feel when they're standing next to a supermodel. He also seems to be bossing Sean around."

That Adonis Vessel must be from one of the Council then. Be careful if you ever encounter one, Roen. They are very dangerous.

Finally, after their conversation ended, Sean returned and sat down. "My apologies. A personal matter, I'm sure you understand."

"When are you getting your personal Ken doll?" Roen smirked.

Sean shrugged as if it was the least important thing in the world. "One day, when Chiyva reclaims his rightful place." He took a sip of his coffee and leaned back. "But back to us; where was I? Oh yes, what we're doing here. Do you even remember what the mission is, Tao?"

"I thought I did," Roen said, repeating Tao's words. "It seems we have differing goals now."

"Oh, I wouldn't say that." Sean shrugged. "It's just that your focus is so... narrow. The Genjix prefer to see the bigger picture, to keep our eyes on what really matters, my old friend, which in this case would be to see the survival of our kind. I would say that we've done a rather fine job of that since our time here. Wouldn't you agree, Tao?" Roen reluctantly nodded. Sean leaned forward and spoke in a more serious tone. "And yes, we have had to crack a few eggs along the way, but the job gets done. And isn't that what's important?"

"Look, I'm just a lowly human that's nothing more than a minor nuisance and a stepping stone to your master plan," Roen drawled, "but just because you believe I'm beneath you doesn't mean I should just roll over and die."

"I'm glad you realize that you're nothing more than a nuisance. Your life, the entire century of it if you're so lucky, is nothing more than a drop in the ocean for us. So, why are you even bothering to get involved?" Sean spread his arms and waved at their surroundings. "Go live life and enjoy it. Don't worry about our little family conflict. Do you really want to waste what precious few moments you have on this planet fighting a war that's not yours? Instead of listening to that delusional voice in your head, why don't you go see the world, get married, have children. Don't be another Edward Blair, Roen, and waste your life."

"Who said Edward wasted his life?" Roen scowled.

"I guess it is all perspective then." Sean paused and studied him for a moment. "Tell me, Roen, what's in it for you?"

"What's in it for you, Sean?" Roen shot back.

"Fair enough. What's in it for me – besides power, prestige, an endless source of knowledge and wisdom, and all the resources I need at my fingertips – is that I will stand with those others that follow the Genjix in the afterlife to a higher plane of existence. You don't realize the great gift that has been bestowed upon you by these divine beings, do you?"

Roen rolled his eyes and said, "I'm not one to fall for religious psychobabble, but then I've always had a problem with a rabbit that lays painted eggs."

Sean drained the last of his coffee and asked for another cup as the waitress dropped off the latte. He looked at Roen and smiled all too knowingly. "And yet, you have an infinitely old being residing within you that's had the experience of a thousand lives. You and I, of all people, should know enough to suspend this standard belief of reality shared by these non-blessed sheep. Don't you realize? We are no longer mere humans. We are chosen beings fighting for a greater cause. We are evolved. We are the shepherds that guide the flock of humanity. Such mundane concerns that you and these Prophus have are quite beneath you."

Roen took the cup and sipped the hot drink gingerly. He said, "The difference between us is that you think being a Genjix host makes you a gift to God's green Earth. You've been Genjix so long now that you forgot what it means to be human. You think you're so above the rest of us that you don't value humanity anymore. Me, I'm quite fond of being human with my primitive beliefs and emotions. Call me old-fashioned."

"It doesn't matter what your perception is. Fact is fact, my young friend, as much as you deny it, you and me, all other Prophus and Genjix vessels, are superior beings. The difference is that the Prophus stoop down to humanity's level. The Genjix choose to rise above it."

The waitress came back with another coffee. Sean politely thanked her and continued. "Don't you see that I'm trying to help you, Roen?"

"That's what the first Genjix in the garage told me right before he tried to kill me."

Sean smiled. "Let's put that behind us, shall we? We're acquainted now. I want to open your eyes."

Roen snorted. "He said that, too."

"You should have listened," Sean said. "Why fight a losing war?"

"Who says we're losing?" Roen snapped.

Sean looked genuinely surprised. "You mean, you don't know? Tao didn't tell you, did he?"

"What's he talking about, Tao?"

Do not listen to him. He is just trying to spook you.

"Well, let me enlighten you then on your precarious situation," Sean continued. "That little Prophus faction – and their philosophy that you have so enthusiastically embraced – are on the brink of collapse. They've been steadily retreating and losing ground since their inception and have had their backs against the wall for centuries now."

"Tao, is this true?"

Tao hesitated before answering. *The war has not been going well, but it is nowhere near as bad as Sean claims. I would not put too much stock in his words.*

"Why don't you sleep on that?" Sean said. "You might wake up tomorrow and realize that this might not have been a wise career choice after all."

"You're bluffing," Roen shot back. "From what I've seen so far, they're doing just fine. Brink of collapse? Give me a break."

Sean shrugged. "Perhaps, perhaps not. I doubt they can survive the century."

"A hundred years is hardly the brink of collapse. It's not like you're the Red Army marching into Berlin."

"A hundred years is a flash in the pan. Roen, we're not only in Berlin, we've surrounded it, blockaded the ports, and we're about to throw a grenade down the bunker you're hiding in."

Roen struggled to control his temper. He said, "You know, that's what your problem is. You're so busy looking at this stupid big picture of yours that you ignore the small things that make the big picture matter. You treat us mere mortals like pawns for your amusement. But remember this; without humans, you superior Genjix are nothing. You need us, yet you treat us as if we're disposable. You keep going down this path, and one day, you'll find that there will be no more lowly humans for you to control."

Sean bared his teeth. "Good thing there are seven billion of you. A few losses are perfectly acceptable."

"We'll see about that. Let's see how acceptable your human losses are after I whittle down your ranks," snarled Roen. He stood up, pulled out his wallet, and put a few bills on the table. "Thanks for the drink, but I can pay for myself. Next time we meet, I won't be so civil." He turned and walked away, not looking back. Roen was so worked up that he stormed back toward his room. He didn't calm down until he jumped into the shower and then prepared for bed.

"Now I know why you think this conference is a waste of time. There's no reasoning with these guys. By signing some rules of engagement, we're just hampering ourselves."

They play dirty. We just have to play dirtier. Be very careful of Chiyva, though. He is extraordinarily dangerous.

"Chiyva, isn't that some Hindu god? God of destruction or something?"

Where do you think the name of the god came from?

"I see. Well, we have our work cut out for us then."

CHAPTER THIRTY-FOUR
DAY ONE

Zoras's host, Armand, decided to slay the Prophus guards escorting the Chest of the Menagerie as a lesson and a warning. For he not only made sure that the hosts died, he made sure that the Prophus inside died as well. The hosts were all buried alive in the very chests that housed the Menagerie. Their cries underground could be heard for hours. This was in many ways, our original sin. For the first time in our history on Earth, the Quasing began to murder each other.

Armand released one prisoner as a warning to the rest of us. From that point on, there was no turning back. The war became one of vengeance rather than control. And to this day, both sides wage this misguided war.

The conference was surprisingly like any other convention Roen had ever been to – except no one was giving out t-shirts, and no vendors were trying to sell him anything. What would a slogan for the Monaco Decennial say, anyway? "Mediating ways to fight since the 1800s"?

The primary purpose of the Decennial was to discuss the return to Quasar and address how the Prophus Command and the Genjix Council could keep their war under wraps. The topic on everyone's mind seemed to be this Penetra scanner and the consequences it could have on their species. Every-where Roen went, Quasings on both side argued the risks it could pose to their species. Neither side was willing to share what they knew, though it was a hotly debated topic.

The Prophus feared that such a device could fall into hu-manity's hands, and with it, knowledge of the Quasing. The Genjix were dismissive of that possibility, hardly acknowledg-ing humans as a concern. The only thing that they cared about was wielding the scanner as a weapon against the Prophus.

There were also a dozen other less important panels going on at the same time. The topic of the panel Roen attended was conflict resolution. The Quasing definition of conflict resolution involved explosives, lots of them. It seemed that within the past decade or so, the loser of any of their major battles felt it was necessary to either plant excessive amounts of explosives or carpet-bomb whatever plot of land they were fighting over. The results led to more expensive repairs and increasingly frustrated public relations groups working overtime to calm the humans. The Genjix's proposal prevented the losing faction from con-tinuing such practices.

"This is stupid, Tao. It's strategically sound to not give your enemy resources they can use. Why wouldn't we blow it up before we leave?"

I agree. They obviously do not think much of Sun Tzu or General Sherman, who interestingly enough, were both Genjix. However, I be-lieve this resolution has a good chance of passing.

"Why would any of us be all right with it? If we lose more encounters than we win, it's to our advantage to blow crap up."

There are other factors involved. The cost of covering up all these situations is astronomical. We do not have nearly as much money as they do. Financially, it makes sense for us to accept the deal anyway. Cleanup teams are not cheap.

Roen shook his head. "Always comes down to money, huh?"

Makes the damn world go round.

The resolution passed just as they broke for lunch. The vote for the resolution went over, even though the support to pass it was overwhelming. Roen looked away in disgust as the Prophus and Genjix who drew up the resolution together congratulated each other. Roen wolfed down his lunch as he tried to figure out which panel he wanted to go to next. His choices were "Political Balances of the Middle East" or "Quasing Metaphysical Mutations." Not knowing exactly what a metaphysical mutation was, Roen chose to go to the Middle East one.

Roen's last panel couldn't come fast enough. It was nearing dinner time and his stomach growled so much he barely paid attention to the discussion. It was something about removing flamethrowers from the list of approved armaments. The only other items on the banned list were nuclear bombs and biological weapons. The former was banned after Chernobyl, while the biological weapon ban was enacted after the Prophus lost control of an artificial strain of polio, one that ravaged the United States in the mid-twentieth century. The Prophus did, however, make a large profit selling the cure.

Supposedly, the intense heat from the flamethrowers toxified the air and killed Quasing trying to escape dead hosts. It was probably true, but again, wasn't that the point? Roen thought that there was little chance this resolution would pass. It became a short panel when it was revealed that the Prophus owned stock in two of the major companies that manufactured flamethrowers. Afterward, Roen decided he'd had enough and headed toward his room.

Sonya met up with him as he walked down to the lobby. She put a hand on his elbow and escorted him to the elevator, giving him not-so-gentle nudges to hurry him along. "Listen, Roen. Tonight, go to your room and stay there. Do not come out no matter what. Remember, all the hotel staff belongs to one of the factions, so if anyone from the staff doesn't give you the code phrase, do not open the door. Barricade your windows with furniture. Take this and keep it with you at all times." She pressed a telescopic baton into his hand.

She added, "The Prophus wing should be safe, but I'm not taking any chances. This is your first night at one of these conferences and you might as well have a bullseye strapped to your back." She pushed him into the elevator and gave him a small smile just as the door closed.

"Does something weird happen at these things at night? She sounded like everyone turns into werewolves or something once the sun sets."

They are all wolves already. They just shed their sheep's clothing once the sun sets. Sonya is right. Newer agents are frequent targets at the Decennial. Do as she says and make sure your windows are barricaded. You never know when an assassin might try to enter through that point. The Genjix side is outside our window, so make sure the curtains are closed and there's furniture in front of it.

"Every time I think you guys can't get any more ridiculous, you prove me wrong."

Imagine what it was like before they forced us to disarm at these things.

That night, the hotel sounded like a haunted house. One minute it was dead quiet, and then the sound of heavy footsteps rumbled down the hallway like a stampede. In the distance, occasional screams and the sound of glass shattering punctured the night. At least twice, the building shook. At one point, his doorknob rattled like someone was trying to get in. On another occasion, Roen swore he saw the faint red dot of a sniper rifle pass through the gaps left open by the dresser he had moved in front of the window. All in all, it was a very restless night.

The next morning, he half-expected to step into the hallway and find dead bodies strewn about or blood sprayed all over the walls, but when he cautiously poked his head out of his room, everything appeared normal. In fact, Roen began to think he imagined everything from the previous night until he met up with several others for breakfast and heard the grim news. The Genjix had struck first. By everyone's count, two Prophus and one Genjix were confirmed as sent to the Eternal Sea last night. Ten delegates were abducted on their way back from a late panel.

"That's twelve Prophus. This is a disaster! How did it happen?"

The rules of the conference are very explicit. There is to be no violence during the tenure of the four days. Anyone proven to cause violence forfeits themselves to the Eternal Sea. The key word is "proven." It seems Jaj was hit through a window while Chau wandered too close to the Genjix wing. The ten delegates must have been a set-up.

"How did you deal with this in the past conferences?"

Are you kidding? I was one of the ones lying in wait.

"You're an evil, evil alien. Doesn't Command disapprove of this? What if you got caught?"

They only disapprove if you get caught.

Roen had a hard time staying focused during the second day. Anyone could be an enemy. Roen had never wished for a gun more than he did at that very moment. The panels flew by in an inconsequential blur.

Some resolution was ratified that disallowed revenge on a host's family after the host was gone. It was a pretty common sense and toothless decree. No one worth their secret agent membership card would ever bother going after a host's loved ones. And if they did, only an incompetent would be sloppy enough to have it traced back to them.

Another hotly contested resolution was the prohibition of assassinating public government figures. Elevating a Quasing to an influential position was a costly and time-consuming en-deavor. An alarming number of these prime targets had been assassinated the past few centuries.

The Genjix had brought up the resolution, and support for it was building, until someone brought up the Spanish

Inquisition. It seemed as if the Spanish Inquisition was a touchy subject for all the Quasing. A few heated words were exchanged and the entire assembly hall degenerated into a full-blown riot.

Roen was about to jump into the fracas – when Dylan pushed him out of the room and into the arms of two security guards. To Roen's dismay, after the guards grabbed him, Dylan left to join in the fighting. The last thing Roen saw was Dylan punching a Genjix representative in the face before he was enveloped by several others.

Marc came up next to him and nudged him with an elbow. "I know you can break free from these two hairless apes. Why don't you do just that and I'll join you in there?"

For a split second, Roen thought it was a great idea and mulled it over. He devised a plan to take both guards out, pull out his baton, and crush Marc's skull. It would take just over two seconds.

No, Roen Tan. Just no.

Roen sighed. "Fine. I could take him, you know."

When did you get so bloodthirsty and stupid? If you are going to be bloodthirsty, at least be smart about it.

The evening found many of the Prophus at the whiskey bar, while the Genjix nursed their wounds at the wine bar. Roen sipped a scotch while he listened to Dylan describe the fight as if he were a Roman gladiator fighting a pride of lions.

"You know I witnessed the whole thing through the door." Roen chuckled.

"Then you saw the half-dozen Genjix I took out?" Dylan said, pressing his cold drink on an angry bruise just below his temple.

"I did see you disappear under a pile of bodies when three of them jumped on you."

"That's how those dirty Genjix fight. It's never fair, those cowards!"

Sonya and Paula came by a while later, looking like two disapproving mothers. Sonya was furious as she scolded Roen for acting so foolishly and getting involved in a brawl at the Decennial.

"Why are you yelling at me?" he asked. "Dylan's the one that did all the fighting. I just stood there. Go yell at him."

She shook her head. "I know better than to yell at that incorrigible jackass. You, I expect more of. I heard the guards had to hold you back. What happened to your innate self-preservation instinct? That was the one quality you had going for you."

Roen shrugged. "Tao happened, I guess."

Damn right. But please remind her that I actually prevented you from assaulting Marc.

"Tao was egging me on the entire time. It's a miracle I didn't kill someone."

And you wonder why Baji thinks I am a bad influence.

Sonya scowled. "You tell Tao that for a wise old alien, he's an imbecile." Her expression softened. "Look, you all should get to your rooms. It's almost 9pm and security is stretched thin enough as it is. Tonight's going to be worse than yesterday."

The warning in her voice was clear. Roen excused himself and made his way toward his room. Like the previous night, he barricaded the window and made sure the doors were locked. He tossed and turned for about thirty minutes before finally dozing off.

He woke to the hotel phone ringing. Roen sat up with a start and looked at the clock: 12.30. Who could be calling him at this time? He waited for the phone to stop ringing before he turned over and tried to fall asleep again. A moment later, it rang again.

Roen sat up and picked up the phone. "Hello?" he said tiredly.

"I'm sorry to bother you, Mr Tan," the voice said on the other line. "This is Leon down in the hotel lobby. There is a Ms Tesser here to see you."

Roen, no...

Roen's mouth fell open soundlessly as he dropped the phone and ran for the door.

CHAPTER THIRTY-FIVE
UNINVITED

After the events involving the Chest of the Menagerie, I do not have much to tell that could show you any insight as to who I am. Because from that point on, it has been nothing but mindless war. I had given up all hope of an enlightened culture or of peaceful civilizations that innovated through stability. We used to be two sides playing chess with humanity's evolution as the prize. Now, we play simply to defeat the other side. In a way, the Prophus fell right into the Genjix's hands.

The hallways were eerily quiet as Roen ran to the elevators. He watched the numbers blink up to his floor, and as the doors opened, was greeted by a tall man in black Kevlar armor carrying a shotgun. His heart stopped as he instinctively sized up the potential threat: military repeating shotgun, two flashbangs, pistol at his waist, and knife in his boot.

"Sir," the guard said. "I don't suppose the ice machine is broken and you're going up?"

"Down," Roen replied, walking in and standing next to him. "Ground floor lobby."

The guard looked him up and down. Roen's own combat gear gave him away. The guard shook his head. "It's past curfew. You seem like you're up to no good. I don't suppose I can talk you out of it."

Roen shook his head.

The guard sighed and said, "Do you at least have a transponder on you?"

Roen shook his head again. "Tao, what transponder?"

Next time, read the security pamphlet.

The guard pulled a small metal box out of one of his many pockets and handed it to him. "Push the button if you require assistance. We'll find you."

Roen thanked him and the two of them waited in silence as the elevator music played. The elevator dinged and the doors opened to the ground level.

The guard called to him again as he sprinted out. "The lobby is no man's land, sir, as is the pool. The security detail is only stationed as far as the wing entrance."

Roen thanked him again and ran to the entrance of the lobby. He nodded at the two men stationed there. They looked tense as he slowed to a walk and tried to appear relaxed. Their eyes followed him as he strolled toward the front desk. There were two more men – not dressed like the other guards – standing in the center of the lobby talking to Jill. Roen tensed, taking in the room: five exits, unmanned main counter, two visible unknowns, and no weapons in sight. Jill seemed unconcerned as she chatted merrily with them. It felt like walking into a lion's den.

They are not ours.

She turned to him with a bright smile that disappeared when she noticed the stormy look on his face. "Hi?" she said playfully, arching her eyebrow.

"Could you come with me please?" Roen said tersely.

She gave him a curious look. "What crawled up your ass? And why are you dressed like Darth Vader? I should be the one that's pissed. Your cell phone is off and Antonio tells me you're here for some convention. How can my boyfriend come to Europe and not tell me? I haven't seen you in two months and Frankfurt's only a train ride away!"

I told you not to tell Antonio!

"It slipped; I didn't mean to."

Then you should have told him it was a Best Western in Utah.

"You know how bad I am at lying."

"Is this the gentleman you were waiting for, miss?" one of the Genjix said.

Jill forced a smile on her face and turned to them. "This is Roen, my boyfriend, the one I was telling you about. Thanks for calling him down for me. I don't know how I was going to reach him with the night clerk gone."

This is a trap. Tell them nothing. Get back to safety.

Roen felt his face go hot as he tried to suppress his discomfort. Jill was chatting with the Genjix as if they were new best friends. One of the smug operatives stuck a hand out. Roen ignored it and grabbed Jill by the elbow, herding her back toward the Prophus wing. He was a bit rougher with her than he'd like, but panic was setting in. If something happened to her, he would never forgive himself.

Halfway across the lobby, Jill stopped and pulled her arm away. "Wait a minute, mister, why were you so rude back there to Leon and Ubei? And why are you acting so weird?"

Ubei is the Iranian Genjix host.

"Go figure. She's best friends with them now."

Careful. They are following.

Roen stopped in his tracks. The two guards at the entrance of the Prophus wing were gone.

"Something is wrong."

The guards are down. Consider them compromised. Genjix behind you are two meters away.

Two more shadows stepped out from where the guards had been stationed, wearing the same black garb as the two Genjix operatives behind him. He would have to fight his way out of this. Appearing as casual as possible, he let go of Jill and put his hands in his pockets. With his left, he activated the transponder. With his right, he gripped the length of cold steel and silently thanked Sonya.

Jill stared at the two in front of them and then looked back at the two approaching them from the rear. "What kind of a convention is this? Why are all of you dressed like you're in the cast of *Cats*?"

The escape route is through the entrance or down the hallway on your right.

"Which route is safer?"

The entrance out of the hotel is longer, but unobstructed. The hallway leading to the pool and garden is a good place for an ambush.

Roen cursed under his breath. "Listen," he murmured out of the side of his mouth. "We need to leave right now. We can't stay here."

"What are you talking about?" Jill's eyes narrowed. "Do you have another girl in your room or something? You do, don't you? Well, I'm not leaving until I get answers."

Roen rolled his eyes. "I can't explain now," he growled. His eyes darted around the lobby. He could have sworn he saw more shadows off to the side.

"You asshole!" Jill fumed, punching him in the arm. "I can't believe..."

She gasped as he suddenly pulled the baton out, extending it as he turned, and striking Leon in the face. As Leon crumpled to the floor, Roen moved on to Ubei. Ubei dodged two wild swings before reeling backwards, the baton hitting him in the face. Blood exploded from his shattered nose as he fell backwards.

Duck!

Roen grabbed Jill and pulled her to the floor as a knife whistled just past their heads. "Run!" he ordered as he rolled to his feet and pushed her towards the entrance. One of the shadows pounced on top of him. An elbow to the side of his attacker's face disoriented him and knocked him back down on the floor. Roen kicked out and connected with his assailant's shins, tripping him.

Get out. Leon is recovering. You cannot take on three.

Roen got back to his feet, blocked a kick to his midsection, and pushed the last assailant away, before running after Jill. He caught up with her as she leaned on one of the columns just outside the front door.

"What is going on?" she said, shaking.

He grabbed her hand and dragged her with him as he took off in a run. "I'll explain later." The two ran hand in hand across the dimly lit streets to the park just outside of the Metropole. Behind him, he could hear the Genjix as they gave chase.

Roen led Jill behind a row of bushes and pulled her to the ground. He needed to get his bearings and stay hidden until the Prophus security team could find him. That damn transponder better work. He had studied the map of the surrounding area before he came. However, it was dark and there were so many trees around; it was difficult to pinpoint exactly where they were. Roen wasn't even sure which direction they were facing. He looked into the sky and scowled. It was too cloudy to make out any stars, let alone a constellation.

You are at the park just south-west of the Metropole. Allées des Boulingrins should be just on the other side of those trees.

"Roen," Jill said, her voice quavering. "Are these people trying to kill us?"

He put one finger to his lips and listened. There was a stiff breeze coming from the east which would help mask their steps in the grass, but it also made it easier for the Genjix to sneak up on them. To the south, he could hear running water. A fountain or a river? There was no river on the map he studied. To the west, he could hear the sound of cars on a busy street. Staying low to the ground, he led her westward toward the traffic. With luck, if there are enough people around, the Genjix would think better than to cause such a commotion just for him.

Suddenly, he heard footsteps ahead and saw a shadow pass in front of him and froze. His heart pounded as he waited. A year ago, Roen would have panicked. Now, he waited tensely for the Genjix to pass.

Jill, however, did not have the luxury of Roen's training. She gasped aloud. The dark figure stopped and looked to the right, then started to turn toward them. Roen had to do something now. He leaped forward, baton in hand, and struck the Genjix across the temple. The man collapsed on the spot. Jill gave him a terrified look that broke his heart. He knew what that look meant: Who is this man I'm with?

Self-defense if I ever saw it.

"Damn, Tao. Should I even bother buying a ring now or just assume she's going to dump my ass before the night's over?"

Let her decide. Do not decide for her.

To his right, he heard someone bark commands and then heard the sound of footsteps.

"We have to go," Roen whispered. They took off running again and burst through a line of bushes to a picturesque walkway with several fountains shooting water into the air. Unfortunately, it was late and there was no one walking about. They continued running south and passed Allées des Boulingrins to a smaller side street. Roen lost track again of which direction he was facing.

Your mental compass stinks.

"I'm sorry. I'm in a foreign country in the middle of the night with no stars and no map."

Make a right down that narrow street. You can get some distance from the Genjix.

Roen looked at the narrow dark street. "Damn European streets. That's an alley, not a street. No good ever comes to anyone being chased in the middle of the night by running into an alley."

Do not be foolish. It is the only direction that takes you away from the Genjix. You need some distance from them until our people can find you.

With more than a bit of trepidation, he pulled Jill toward the alley. She frowned and stopped. "Are you sure you want to go this way? I mean, this is usually the part in a movie where something jumps out and kills us."

"I know, I know." Roen shook his head. "Trust me on this."

Despite their hesitation, they took off down the alley, running blindly at a full sprint, when they heard footsteps fast approaching from behind. They were just about to round the bend when a shadow charged from the corner of Roen's line of sight. He twisted out of the way and dove to the ground. Instead, the shadow barreled into Jill, and a horrified Roen watched as her small body flew in the air and bounced off a brick wall with a sick thud.

With an enraged roar, he moved before he knew what he was doing. The baton materialized in his hand, and Roen struck Jill's assailant on the back of the neck, and then finished him off with two more vicious blows to the head. He turned and knelt down next to Jill. She moaned. She had an ugly welt on the side of her face and what looked like a broken arm.

With the way she is breathing, she might have cracked ribs as well. You have to leave her or hide. Or fight.

There was no way in hell Roen was going to leave her. Grimacing, he grabbed her by the waist and dragged her around the corner. She moaned in pain as they moved. His blood froze when he ran his fingers down the length of her arm and felt a bone protruding right below her elbow.

If you leave the transponder with her, our people will find her. You have to go. These men might not have guns, but be assured there is another fully armed Genjix team on their way now.

Roen hesitated. What could he do? He had to protect Tao and keep him from capture, but he couldn't leave Jill here. What would Edward do? The footsteps were getting louder. Roen dug out the small transponder and stuffed it into Jill's pocket. At the very least, the Prophus would find her. He was about to take off again when he stopped. With a curse, he pulled out the baton. "I'm sorry, Tao. I won't leave her."

Roen...

"I don't care. Help me, God damn it. I'm not leaving her!"

Roen peered over the corner and saw a group of dark figures charging closer down the street. He crouched and gripped the baton in his hand as the first of them reached the corner. Roen leaped at the closest figure just as he got into range, dropping him with a punch. And then Roen was surrounded. He barely ducked another baton swing before he connected one of his own to an assailant's knees. Then a rain of blows fell on top of him and his vision got fuzzy.

"Careful, you idiots. We need him alive. If he dies, Tao will escape," he heard a familiar voice fade in and out from close by.

Marc Kenton!

"I think I owe you one, Tao," Marc said as his voice came closer. A kick connected to his head and everything went dark.

Roen! Snap out of it!

Roen ebbed in and out of consciousness as he felt them move his body. Jill. What were they doing with Jill? He kept his eyes closed while he got his bearings and waited for a chance to escape. That opportunity came when he was suddenly dropped as another battle erupted all around him.

Roen opened his eyes and saw the most beautiful thing in the world. Sonya and her team had found him! The Genjix had all converged on them, only leaving one agent guarding him. Roen waited until the Genjix agent was distracted; then he jumped up, grabbed him by the neck and twisted. The Genjix collapsed. Roen looked around and saw Marc standing a few meters away, barking orders.

"All right, Tao. I think it's time I do Kathy a favor."

Roen found his target in the melee, and tackled Marc from behind. To his surprise, the man reacted immediately, turning his waist and wrapping his large arms around Roen's torso. They both crashed to the ground. Roen rolled and pulled out Marc's knife out of his belt sheath. Marc kneed him in the ribs, and the two wrestled for the knife. It flipped out of Roen's grasp and slid across the ground. They scrambled to their feet.

"You think your new toy is man enough to take me, Tao?" Marc snarled and attacked.

The first time they met at the club, Marc had seemed an impossibly massive man that was much stronger than Roen. Now, they were better matched. Roen stayed alert, defending himself when he could and retreating when he had to.

From what he could tell, Marc utilized a hybrid form of tae kwon do and possibly wing chun. The momentum was one way as Roen slowly retreated. Try as he might, he barely held off Marc's offense as he struggled to dodge a barrage of leg kicks.

Watch his attack pattern! An image of Marc moments before throwing the same combination of kicks appeared in Roen's head. As the fight progressed, he began to recognize the pattern.

"You're like a punching bag," Marc sneered. "Tao, I thought you had a better-trained vessel, considering how formidable Edward was."

"It's not over yet," Roen snapped back.

He attacked again, blocking Marc's kick and pressing forward. Roen took two quick punches to the face as the other man retreated, but Roen refused to back down. He would have to smother Marc in order to beat him. They fought on, attacking and defending in succession.

Marc was quicker and stronger, and Roen was eating a large
number of blows. It was a fight he was going to lose at this
rate. He missed blocking another high kick that floored him.
Roen sat up and scrambled away on his hands and knees. He
was bleeding from several places and tiring. Then his hands
felt a sharp smooth metal object – the knife! Roen picked it up
and brandished it.

Marc sneered. "What's the matter, boy? No fair fight?"

"You mean like when you had ten of your goons jump me,
you piece of garbage?" Roen spat.

"Semantics." Marc shrugged and grinned. "I thought we
were having a gentleman's mano-a-mano fight. Well, no matter." He pulled out a baton.

*You can take this guy. Watch his footwork. He favors stepping into
his swings and pushing. Take advantage of his forward movement.
When Marc is injured, he loses his temper.*

The two stalked each other for a few moments, until Roen
made the first move. Their weapons clashed several times as
he feinted and thrust low, trying to find an opening. His attacks
fell short and Marc attacked. Roen backpedaled, staying just
out of range of the longer weapon, weaving and dodging the
swings of the baton as Marc pressed him even harder. Then
Roen suddenly ducked, slipping under the large man's guard.
Marc had overreached and Roen sliced a gash across his
ribcage. Marc stumbled backward.

"Is that the best you got, Tao?" he growled.

Marc came in again. Roen, watching for the opening Tao
had advised, dodged the first swing and nicked Marc in the
arm. Marc roared and moved again, this time coming from the
opposite angle. Roen ducked low, slipped under his arm, and
buried the knife into his ribcage. Marc shuddered as he stared
down at his chest.

Roen could have sworn he heard Tao growl as he pushed
the knife into Marc's chest. This man killed Edward, was all

Roen thought as he drove forward, shoving Marc back against the wall.

Roen leaned close to Marc's ear and whispered, "One day, I'm going to tell my kids about how great a man Edward Blair was, and how a worm named Marc Kenton shot him in the back. And then I'm going to tell them how I avenged Edward. Edward will live forever through Tao. You, on the other hand..." Roen twisted the knife in Marc's chest and pulled it out. Marc gasped and collapsed onto the ground, breathing shallowly as blood poured from his mouth.

Thank you, Roen. This meant everything to me.

"Should I put him out of his misery?"

No. Leave him. He has a punctured lung and can survive for a bit. If you kill him, Jeo will escape. Hurry and get to Sonya.

Roen turned and saw Genjix enveloping her as she flashed through a cloud of dark bodies. The bodies of all the other Prophus agents were lying face down nearby. She wielded a knife in one hand and a baton in the other. Blood was streaming down her face. One Genjix grabbed her arm even while Sonya slit another agent's throat with the knife. A third disarmed her, forcing the knife out of her hand. And then a fourth agent punched her in the face.

Sonya twisted free of the Genjix holding her right arm, elbowed him in the neck, and finished him off with a swing of her baton. She pulled back just as the first agent who punched her swung again. The punch missed her by scant centimeters and she retaliated with a low kick to the shin, snapping the bone. Despite that, she could not handle the rest as several more took his place.

With a roar, Roen charged the remaining Genjix and bowled one over. He struck blindly, cutting his way through to her. However, there were too many. The Genjix agents turned on him and overwhelmed him with their numbers. Finally, a blow to the side of the head staggered him and everything went dark again.

When he came to for the second time, Paula was kneeling over him, propping his head up. "You took quite a beating there, Roen," she said as she looked him over.

"Sonya?" he said weakly.

Paula shook her head. "Taken. The Genjix were trying to escape with all of you when we descended on them. I shot the two men carrying you and Marc." Roen struggled to sit up, but she kept him pinned down. "Easy there. Rest a bit. Things are under control now. We captured Jeo. Marc is still alive."

"I have a friend. Is she all right?"

Paula looked at him solemnly, then looked away. "The Genjix escaped by car with two prisoners. I'm assuming the other body is your friend. We chased them to the airport, but they escaped. We're moving a satellite in now to track them. Don't worry, we'll find them."

Roen's mind went blank as his entire world came crashing down on him. They had Jill! He screamed as loud as he could, then pushed Paula aside. He looked down the dark alley, at where he last saw her, and took off at a full sprint. It took half a dozen Prophus agents to subdue him.

CHAPTER THIRTY-SIX
CAPULET'S SKI LODGE

The last few centuries, we were involved in nearly every war. The Prophus inspired the French and American Revolutions. The Genjix started the War of 1812 and the Great War. Both sides blamed the other for World War II. The blame for the Vietnam, Korean wars, and the events in the Middle East could be laid at both our feet. We keep declaring that we fight for humanity and this planet, but at every turn, our actions speak otherwise.

Roen marveled at the state-of-the-art submarine that was the Prophus flagship, the Atlantis. Once all the agents had gotten on board, the submarine was underwater within seconds and speeding off toward its destination. He would never have believed the Prophus had such technology at their disposal if he hadn't seen it with his own eyes.

Following the rest of the group, he went into a conference room packed with agents for the briefing. It was standing room only, so Roen leaned against the cold steel wall and looked around at the sterile layout of the submarine, studying the metal frames that supported the room like a ribcage. He supposed he would be in the stomach, then.

The transponder Roen put on Jill had stopped working

shortly after her capture. Fortunately, by that time the Prophus had oriented a satellite over the Mediterranean Sea and tracked the Genjix craft east toward northern Italy, to a base known as the Capulet's Ski Lodge. Roen had thought Sonya and Jill were out of reach until Abrams, the admiral of the Prophus fleet, informed him that an attack on the base was already on the books for that night. From there, it was a short helicopter ride to the *Atlantis* and soon they were on their way toward the base – with the assault commencing within a matter of hours.

The lights dimmed briefly as the submarine descended deeper into the sea's depths. Unlike most submarines Roen saw in movies, the *Atlantis* was very spacious, almost like a luxury submarine, if there were such a thing. The lights dimmed again as Admiral Abrams stepped up to the podium.

The crowd grew silent as the admiral cleared his throat and spoke. "The bulk of the Genjix are still at the Decennial. We need to complete this mission before the enemy can reroute their forces. As you all know, this was originally an assault to steal the Penetra scanner prototype while the Genjix were focused on the party at Monaco. Now it is also a rescue mission. Several Prophus delegates and a civilian were kidnapped at the Decennial. Satellite tracking has pinpointed their trajectory toward the Capulet's Ski Lodge.

"The Capulet's Ski Lodge is currently the headquarters of Genjix European operations. We've heard no chatter from the Genjix regarding our rapid deployment, but they are likely on heightened security. If we take this base, it'll cripple their operations.

"Team formations have been altered to accommodate the rescue mission. We need to hit them hard at the very last minute in order to minimize the danger to the hostages. We reach the beach in two hours, so rest up and get some chow after this meeting. They have our people, ladies and gentlemen.

We want them back! Good luck, and send these bastards to the Eternal Sea. The floor's yours, Stephen."

For the rest of the meeting, Stephen and Dylan laid out their tactical attack plan. It was a complex and large assault. The base was built into a mountaintop and would be difficult to breach. All five teams had separate entry points and objectives.

Roen's Echo team was augmented from the original plan, and would infiltrate the base from the rear to locate the hostages. Roen lost track of what the other teams were supposed to do, and decided to focus on the specific objectives for his own. He'd have to rely on his squad commander for guidance. All he cared about was Jill and Sonya's safe return anyway.

As the briefing wrapped up, Roen decided to get a final meal before the attack. His stomach had growled all through the meeting, constantly reminding him that he was famished. He went down to the mess hall and sat down with a plate of food. He found he had no appetite for food as his thoughts went to Sonya and Jill. What was Roen doing eating while they were in danger? How could he have failed both of them? It was his fault they were captured. He would never forgive himself if anything happened to them. Tears welled up in his eyes as he pushed the plate away. He got up to leave, ashamed that he was crying.

"Roen, good to see you're all right," Stephen said as he came up and put a sympathetic hand on Roen's shoulder. Taking an apple and cutting it in two, Stephen offered him half. Roen shook his head and tried to wipe away the tears. Stephen shrugged and took a bite with a loud crunch. "Don't worry, son, the girls will be all right. They'll keep Sonya alive until they can interrogate her. Your friend will be used as leverage against you. We'll be on them before they can do anything. I promise."

"It's my fault they got captured," Roen mumbled.

"Nonsense, son," Stephen said. "It's the Genjix's. Make no mistake about it. Don't beat yourself up. Just make it right in two hours when we land and make them pay."

He is right. If you let your emotions control you, we will not be able to save them. Focus on the task ahead of us.

"What if we're too late, Tao? I don't think I can live with myself."

I swear, if you continue wallowing in self-pity, I will kill you myself just to switch hosts. Get yourself together. We have your future wife to save.

"Look," Stephen reassured him, "you'll see them both again. I put you in charge of the retrieval team; you'll find them." Stephen gave him one last pat on the back before leaving. "I'll see you on the beach."

I cannot believe I am saying this, but you should eat. You will need your strength.

Roen couldn't help but feel guilty about eating at a time like this, but Tao was right. He needed to be ready for the rescue mission. He pulled the plate back and chewed with conviction, intent on not enjoying any of it. However, the submarine mess hall's food was actually pretty good. In fact, Roen warranted it a step up from the crap he usually ate. At least if he died, he would do so with a full stomach.

"Small solace," he muttered as he stuck his fork into a piece of potato and lifted it to his mouth.

Feeding you well is the least we can do.

"Is that some kind of rule? Never kill people on an empty stomach?"

If it is not, it should be.

Roen sighed. "I never dreamed my life would come to this."

Your life will be whatever you make of it. You always lamented about wanting to get out of that... what did you call it, middle-class rat race? Well, now you are making a difference. Is this not what you always dreamed of?

"You know what that taught me? To be careful of what I wish for. I should have spent all that mental energy dreaming of a Brazilian lingerie model instead. Think of how much happier I would be."

I am glad you still have your sense of humor.

"Who says I'm joking?"

Well, I would rather you be with a Brazilian lingerie model instead of being here as well. Does that make you feel better?

"Surprisingly, it does. Shows you're not all work and no play."

You sound like a bitter girlfriend. You never take me anywhere. You are not funny. You are not romantic. You do not buy me things.

Roen chuckled. "I do feel like a bitter girlfriend."

Really? Is that what you think of me?

"Well, everyone tells me you're a hard-ass. I mean, just look at Yol and Paula. It's like they're having a party in her head every day."

You do realize that Paula is highly trained and very experienced. She has been involved with us for a decade now. Yol has it easy. He moved into a penthouse while I got a fixer-upper. You needed my hard-ass-ness.

"I'm a fixer-upper?"

Actually, you were a complete demolition and rebuild.

"That would be insulting if I didn't know it was true. Was I that bad?"

You want me to be honest?

"No, lie to me."

You were a natural. There was a pause before Tao spoke again. *But I have to say, Roen, I am extremely proud of you. You have come unbelievably far and become a fine agent.*

"Like Edward Blair fine?"

Keep aiming high. It is hard to be Edward Blair fine.

"So everyone tells me."

"Excuse me, sir?" A lieutenant walked up to him.

Roen looked up from his meal. "Yes?"

"Admiral Abrams is requesting all personnel report to the launch deck. We're deploying in ten."

Roen leaned over the side and hurled his dinner into the dark depths of the Mediterranean Sea. The skiff bounced up and down over the thick waves like a bronco trying to buck him off. He wiped his mouth and sat back down in his seat. Around him, the men in his squad looked as if nothing happened. Morgan, Roen's second in command, leaned over. "You all right, sir?"

"Just a little seasickness." Roen retched.

They might have believed that if you had not vomited before we launched.

"Well, this boat ride isn't helping matters much. Are we almost there?"

0400. Any minute now.

Roen watched the other two skiffs skim along the water. Watching them move around made the nausea creep back up his throat. His skiff banked sharply to the right, throwing him toward the far side. He almost lost the rest of his dinner right there. Roen tried to take his mind off the waters by going over the tactics in his head. With Jill and Sonya's lives on the line, there was no room for error.

Moments later the captain gave the signal to cut the motors. The skiffs went dark as their forward momentum carried them quietly to shore. The men began preparing for the landing, checking gear, supplies, and ammunition. When the skiffs neared the edge of the water, they jumped out and waded the rest of the way. The groups separated into their teams while Stephen gave last-minute instructions to the commanders.

Roen looked up at the mountain in front of him and then at the sky. It was a pitch-black night, which offered plenty of cover, but would make traversing the mountain very treacherous. Thunder rumbled in the distance; rain could make the climb even more dangerous than the Genjix.

After the last-minute instructions were finished, the teams began the long trek up the mountain, each taking a different path. Roen's team was assigned to the ventilation shaft, the highest but safest point of entry. They filed into a loose line and moved at a brisk pace up the mountain. Roen looked back one last time as the rest of the invasion force disappeared into the thick foliage.

"How did the Genjix build this fort? From the photos, it seems carved into the mountain."

They did not build it. The Germans built it during the war as a secret V-2 rocket research lab. They thought putting it in Italy would keep the Allies from bombing it. Only a few in the Nazi high command knew of its existence. It was very top secret. An accident in 1943 caused a cave-in that sealed it off. We moved in during the Cold War.

"If it was so secret, how did we know about it?"

We had people in the Nazi high command.

Roen almost stopped walking, shocked. "We were Nazis?"

As were the Genjix. We were many things. Some we were proud of, others not so much. One of us was the centurion who crucified Jesus of Nazareth. Another of us helped design the atomic bomb. Several of us sacked Carthage.

"So why didn't you guys do something about the Nazis?"

We tried, and failed. Nazi fascism was the brainchild of a certain Genjix named Zoras. We had people in the government, but he arranged to have them all removed.

"Is there anyone in the current administration?"

In the cabinet, as a matter of fact.

"Really? Then why doesn't he do something about the Middle East?"

She is doing something about the Middle East. But we have to be careful not to blow her cover. Our influence needs to be subtle.

"I guess. Have you been to this place before?"

It used to be our Eastern European command center until we moved after the Cold War. All the execs were getting annoyed with having to make the trip to the middle of nowhere. Then the Genjix moved in.

"Where did you move our headquarters to?"

Prague.

"That doesn't seem like a great place to have a secret head-quarters."

It makes traveling a lot more convenient. Secret headquarters are so last century. We just bought a building and took over the top offices. Welcome to the new millennium.

"Why is it called Capulet's Ski Lodge?"

The Keeper likes to name our bases after references from her old plays.

The rough path they were following became more difficult. Roen did not have much experience with this terrain but was determined not to show his uneasiness.

"How is our progress so far?" he asked as he moved up alongside Morgan. He knew the commander was in control of the situation, but Roen was still the ranking officer and intended to lead them as much as he could.

"We're five minutes behind schedule, sir," Morgan said in his no-nonsense way. "But that is expected, considering the conditions, and allowances have been padded into our mission timetable."

"Make up the time," Roen said anxiously.

"Of course, sir," Morgan replied. He signaled the men, and they picked up the pace. If the mission went as planned, the other four teams would have already engaged the Genjix by the time Echo team penetrated the interior of the base. With the attention on the front of the base, his team would surprise the Genjix from the rear. The upside of this assignment was that they would most likely meet the least resistance. The downside was they had no path of retreat.

They reached the apex on schedule. Stephen and the rest of their forces should already be in place by now. Radio silence kept them from communicating until the first shot was fired. Morgan took out the map and spread it on the ground. The men gathered around to cover the small light he was using. He compared the coordinates on their GPS to the map and nodded to Roen. This had to be the right spot.

Roen looked around. He did not see anything remotely resembling this ventilation shaft. One of the men tapped him on the shoulder and pointed up. The ventilation shaft was about ten meters above them, jutting from a sheer cliff. Roen began to look for another way up when he noticed two of the men unpacking climbing gear.

"We anticipated this," Morgan said. "There will only be a small delay while we rappel up."

Roen sighed and shook his head. Morgan might have thought Roen was just being irritable, but the real reason was because he hated heights. Walking up a mountain was one thing, but rappelling up it was another matter entirely.

Before long, the two men had scaled those ten meters and were at the top of the cliff, using some sort of grappling gun. Once there, they set up a pulley system to pull the others up. One of the last to ascend, Roen closed his eyes and tried to keep his cool. He did not want to appear weak in front of the men. Thankfully, the trip up was short. In mere minutes, they were all huddled around the metal shaft while one man used wire cutters to cut through the grating. Roen looked over and tapped his watch. Morgan nodded in return. They were still on schedule.

"Tao, do you think there might be traps in the shaft? Like wired bombs or mines?"

Doubtful. Birds fly in here all the time. Besides, if they blow up the main ventilation shaft, how is anyone going to breathe down there?

"I didn't think of that."

Good thing I am here to think for you.

In a matter of minutes, they had cut a man-sized hole through the shaft and bent in the rest of the covering. Another agent took out a small box and handed out something that looked like large fuzzy slippers to each of them. Roen frowned at the slippers in his hands.

"What is this for?"

Put them over your shoes. It will dampen the sound of your footsteps in the metal shaft.

"Wow, we think of everything."

We have been in the breaking and entering craft for a long time now.

"Infiltration craft, you mean."

Welcome to the family business.

They filed in one by one, silently moving through the large shaft. It was surprisingly clean. Roen looked down to see his gun strap swaying back and forth. There must be a fan that was pulling the wind into the base. They continued as the shaft split into a few smaller side paths. They ignored most of them, following some predetermined route through the confusing metal maze. Roen could probably wander around in circles for hours without knowing which way to go.

"Do you know where we're going?"

Did you fall asleep during the briefing?

"No, but we've made so many turns."

I can get us back to the entrance if that is what you are asking.

"Good, because I'm completely lost."

The humming became louder the deeper they traveled through the shaft; they must be near the generator. The point man held up a fist and illuminated with his flashlight a metal grate in front of them. The rest of the squad stopped and knelt down.

"Is that the drop-off point?" Roen whispered to Morgan.

Morgan took out the GPS and checked the coordinates. He nodded. Immediately, the men began to shed any excess gear they were wearing. From this point on, it was guns and ammunition only.

Roen stared at the grate. This was the point of no return. During the meeting, Intelligence had estimated that there most likely could be up to two hundred personnel. That was twice their number, but hopefully with their element of surprise, it would be enough.

Two men picked up the heavy grate and moved it to the side. Another agent took out a small probe and scanned the room below. When he finished, he moved to Roen and Morgan to report his findings. "It's the back storeroom, all right; no heat signatures, just boxes and crates. No motion detectors or cameras either. We're looking at a six-meter drop to the floor."

"Shouldn't the other squads have started by now?" Roen asked. "We should have heard shots."

"There might have been some delays getting into position. We all move when Stephen's team is ready," Morgan said. "But this is our go-no-go point. Get the rope ready to drop down but we won't move unt..."

A loud bang punctured the air, followed by a series of other rapid bangs. In the distance, the muffled sound of an explosion shook the walls around them. Thick dust sprinkled down, covering them.

"Get the rope lowered," Roen snapped. "I want us down there in thirty seconds."

Easy there, General Patton. Remember, a leader always stays in control. Do not let your emotions get the best of you here.

One of the men lowered a long rope, and the team shimmied down one at a time. Roen watched as twenty men dropped down with catlike quickness and formed a defensive perimeter. Roen went down almost as fast, though he almost lost his grip midway down. His heart was pounding as he dropped to the floor and took up position behind a crate.

Somewhere in the distance, a muffled explosion rocked the base and a siren began to blare. Shouting and footsteps added to the cacophony. Roen ran through his pre-fight mental checklist, checking his clip and making sure the safety was off. His mind raced and he worked at keeping his breathing steady. The squad waited with professional patience for the signal to move. Morgan looked at him, waiting for his go.

Give it another sixty seconds.

Those sixty seconds felt like an hour as Roen counted the time out. Another explosion shook the base again. And then another. "Fifty-four, fifty-five, fifty-six..."

Now!

Without any hesitation, Roen stood up from his hiding spot and waved his arms forward. "Move, move! Weapons hot, we're going in!"

CHAPTER THIRTY-SEVEN
THE ASSAULT

After the turn of the twenty-first century, man has evolved to such a point where the Quasing can no longer treat man as errant children. The recent development of the Penetra scanner has raised new concerns for our safety. Now, for the first time, we can be detected by humans. It is a powerful weapon for either side in the war, but even more importantly, if it falls into the wrong hands, it has the risk of exposing us to those not involved with the Quasing. Now is the beginning of the end. Human and Quasing fates are converging. With the Penetra scanner, humans will soon learn that they are not alone. How will they react to us?

The door opened a sliver, just large enough for the scope to scan the outside room. The agent held his hand in the air in a closed fist pointing forward and waved it from side to side. Immediately, the door swung open and the others poured into the next room.

Morgan put a hand on Roen's sleeve as he rushed forward and shook his head. "Commanders go last."

There are different sets of rules for leading and following. As a leader, your safety comes first.

"I don't want them to think I'm a coward."

This is your first command. Your men will value your judgment more than your bravery.

Roen and Morgan were the last to walk out of the store-room. They entered a deserted industrial-sized kitchen with food still cooking over the stove top. Two Prophus agents were stationed at the double door at the far end, and the rest were scattered throughout the room. Morgan walked up to one of the boiling pots and turned the fire off. "They'll set fire to this place if they're not careful," he muttered.

Roen looked at the row of ovens cooking different varieties of meat and frowned. "That's an awful lot of food to cook for a midnight snack."

"Probably operating on American time," Morgan said. "That's where most of the major action is these days, and if you're holed up in a cave, it doesn't matter what time zone you're in."

Roen did a fast inventory of everything being cooked and looked back at Morgan. "There must be several hundred men here. That or they're feeding a professional football team."

Morgan nodded and turned to one of the agents. "Daniels, stay in the rear and establish communication with the other teams. We should be out of radio silence now. All right, gentlemen, our primary objectives are the control room and the security cells. Once we gain control of those facilities and free the delegates and the princesses, we'll work our way forward and jump these bastards from the rear."

Roen ordered the two men at the door to scope outside and signaled for the others to gather around. Morgan stood by and watched as he gave the proper signals. "You sure you never led a team before, sir?" he asked with a wry smile as Roen walked by.

"Just cover for me when I screw up," Roen replied, lifting his gun and following the last of them out the door.

They filtered out to the main corridor with half the squad

on one wall and half on the other. Roen took the right flank and stayed low as they moved in a double line down the hall. The walls were made of cement blocks, painted dull white. It reminded him of the hallways in his high school. There were even lockers lined up at the wall. The florescent lights added a touch of the surreal as the group of hunched-over men, dressed in black, skittered forward like oversized centipedes.

One of the agents pointed at a camera in the corner and another pulled out a pistol with a silencer. He took aim and destroyed it with one shot. In the back of his mind, Roen ran through all the things that could go wrong. Were they going to be late? What if his team was out of position? Those fears overrode his usual strong sense of self-preservation.

"We need to step it up!" he growled. "We have men depending on us."

Easy there. We are on schedule.

"Are you sure? The noise of fighting has been going on for a long time now."

You really have no internal clock, do you? It has only been three minutes. We will engage when ready.

Daniels, standing next to Morgan, spoke up. "Sir, group communication has been established; all except Delta team are in place. They are reporting heavy resistance at their entry point. They are unable to advance."

Delta is Dylan's team.

"Tao, Delta's objectives are the main hallway and securing the scanner, right?"

I see you were not completely asleep during the briefing.

"I take my breaking and entering very seriously. Are we close to them?"

We are not too far away. It is on the west side one level down. His team's objective is crucial.

"Echo has too many objectives already. If we don't secure the control room, we stall the offensive. If we don't rescue our people fast enough, they might be killed. If we don't help Delta, the teams won't be able to converge. What should I do, Tao?"

You do not have a choice. Split the team into squads and divide the objectives.

Roen nodded. He looked at Morgan and ordered, "Send one squad to the control room and one to the security cells. The rest will spring Delta team. The squad at the control room needs to coordinate with the rest of the squads once they obtain access to the base. The squad at the security cells stays put until the rest of us can rendezvous with them."

Morgan replied, "Affirmative."

Then Morgan split the teams off, and the rest of them hurried down toward Dylan's location. The hallways were filled with smoke and broken lights as they made their way through, occasionally meeting light resistance. Roen was surprised that they had found so few guards so far. Stephen really had made sure he would be in as little danger as possible. The sound of heavy gunfire, however, increased as they reached the upper level of the main hallway. They arrived at a large set of wooden double doors and fanned out on both sides.

Morgan opened one door a crack and scoped out the other side. "Heavy enemy presence engaged with our people. Let's crash the party. Will you do the honors, sir?"

Roen gave the signal and watched his men burst through the doors, spreading out as they moved down the stairs. They encountered resistance immediately as they proceeded toward the lower level. A group of Genjix soldiers had taken up position at the bottom of the stairs, setting up a barricade to fight what should be Dylan's Delta team. Roen's Echo team descended upon the Genjix furiously, catching them in a crossfire. Roen positioned himself behind one of the banisters and fired, carefully picking his shots as they presented themselves. He estimated the enemy strength to be about forty men at the base of the stairs. Out of the corner of his eye, Roen saw

Delta team moving forward when they realized the Genjix soldiers had been outflanked.

A sudden shock knocked him onto his back. He gasped and began to tumble down the stairs. One of his men grabbed him by the collar and pulled him back up. Roen took shallow breaths as his eyes watered from the pain. Morgan moved next to him and checked him for wounds.

"Where were you shot?" he asked.

"It feels like someone just took a cattle prod to my shoulder," Roen gasped.

Morgan moved his hand to his shoulder. Roen grimaced with pain. When Morgan pulled his hand back, there was blood on his hands.

"Shoulder wound, all right," Morgan said. "Can you move your arm?"

Roen raised his left arm, winced, and then made a fist with his hand. "Well, it doesn't seem like it struck bone. You should be fine," Morgan said, helping Roen to his feet. "First time being shot?"

He nodded.

"Welcome to the club." The man actually grinned. "Why don't you hang back while we finish up here? We seem to have this under control anyway."

Roen gritted his teeth. "No, I'm fine. Hand me my rifle."

"Take five... sir."

Roen saw the look on Morgan's face, sat back down, and leaned against the wall.

"Really? Welcome to the club?"

Hey, it was bound to happen, might as well happen now. At least you were not shot in the stomach. Now that is painful.

"You guys are nuts."

Several minutes later, the sound of the gunfire finally died down. A few minutes later, Dylan met him at the top of the stairs. The older man grinned as Roen picked himself up to shake his hand.

"I see you got your initiation," Dylan said, gesturing at his shoulder.

"Am I supposed to be happy about that?" Roen replied.

"Nah, getting shot sucks. Anything broken?"

"Just a flesh wound, I think."

"Good, we need to help Stephen secure the level, then we'll make the push to the Penetra scanner housing unit. I'll see you at the end of this, eh? Godspeed, Roen." Dylan patted him on the non-injured shoulder and ran back downstairs.

"Sir." Morgan ran up. "We have control of the security cells. The squad rescued six delegates. Two are dead. There are no sign of the princesses or the other two delegates. Retrieval team is pinned down and is requesting support. The squad at the control room is reporting a large concentration of enemy activity at the helipad. If the Genjix are trying to escape, they might have the princesses and the two delegates with them."

Roen clenched his uninjured fist and looked at Morgan. If he didn't reinforce the security cells now, there might not be a squad left by the time he got there. There were also the lives of the six remaining delegates to consider. However, if the Genjix at the helipad had the girls and they escaped, he might lose them forever. He could split his men again to tackle both objectives, but it was too risky; they were already stretched too thin. None of the options seemed acceptable.

"Tao?"

Conventional wisdom is to take the security cells as planned. The six delegates' lives have to be the priority. Pray that the Genjix at the helipad do not have Sonya and Jill.

Roen shook his head. It wasn't a gamble he was willing to take. If he was wrong, he could never live with himself. "Commander Morgan," he said. "I'm taking five men to the helipad. Take the rest and reinforce the security cells."

That is not wise.

"I'm calling this, Tao."

Morgan shook his head in protest. "We shouldn't be splitting..."

"That's an order!" Roen growled, giving him a look that left no room for argument.

The commander hesitated slightly before nodding. He waved at several of the agents. "Seven through eleven, assist the commander. Everyone else, let's keep moving."

He grabbed Roen's arm as he passed by. "Stay low and keep safe. Watch your six, sir."

Roen and his men broke off from the main group. Since they deviated from the planned route, he depended on Tao to help navigate through the complex to the helipad. When they reached the first corner, Roen held up his fist. The group stopped and leaned against the wall.

He took out a probe and looked around the side. There were four guards at an intersection on the far end of the hallway. Roen turned to the others and signaled, holding up four fingers, closing them into a fist, and then flicking his thumb out. He took out a grenade and pulled the pin. With a deep breath, he turned and rolled it toward the guards. The resulting explosion almost knocked him off his feet. Roen turned the corner and charged.

Commanders go last.

He stopped and pointed. "Go, go!"

The others, rifles up, moved forward into the thick smoke. Roen followed, staying low and moving in the rear. They reached the intersection and inspected the scattered bodies on the floor, taking position at the corner. Roen saw a group of guards approaching from the left hallway. He held up three fingers, counted to three, leaned around the corner, and opened fire. The Genjix soldiers scattered and returned fire.

Roen pulled back to reload and let two of his other men take his place. All his men were on one side of the intersection. They had to get on the other side to take advantage of the corridor space. He gritted his teeth as the two currently engaged pulled back around the corner to reload.

"I need suppressive fire," he yelled over the din of the noise. He looked at the agent in the back and pointed at the corridor behind them. "Watch the rear!"

After the next round of enemy fire, he waited while his men laid down covering fire. Roen took a few steps back, ran forward, and dove across the intersection to the other side. He had become used to such acrobatic moves through his time training with Sonya and Lin. However, carrying out these maneuvers with heavy gear through gunfire made this dive feel like he was swimming through molasses.

Bullets zinged past his body. Time seemed to slow as he seemed to float in midair. The yellow explosions from the muzzles of their guns pulsed like dancing flames. Then Roen felt a heavy thud as he hit the floor and rolled onto his knees. It took him an instant to catch his breath as he scampered up to the corner and leaned against the wall.

What the hell are you doing?

"I'm fine. We needed more cover, so I came to this side."

Next time, tell someone else to do it. You are the commander.

Roen watched his men on the other side lay down a fresh barrage. He joined them, spraying bullets at the Genjix soldiers. The exchange continued for several more seconds until the sound of enemy gunfire eventually died. One of his men crept forward to confirm the kills. When the agent finally signaled the all-clear, Roen's men came out of their positions.

Check the men. Always put their safety first.

"Anyone hurt?" he asked as they checked the bodies.

"Two of us with minor wounds, sir," the man next to him reported. "Carlberg suffered a head injury, but he's fine. Perez might have a cracked rib."

The thought of losing men never occurred to him. Roen turned and looked for his men. He counted only four as they reported in.

"We lost Hutchinson," another man said.

That hit him like a mild shock. Roen stiffened and looked down at the floor. While he had expected that some of his people might die, it had never occurred to him that the burden of command would make their deaths his responsibility. Now, that statement weighed heavily on him: "We lost Hutchinson."

Roen, do not dwell on it. We have a job to do.

"Sir?" his man said, waiting on his orders.

Think about the rest of your men. You still have their lives to worry about.

Roen nodded and looked at the agent. "Kwan, right?"

The agent nodded.

"Let's go. We have a job to do."

CHAPTER THIRTY-EIGHT
VINDICATION

I live in fear of the day when humans learn that we have been playing them like puppet masters since the dawn of their time. I can only hope that they understand that we tried to do right by them, that no matter how much evil the Quasing has brought to their planet, some of us are still fighting for their best interests. I do not think humanity will have that forgiveness. As is your saying, may God have mercy on all Quasing's souls, for I do not believe humans will, once the truth is out.

Roen's small group continued toward the helipad. When they reached the stairs, they gathered at its base and used a scope under the door to assess the enemy strength. There were two guards on the other side of the door and at least a dozen men near the center of the helipad.

A waiting helicopter hovered directly above them, readying to land. There were four prisoners, with hoods over their heads standing off to the side, flanked by two guards. Roen recognized Jill and Sonya by their clothes. Both seemed no worse for wear. Roen felt renewed rage when he saw Sean giving orders on a handset and standing behind Sonya.

"How should I play this, Tao?"

Incendiary to the right, away from the prisoners. Send two left and

the rest right, providing suppression fire. The guards in the open are
not wearing armor, so they should go down easily. Have the men stay
near cover. Be careful of Sean and take him down last.

Roen pointed to two of his men, pointed at the door, and
then pointed left. He pointed at the other two men and
pointed right. Then he held up his open hand and counted off
from five. His men ran up the stairs and quickly took out the
two door guards and then took cover. Roen came out last and
hurled his grenade toward the enemy but away from the two
women. The explosion shook the ground and threw up a cloud
of smoke and debris. He felt a rush of cool air and raindrops
on his arm as he burst outside and opened fire.

Roen waited a beat as his men moved to flank the enemy,
then he dove behind a crate near the door and took aim at the
soldiers at the far end. A quick burst of gunfire took them
down. A grenade flew right over his head and landed a few
meters behind him. He took off running and stumbled as another explosion damaged the entranceway to the helipad.
Roen rolled to his feet and continued to fire, staying low and
constantly moving. Out of the corner of his eye, he saw one
of his men fall. And then another. There were still half a dozen
Genjix guards left.

Keep moving down the right. Order the left flank back, and get
someone on that guard making his way toward the back. Be careful
with the two near the women.

Roen shouted orders at his remaining two men as he followed Tao's lead and continued to shoot. One of the Genjix
guarding Sonya and Jill fell, and then another fell. Sean pulled
out his pistol and took cover behind the two women.

"You coward!" Roen roared.

Smart move if anything. Order your men to get behind him.

Roen looked to both sides and suddenly realized he was
alone. Where were his men? By his count, there were still at
least two Genjix guards and Sean to deal with. He reloaded

and crawled back toward the door. It had gotten eerily quiet on the helipad, with only the crackling sound of fire interrupting the otherwise dead silence.

Roen saw one of the Genjix poke his head out of a corner. Roen aimed quickly and took him down. The last guard he found trying to flank him. Roen's life flashed before his eyes for a split second when the guard fell. Kwan, it seemed, was still alive. The agent gave him a quick nod as they warily headed for Sean.

Sean, still standing behind Sonya, looked more annoyed than worried. "Now that you two can hear me," he said mildly, "I suggest you drop your guns before I put a bullet in your precious Prophus here."

"Fat chance, Sean," Roen shouted. "You should think about surrendering right about now."

Sean cocked his head. "Is that you, Roen Tan? You came all the way here for your girlfriend, did you? I'm just not sure which one she is."

Roen and Kwan slowly closed in on Sean. Sean glanced back and forth at the two with a bemused expression. Roen didn't know how the man could be so unconcerned with the situation. The helicopter had long since pulled away and the entranceway had been damaged. There was no way for the man to escape except down the mountainside.

"I'll make you a deal, Roen," Sean said. "Why don't we all put down our weapons? And then I'll release your girlfriends and these two gentlemen here. In return, you give me a one-minute head start, and then you can pick up your weapons and come after me. Is that reasonable?"

Sounds too reasonable. You cannot trust Chiyva.

"Or I can just shoot you," Roen responded.

Sean chuckled. "Here's why you won't. If, let's say, you happen to miraculously be a crack shot with an automatic assault rifle, which I don't believe you are, and you do manage to kill me, where do you think Chiyva will go, girlfriend number two or your man here? Think about it, son." The thought of the Genjix being in Jill gave Roen chills. That would be a fate almost worse than death. What could he do then? Roen frantically tried to think of a solution.

"How do I know I can trust you?" he asked.

Sean shrugged. "You don't. But I can't take on two fully armed men and you won't shoot at your woman here. And since I only care for Chiyva's survival, which is guaranteed, I really have a lot less to lose than you do. You should give me that one-minute head start before you hunt me down. It's your best chance."

Do not do it!

"Tao, I don't have a choice. I'll still have a pistol on me anyway."

Roen shouted out, "Fine, Sean. Put down your gun and we'll put down ours."

Sean let go of his pistol and dropped it with a loud clatter onto the metal grating. He held out both his hands to show that he was completely unarmed. Roen gestured to Kwan, and the two slowly placed their rifles on the ground. Roen stood up and put one hand near his holster, ready to pull his pistol out. And then – faster than he thought possible – Sean drew another pistol from his hip pocket and shot Kwan in the head.

Roen pulled out his pistol, but dropped it when he felt a hammer-like blow. He fell backward, clutching his chest. His armor had taken the brunt of the blow, but it hurt nevertheless.

"Stupid, stupid," said Sean. "Why would you make a deal, boy, when you already know I don't care about the consequences? And now look at the mess you've made." He brandished the gun in his hand and looked at all the bodies littering the ground. Then he looked at the crushed door at the entranceway. Sean added, "You've built quite a body count, son. There is no escape from the helipad for any Quasing here, so this one is insurance." He gestured at Jill and clubbed her on the head with the pistol. "And since no Quasing wants competition for available vessels, these three won't be needed anymore either."

Roen watched, horrified, as Sean put his foot on the backs of the two Prophus delegates and pushed them off the helipad over the cliff. Their screams faded as they fell down the side of the mountain. Sean was about to do the same to Sonya when he hesitated and turned to Roen.

"You care for this one, don't you, boy?" he said slowly. He pulled out the small glass figurine of a turtle and looked at Roen. "I believe it's time Tao pays a debt owed to Chiyva. Do you remember Paneese, Tao?" Sean pointed the gun at Sonya's back and pulled the trigger.

Bam. Bam. Bam.

Sonya gasped. Roen watched as her body shuddered and contorted before collapsing onto the platform. A pool of blood began to expand on the ground around her.

"No!" he screamed. He dived to the right, rolled up onto his feet, and began to run. Roen continued running, dodging and weaving behind a few crates on the helipad. A bullet ricocheted dangerously close to his head as he dove behind a generator.

Stick your head out of the right side and pull back!

"What? I have to get to Sonya!"

Trust me. And do it quickly. You cannot save her until you handle Sean.

Roen complied, peering out from the right edge and pulling back. Two bullets spit up the ground at that side, and he huddled back toward the center.

Five. Six. Now do it again.

"Are you crazy?"

Just do it.

"Come on, boy. Why do you delay the inevitable? Do you know how to die like a man? Come out and show me!" Sean's voice echoed through the mountain air. "You better stop hiding. Your girl will bleed out in a few minutes."

Roen stuck his head out and peered at Sean, having just a split second to pull back behind the generator before two more bullets flew right past his head.

Seven. Eight. Now, stick your head out the other side.

"I'm not getting this."

I will teach you if we ever survive this. Just follow my directions.

Resigned to trusting Tao, Roen stuck his head out and pulled back just as a bullet struck the railing close to his head.

Good, now run to the right, past that debris toward the edge. Cut in and charge Sean when I say so. Go!

Roen took off, keeping his head low and charging across the length of platform. He sprinted past a row of crates and heard a bullet pass by. He almost stumbled as his momentum carried him forward. Roen put his hand down to keep his balance as he turned and dived behind several large fans.

"Now what?"

Keep going.

Roen continued running and rounded the platform corner. He felt a sharp sting as a bullet grazed his armor, just missing his elbow. He pivoted and stumbled, almost falling down.

Now! That was his last bullet. Take him down!

Roen regained his balance and charged. His body throbbed everywhere, but he pushed the pain out of his mind. There was Sean with Sonya lying at his feet. Sean looked up and realized that he didn't have time to reload. He hurled the gun at Roen. Roen tried to duck out of the way, but the pistol struck him in the shoulder, making him lose his balance. Miraculously, he stayed on his feet and closed the distance between them. He moved in close and attacked Sean with everything he had.

Control your momentum. Stay in control.

He threw a hard right cross that passed harmlessly by Sean's face as the man easily sidestepped the attack. Sean countered with a quick right backhand on Roen's cheek that sent him staggering. Roen attacked again, throwing a combination of kicks and punches. Again, Sean easily evaded him. He retaliated with another backhand that sent Roen crashing to the ground.

Sean chuckled, shaking his head. "You disappoint me, Tao. This is the best your vessel can do? I shot her through the lungs, Roen. She's choking on her own blood as we speak."

He is trying to rile you. Stay focused.

Growling, Roen picked himself up and took a few steps back. His shoulder and chest were throbbing, and he barely had the use of his left arm. Exhaustion was setting in as well. It was all he could do to stay upright. He watched warily as Sean stretched his neck and arms lazily, sauntering closer and closer.

He is trying to intimidate you.

"He's doing a good job. I don't think I can beat him. He's too good."

Now is not the time for self-doubt, Roen. He might have more experience and skill, but you have youth and strength on your side.

Gritting his teeth, Roen charged again, slipping outside of Sean's guard to attack at an angle. He pressed forward and threw a right hook toward Sean's exposed ribcage. Sean twisted out of the way. He grabbed Rocn's forearm and sent him tumbling head first to the ground. Roen found himself lying on his back as fresh waves of pain rippled through his body. The man was toying with him.

"I can't beat him. I can't even touch him. What style is he using? What do I do? He moves like Lin!"

I believe he is using a form of aikido or possibly Ba Gua Zhang to neutralize your speed and strength. He is good, but not that good! You can beat him! He would not hold a candle against Lin.

"That doesn't make me feel better. Sifu Lin never broke a sweat tossing me around."

Roen scrambled back to his feet and retreated, watching with unfocused eyes as Sean stalked him. Sean still wore that bored smug smile as he yawned. He said, "Why don't you make it easier on yourself?"

"What?" Roen growled. "Just lie down and die for you?"

Sean chuckled. "You might as well. You have no chance, but who can blame you? You're only human."

"Tao, I... I can't beat this guy, not by myself. I can't do this alone."

Roen, listen to me. You will beat him, because you must. Sonya and Jill are depending on you. If you fail, they die. You are stronger than you give yourself credit for. Do not let anyone tell you that you are not able. Not me, not you, and damn it, not Sean Diamont. So, forget about me, the Prophus, and this ridiculous war. Think about those who love you and depend on you. What else is worth living and dying for? And Roen?

"What?"

You are not alone. What is the capital of old Assyria?

Roen closed his eyes and chuckled involuntarily. "The capital of Assyria?" He looked up at the early morning sky. "Well, heck, everyone knows the answer to that. The capital's Assur!"

Exactly. I will always be with you. You want to change the world? Now is your chance! Go show this bastard what you are made of!

Roen's anger reached a boiling point as he glared at Sean's smug grin. The man was standing very close to him now. With a snarl, Roen took his pent-up energy, focused it into his right fist, and threw with all he had at Sean's closest body part – his left hand. His fist struck the lower half of Sean's palm. He heard the satisfying crack of bone breaking as Sean's wrist and forearm took the brunt of the blow. Sean had only a moment's look of pain and surprise before his head snapped back from a second punch that sent him tumbling to the ground.

"Last I checked," Roen growled, "you're human too. Or did that not hurt?"

To his credit, Sean recovered quickly. Within seconds, he stood up, and the look of serenity was back. If he was in pain, he didn't show it. His left arm dangled at his side, useless. Sean gave it one dismissive glance and smiled. "Not so toothless after all? Now, let's see..."

Before he finished talking, Roen bounded forward to take advantage of the situation. He slipped toward Sean's weakened side and pressed the attack, punching the broken left arm repeatedly. Sean grunted with each shot, but deftly avoided most of Roen's attacks.

Be careful. You are too aggressive.

Roen kept up the pressure, throwing a jab at Sean's head, followed by a kick to the ribcage. Even injured, Sean was quick enough to dodge them both. He hit Roen with a right elbow strike that sent him sprawling to the ground. Within moments, Sean jumped on top of him, pinning him with one knee on his chest and raining punch after punch down on him.

"You want to play rough, boy?" Sean laughed. "I have killed men far worthier than you will ever be! You are nothing but an insect, and now it's time to die like one!"

He tried to cover his face with his hands, but Sean just punched through them. Then, while desperately trying to find something to cling to, Roen grabbed Sean's limp broken wrist and twisted. Sean gasped as Roen twisted it even harder. And harder. Finally, he cried out when Roen found enough leverage to lean forward and punch Sean in the jaw. This gave Roen enough room to push him off and scramble to his feet.

With Sean still clutching his broken wrist, Roen went on the offensive again. He threw punches that Sean was only able to partially block, followed up with a kick that snapped Sean's head back. Then Roen twisted the dangling arm until he heard a pop and a snap as bone and ligament broke. This time, the skin around the elbow tore. Sean spun quickly and Roen felt the air whoosh out of his chest as a spin kick caught him square in the solar plexus, sending him tumbling back.

Roen gasped for breath as he tried to pull himself up. His insides were on fire and his legs refused to cooperate. He desperately tried to crawl away. He looked over and saw Sean staggering away in the opposite direction. "My God! I almost tore his arm off! How is he still kicking my ass?"

Sean Diamont is tough. You were holding his broken wrist when he executed the spin kick. He dislocated his own shoulder doing that.

Roen looked behind him just in time to see Sean pick up a pistol from the far side of the helipad and stagger toward him. "Die, betrayers!" he screamed.

Roen tried to crawl behind a metal generator, but instead his hands found cold metal. Looking up, Roen saw the dark metal sheen of an assault rifle. Using what was left of his strength, he grabbed the rifle, rolled over, and pointed it at Sean. "Let's see how immortal you really are," Roen growled, pulling the trigger.

A quick burst nailed Sean across the chest and he fell. It became quiet, save for Sean's final gasps. Very slowly, Roen pulled himself to his feet and limped toward his nemesis. He had to finish this. Sean's beaten, bloody body lay against one of the generators. He was alive... barely. His breath came in shallow, ragged bursts. Roen stood over him and pointed the muzzle at Sean's forehead. This might be his only chance to kill him.

"For Sonya, you bastard," he growled.

Roen! No! You cannot kill him.

"Why?" Roen turned and saw Jill's crumpled body. He turned cold at the thought of what almost just happened. She was the only viable host for Chiyva. He would be condemning her.

"What do I do, Tao?"

Sean's time is short. You need to throw him off this platform before he dies.

Roen grabbed Sean by the collar and pulled. Sean barely budged. Grunting, he tried again, willing his body to summon the strength to drag the body to the ledge. This time, Roen's legs gave out and he collapsed onto the floor. He had lost too much blood and was too weak.

"I can't, Tao."

Let me think. Let me… damn it! We have no choice then. See to Sonya before it is too late.

"Too late for what?"

Sean will pass any second now. You have to think about Baji's safety.

"I don't understand."

Yes. You do.

Then the sudden realization struck him and his chest seized. The air became difficult to breathe. "No, no," he moaned.

I am sorry.

"There has to be another way."

Think about Jill.

Roen looked over at the unconscious Jill again and then crawled to Sonya. He removed the hood from her head and caressed her face. She had lost a lot of blood and looked very pale, but was still conscious. There was blood everywhere and her breathing was becoming uneven. He cradled her head gently while she shook uncontrollably. Tears streamed down his face as he brushed her hair aside.

"So… cold," she murmured, choking up blood.

"Sonya," he said gently. "I'm here. You're going to be…" He wiped the tears falling down his face. The words wouldn't come out.

She is not going to make it. Her wounds are too severe.

"Roen," she whispered, caressing his face with her hand. "I'm glad you're all right." She coughed again and more blood poured out of her mouth. "What about your friend?"

"She's fine," he choked through his tears.

He picked up the rifle and pointed it at Sonya's heart. The seconds ticked by as he stood there, unable to pull the trigger. "I'm sorry," he said softly, between choked breaths.

Sonya's eyes fluttered and she looked at the rifle muzzle pointing at her chest, the realization dawning on her face. "Baji or Chiyva... your friend?" she whispered.

Roen could only nod.

"It's OK," she murmured. "Save Baji."

Roen's hands trembled as he knelt over her, eyes fixed on her face. "I can't do it," he cried.

Time is running out.

She gripped the muzzle of the rifle with her other hand and pulled it down to her heart. "Who would have thought you'd be the one to rescue me?" She smiled.

"I'm sorry, I'm sorry," he moaned over and over.

Sonya put a finger over his mouth. "Hush," she murmured. Her breathing became labored as she clutched him tighter. "You... you know why Baji never liked you?"

"Why?" Roen sobbed.

"Because," she said softly. "Because I thought you were cute, in your own goofy way. Baji's funny when she's protective."

Roen smiled through his tears. "She didn't want you slumming it with me."

She laughed, choking up more blood. "Do it. Now. It's an order. I'm at peace."

Pulling the trigger was the hardest thing Roen ever had to do in his life. The crack of the rifle punctured the air as Sonya shuddered and went still, her eyes blank and looking off into space. A sparkle of light left her body and floated toward Jill. It hovered over her for a few seconds before finally resting on top of her like a blanket. The sparkle dissolved into her and Jill gasped. She began to cry for several seconds before drifting back into unconsciousness.

Roen screamed.

Behind him, Sean uttered one last gasp as well before going limp. Another sparkle of light sprang into the sky. Chiyva swam in a large circle over the helipad, moving desperately from body to body. Unable to find a suitable host, it rose into the air and tried to look elsewhere. Then a strong gust of wind blew it into the sky and out of sight.

Roen didn't know how much time had passed as he cradled Sonya's head, weeping. Tao tried to say a few comforting words, but Roen tuned him out. Nothing Tao said would ever make this all right.

He didn't move when there was a large explosion behind him which blew open the damaged entranceway and the helipad was suddenly filled with agents. He shrugged off the first hands that tried to pull him away and pushed away those that tried to move her body.

Stephen appeared and rested a hand on his shoulder. "It's over, son. Let's take her home."

Roen stood, numb, and listlessly watched as they wrapped Sonya's body up and took her away. He turned to follow Stephen back into the base when an ashen-faced Dylan ran up to them.

"Stephen," he said, sucking in deep breaths. "You're needed at the research lab. There's something you have to see."

Stephen frowned. "Can it wait?"

Dylan shook his head. "There's half a dozen large vats of red liquid in a holding room. There's dead Quasing inside."

CHAPTER THIRTY-NINE
EPILOGUE

It would be amiss for me to not say a few words about Edward Blair. I met the young man at the height of the Cold War. Edward was a rare man, a treasure: raw, but confident, cocky, but with a soft heart. I had chosen well when I first met the young West Point student interning at the United States House of Representatives. In a way, he reminded me of a Zhu Yuanzhang before I failed him.

With Edward, I was determined not to make the same mistake I made in the past. I chose to put his priorities at the same level as mine. We were true partners and did great things together. That is my vision for the future. The world will never know his name, but humanity owes a debt of gratitude for the work he has done on their behalf. I would do you and Edward a disservice if you did not learn about the great man that was your predecessor.

Roen sat in his parked car along the side of a narrow road and waited, tapping the window with his finger as he turned his attention to the grassy knoll. He looked down at his watch and then looked out again. He had just returned from Italy this morning and the jet lag was killing him. However, there was much to do and little time to rest. The Penetra scanner prototype was damaged during the battle and the Prophus scientists were hard at work re-engineering it. It was now a race to see which side could utilize it first in the war, and which side could develop a counter for it.

He glanced down at the report Command had compiled on the attack at the Capulet's Ski Lodge assault. The disturbing news about the mysterious red vats was confirmed. Scanners detected the remains of over fifty Quasing in those vats. The chemicals stored in the vats were being analyzed by multiple Prophus research divisions. Was this related to the P2 and P3 projects? What were the Genjix trying to achieve? Theories about its use ranged anywhere from a biological weapon to forced body expulsion formula to reproductive incubators. It would take time to unravel what the Genjix were up to.

He picked up his phone and called Jill's number again. As with the rest of his calls, he only received a busy signal. It was killing him to not speak with her. Roen sighed and rubbed his eyes. He was too tired to be frustrated today. On the horizon, a row of people dressed in black were gathering on the crest of the hill next to a lone tree.

It is time.

"I know. It hurts."

It never gets any easier.

Roen looked in the mirror, adjusted his tie, and stepped out of the car. It had rained earlier and the sun was still hidden behind the cloudy sky. Roen looked to both sides of the road and began the long trek up the hill. He walked up next to the tree and looked down at a small clearing where a larger group of people had gathered. Dylan and Stephen gave him a nod and Paula hugged him.

The four of them stood and watched as the funeral service continued in the distance. Sonya was about to be buried next to her mother. Gathered at the service were her extended family, friends, old classmates, and anyone else she had touched during her short-lived life. Anyone except the Prophus, that is.

It would have been too difficult to explain, Tao had said. *It is Quasing tradition to stay in the shadows and grieve on our own.*

While it hurt Roen to not be down there to properly pay his last respects, he understood. He had never thought of Sonya's life outside of the Prophus. Now, he realized that there was much more to her than that. She had a life like everyone else. He wished that he had gotten to know that side of her better. The four of them waited until the service was over and the mourners, one by one, had paid their final respects. Roen's eyes welled up with tears when they lowered the casket into the ground. The last ones to leave were her grandparents and her aunt's family. They stayed until the last shovelful of dirt was patted down over Sonya's grave.

The sun had almost set by the time the last of them left. Stephen, Dylan, Paula, and Roen walked down the hill to Sonya's gravestone and stood around the burial plot. Roen stared at the simple markings on the headpiece. Lyte. That was her last name. Sonya Lyte. Roen hadn't even known that.

He pulled out a single red rose from his coat and placed it with the other flowers. He closed his eyes and murmured a prayer as tears streamed down his face. The others turned to leave. Stephen put one hand on his shoulder and told him to take care. Paula hugged him again and told him to get some rest. And then he was alone.

The sun had long since set and the crickets chirping reverberated in the empty night. Roen sat on the ground, with his back to the tombstone, and looked up at the sky as the moon poked out behind the clouds, bathing the plot with a soft white glow. He looked at Dania's plot, and then back at Sonya's. The Prophus giveth, and the Prophus taketh away. When would his time be up?

"Hello, stranger," a voice spoke from behind him.

Roen looked up with a start, his eyes filling with tears when he saw Jill walking up. He hadn't seen her since that night in

Italy. The Prophus had whisked her to a hospital in Rome and then sent her back to the States in a private transport. Roen had to stay with the Prophus for a week in Italy to analyze the data they found at the base. There was a treasure trove of information there.

Later on, he received word that Jill had suffered a concussion, a broken arm, and several broken ribs from the ordeal. He had been unable to reach her ever since.

"Hey you." Roen gave her a fierce hug. He held her tightly and felt the brace around her chest. He pulled back and studied her beautiful face. Jill also had a fading bruise on her cheek and her hair was cut short. It killed Roen to know that her injuries were because of him. Wiping the tears from his face, he studied her delicate features and promised himself to never let her go. He brushed his fingers along her chin and kissed her gently on the lips.

"I see the doctor let you out and about."

"I can't spare the vacation days," she replied solemnly with a small smile. "Your people told me you were here and gave me permission to come." Jill melted into his arms again and they stood there together for several moments. He felt her beating heart and the heat from her body. Roen hoped this moment would never end. He knew right there he could never live a full life if she wasn't by his side.

Roen kissed her again, inhaling her scent deep into him. "Gave you permission?"

She nodded. "I have a lot of new rules I'm supposed to follow now."

"I was so worried about you. I tried to call you for days, but the Prophus had already changed your information. How are you dealing with everything?"

Jill bit her lip thoughtfully. "I'm not sure yet. This is so new and strange. Did you have one of these Prophus with you the entire time we were dating?"

Roen nodded. "Tao gave me the courage to ask you out. How is Baji?"

Jill held his hand and looked down at Sonya's gravestone. "Baji seems nice enough. To be honest, she's in worse shape than I am." She pulled out a white rose and put it on Sonya's gravestone and murmured a small prayer. "Baji loves you, Sonya, more than you can ever know." She turned to Roen. "This is so much to take in. How did you make sense of any of this?"

"It took me a long time," Roen said. "But my Prophus helped me learn who I was, and what kind of man I should be. I believe they're here to help us. Trust them and learn from them."

Jill hesitated. "I think I need to take some time away from you to sort things out. Baji and I need to get acquainted. Is that OK? Will you still be here when I come back?"

"I'll always wait for you," Roen replied, a lump in his throat. "However long it takes." Inside, his heart broke. Just when he had gotten Jill back, he lost her again. It was more than he could bear. If she needed as much time as he did with Tao, when would he see her again? Would he ever see her again? His relationship with Jill just became another casualty of the war. It was the right thing for Jill to do though, and because he loved her, he accepted it.

She squeezed his hand and gave him a long, deep kiss. "I love you, Roen." Then she turned and began to walk away.

"I love you." He watched her walk up the hill. The thought of Baji telling Jill what she thought of him suddenly made him very uncomfortable. "Wait, Jill," he said, quickly following her. "Whatever Baji says about me..."

She turned and, with her trademark bright smile, said, "Oh, Roen, if you could only read my mind."

Devin Watson crumpled the report in his hands and threw it against the wall. How could this happen? The entire operation was an unmitigated disaster. The Capulet's Ski Lodge fiasco had crippled their entire European operation. Already, several of their troops had been captured in a wide net thrown by the Prophus from the intelligence gathered at the base. Three factories, two stockpiles, and multiple safe houses had already been compromised. The Prophus had also taken control of two satellites! Devin looked for something else to throw.

He pounded his fist on the fine Brazilian cherry desk and stared at the crumpled paper on the floor. With a sigh, he walked to the other side of his office and picked it up. He couldn't stand messes. His left leg ached again today, forcing him to walk with a noticeable limp. Rain must be coming. Walking back to his desk, he lit a cigar and puffed earnestly, staring out the window at the Potomac. It rained far too much this time of the year.

The Genjix hadn't experienced such a defeat since the American Revolution. It would take decades to recover from this. With the scanner prototype stolen, the advantage that the Genjix had was effectively nullified. And now, with their discovery of the vats, the P2 ProGenesis project had been exposed prematurely.

Curse those Prophus. Damn that Chiyva! It was unlike him to be so sloppy. But then, after reading the report, Devin could hardly blame him for any of his mistakes. In most cases, he would have done the same thing.

Both Chiyva and Jeo were gone, probably captured and most likely sent to the Eternal Sea. It seemed all of them had underestimated the resolve of their wayward brethren. Well, it was one mistake that Devin wouldn't make.

Devin. That is enough. There is no more use in thinking of the past.
"My apologies, Holy One."

Zoras was right, as always. Devin was fortunate to have such a wise Holy One. Though he was furious with the failures, Zoras was able to see past the issue – and focus on the tasks ahead – and not allow the sins of the past to cloud his judgment.

What's done is done, Devin thought. They must now plan for the future.

There is much work to do. We need to rebuild and reorganize. I will not tolerate these temporary setbacks. Suspend all major operations in Europe until we have assessed the damage. Reroute our resources to China.

"I shall call a meeting of the Council and re-prioritize immediately."

See to it. The Prophus conceded much during the last Accords. We should take advantage of their concessions in India.

"As you wish, Zoras."

Resources would have to be moved out of the European Union to China through back channels. Zoras was wise to see that the lost base in Italy was only a minor setback. After all, the Genjix had an eternity. Devin put out the cigar and pushed a button under his desk. A hidden door slid open and a tall dark-haired man walked in, impossibly beautiful, with chiseled features.

"Yes, Father," the man said.

"Enzo, prepare the plane. I want to be in China by tomorrow morning, to personally oversee the continuation of the ProGenesis at the new facility. See to it. I'm not leaving anything to chance."

Enzo bowed and left.

Then Devin called his secretary in. He wrote several names down on a list and handed it to her. "I have an unexpected trip to take. Clear my schedule for the next two weeks. However, I need to meet with the cabinet in the next twenty minutes. I don't care what time it is. Tell them to drop whatever they're doing. We have a world to rule."

She read over the list and nodded. "Yes, Senator, will that be all?"

ACKNOWLEDGMENTS

I couldn't have gotten this far without a small army of people (robots?) believing in me. If I miss you during my shout-outs, beers on me. Here goes...

First of all, thanks to the blurbers who liked *The Lives of Tao* enough to put their stamp of approval on it. You guys have paved the way for newbies like me. I won't forget to pay it forward.

To Russell Galen, my agent who helped got this deal done. Your guidance has been invaluable and your faith in my potential humbles me.

To Amanda Rutter, the editor of Strange Chemistry, who discovered me in the Great Angry Robot Open Submission of 2011. I wouldn't be here if it wasn't for you. To my editor, Lee Harris, who smoothed the rough edges until the story shined, it's been so nice, let's do it twice (or thrice). And thanks to Marc Gascoigne, Darren Turpin, Michael Underwood, John Tintera, and all the other fantastic people in the robot army, let's go assimilate someone!

To my fellow Anxious Appliances, who climbed Mount Midoriyama alongside me, you've shown that writing can be a team sport. A very special thanks to my best literary friend

Laura Lam, who laughed, cried, and shared angst with me every step of the way.

To my beta readers: Amber Kuo, Tiffany Moy-Kang, Michael Huchel, Rob Haines, Peter Friedrichsen, and all the others whose invaluable feedback helped shape the book. You guys kept me steering straight.

To my grandparents A-gong, A-ma, Nay-nay, you're in my youngest and fondest memories, which I'll cherish until the end of my days. To my parents, Mike and Yukie Chu, thanks for raising me right and letting me be wrong.

To Eva the Airedale Terrier, for dragging me out of my writing cave to see the sun once in a while.

And finally, to the love of my life, Paula, whose steadfast love and support (and editing and more editing) made this dream a reality. You deserve your name on the cover of this book as much as I do.

Tao is now insisting that I thank him as well. So thank you, Tao, for yammering in my brain all those years, demanding I tell your story. There, you happy?

Wesley Chu, Chicago, February 2013

ABOUT THE AUTHOR

Wesley Chu was born in Taiwan and immigrated to Chicago, Illinois when he was just a pup. It was there he became a Kung Fu master and gymnast.

Wesley is an avid gamer and a contributing writer for the magazine Famous Monsters of Filmland. A former stunt man and a member of the SAG, he can also be seen in film and television playing roles such as "Banzai Chef" in Fred Claus and putting out Oscar worthy performances as a bank teller in Chicago Blackhawks commercials.

Besides working as an Associate Vice President at a bank, he spends his time writing and hanging out with his wife Paula Kim and their Airedale Terrier, Eva.

chuforthought.com

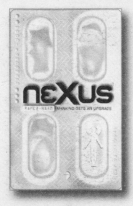

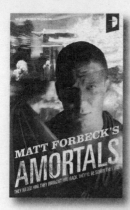